Afterwards, Nancy couldn't remember when it had all started. Or just how they'd taken the first intimate step.

She did remember that, when she and David had first met their next door neighbors they hadn't liked them. Horace was too out-going, and Tanya's exotic beauty made Nancy jealous. Then they'd become friends . . . and after that, something much more.

Nancy had never dreamed she could be so sexually free—with her husband, let alone with another couple. David was beginning to realize that he could physically and emotionally love two women at once.

But it wasn't until one perfect weekend in New Hampshire that they all knew they could never live monogamously again—that they loved and needed each other and that they were proud of it—that the years ahead would be difficult for all of them—but that now there was no turning back . . .

Other SIGNET Bestsellers
You Will Enjoy

PROPOSITION 31

by

Robert H. Rimmer

A SIGNET BOOK

Published by
THE NEW AMERICAN LIBRARY

Library of Congress Catalog Card Number: 68-57495

The author and publisher express their gratitude to:
Ralph Borsodi, for permission to quote from the book *Education and Living,* published by Melbourne University Press. Copyright 1948 by Ralph Borsodi.
Hawthorn Books, Inc., for permission to quote from the book *On Being Human,* by Ashley Montagu. Copyright © 1960 and 1950 by Ashley Montagu. Published by Hawthorn Books, Inc., 70 Fifth Avenue, New York, N. Y.
The Indiana University Press, for permission to quote from "The City as a Mechanism for Sustaining Human Contact," by Christopher Alexander, published in the book *Environment for Man: The Next Fifty Years.* Copyright © 1967 by Indiana University Press.
Abraham Maslow, for his kind permission to quote from two of his various papers published in the *Journal of Humanistic Psychology* and the *Journal of Individual Psychology.*
Random House, Inc., for permission to quote from the book *The Age of Anxiety,* by W. H. Auden. Copyright 1946 and 1947 by W. H. Auden. All rights reserved under International and Pan-American Copyright Conventions.

This is a reprint of a hardcover edition published by The New American Library, Inc. The hardcover edition was published simultaneously in Canada.

SIGNET TRADEMARK REG. U.S. PAT. OFF. AND FOREIGN COUNTRIES
REGISTERED TRADEMARK——MARCA REGISTRADA
HECHO EN CHICAGO, U.S.A.

*SIGNET BOOKS are published by
The New American Library, Inc.,
1301 Avenue of the Americas, New York, New York 10019*

FIRST PRINTING, JUNE, 1969

PRINTED IN THE UNITED STATES OF AMERICA

THIS BOOK IS DEDICATED NOT ONLY TO
THE OUTNUMBERED BUT GROWING
ARMY OF MEN AND WOMEN WHO
DARE TO SEARCH FOR A WORLD WHERE
LOVE, COOPERATION, AND
UNDERSTANDING ARE THE KEYNOTES
OF DAILY LIFE, BUT ALSO TO THE
MILLIONS OF READERS OF *The Harrad
Experiment* WHO HAVE ASKED:
AFTER HARRAD, WHAT?

A word
to the reader

When Nancy Herndon asked me to put her story in perspective from a sociologist's point of view, I told her that my saying anything after all the furor she had created with Proposition Thirty-One would be a little like gilding the lily. I am convinced that her book, and the law it proposes, have a good chance to restructure the institution of marriage and to modify, in a startling way, the sexual practices of the married. These few words, then, are my small contribution—however superfluous—to the cause Nancy has taken up.

The newspaper and magazine stories that are beginning to appear, praising or excoriating Future Families of America, have scarcely scratched the surface of the fascinating motivations that brought this organization into being. Whether Nancy has exercised good judgment in telling the true story, without any attempt to disguise the individuals or most locales, is still a subject of hot debate in the Herndon and Shea* home.

A few weekends ago, while David Herndon and Horace Shea were sailboat-racing with their children, Nancy, Tanya Shea, and I, all three of us naked, were lazily basking in the late afternoon sun and occasionally swimming in the huge pool within the spanking new Herndon-Shea compound.

"Horace is not so sure that I shouldn't be locked in the attic." Nancy laughed at my reaction. "Like that character in *Jane Eyre*. Either that, or I should have my behind spanked. But I warned them all long ago the world wouldn't leave us alone. After that police raid, I became convinced. For the sake of the

---

* Very recently the Herndons and the Sheas changed their last names to Hershe. I use their older, more familiar last names here, to avoid confusion, just as Nancy has done throughout her book.

vii

children I would leave no stone unturned to *normalize* our family."

I asked Tanya for her opinion. "Of course, Nancy's book is very personal and revealing," she told me. "I could disagree with her on the first part where she plays God. But the thoughts she attributed to me are not too far from the truth. When she first started to read us parts of her manuscript, I guess Horace, David, and I thought she was writing as a kind of therapy or, as Nancy put it, "to untangle the threads, so that we could all see how we arrived at this point in our lives." We never suspected that it would become Nancy's Manifesto. Now she's trying to convince us that when the book is published it will help people identify with us better; to understand our motivations. It might even assure a sweeping victory for Proposition Thirty-One."

I was sitting on the edge of the swimming pool, dangling my feet in the water, enjoying the serenity of this world within the world. A half-acre compound of flowers and trees and an interrelated house that Peter Alberti had built for them. Nancy was lying on a chaise with her eyes closed, a tiny smile on her lips.

"I personally don't give a damn," Tanya continued. "It's an honest book. That's more than you can say for most. But David and Horace are acting as though they uncorked the genii from the bottle. Only this one doesn't bow and scrape and do their bidding. In their opinion all of us have been vocal enough, and there's no need to expose our personal lives. We have to think of the children. If Proposition Thirty-One becomes a law, then we will have proved ourselves legally. If it doesn't, then someday we may be considered Pied Pipers who played a mad tune that led the younger generation into the mountain caves. David is afraid that we might leave a Mormon heritage. It took the Mormon children over a generation to live down the so-called disgrace of plural marriage. He's even worried that the Herndon Showcase Corporation may get identified as a kind of Oneida Community. He insists he's no John Humphrey Noyes."

Nancy smiled. "We're not operating under any religious imprimatur. Even if we don't succeed, I'm confident that our family and our way of life will survive. It's no Piper's tune we're playing. In a society that largely negates the individual, this is the way for human survival."

"Your book will be quite shocking to middle-class suburbanites," I told her. "They play on the fringes of unconventional sexual behavior, but retreat into monogamy or divorce when a

viii

crisis rears its head." I was needling Nancy purposely. "Already one California newspaper has speculated that the Albertis didn't contribute five million dollars to Future Families of America out of altruism. Despite everything you've said, you'll be linked to the swingers and wife-swappers. Many people will be certain that Proposition Thirty-One is little more than a license for lust and sex gone amok."

Nancy shrugged. "The world is composed of people who would rather stagnate than embrace a new idea. Proposition Thirty-One unsettles their minds. Don't forget we have thousands of enthusiastic supporters and we have more than enough signatures to put Proposition Thirty-One on the state ballot this fall. Now it will be up to the voters. I've a feeling there is still considerable pioneering spirit in California. In a sense we're offering the only real adventure left in the world for men and women. If Proposition Thirty-One becomes law, a great many couples are going to experiment with corporate marriage. Even if they fail, the failure will do little harm to the participants, certainly nowhere near equivalent to divorce in a monogamous environment."

I had been casually examining the naked beauty of Tanya and Nancy, one a natural blonde, the other a dark-skinned brunette. An interesting contrast to my own untanned brown nudity. Even in their late thirties, their faces reflect a lovely ingenuousness that many females lose early in life. It occurred to me to test the depth of their conviction.

"Doesn't it bother you that my presence here on occasional weekends is a disrupting influence, at least for Horace?"

Tanya smiled. "In a typical monogamous situation, I simply couldn't tolerate you. But in that situation you wouldn't be here in the first place. Obviously, if Horace or David wanted to have an 'affair' with you (Such an ugly word!) you'd have to meet in your apartment. Your very existence would undermine the strength of a monogamous home. In this environment it is different. Because you are our friend, if you sleep with Horace or David occasionally, *here in our compound,* you're accepting an involvement with our total family. What's more, if you do, knowing you, you would *want* to be involved. Of course, I'm speaking for myself. Why don't you ask Nancy?"

"Sylvia!" Nancy grinned at me. "Neither Tanya nor I are sex-starved. If David or Horace wants to go to bed with you, it will be because they can come to you the way they come to Tanya or me, not for seduction or possession, but for the joy of complete surrender to a person who warmly understands them and can surrender to them. I'm sure that all of us, in the past year, have had opportunities to fuck with another person —I use the word fuck advisedly, because it sums up for me a sexual act devoid of meaning—yet I'm quite sure none of us has."

Some books are written about sex. Some are written about love. Nancy's story is about friendship, the sine qua non of both sex and love. Since, in its fullest flowering, friendship is a learned response rather than a genital reaction, the cerebral ability to sustain friendship may bring man closer to God than sex or love.

And that is what this book is about—a story of four people who have posited for themselves, and possibly for many men and women, a solution which may be the *only way* the individual can make his technologies and his society *serve* him for complete self-actualization.

Nancy, Tanya, David, and Horace are my friends. I hope they may be yours.

SYLVIA MAI
Professor of Sociology
California Institute of Sociology

If I am not for myself, who will be for me?
If I am only for myself, what am I?
And, if not now . . . when?

HILLEL THE ELDER

PART ONE

The Entanglement

~~~~~~~~~~~~~~

A giant with seven-league boots might have straddled the rooftops or walked an asphalt-shingled highway from the Shea and Herndon homes to the Pacific Ocean shimmering in the distance. With one gargantuan step he might have spanned Los Angeles Harbor and put his foot on Catalina Island, twenty-six miles at sea.

Lesser people, like the Herndons and the Sheas, sat on their porches, or stared through sliding glass-window walls at the vast unpopulated ocean, a constant reminder, like Tantalus's apple, of space still untrammeled by man. If they couldn't piss on San Pedro or Long Beach, as Gargantua pissed on Paris, they could at least console themselves that somewhere in the world it was still possible to flex one's elbows without jabbing one's fellow men.

Having lived in their fifty-thousand-dollar home sixteen months longer than the Herndons, who had just arrived from Boston, the Sheas, at least Horace Shea, had grown crass enough to label this magnificent, Balbonian view of the Pacific "a case of sea but not touch." Unless, of course, unlike the Sheas or the Herndons, a family became wealthy enough to buy a yacht or spiritual enough to walk on water. For the rest of mankind, perched like chickens and roosters in miles upon miles of semicircular hatcheries, rimming the sea and holding together the unvegetated hills of California, it was charming—always provided the November and December rains didn't wash the entire jerry-built mess, like a modern Atlantis, to the bottom of the Pacific.

Two evenings after the Herndons had moved into their home next door to the Sheas, Horace Shea, usually quite introverted, but at the moment expansively bolstered by three quick Scotches, told his wife Tanya that they owed it to the Easterners' image of California to constitute themselves a welcoming committee. After all, as Tanya should well appreciate, these Herndons were only a few generations removed from our covered-wagon forebears. Hardy pioneers, really, they had arrived on wings, sipping highballs, while they watched the latest in-flight movie, secure in the certainty that their possessions, carefully wrapped and crated, were following at a somewhat slower pace in a huge transcontinental van.

Despite Tanya's insistence that some people were not gregarious (And didn't Horace himself, when sober, resent neighborly intrusions on his privacy?), Horace persisted in his notion. "Welcome to the Golden West," he boomed at Nancy Herndon, who timidly peered at him through a crack she had opened in her front door. "We are your neighbors, the Sheas. This is Tanya, my spouse. I'm Horace."

Unable to support the front door against Horace's weight, gasping in proper New England dismay, Nancy clutched her thin housecoat tightly around her, thus inadvertently displaying her breasts in some detail to Horace, who chuckled approvingly.

"Do not be embarrassed by the state of your undress," Horace said, as he calmly walked into a living room that was a chaos of packing cases, cardboard boxes, loose clothing, toys, and even, on top of the television, a pair of boy's ice skates. "In California we take nudity somewhat lightly. Tanya and I have come to drink a quick libation to your happiness and success in this smoggy land of dreams."

Tanya, more appreciative of feminine propriety, clutched Horace firmly by his arm. "We'll come back later, Mrs. Herndon. Welcome to California!" She attempted to edge Horace toward the front door, ignoring his happy insistence that he had brought a magnum of California champagne that

14

had been cooled just right. What better, more spontaneous time than right now?

"We're still unpacking," Nancy apologized, as she looked around for something more to put on. "David, where are you? We have company. Come upstairs!" She glanced down the stairwell that led to the bedroom below. "Oh, dear, I can't get organized in this house. Back home our bedrooms were upstairs. David, where are you? We have visitors."

With a sigh of relief, Nancy slipped into her husband's trenchcoat, which she had found in a pile of clothing.

"Our house is identical with yours," Tanya said, looking nervously at Nancy. To herself she silently admitted that with her wide-apart, brown eyes and a flustered look on her face Mrs. Herndon, who must be about her own age, was quite pretty. "You can see the Pacific from all your bedrooms. Even the laundry." Tanya tried to convey with a shrug that Horace, who was swaying toward a bar and counter that separated the living room from a rail-car style kitchen, would be impossible to divert. "Drink a little champagne," she whispered to Nancy. "It may be our only chance to get acquainted. When he's sober, Horace never talks to strangers."

Feeling as if she were a guest in her own house, Nancy watched Horace search the empty kitchen cabinets for glasses. "The glasses are not unpacked, Mr. Shea. I'm sorry." She smiled helplessly at David, who had finally emerged from the bowels of the house and was frowning at Horace and this un-New-England-like invasion of his privacy. "These are our neighbors," Nancy said timidly. "Mr. and Mrs. Shea."

David stared at Horace, who clasped the huge bottle of champagne between his legs and was carefully extracting the cork. "As you can appreciate, Mr. Shea, we're scarcely prepared for entertaining. Why don't you save it . . ."

His sentence was cut short by Horace's whoop of joy and the sound of the cork exploding from the bottle and bouncing off the ceiling. "Quick, stick your mouth over it. It's too good to waste," Horace roared as he shoved the bottle under David's nose. The gushing liquid sprayed across David's face. He swallowed, sputtered, and choked. Tears of rage gathered in his eyes.

Chuckling, Horace patted him on the back. "Too damn bad you got so many clothes on, ol' man. Not every new resident of California gets a champagne shower bath." He ignored the wrath on David's dripping face. "Some day you'll laugh about this. Nothing tragic in this world. Only thinking makes it so." Horace offered the bottle to Nancy. "Here, Mrs. Herndon, have a slug. There's plenty left."

"Horace," Tanya wailed, "our new neighbors will think

15

you're a boor." She tried to dry David with a tiny lace handkerchief as she promised the Herndons they would learn to like Horace when they got to know him better.

"God forbid," David replied.

Horace ignored his cold glance. "No time like the present, is there?" He grinned as he clutched David around the shoulder. "Don't mind us, old friend. Tanya is stickier than you are when she's sober."

"Oh, I do hope you'll forgive us, Mr. Herndon." Tanya scowled at her husband. "Horace is really quite harmless. On Saturdays, after a hard week at the Institute, he tries to sail with both jib and spinnaker. I'm afraid he gets windy."

"Loquacious, darling, not gaseous!" Horace beamed at all of them. "You see, Mr. Herndon, it's a professional handicap. After five days of lecturing to the younger generation—I teach sociology at Cal Institute—I can't stop talking." Horace pointed at David, who was still mopping himself. "What do you do for a living?"

"David is in the fixture business." Nancy's lips curved in what she hoped was a neighborly smile. Suddenly she realized she was holding the huge bottle of champagne.

"I'm in woodworking; I manufacture showcases and fixtures." David's voice had a stern tone of dismissal in it. "We really appreciate your visit, Mr. Shea." He moved Horace toward the door. "But, as you can see, we are quite unprepared for a party."

"Wait a minute, you're a builder?" With a smile that indicated they had at last achieved rapport, Horace plumped on the arm of a chair that was piled with Nancy's bric-a-brac. "You're a builder! By God, Mr. Herndon, I insist on a toast. Mrs. Herndon, take a swallow, and pass what remains of that nectar. I hereby propose a toast to the building fraternity, those noblemen who, with little regard for their fellow man, though with ample respect for the buck, have crammed these lovely fifty-thousand-dollar homes so close together."

With a warning scream, Nancy gathered up her figurines just before Horace slumped down into the seat.

Horace blinked to get his bearings. "I also propose a toast to the contractors who connived with them and built these houses not only so close, but of such porous material, Mrs. Herndon, that your sleek modern bedroom, where you will patter barefoot each night up to your ankles in broadloom, where nightly you will consort with your husband, and your bathroom, where you will perform the excretory and micturitory functions necessary to the maintenance of a healthy life . . . What was I saying? Yes! So close that your bathroom and bedroom are separated only visually from ours. Auditorially, from this evening forth, without benefit of hearing aids or bugging devices, we are to all intents and purposes roommates."

Seeing the amazement on Nancy's face, Tanya giggled. "Horace exaggerates," she said. "He just means that sometimes when you flush your toilet, we can hear it."

"I am a man who uses words carefully, Mr. Herndon." Horace ogled David. "That toilet is not all. I would suggest that you oil your bedsprings unless, of course, you enjoy the delights of bellybumping in an extremely unathletic manner. Still, you will have no secrets from me. Like Abou Ben Adhem, I am pleased to offer my services. I will function as your guardian angel and record the lubricities of your bedchamber for posterity." Unable to withstand the shocked and righteous glare in David's eyes, Horace grinned sheepishly at Nancy. "I hope, Mrs. Herndon, that you will forgive my high spirits. Really, it is a joy to have a couple living here who, I would guess, are our own age. Already our children seem to have got acquainted, and unless, as they say in old New England, you have another in the oven, we are matched in that respect. The previous owner of this house was in his late sixties. Diminished bladder capacity forced him to take a leak several times a night, but what was far worse was that he gave so little thought to his neighbors' comfort that he punctiliously flushed the hopper each time he pissed."

Nancy tried to smile, but failed; David's face was frozen into a stern frown. "I'm sure ultimately we will become good neighbors, Mr. Shea," he said stiffly. "Back where we come from it is something of an adage—good fences make good neighbors."

Tanya, embarrassed by the glare of disapproval in David's eyes, pushed the reluctant Horace to the door.

"I like you, David," Horace grinned at him. "You're a man after my own sober, nonalcoholic heart. I propose a toast! Here's to the end of our friendship. In this alienated world, the idea of friendship is a boring responsibility." Horace recovered the open bottle of champagne from Nancy and tipped it to his lips. "May we always disagree. The back of my hand to you, Mr. Herndon, may the flushing of our toilet in the wee hours of the morning precede the flushing of yours."

17

Chapter 2

Close proximity can give birth to many things, including laughter and ulcerating anger. The Herndons and the Sheas spent several weeks annoying each other with their noisy toilets. On at least two Sunday afternoons, as they frigidly refused to exchange greetings, they sat on their respective back porches and stared at the blue Pacific in the distance. Conversations between legal mates were carried on with excessive interest and avidity, punctuated by high laughter. Thus they proved, at least, that there was strength in union against each other.

It was nearly two months before it became apparent that they had at least one thing in common besides noisy toilets —a lack of dependable baby-sitters. Not that the Herndon children, Jimmy and Sue, age eight and ten, were actually babies, or that the Shea boys, Mitch and Sam, age six and eleven, were in their nursing years. But the inescapable truth was that neither the Herndons nor the Sheas could simply walk out for a Saturday-evening respite from the routines of marriage to leave their broods to shift for themselves.

Nancy noticed that the Sheas occasionally employed Franny Materi, who lived three houses up the street, to mind the Shea boys. One Saturday, a few minutes after the Sheas had left Franny in charge on Saturday night, a pimply-faced boy arrived. Despite David's objections that she was nothing but a voyeur, Nancy stood on a chair in the living room and confirmed that the boy was simply holding hands with Franny while they watched television, except during the commercials, when they ate popcorn and consumed innumerable Coca-Colas.

While David, who was appalled at the amount of traffic on the freeways on a Saturday night, might have been willing to stay forever nested in the little womb of their home, Nancy insisted that if she didn't escape the house at least once a week she would go stir-crazy. A discreet telephone call to Franny's mother, in which the price of Franny's services for an evening moved from four to five dollars, brought Frances, grinning and ready to talk business. Nancy assured her that

18

the television was working and that the Herndon children would probably sleep all night and, yes, Franny could use the kitchen to make popcorn. It was agreed that Franny was to arrive promptly at seven thirty the following Saturday.

"It's ridiculous," David told Nancy, as he reluctantly dressed for their first California evening out together. "Where are we going that's so damned important that you had to pirate the Shea's babysitter?"

"Out!" Nancy said irritably. "Just out. We are going out! I've been cooped up in our dream house for six weeks, and I'm bored; I hate sunny California. You can at least take me out to eat. If you have no better idea, after we eat you can take me to a drive-in movie."

"A drive-in movie?" David exploded. "For God's sake, Nancy, are you regressing? Drive-in movies go on forever. Have you forgotten those interminable intermissions while the kids glut themselves on hot dogs and pizzas and play feelies with each other when there's nothing left to eat?"

"You used to think it was romantic."

David sighed as he patted Nancy's cheek. "That was fifteen years ago. We've grown up!"

"No, we haven't. We've grown down! Down to boredom." Nancy gestured out the bedroom window to the Shea house. "If you could take *her* to a drive-in, I bet you wouldn't be so damned grown up."

David smiled. He knew his silence would irritate Nancy, but it was probably true. After a certain number of years of marriage, the grass in the sack next door did look a little more virginal. In recent years Nancy had become somewhat methodical. Making love to her was like putting the same old Tchaikovsky symphony on the turntable. He could anticipate the climaxes and denouements. There never seemed to be a new phrase or motif. Maybe, if the truth was said, Nancy felt the same way about him. Maybe Nancy would be exciting and mysterious in a drive-in movie with Horace Shea, who didn't know her so well. Tanya was a natural blonde. Grinning at himself in the mirror as he tied his necktie, he had a sharp visual impression of a naked female stomach. Milky-white, it curved into the soft blond hairs of a female triangle; the cleft below it, darker and inviting, was lost in a love-tangle, waiting to be pierced by the touch of his fingers. That was the lure of the unknown. It occurred to David that his knowledge of females was somewhat limited. Prior to marrying Nancy, nearly fifteen years ago, he had known only two other women, both of them brunette. He chuckled; so he owned a brunette love nest, or it owned him. The truth was that copulation was only a minor motif in the symphony of

19

marriage. Most marriage counselors insisted this was true, and sensible people knew it, too. What was more, not all daydreams could become realities.

David suddenly realized that Nancy, fully dressed, was staring at him with tears in her eyes. Had she read his mind?

"Didn't you hear the telephone?" Nancy sobbed. "It was Franny's mother. Franny is going to the Sheas tonight. Franny's father is a friend of Horace Shea. He told her it wasn't proper for her to disappoint the Sheas."

"There must be other baby-sitters," David said, somewhat relieved that mind-reading wasn't one of Nancy's accomplishments.

"Well, you just try and find them!" Nancy shouted. She knew her hysteria was not justified by the circumstances, but she couldn't help herself. "It was *your* idea to move to California. The teen-agers out here are all too busy trying to make babies. They haven't time to mind them."

"Then let's have a romantic evening at home," David said as he put his arm around her. "I'll call Rizzo's and order veal cutlet Parmesan to take out. I'll make you a drink, and I'll open a bottle of Chianti. We'll eat after the kids are in bed; then we can look at television."

Nancy scowled. "Maybe Jimmy'll lend you one of his cap guns. Then you can have man-fun together while you watch the Saturday night cowboys and help him shoot the bad guys. As for me, I'm going to bed alone."

Three solitary drinks later, after listening twice to the Sheas' toilet being flushed with an awe-inspiring gurgle that took at least four minutes to subdue before quiet and equilibrium were restored, David decided to give Horace Shea a piece of his mind. As he raised his clenched knuckles to pound a second time on the Sheas' front door, Horace, grinning, opened it. He returned David's salute with a closed fist. "Comrade Herndon, don't knock so loud. You'll alert the police and have us all in the jug for subversion."

"You took our baby-sitter," David fumed. "It was an unneighborly thing to do. You are purposely making your toilet a braying nuisance. If I were bigger than you, and I had one more drink, I'd punch you in the nose."

Standing behind Horace, Tanya, a drink in her hand, offered it to David. Most friendships can be traced to the simple art of communication.

Staying friends, as millions of families have discovered, is even more difficult than staying married. Since both marriage and friendship presuppose a mutuality of interests and common achievement goals usually lacking in a society where male specialization reduces communication to the level of communally shared bridge, television, golf, or amorphous Saturday nights drinking and eating out, it is easy to predict that friends will eventually tread on each other's toes. When this happens the proper spouses will return to the bastions of their married existence, and from this vantage point are likely to excoriate "those so-called friends of ours" with newer friends who, at the moment, may be more sympathetic.

Thus far the Herndons and the Sheas had become deeply enough involved to grin, or to laugh a little at each other's peccadillos, or sophisticated enough to see, in the superior quality of their friendship, something unique and thus quite satisfying. Unlike most friends they were unafraid to analyze themselves. "We must not become victims of the Saturday Night Syndrome," Horace, the self-appointed philosopher of the group, told them. "As the song says 'everybody loves Saturday night.' But people get as mad as hell if Saturday night doesn't love them. Ultimately, it means that most people expect a Constitutional guarantee that man is entitled to pursue happiness even if he is unhappy doing it."

Nancy wasn't wholly convinced. "In Boston, David always took me out to dinner on Saturday night; Mother sat for us. Since it's so difficult to find baby-sitters out here, why couldn't we sit for each other on alternate Saturdays?" Nancy pointed out that Tanya got out of her house every day to her job at Bayberry's. "The rest of you can afford to feel superior; I'm the only one who's cooped up here all week. I need Saturday night to love me."

Though they tried Nancy's plan, later on they agreed it was really more fun when they were all home together. Then they could visit back and forth, and when they were together the conversation was brighter than when they weren't.

"David can sit opposite me, stare at the other diners, be

pleasant as hell with the waitresses, and not offer one interesting bit of conversation through an entire dinner," Nancy told Tanya.

"Years ago Horace talked incessantly," Tanya said. "He would spend whole evenings trying to explain how he felt about the tiniest thing. Nowadays when we dine out we often end up just grunting at each other like a couple of old sows."

The men agreed with the women that years of marital togetherness had put a damper on extended conversation. But they all discovered an interesting phenomenon; together, as a foursome, some of their premarital curiosity was restored. Since their proximity was limited to a few hours on Saturday night, with an occasional Wednesday or Thursday thrown in to break up the week, the process of getting acquainted was a little slower than in ordinary courtship. And while David and Horace could talk directly to each other, as Nancy and Tanya did, David could only learn about Tanya or Horace come to know Nancy, somewhat casually, through their general conversation.

To save running back and forth between houses David wired an intercom from the children's bedrooms to the two living rooms. When the project was finished they had become such good friends that it was even possible for David to suggest, in jest, that he could also wire up the adults' bedrooms. "Then we could spend Saturday nights in bed and converse with each other," he said. He winked over his highball glass at Tanya.

"Or we could listen to each other," Tanya laughed. "Who knows, it might be stimulating for Horace."

Nancy glared at David. "Mostly you would hear David snoring," she said. He embarrassed her. More often than not lately his conversation seemed to ramble into bedroom subjects.

As she came to know the Sheas better, Nancy discovered that she and Horace were the steady members of their respective families. Unless he had a few drinks, Horace was somewhat introverted, just as she was. He lacked the carefree and effervescent temperament of Tanya. And she had noticed that, though David was often taciturn when they weren't with the Sheas, he seemed to be recharged whenever Tanya was around. At such times he assumed a bantering ease and debonair attitude that reminded Nancy of the days when he was courting her.

Once Nancy tried to explain this to Horace and received a rather surprising reply. "I think Tanya and David enjoy flirting in front of us," he told her. "Our apparent stodginess becomes an exciting foil for them." Nancy was not quite certain

22

what Horace meant. She was aware that their marriages had been guided by the theory that likes attract but opposites marry, but she was confident that she and Tanya were reasonably good middle-class wives and mothers. Perhaps their marriages were nothing to write a book about. But really, except for those bedhopping actresses over in Hollywood, whose normal marriage was an interesting subject for fiction, or even for a factual book, for that matter? Nancy was at least sure that the dull life of predictability was preferable to passionate love followed by drugs, tears of penitence, and an overdose of sleeping pills.

Chapter 4

It took the Sheas some time to acclimate themselves to the ear-shocking Herndon accent with its broad Boston "A." But even more surprising to Horace, who had received his doctorate from U.C.L.A., was the discovery that David, who had a B.S. from Dartmouth, was politely but not deeply educated. Yet Horace had to admit that David was a refreshingly blunt escape from the academic world and the pressures that often made the acquisition of knowledge seem more vital than the ability to use it.

"I haven't time to worry about the state of the world," David insisted. "I am a downright materialist. Other than electing a Republican President, and lately I am not at all sure there's any essential difference between the Republicans and Democrats, or praying that whoever runs the country will keep us out of nuclear war, I'm just too damned busy trying to survive to worry about the divorce rate, or censorship, or civil rights, or the high birthrate. Really, Horace, I'm the sociologist's dream-man. The perfect economic unit. I run a business, employ fifty people, sire the right number of children, support my family, and generally stay out of trouble. If everyone did that much, we wouldn't need starry-eyed theorists like you figuring out new ways to share the wealth with those too lazy to work."

Nancy, too, was somewhat of an intellectual disappointment to Horace. She admitted that her destiny in life was to be both a sex machine for David and a reasonably good mother for her children. "When I first married I used to fret about it," she told Horace. "After four years of Smith I wasn't settling for suburbia. I was going to be famous, do something in the world. But after a day with the kids it takes more energy than I have left, and anyway, what does it all add up to? Before long we all die, and in the interim a woman's job is to devote her life to her children and to her husband's ego."

Though Horace guessed Nancy didn't really believe that, the truth was that she did, or at least had until they moved next door to the Sheas. From the moment that Tanya Shea had appeared in her living room, smiling so sweetly at David while she apologized for breaking in on them, Nancy had begun to feel somewhat frowzy. Somehow Tanya always managed to appear both casual and feminine, as well as crisp and self-assured. Yet Tanya was no brain. Nancy knew that, given the opportunity, she herself could really converse intelligently with Horace, even read his sociological stuff and understand it too. After all, she had majored in psychology at Smith. But all Tanya had ever done was graduate from high school; then she had studied art and fashion designing at some unknown college in San Francisco. Yet, though Tanya might be a flit-brain, she somehow managed to put her small talents to work. She of all people had successfully combined the joys of motherhood with a satisfying career.

She tried to avoid thinking too much about Tanya. In the morning, if she happened to be gardening in her tiny front yard, Tanya would gaily wave at her as she drove off with Mitch and Sam in the front seat of her car. Nancy knew that Tanya left them at the Andrew Jackson Grammar School, and then she could forget her maternal responsibilities until midafternoon. From nine to three Tanya enjoyed the professional world of fashion as artist and advertising director for Bayberry's in Long Beach. What's more, the seventy-five hundred a year she earned made her not dependent on Horace. Nancy stressed the *not dependent* rather than independent. She believed a female should give her male a feeling that she depended on him, though she wished she wasn't quite so dependent on David. If she ever had any possibility of being her own woman, it was lost forever. For security she had traded the only thing most females have to offer. Instant, hot-off-the-griddle sex. Of course, she loved David and the kids, but lately she had begun to worry. He didn't seem to mind that she served him a more hurried, cooler version of . . . what did David call it when they were first married? Nookie! "His little nookie." Ugh! Well, it wasn't the female's role to be the aggressor. Maybe Tanya Shea didn't believe that, but Nancy Herndon did. And it was too late to change now.

Nancy knew she must have some exceptional abilities; the trouble was she hadn't been able to define them. Once in college she thought she might become a writer, but after her first short story came back with a printed rejection slip she felt ill for a week, and that was the end of her literary career. Well, she might not have a career, but at least she was a better cook than Tanya. And kept a tidier, more organized house! Tanya seemed constitutionally unable to hang up her clothes, or put the dishes in a dishwasher until the last clean plate or glass was used. Nancy was sure that David, who was so finicky neat, couldn't live under the same roof with a woman like Tanya. She wondered if David appreciated her firmer grasp on the realities of homemaking. She knew Horace did.

David often felt that Horace, with a perpetual pipe in his mouth, was attempting to build an image of sagacity and wisdom that was unrelated to the actualities of existence. David never made an issue of it, because he knew that friendship seldom survives rash criticism, but he was certain that men like Horace were completely unaware that without the entrepreneur types like David—the men who had the drive and nerve to take risks and carve new shapes in the economic environment, the men who actually produced the economic wealth—society would be unable to afford the luxury of its philosophers. He suspected that Tanya, who was closer to the realities of the business world, appreciated his firmer grasp on the grim economics of working for a living. He was sure that Nancy didn't. It irked him a little that the Sheas' combined income was probably a few thousand dollars more than David managed to earn by the sweat of his brow from his own brainchild, the Herndon Showcase and Fixture Corporation.

While the Herndons and the Sheas often played bridge for an hour or so as the entrée to an evening together, they gradually discovered that none of them was really a bridge addict. After bridge they switched to penny-ante poker, and once Horace even suggested they play strip-poker. If it had been David's idea, on some other evening, they might have tried it. But the suggestion from a fully sober Horace seemed out of character, and the idea was squelched when Tanya said, without so much as blushing, "Sorry, Horace, I've got my period. I'm not betting my sanitary belt and pad against David's jockey shorts."

Sometimes they tried television. But while David liked Westerns, Nancy liked good dramas with social meanings, Horace preferred news commentators and world surveys of this and that, and Tanya thought everything on the tube was a horrible bore.

Often before dinner they tried alcohol and hors d'oeuvres. This led to conversations about their views on religion, the affairs of the day, current novels, moving pictures, television, Russia, China, and politics. Horace was a proselytizing Democrat. David was an unshakable Republican. Tanya was nonpolitical. Nancy didn't really care, but was loyal to David. Nancy admitted to Horace that she had admired President Kennedy and Jacqueline, and she thought Franklin Roosevelt

26

had done some good things, like getting rid of prohibition and starting Social Security.

Horace played golf for the exercise. David played because he liked it. Since neither of them played better than the middle nineties, they discovered that the game was a pleasant excuse to spend Sunday mornings together and thus eliminate the problem of whether to go to church. Tanya's Swedish parents had been Lutherans. Horace had been brought up Catholic, but was happy to tell anyone who was interested he had "thought his way out of all religious traps." For Tanya the path of least resistance was not to go to church at all. Besides, as she told Nancy, Sunday was cleaning and resting day. Being a working wife, she had to cram housewifely duties into Sunday morning.

Nancy had been brought up a Congregationalist, and was married in a Congregational Church. After they were married, David, who had been an occasional Unitarian, went to church with her on Easter and Christmas. "I'm glad you're a good wife," he told her. "You take the kids to Sunday school. Frankly, it bores the hell out of me to sing those damned hymns."

Nancy tried to explain to Susan and Jimmy that their father worked hard and needed Sundays to relax. To herself she had to admit that listening while Reverend John Winter attempted to relate current moral problems to biblical precepts was not always inspiring. Nevertheless she considered it her duty. She even managed to corral Mitch and Sam most Sundays and bring them to Sunday school along with Susan and Jimmy.

As they became closer friends Nancy had been somewhat concerned that their Saturday evenings, even while they were playing bridge, seemed to creep with increasing detail and hilarity into the subject of sex. Not just general sex and dirty stories, though David and Tanya seemed to pick up in their business contacts an endless fund of stories. Neither David nor Tanya seemed embarrassed to say any of the dirty words that made Nancy shudder when she heard them. But even worse, the stories often led to blushingly frank personal observations on the sexual idiosyncrasies of their respective partners.

"Horace doesn't waste time," Tanya chuckled. She patted Horace's cheek. "Each year it gets faster and faster. Pretty soon I guess all we'll do is talk about it."

Horace wasn't angry. "The trouble with Tanya is I have a feeling right at the crucial moment she's planning a new advertising campaign for Tom Bayberry." He stroked her arm. "Or maybe she is pretending I'm Tom Bayberry."

27

"Tom Bayberry is fifty-two years old," Tanya rolled her eyes. "He has grown such a belly I doubt if he has seen his instrument for several years."

"His wife must have to climb on him," David laughed. "It would be interesting to watch. Intercourse on a bowl of Jello. The trouble with Nancy is that she's a perfectionist. The kids must be asleep. The candles sputtering. The hi-fi playing Mantovani."

Nancy was angry, but she was careful to hide it. What would the Sheas think if she told them that many times she had waited for David, prayed that tonight was the night; had prepared herself for him. Then, more often than not he would simply kiss her, say, "I love you, Sea, but tonight I'm pooped," and calmly David would go to sleep. Maybe it was better fast than *not at all!*

But, while the Herndons and Sheas discussed the intimacies of sex, tried to evoke the true meaning of love and marriage, and inveighed against divorce and wife-swapping, they maintained a very proper relationship. Horace was always friendly with Nancy, but never so much as touched her. Often, it seemed to Nancy, he went to awkward extremes to avoid physical contact. David teased Tanya that she had a shape like a burlesque stripper. While occasionally Tanya might have wiggled her pelvis at him with what Nancy might have considered more than neighborly interest, yet on Christmas under the mistletoe and on New Year's Eve at midnight they kissed their respective spouses on the lips and each other's wives on the cheek.

Chapter 5

Perhaps it might have continued that way if the Sheas hadn't decided to build a swimming pool into their rather crowded backyard. It wasn't really Horace's idea. Tanya had done the artwork and illustrations for a construction company that installed the pools. In payment she had the privilege of purchasing their best pool at cost. As Tanya said, "While I'm not the mermaid type, it's such a bargain that we can't afford not to buy one."

The Saturday after the pool was finished the Herndons were invited to christen it. Nancy Herndon, wearing a discreet two-piece flowered bathing suit, sat in a sun-chair beside the pool and sipped a vodka collins which melted ice had reduced to a pale potency. She watched David and Tanya, who were in the deep end of the pool. They were playing water volleyball against the boisterous, combined forces of the Herndon and Shea children.

"Come on in and help us, Nancy," Tanya yelled. She leaped out of the water to return the ball across the net. "These kids are too much for us."

Nancy shook her head. Your breasts, practically falling out of your bikini, are too much for David, she thought. Nancy looked at Horace. He was reclining in a beach chair, his face tilted to the late afternoon sun; he didn't seem to give a damn. Nancy felt grim. She wanted to poke him and say, Wake up, stupid! With that tiny bit of cloth across her nipples, and that abbreviated diaper between her legs that scarcely covers her cleft and leaves nothing to the imagination so far as her behind goes, your wife is seducing my husband!

When Tanya had sauntered toward the pool and David saw her for the first time, hadn't Horace noticed the glazed look in David's eye? Nancy did, and she would bet Tanya knew what she was doing.

"I wouldn't dare wear it to the beach," Tanya had confided. Nancy complimented her but thought, like hell you wouldn't. "But here in my own back yard," Tanya added, "among friends, it's different."

Nancy was quite certain that it wasn't *that* different. She had breasts and buttocks and a mound with hair on it too, but she wasn't displaying them or wiggling them just to drive Horace crazy. Still, Nancy knew she was being petty. Tanya was just Tanya; she was much too ingenuous to tempt David. Subtlety and the femme fatale approach were definitely not a part of her character. Really, after three years of friendship, she should be used to Tanya's lack of restraint. Last night when they were playing bridge was typical. Tanya had asked David if, like Horace, he was inhibited in the bathroom. Despite Horace's protest that bathroom habits weren't an appetizing subject, Tanya rambled on.

"I'm not like Horace," she said calmly. "Traffic in the bathroom, even if I am trying to shit, doesn't constipate me."

Shaking his head in dismay, Horace asked if it was necessary that Tanya be so vulgar; but he was too late. Tanya was already well into the details of the size of an amazing bowel movement she had had the day before. David, choking with hysterical laughter, encouraged her. Nancy told him later that she didn't think the subject was that funny.

"Oh, Nancy, for God's sakes, can't you relax? You're a big girl now. Thirty-six years old. You don't have to act the shy virgin any longer."

I don't have to act and talk like a prostitute either, Nancy thought. She watched Tanya splashing in the pool with David. Of course, it wouldn't pay to underestimate Tanya. Nancy remembered fifteen years ago and more, when David was dating her. Then, by gosh, he liked the shy virgin type. Back in New England, in those days, he hadn't been so sophisticated, and a female like Tanya, saying any damned thing that came into her head, would have scared him half to death.

Nancy remembered that once, three weeks before they were to be married, she had confided to David that she was ready for him. By inserting her new diaphragm before David arrived for their date she had hoped to avoid embarrassment, and she wanted to convince him that they didn't have to wait for their wedding night. But David had been shocked. Though he had tried to hide his dismay, clearly he didn't want *his* virgin bride to take the initiative. For many years after that Nancy had let David take the preventive measures. But now all she had to do was take a pill once a day; that, at least, eliminated the sort of female premeditation David had objected to.

"Of course, I'm not so naive myself any longer," Nancy murmured.

"Talking to yourself?" Horace asked. He picked up her

30

glass and his own and refilled them at a portable bar beside the pool.

"I don't know whether I should drink any more. I'm getting a little woozy." Nancy turned the glass in her hands. "I was thinking of a poem I memorized a long time ago:

> The little toy dog is covered with dust,
> Sturdy and staunch he stands.
> The little toy soldier is covered with rust;
> His musket molds in his hands.

"You're obviously not thinking of the situation that inspired the poet."

Nancy smiled. "Only the mood. Life goes on. What once was, no longer is. Fifty years from now who will be sitting here? Fifty years ago who sat here, unaware that on these hills would be the bedrooms of Los Angeles?"

"What is may be better than what was."

"Probably, but the past is blurred. The outlines are purple, not jagged and sharp. The rough edges are obscured."

Horace shrugged. "To look at your problem sideways, let's start afresh. I read a book once by a fellow named Robert Heinlein. He added a new word to the vocabulary. *To grok.*"

"I read that book," Nancy said, delighted with her sudden rapport with Horace. "Grok means to understand so thoroughly that the observer becomes a part of the observed, to merge, blend, intermarry, lose identity in group experience." Nancy looked at Horace thoughtfully. "It's a nice idea, but I'm a New Englander. We're raised in the tradition of rugged individualism."

"You mean you're not grokking Tanya and David?"

Nancy looked startled. Was her expression so obvious? "Tanya is Tanya. If I tried to act like her it would be contrived sexiness. I was taught that little girls should be modest. But Tanya isn't acting. I know she's just buoyantly unfettered. The thought occurred to me that in her innocence she may be underestimating David."

Horace was amused. "Don't delude yourself. Tanya's not *that* innocent."

Silently Nancy watched David and Tanya. One thing was certain. She and Horace were acting like old fogeys. Why didn't they jump into the pool and play volleyball with the kids, too? Why couldn't she be provocative with Horace— just a little? Tease him the way Tanya was teasing David.

She handed her glass to Horace. "In that book to grok meant to drink. We are water brothers, Horace. Get me a refill."

31

Later, Nancy insisted that she wasn't really inebriated. "I never drink to excess," she smiled blearily at Tanya, who was trying to rouse her from the redwood lounge chair. "Jus' go away and let me sleep a little bit." She closed her eyes and then jumped up. "My God! Where are Jimmy and Sue?"

David offered her a hot dog. "Horace barbecued them. It's nine thirty. Don't worry, I put them to bed. Tanya helped. Then we tackled Mitch and Sam. Horace watched over you and got the charcoal going."

"We told the kids that tomorrow is Sunday, and the pool won't vanish," Tanya plopped on a chaise. "Ah, it's nice to have it quiet. The night is ours."

Though she was still a little groggy, the conversation filtered through Nancy's beclouded brain. Tanya and David had been in her house. Had they been in her bedroom? Would Horace have stood idly by and waited? Eating a hot dog, she asked Horace if he had spiked her drink.

"It did you good to relax," Tanya said. "Nancy, your children are lambs. How did you ever subdue them? They went to bed like little angels, but we had to use a club on my two."

"David makes them mind," Nancy said. "I'll lend him to you. He'll straighten out Mitch and Sam. He just acts like a big grouchy bear. He's a boss, after all. No one tangles with a boss."

David, sitting on the edge of the pool, dangling his feet in the water, ignored Nancy's attempt to have herself contradicted. "This is a very lovely pool," he remarked. "Back where I come from everybody knows in California they swim naked in their swimming pools and have orgies when the sun goes down." David's words sounded slurry to him. Without the cover of liquor he probably wouldn't have dared. Now happily tipsy, he grinned at Tanya. "Come on, take off those handkerchiefs and swim in your skin."

Horace pointed at the reflection of the moon in the pool. "Let's be bare-assed astronauts," he agreed. "We can jump on the moon."

"A good idea," Tanya said brightly as she fumbled with the strings holding her bikini.

"The children!" Nancy wailed. "Besides, I can only swim dog paddle." She knew she just couldn't wiggle out of her bathing suit while everyone, especially Horace, watched her. "What if the kids are awake?" she asked. "What if they got up and discovered us all naked?"

Tanya agreed. First they should make certain the children were asleep. Conspiratorially, she led Nancy first to check Sue and Jimmy's bedroom. "I'm afraid I'll be embarrassed," Nancy whispered. Actually, she was both frightened and intrigued. She got Tanya to help turn out all the lights in both houses, so that the neighbors would think they had gone to bed. In Tanya's bedroom she slowly slipped out of her bathing suit as Tanya, already naked, urged her to hurry back to the pool. All four children were sound asleep; Nancy was sorry she couldn't use their presence to dampen the idea. Tiptoeing through the Sheas' kitchen, she was aware of her breasts swaying against her chest. Tanya opened the back door. They were both quite naked. Suddenly Nancy had to go to the john again.

"Silly!" Tanya said, and pushed her onto the patio. "You just leaked. Horace won't bite you, and after all these years David must have seen you in your birthday suit."

With the moon briefly behind a cloud, the pool was so shadowy that Nancy could see only the vague outlines of Horace and David placidly floating on the water. In hoarse whispers the men urged the women to hurry up, because the water was so erotically fine.

Horace soon discovered that Nancy's breasts were larger than Tanya's. With a large aureola framing each erect nipple, they seemed to be so friendly that they were extending an invitation to be caressed independently of what Nancy might want; she herself seemed rather shivery and grim, but at last she lowered herself into the water a respectable distance from Horace. Nancy noted that David and Tanya were diving and submerging together like playful porpoises. It was too dark to be sure, but she thought she saw Tanya clinging to David as they went under the water.

But Horace wasn't watching Tanya. Suddenly he dove for Nancy's legs and dragged her under with him. As she was pulled to the bottom, she struggled to escape Horace's quick, tingling embrace.

Nancy came to the surface gasping indignantly. "Horace," she whispered, frightened. "Don't do that again! I don't swim very well. You'll drown me. And I'm not *that* tight!" He watched the oval of her behind as she pulled herself onto the edge of the pool.

"I'm not tight," Horace muttered. "Just dangerously priapic." He hoisted himself out of the water and sat beside her. In spite of herself, Nancy grinned at him. "If the children woke and saw you like that, what would they think?"

"I'd tell them I'm practicing for the pole vault at a track meet." Horace smiled happily at her. "You obviously have unique powers, Nancy. You can raise the dead." He pulled on his bathing trunks and flopped in a chaise at a respectable distance from her.

Did David and Tanya, still heedlessly naked, join them

33

somewhat reluctantly? Nancy was quite sure about one thing. David and Tanya both felt that Horace and Nancy were party-poopers. But they didn't voice the thought.

That was a month ago. Although there had been some very warm nights since, no one broached the subject of swimming in the Shea pool late at night—with or without clothes.

Chapter 6

~~~~~~~

Lying in her bed a few weeks later, listening to the early-morning bathroom sounds, Nancy felt a momentary annoyance. David's blood must flow faster than hers. Forcing her eyes open, she glanced at the clock on David's dresser. Five thirty. Impossible! Given any encouragement, if he knew he wouldn't awaken the children, David would be singing. Nancy buried her face in the pillow. What was wrong with her? Why after three years hadn't she adjusted to California as well as David? Was it California, she wondered, or was she antisocial? There were the women's clubs. She had joined two. One for mothers, the San Pedrans, the other for culture, little adventures in literature and the arts with frustrated school-teachers, or women in their fifties who, now that their bellies had grown larger, extolled the virtues of the mind over sex.

But she really didn't have a typical case of suburban boredom; the trouble was that she was too introspective. Constantly trying to evaluate her life, the meaning of marriage to David, and the roots of her own existence only led to sleepless nights, like last night. Usually she stayed up and read until she was exhausted. But last night, deciding to be more compatible, she had gone to bed early with David to watch television. Promptly at ten o'clock he had pecked her on the cheek, patted her behind, and said: "It won't keep me awake; you watch it." In ten minutes, thus verbally reassured that she still was David's beloved, she was left alone with her thoughts. David was efficient; he could sleep on schedule.

She lay there tossing. It wasn't sexual frustration, she thought. David was systematic. The whole sex business occupied less than two hours a week. But in that time at least three orgasms were arrived at without too much effort. So the trouble was not sexual frustration.

Through her eyelashes she watched the warm glow of a new day piercing the night sky over Catalina. As David often pointed out, not every female in the United States could wake in her bed to the expanse of the Pacific Ocean stretched to the horizon. It was November, and the sky was cloudless.

35

Another perfect day. A happening in the sum total of happenings, adding up to what?

Today maybe she would magically climb out of the rut she was in. She didn't have to be merely the wife of David Herndon, the mother of Sue and Jimmy. She didn't just have to spend the day waiting for David to come home, only to realize he was scarcely aware she had actually cooked his dinner, instead of defrosting it, as most women did. Maybe, Nancy thought, I should write down all the brilliant ideas that keep me awake. I could write them into an article; I could be a free-lance writer and sell all my brilliant intuitions to women's magazines. I would be invited to appear on television. Not like that hard-looking, bejeweled woman who wrote a nasty novel about her Eastern college and the sexual frustrations of middle-class women. She had divorced three husbands and publicly proclaimed that sex was a grim business, of very little value in the wider scheme of things. What had David called her? A bull dyke? Nancy wouldn't admit she didn't know what the term meant. Later she looked it up in *The Dictionary of American Slang*, the book that had all the dirty words in one place, as someone in her literary group had told her.

No, not like that woman, nor like Betty Friedan, who wrote about the feminine mystique. Because last night a brilliant new idea had occurred to her. The *real* trouble with the world was that both males and females were so unsure of each other their lives had become a series of indirect, half-embarrassed contacts. Couples long married, who could freely give their bodies in mutual embrace, only reluctantly shared their thoughts. What she wanted to tell David was her new idea. Television, movies, novels, biographies, alcohol, sex, drugs like marijuana and LSD, even concerts, opera, spectator sports, aimless automobile driving—all the myriad forms of escapism added up to a lot more than proof of boredom. They were symptomatic of a world where no one was ever taught how to step out of his own skin and find mystery and wonder and adventure in another person. So human beings used all these other means of indirect contact. They touched each other like carom shots in billiards. An indirect attempt to impel someone in the direction you wished, because most men and women were afraid to reveal their poor little egos to each other in any other way.

Nancy was certain, after fifteen years of marriage, that David would only half listen if she started to rattle on to him about this wonderful new perception of hers. He would be convinced that the feminine mind was really quite unstable. With a flash of honesty Nancy realized it was a two-way

36

street. If David came home worried about the problems of getting orders or manufacturing showcases and fixtures, she too would probably only half listen. She would try to divert his thoughts to matters of more interest to her. Why? Why couldn't she momentarily, at least, try to see David's world through David's eyes?

Still half lying on the edge of the bed, Nancy slowly let her feet touch the floor. Suddenly, unaccountably, a clear vision of Horace's penis flashed across her mind. Swollen and erect, it pointed at her, ready to penetrate her. Nancy shivered. Why, for God's sake, when she was thinking something entirely different should she have that thought? What unspeakable ideas were churning in the subterranean layers of her brain? Why did the image of Horace, naked, as she had seen him only on the night they went swimming, pop into her mind?

She slid out of bed. The dismaying thought occurred to her that it would take extremely courageous males and females to divulge *all* the thoughts that flickered through their brains. Exasperated, she knew that she was trying to erase the even deeper image. Momentarily she had been willing, no actually wanted, to kiss Horace's penis. It was a gesture she had often refused David.

The hot Santa Ana wind was blowing, and Nancy wished it would rain or, better, snow. That would be wonderful. A gray, sputtery, grim kind of day, such as they were probably having in Massachusetts right now. A day so anti-man outside that you were content with the relative simplicity of a roof overhead, an oil burner humming merrily away in the basement, and something to eat in the refrigerator.

But days in San Pedro were laughing days. Except for the rare hot days like today, they beckoned you to come outside to forget your worries. Come outside and be doing something! But do *what?* Ah, that was the rub. Outside was a scrubby lawn about six feet wide by fifty feet long. When they were outside, she and David lived on a balcony, and from there they could look only at the rooftops below them and at the Pacific Ocean, a remote stage, miles away, placid, unchanging, unconcerned.

It was quarter to six. Nancy brushed her hair and slipped a thin, new housecoat over her nightgown. She could hear David, upstairs, padding around in the kitchen, and she knew that if she didn't join him in five minutes, David, immaculately dressed, with the spicy odor of aftershave lotion on his cheeks, would be giving her his goodbye kiss on the nose, saying: "You don't have to get up, Sea. I can get breakfast in town."

37

"No," she smirked grimly at herself in the mirror, "I refuse to be a soap-opera cliché. I will not be the dissatisfied hausfrau, bored with her lot in life. I'm still presentable: no jowls, few wrinkles." As she ran upstairs at least she felt physically alive and in good shape. That was half the battle.

"Hi and good morning!" She brushed her lips across David's cheek He was perched on a barstool, adjusting the lens on his large telescope.

Grunting his greeting, David pointed the telescope on its easel toward Los Angeles Harbor. Nancy watched him out of the corner of her eye and wondered why he spent so much time staring through his telescope at the ocean and at Long Beach. She put water on to boil, measured instant coffee into two cups, poured some frozen orange juice into two large glasses, poked around in her combination refrigerator and deep freeze and unearthed a package of precooked frozen waffles Soon the waffles popped out of the toaster.

"Breakfast is ready. See anything new this morning?"

"A tanker going out." David spread some jam on his waffle.

"I never can figure out why that telescope intrigues you so much."

David chuckled. "I'm a voyeur. Every morning at about six, four streets below us, a little old lady gets out of her bed and stares out the window while she scratches her belly."

"She's naked?"

"Of course not. She sleeps in her girdle."

"Why should that interest you?"

"I like to speculate on what is going on in the lives of other people."

"Because your own life is so dull?" There was a tremor of anger in Nancy's words.

David just grinned. "You and I are the salt of the earth. A dull husband, a dull wife, and two dull children. There's millions like us " He drank his orange juice. "We did, presumably, move to the land of fresh oranges."

"If that's sarcasm, I don't appreciate it. I'll be glad to buy you fresh oranges."

David shrugged. "You seem a little edgy this morning. Why didn't you stay in bed for another hour and get your beauty sleep."

"I most always get your breakfast." Nancy angrily brushed the tear from her eye. Why was she so tense today? She couldn't help it. "I suppose you would deprive me of getting your breakfast."

"Now what in hell does that mean?"

"Oh, I don't know." It really was impossible to explain.

"Here, put this maple syrup from good old Vermont on your waffle. It's snowing there. I wish it would snow here."

"Overshoes, snow shovels, snow tires, slush, runny noses." David smiled. "It's better thinking about it than being there."

"If it snowed here, maybe all the millions of automobiles on the freeways would skid together and crack up all at once instead of piecemeal. David, why do you have to go to work so early? Joe Casey, across the street, doesn't even own his own business. He works in downtown Los Angeles. He never leaves until seven thirty."

David munched on his waffle.

"David, did you hear me? Why do you . . . ?"

"I heard you, Sea. For the fortieth time, in the three years since we've lived here, I'll tell you. There are three reasons. All my life I woke up early. My New England heritage. I can't sleep after five thirty. The early bird catches the worm. Look around you. This is a pretty expensive worm I've caught. The average income in these United States is about six thousand dollars. I make nearly four times that much. I'm thirty-six years old, and I believe that if I keep getting up early, someday I may make four or five times what I now earn. Since you obviously enjoy some of the luxuries of living, like that housecoat you're wearing—it probably cost at least fifty dollars—you can't possibly object to that. The second reason is: A man who runs a business *has* to set a good example. Arrive before his employees. Give them the evil eye when they are late. Convince them that the American dream can be theirs, too! Convince them that the way to wealth and happiness is through their own efforts. They, too, can catch the worm."

Nancy was aware that David was baiting her. She just stared at him, her eyes round and wide, an indication that she was in her story-listening mood. David finished his coffee. "As I've often said the third and most important reason is that between six and seven on weekday mornings only worm-catchers like me are on the freeway. This means that I can drive to the plant in forty-five minutes instead of an hour and forty-five minutes." David kissed Nancy's nose. "There's a tear in your eye. Don't cry, Nancy; I'm not going on a world tour. I'll be home tonight by seven."

"David, can't I go to work, too? Tanya does. Couldn't you use another secretary? Once I was a very good typist." Even as she said the words Nancy was angry at herself. Why was she pleading? If she were getting her period it would make sense, but that was at least two weeks ahead.

David walked toward the front door. "The trouble with you, Sea, is that you've been reading too many of those

39

damned books. Some women haven't a thing to do except irritate other women into a frenzy because the modern American female supposedly isn't fulfilling herself. If you *had* to join the rat race, if you *had* to go to work every day, you'd be sick of it in a month. You're not aggressive like Tanya. What good would it do, anyway? If you earned a hundred dollars a week, you would have to pay a woman seventy-five to take care of the kids." At the door David kissed her feebly on the lips. "I'll see you tonight, hon."

Nancy watched him drive off in his Pontiac toward the freeway. She brushed the tears from her eyes. Damn him anyway. Not so aggressive as Tanya! Someday she'd show him just how aggressive she could be.

Chapter 7

~~~~~~~~~

Nancy poured two more glasses of orange juice and two glasses of milk, and started to hum softly. No, she wasn't going to waste today in a depressed mood. David was probably right. They had two wonderful children and a lovely home, and she had David, who really was the salt of the earth. Maybe all she needed was a hobby to exercise her brain on.

During breakfast another thought kept recurring to her. We are really Martha and George, not Nancy and David at all. Really characters out of a play like *Who's Afraid of Virginia Woolf*. This kitchen was not a kitchen at all, but a stage. She and David were actors being watched by some other David with a telescope in his living room.

Nancy looked at the clock on her electric stove. It was only six fifteen. No need to wake Sue and Jimmy yet. She had an hour. She wandered around her living room enjoying the feel of the deep-pile broadloom beneath her bare feet. If they were really actors on a stage, she would bet she could write the play better than Albee. After all, what did a man know about a woman's point of view?

Nancy rolled up last night's newspaper and emptied two ashtrays into it. Tonight was a Shea night, but she didn't have to clean house. There wasn't even any dust on the tables. Back home in Boston. No . . . not home. This was home. Back in Boston, she had to dust the tables at least twice a week. But that really was a nuisance, too.

She walked downstairs to the laundry and examined the dirty clothes in the hamper. Methodically, she sorted them for the washing machine; tossed in a few shakes of detergent and closed the hatch. She would start the washer later, when the kids were in school. Momentarily, she had a vision of that old television commercial with a strong male hand reaching out of the machine. She smiled. If a male hand came out of her washer, she would grab it and pull until the whole man emerged. He would be bald, like Mr. Clean, but since he lived in a washing machine he would be naked, too. Seeing her standing there, dumbfounded, with her nipples taut and

41

her pubic hair tantalizingly visible, he would have a gleam in his eye and be wonderfully and even alarmingly erect. It would be nice to spend the day in bed with the man in the washing machine for a loving companion. David might think she wanted the jolly bald giant only for his hard-on, but David would be wrong. The real trouble was that she was lonesome. If there ever should be a giant in the washing machine, he would have to love her for her brains, too.

Nancy looked in Jimmy's room. He was stretched out flat on his back, sleeping soundly, his face cherubic. Sue, in her bedroom, was curled in a ball, a finger in her mouth. It was only six thirty. She could go back to bed for an hour. No! Today, she would turn over a new leaf. Why shouldn't she really try to write a play? She dashed upstairs to the kitchen and pulled her portable typewriter out of the closet. She inserted a sheet of paper and started pecking.

> *The curtain rises on the living room of the home of David and Nancy Herndon. Sliding glass-window walls overlook the Pacific Ocean and Catalina Island in the distance. Beyond the windows is an open porch that flanks the back of the house. The room is carpeted in white broadloom. Modern low sofas, coffee tables, a white brick fireplace on one wall with an abstract painting over it, and a television set are arranged with the clean-cut simplicity and impersonality of a hotel room. Do people really live here?*

Nancy smiled as she typed. That was good.

> *The general impression is that the interior decorator of an expensive department store furnished the room and ordered all the appointments at once. Nothing has been added since. To have done so, according to the decorator, would have weakened the total effect. It is a room for viewing. A room that requires a minimum of housework to retain the original, simple luxury. A room in which a cluttered mind could unclutter itself. A staircase descends to bedrooms below.*

Nancy stared at the paper in her typewriter. This was silly. There was no need to describe her own living room. The set designer would quickly get the picture.

> *David Herndon, a man in his middle thirties, comes up the staircase into the living room. He is fully dressed in a business suit. Ivy League in appearance, he gives*

*the impression of brusque efficiency. The kind of man
who has worked hard to build his own image, and now
he lives by it. Whistling softly, he walks into the kitchen
that flanks the living room, pours water from the sink
into a pot and puts it on to boil. He fumbles in the refrigerator, finds orange juice, pours himself a glass, sits on
one of the barstools, walks back to the living room, ad-
justs a telescope that is on an easel, and scans the distant
harbor.*

Nancy smiled. This was getting better.

*While David is looking through his telescope, Nancy,
his wife, in her early thirties, appears on the staircase in
white panties and bra. She puts on the pink housecoat
she is carrying. Her hair is disheveled. With no makeup,
she looks the worse for wear.*

Nancy was enjoying herself. *This* Nancy wouldn't spend
the night looking at television while her husband snored.

*She stares at David for a second, and then notices the
pot boiling and the dirty glass.*

NANCY (*pouting*) I suppose you'd deprive me of getting
your breakfast, too?

DAVID Why didn't you stay in bed? Get your beauty sleep.
The kids won't be up for an hour.

NANCY (*Puts instant coffee in the cups and drops a frozen
waffle in the toaster*) After fifteen years of marriage, is it
more interesting to look in other people's bedrooms?

DAVID (*relinquishing the telescope*) I'm not looking in bedrooms. I was watching a freighter coming into the harbor.
Really, it's silly for you to get up so early. I'm perfectly
capable of boiling water and dropping a waffle in the
toaster.

NANCY You're so damned capable, I'm beginning to wonder
why you got married in the first place.

Nancy smiled. This was more like it.

DAVID How am I supposed to answer that?

NANCY Tell me you need me!

43

DAVID I need you.

NANCY Great!

DAVID I'm not twenty-six anymore.

Nancy pondered. Should David tell the truth? What the hell.

DAVID Besides, last night with your hair in those god-awful rollers, yelling at me that because I didn't take the kids to Sunday school I couldn't possibly be a good father. And when you finally took off the curlers, you lay there like a lump of dough waiting to be kneaded.

NANCY (*indignantly*) You should have married a burlesque queen. I'm a wife and mother!

DAVID You're not *my* mother.

NANCY Let's not bring your mother into this.

DAVID Into what?

NANCY Into our dull marriage.

DAVID What do you want from marriage, anyway? I love you. You live in a fifty-thousand-dollar home. You spend more for clothes than any of your friends. You have two nice kids.

NANCY (*loudly*) I want it to snow! Tanya spends more for clothes than I do. (*She shoves a bottle of maple syrup at him.*) It's snowing in New England. Try some Vermont maple syrup. It will sweeten your disposition.

DAVID My disposition was perfectly sweet until you came upstairs. (*he sings*) "Oh, what a beautiful morning. Oh, what a beautiful day!"

NANCY I hate California. I want to snuggle in front of a fireplace with the snow howling outside. I'm sick of sunshine.

DAVID There's smog. You could wrap yourself in that.

NANCY There's Tanya Shea!

DAVID What in hell has Tanya to do with this?

NANCY You think she's sexy.

DAVID (*shrugging*) I'm a man. Men like women who react to men like women.

NANCY   (*Sadly*)   I know I'm not sexy.

Disgusted, Nancy ripped the paper out of her typewriter, put it with the other sheets she had written, and tore them in small pieces. It seemed that after all these years of marriage she still didn't know what made David tick, though she did know he liked Tanya. Yet he had never seemed too close to her, except possibly on the night of the swimming party. Tanya, like Horace, was just a friend, but David—she had never found the key to him. Oh, nonsense! She sounded like the heroine in a women's magazine story. David wasn't subtle; he was just a good man trying to build a business. Still, didn't everyone need a raison d'être? Something to live by until they carted you away to listen eternally to the music of the spheres at Forest Lawn? She was sure David believed in God, though he refused to go to church. He loved his children, but not so much that he couldn't be stern with them. He went fishing occasionally, he played golf occasionally, he watched television, he managed always to have read one or two bestsellers, he played bridge unenthusiastically. But with all the things he did, Nancy couldn't remember his being keenly interested in anything but the Herndon Showcase and Fixture Company.

Nancy sighed. David was right. "My husband is a dull man. I'm a dull woman. We're well mated."

"What's well mated, Mommy?"

Susan was standing beside the table. She was dressed for school, watching her mother with wide brown eyes.

"Susan, you startled me. Was I thinking out loud?" Nancy asked. "My God, I really am getting loony. What did I say?"

Primly, Susan poured cereal into a bowl. "I talk to my dolls out loud, sometimes. You said, 'I guess I'm a dull woman. We're well mated.'"

Jimmy appeared at the top of the stairs. "Nancy needs to be sharpened, that's all."

Nancy tried not to smile. "I told you not to call me Nancy."

"Daddy said now that I'm nearly eleven I can call him Dave."

"I don't care what Daddy said. Hurry up and eat your breakfast."

"What's well mated?" Susan asked again.

"It's like chess," Jimmy explained. "The king and queen are well mated. Then the king is checkmated."

Chapter 8

~~~~~~~~

Nancy backed her Chevrolet out of the garage. Susan and Jimmy sat in back. With the doors locked and the seat belts fastened, they seemed safer back there. Nervously, Nancy threaded the car onto the Harbor Freeway. The traffic whizzed by her. Ten minutes of this, and then a turnoff that led to the Andrew Jackson Grammar School. People! Had God ever intended there to be so many of them? Every family had a minimum of two automobiles, and some three or four. All these smoking monsters crammed into God's lovely scenery, fouling it with gasoline fumes. People! People who erected nasty little metal dinosaurs in the few remaining weedy sections of land. Unthinking metal robots, they glared at you from the empty holes in their metal heads as they pumped insanely twenty-four hours a day to capture a little more of the oil that would later become gasoline. And the gasoline became smoke that hung like a pall of death over its creators. People! People caught like mice, people insisting that the treadmill they raced on was freedom! It would be only poetic justice if they all died breathing the noxious mess they had made of this once beautiful world.

As they neared the school, Susan reminded Nancy that she was staying after school to practice her part in the Christmas play. Jimmy groaned and said he wasn't hanging around school until four thirty, but Nancy insisted she wouldn't make an extra trip just to bring him home. He must wait until Mommy could bring them home together.

The trip to school and back took exactly twenty-four minutes. As Nancy turned into her driveway, Tanya backed out of hers. Mitch and Sam were in the front seat with her. "I'm late, as usual," Tanya yelled. "See you tonight."

Nancy waved. "Tell your boys to wait with Jimmy. I'll pick them all up at four thirty."

David was at work and the children were at school. And now what would Nancy Herndon do today? She could have joined her club's bowling team, but she had tried bowling for a few weeks and then dropped it. The trouble wasn't her aching back, she told David, but her aching mind. She couldn't get interested in the boring details of intimate family life that these women spouted to each other. If David wasn't the world's best man in bed, she wasn't going to discuss his short-comings with other women.

Maybe she ought to take some courses. Maybe learn how to write a play, or take a sociology course . . . under Horace! That was good; she grinned at the sudden picture the words conjured up in her mind. What would it be like under Horace? Different from being under David?

Suddenly she knew she couldn't stop herself. Horace didn't leave the house until nine o'clock on Wednesdays. By now he was in his bathroom, and she hadn't watched him there for the past two weeks. Well, damn it, merely watching wasn't sexual, it was only a kind of relief from ennui. Anyway, it was too early to go shopping.

It was by accident that she had discovered that by standing on a chair in her upstairs guest bedroom, she could look through the high corner window right down into the Shea bathroom. She had seen a cobweb in the corner of the room and stood on a chair to knock it down. Could she help it that Horace opened his bathroom window in the morning, or that he stood beside the window, not twenty feet away, shaving without a damned stitch of clothing on? David always wore shorts when he shaved, and David's body was as smooth as a young boy's. Just a dark bush of hair around his genitals and under his armpits. She had been startled to observe a man as hairy as Horace, and that night in the Shea pool she hadn't really dared to look at him. Not much! Anyway, she told herself, her interest wasn't sexual. It was just that she liked to watch the firm stance of Horace's hairy black legs and the shifting of the gluteal muscles in his small, hard buttocks in sympathetic response to the grimaces he made in the mirror while shaving.

Today she didn't bother to ask why. She flung off the polo coat she had put over her housecoat and nightgown to drive the children to school. Then, with a sigh, she took off her housecoat and nightgown. Standing on the chair, naked, look-ing down into Horace's empty bathroom, she felt very silly and stupid and disappointed; Horace wasn't in sight. Sud-denly, the bathroom door opened and he walked in, naked. He lifted up the toilet seat.

Nancy could feel the blush seeping over her body; Horace was going to take a piss. She had never seen him do that. Of course, she shouldn't look but, then again, why not? David never let her see him urinate. He said he couldn't do it if he was watched. If Nancy had told him she would enjoy watching him, David would have jabbered to her all that nonsense about female penis envy.

"My God, David," she had told him once, "penis envy is utter nonsense. I never wanted a handle. I'm perfectly happy with my female urinary and copulating equipment."

Ashamed or not, blushing or not, Nancy couldn't help herself. Horace was directing a powerful stream through his stubby instrument, and she was watching him, delighted to be an unseen observer. Then, just as he finished, with that second sense that often warns that someone is staring at you, Horace glanced toward the Herndon window directly into Nancy's hypnotized eyes. Shocked, Nancy twisted away from the window, causing the chair to skid out from under her on the waxed floor. With a loud scream, she plummeted into a naked heap on the bedroom rug. Fortunately she hadn't crashed into anything. She heard the click of footsteps up the front walk. The front door burst open. Still stunned, she squatted on her knees. Horace yelled, "Nancy, are you all right?" and dashed into the bedroom. Now he had shorts on.

"Get out of here at once!" Nancy screamed, trying to cover herself with her arms. "Can't you see I'm naked?"

Horace grinned. "I thought I was going to find you dead. Being naked and breathing is much better." He helped her to her feet, quickly surveying the room. "Good lord, you took quite a fall. I didn't know you were a nudist."

Grimly, Nancy slid into her polo coat and buttoned it up to her neck. "I'm not a nudist. Horace, please get out of here. By now Marsha Carey and God knows what other neighbors know you're here."

Horace shrugged. The vision of Nancy, disarrayed, naked, looking fragile and feminine, with tears on her cheeks, was imprinted on his mind. He was tempted to tell her that they might just as well give substance to the gossip. But that was silly. Even if Nancy would jump into bed with him, what would it accomplish?

As Horace turned to leave, Nancy said, "I want you to know I wasn't watching you. I was trying to knock down a cobweb."

"I don't mind if you were watching," Horace smiled. "The National Safety Council reports that hundreds of people every year try to knock down cobwebs, and then it happens. They sail right out of their clothes. From now on you better stay dressed when you clean house. God knows who might have to rescue you!"

"Horace, get out of here this minute," she said.

"Okay, Nancy. It's our secret." Horace chuckled. "And don't worry; I don't tell Tanya everything."

48

Chapter 9

The clock in Ralph's Supermarket read ten fifteen, and she had only been out of bed three hours. Most of the day was still ahead. As she collected groceries into her wagon she kept trying to convince herself that Horace believed her. If she had kept her wits, she could certainly have been more convincing. Instead of brushing away cobwebs she could, for example, have been trying to hook her curtains back on the track. But why naked? Damn it, why not? The temperature was sure to hit a hundred again today. Psychologists said that the hot Santa Ana wind made people do strange things, and the crime rate went up. Well, was it a crime to be naked? Not in weather like this. Of course, her house was air-conditioned, though she never kept it very cool. Nancy grinned. Her mind was attempting to run away from the basic question. Of course, the shedding of her clothes when she watched Horace had strong sexual overtones. She shivered. Was she a nymphomaniac? Would she have masturbated? Now, that was a silly thought. But maybe someday she could honestly try to discuss her motivations with Horace. After all, he was an educated man. He had collaborated on a textbook about marriage and the family that was used by a great many colleges. If she was a little crazy, had a complex of some kind, no doubt there was an answer in one of those horrible books on sexual abnormalities. Horace would have read them.

After she put the groceries in the car, Nancy sat behind the wheel for a moment. Should she go shopping in Long Beach? Maybe she could find a new bathing suit. Not a bikini, but maybe a one-piece suit with fishnet sides. Since it had been so warm, perhaps Tanya would suggest swimming in the Sheas' pool. Anyway, tonight she would simply refuse to be Horace's bridge partner. How could she play intelligently while Horace sat across the table and stared at her, his eyes blue-black and remote? Why couldn't she be David's partner at least one night? It was Tanya who always insisted that they not play bridge with their own husbands. "Let him have a change of partners once in a while," Tanya said, delighting in the innuendo.

Nancy felt sure the whole business this morning was David's fault. If he had made love to her last night, she probably would not have climbed on the chair to watch Horace. Without normal sex she was madly restless right after her period. After that she might go through the rest of the month and not give it much of a thought. But last night, today, she was itchy, hot! Yes, hot. There was nothing shameful about it. It was a female fact of life, of her life anyway. Of course, she could easily have teased David into action last night. Why couldn't he sense her need; why must she make overtures? She had never refused David, but she was damned if she was going to play-act the whore with him.

Nancy drove to San Pedro Harbor, where she parked her car and wandered toward the gift shops. But today she wasn't interested in the imported gifts. Inexorably, her footsteps were taking her toward the Port-o-Call Restaurant. She almost hoped Peter Alberti wouldn't be there today. No, that wasn't true. She wanted a little companionship, that was all. She knew that Peter occasionally came over from the yacht club at around eleven thirty to sit at the bar. After nursing his drink for a while he would leave on his Chris-Craft, which was tied up in front of the Port-o-Call. About a month ago, after she had watched him at least four different times, his searching glance had caught hers. She had been sitting at a table that overlooked the harbor, sipping a Manhattan. Eventually she planned, as she had done before, to order a club sandwich, eat it slowly, and then leave. It was a harmless pastime; a lot of women did the same thing. At least they weren't like those females who hang around the house all day in shoddy housecoats, their hair piled high in curlers.

Peter had bought her a second Manhattan and they talked. Afterward she realized that she had done the talking while he had listened, and all she could really say about Peter Alberti was that he was obviously rich, about fifty-five years old, handsome, and a gentleman.

A few days later at a P.T.A. meeting she discovered a few more things. Wouldn't you know it? The one time she had slipped from the straight-and-narrow and let a stranger buy her a drink, someone had to recognize her and then make a point of it.

"I think I saw you at Port-o-Call Restaurant last week." That dreadful Mrs. MacNamara, one of her neighbors, had caught her arm, making her lose her place in line to talk with Susan's homeroom teacher. "Wasn't that Peter Alberti I saw you sitting with?"

Nancy smiled, but didn't answer. You don't *think* you saw me; you *know* you saw me, you old biddy.

Mrs. MacNamara ignored her silence. "I suppose you're old friends."

Nancy shook her head. "We're better acquainted now. Next time you see us, come over. Peter may buy you a drink, too."

"Oh, thanks, Mrs. Herndon." Mrs. MacNamara stared at her coolly. "But *I* wouldn't dare. If John ever found out that Peter Alberti had bought me a drink, he'd suspect the worst."

"What do you mean?"

Mrs. MacNamara smiled coyly, as if inviting a confidence. "I'm not saying the worst might not be the best. You know the story that came out last year. Peter's worth at least sixty million, and if he divorces his wife, she gets half."

"I'm sure the next wife could manage on the other half." Nancy grimaced. "Anyway, my conversation with Mr. Alberti was very impersonal, mostly about the weather."

As she walked into the Port-o-Call Nancy knew she was twinkling. It occurred to her that the only subject Peter Alberti had really pursued was "whether." He asked whether she was married, and her affirmative answer was evidently a plus in Peter's notebook. Whether she was happy? Yes, she was. And that appeared to please him, too. Unhappy women from suburbia were a bore. Whether she would like a spin around the harbor in his Chris-Craft? No, she wouldn't; she had to pick up her children at school. She had thanked him for the drink, and left with his assured voice caressing her ears. "It was pleasant. See you again, Nancy."

Four weeks ago, no argument would have convinced her that she would return to the Port-o-Call deliberately hoping to set the stage, to be with Peter Alberti, to see where acquiescence led. As she walked by the bar, toward a table, her legs trembled. He was here, alone! Would he buy her drink today? If he asked her this time to take a ride on his Chris-Craft, would she refuse? Really, when you stopped to think about it, who could be hurt if she accepted? Harmless!

Peter recognized her. "Hello, Nancy Herndon. Nice to see you again." He smiled at the bartender. "Mrs. Herndon will have a Manhattan."

And there she was, sitting beside him at the bar, trying to avoid the obvious question in his wide-apart brown eyes, trying not to be entranced by his bronzed face and pure white, wavy hair. She warned herself that she had had only coffee and a piece of toast for breakfast, but she sipped her Manhattan and only feebly—too feebly—refused a second one. She tried to ignore the happy numbness in her legs and giddy inability to concentrate. According to a ship's clock on the wall, it was still only quarter to twelve.

Already Peter had passed beyond the inanities of weather, health, and how lovely she looked today. He was swimming in deeper waters. "Today, you simply can't refuse me. With this heat drying us all over, you have no excuse. A few hours out in the harbor, where there's still some moisture left in the air, will be cooling and refreshing." He gestured out the window. *"The Wanderer* is tied up ready to go. It's windy, but not impossible. Come out with me for a few hours while we fill our lungs with moist Pacific air."

She went through the motions of refusal. She warned him she would have to be back by three thirty to pick up her children. She listened while he commandeered a take-out luncheon for two, and then followed him docilely, slipping easily over the rail into his boat, amazed that what she had planned at six in the morning, when she wouldn't admit it to herself, was happening now.

"Go below," he told her. "You'll find some dungarees and a jersey and sneakers. The pants may be too big, but you can hitch them in. You'll find them more comfortable on a sea voyage than a dress and girdle."

She wondered why she didn't say no. She could have told him that her dress was just fine. Instead, she poked around in one of the compartments and found several pairs of pale-blue denims that had obviously been purchased for female hips. Hesitating, wondering whether to try them on, she suddenly realized that Peter had cast off. He was steering the boat toward the harbor breakwater.

She looked up at him through the hatchway to see him grinning at her, the wheel in his hand. "Hurry up and change. The Pacific is calling you."

You're in up to your ears, Nancy, she sighed. She stepped out of her dress, contemplated her nylons for a second and then, shrugging, unhooked them from her garter belt. Barefoot, the levis and jersey her only clothes, her hair blowing crazily in the hot wind, she felt wonderfully free.

"How come you carry female clothing aboard?" she demanded. She stood beside him as he steered the boat through the choppy waters.

"I'm ready for all contingencies—size twelve through eighteen."

Nancy shuddered. "I'm not the first, obviously."

Peter laughed. "You'll be one of the first to wear clothes. Most gals who come aboard welcome the opportunity to toss off the shackles of civilization."

"Meaning what?"

"Meaning you don't have to wear clothes at all if it suits you. The ocean is a big place. This afternoon, while the husbands perspire in Los Angeles, we have the Pacific to ourselves."

Nancy suddenly realized he was going to be hard to handle. She tried to be firm but not haughty. "I'm not a gal," she began, "I'm thirty-six years old, and I have a husband and two children—and I don't walk around naked."

She noticed Peter was steering the boat in the general direction of Catalina Island and, though he didn't look at her, she could see he was smiling. "Mrs. Herndon, you haven't lived thirty-six years without knowing that most men don't seek Platonic friendships with women."

"You offered me a ride. I thought you were a gentleman."

Peter laughed pleasantly. "Rest assured, Mrs. Herndon, I would never take a woman by force." He was silent for a minute. "It would be interesting to know why you came."

Tears in her eyes, Nancy sat on the railing as she tried to think of an answer. But how could she? No sooner had she climbed in the boat than she was sorry. Now, somehow, she must endure it. "I don't know why," she mumbled. "I'm really not trying to be difficult; I just thought it would be nice to talk."

"And so it shall be, Nancy." He turned off the engine and ran forward on the upper deck. He tossed out an anchor, gave it plenty of rope and then tested it to make sure it had caught.

With the engine silent, Nancy was vaguely aware of the wind burning her face. The boat dipped and then rolled. There wasn't another boat within miles. It suddenly occurred to her that if David were looking through his telescope, he could easily pick out Peter's boat. She shaded her face from the sun; it would be better not to have to explain a sudden sunburn.

Peter had gone below, and she could hear him moving around. Then he emerged on deck with a pitcher of Manhattans and a tray of chicken sandwiches.

"So, Nancy Herndon . . . let us drink and talk." He poured her drink in a plastic cup.

Nancy accepted the drink dubiously. "I've had two already. Are you trying to get me drunk?"

"Never," Peter smiled. "I dislike women who don't know what they're doing. Let's say I'm trying to make you amenable."

"How amenable?"

Peter lit a cigarette. "I'm fifty-seven; you're thirty-six. If I had had a daughter during my first marriage she could be your age. I enjoy making love to women who remind me of the daughter I never had. If you took off your clothes, and I took off mine, no one could see us. I'm sure we wouldn't catch cold. We could lie down on these air cushions, and you would find how exquisitely enjoyable it is to make love with the warm air blowing around your genitals."

Nancy didn't dare look at him. "Do you have binoculars?"

Peter smiled. "That's an interesting non sequitur." He went below and returned with a pair.

Nancy looked through them toward San Pedro. "I see my house," she said excitedly. "Look. It's near the top of that hill, about five houses in from the right."

"I'm not really interested, Nancy."

"My husband would be. Sunday afternoons he looks through a telescope at the ships in the harbor. He could see us, if he were looking now." Nancy handed the binoculars to him. "But David's working today," she added.

Amazed, she watched Peter take off his tee shirt. He unzipped his pants and kicked off his sneakers. Grinning at her, he stood calmly naked—lithe and completely tanned—in the stern of the boat. "Come on, Nancy." He laughed at her consternation. "David can't see you. Swimming bollicky is great fun." He dove off the side and emerged in a few seconds, blowing water from his mouth. "Come in. Put your suburban conscience away for a few hours and live a little."

Nancy finished her drink. As she watched him swimming she realized that Peter's face and shoulders seemed occasionally to come apart and then remerge. Was it the boat tossing on the waves, or had she drunk too much? Or was it the overwhelming desire just to give in and let Peter take possession of her? Whatever it was, she was beginning to feel nauseous. It really was impossibly hot in the sun. She kicked off her sneakers and slowly unzipped the levis. Maybe she could just sit at the stern and dangle her legs in the water. That might straighten out her sudden dizziness. Dimly she heard Peter's shout of pleasure; he was delighted with her nakedness. Was he looking between her legs? The hell with it; let him look. The water felt refreshingly cool on her ankles. Could she hold down those drinks and that chicken sandwich? She felt the boat pitch and yaw. "I'm going to be sick, Mr. Alberti. I'm sorry."

Puffing, in the water below her, Peter grabbed at her ankles. "Come on in, the cold water will shock you out of it."

She felt her naked behind sliding across the hot rear deck. "Let go! I can't swim!" she yelled. It was too late; he had pulled her over the side; down and down she went. The pressure of the water pounded in her ears. It was all over. She was drowning. I really want to die, she thought. Then there was no coherence. Just pictures flashing across her brain. She was kissing a man madly—his lips, his eyes. She was slithering down on him, lapping him, burying her face in his belly. His penis deep in her mouth was gagging her; her cheeks would explode. Her jaw was going to crack. David! Horace! She heard herself scream. Don't!

She opened her eyes and stared into Peter's face. He was straddled over her. They were both naked. She could feel the pressure where his mouth had been on hers. "Jesus Christ," he puffed. "I thought you were gone for sure. Why in hell didn't you tell me you couldn't swim?"

"I didn't drown." Nancy smiled feebly. "You saved me."

Exhausted, Peter flopped beside her. "Lady, if you think it was easy to pull a slippery, half-naked female back into this boat and then pump water, Manhattans, and a chicken sandwich out of her, think again."

Nancy closed her eyes. She felt his hands on her breast. Her head was pounding. "Oh, Peter, I *am* sorry. You should have let me drown." His fingers had lightly parted her legs. Gently he probed her. "I'm married, Peter. Really, I can't let you."

He smiled and kissed her nipples. "I've earned the privilege," he said. "In the last fifteen minutes I've become as well acquainted with the physical Nancy as David or Horace. Who is Horace? Your lover?"

Nancy tried to pull away. Her hand brushed across his staring penis. "Oh, my God, Peter. Don't force me. I can't. I can't." Sobbing, she buried her face in his chest. "I hate myself."

He held her, quietly stroking her back. I am going to make love to him she thought. I am. I can't stop myself. She felt his arm stiffen on her shoulder. "There's a boat coming this way. Scrunch down," he whispered hoarsely. "It's probably just kids water-skiing."

She heard the thunderous roar of a powerful engine. Terrified, she tried to crawl toward the cabin. It was too late. The speedboat was pulling alongside them. A blond woman, her hair streaming behind her, stood at the wheel; she was laughing uproariously at them. Beside her, a man in a bathing suit, a small camera in his hand, was snapping pictures of them. "Get a little closer to the broad, Alberti," the man yelled. "Brother, what an erection! Hey, sister, hold onto his jellung; it'll make a better picture!"

Cursing, scarlet with anger, Peter tried to spear him with a boat hook, but missed. "You nasty little bitch, you bitch," he shouted. Still laughing, the blonde kept the speedboat idling out of reach. Peter threw a boat cushion at them. Ducking, the man continued to snap pictures.

Stunned, Nancy watched the woman turn the speedboat away from them and heard her shout, "Don't call me a bitch, you bastard! Wait until you see these enlarged." She gunned the boat, racing around them in circles until the Chris-Craft was pitching and careening in the waves.

Nancy tried to pull on her levis, but lost her balance and sprawled flat on the deck cushions. Peter, still naked, pulled her to her feet. The speedboat had disappeared toward the south. Nancy suddenly realized she had pulled her dungarees on backward. Peter exploded with laughter.

"Oh, it's very damned funny," she screamed. She pulled them off and flung them at him. "Who was she? What will she do with those pictures?"

"She must have been tailing us," Peter replied. "It's my wife, and it's the third time she's caught me. Damn her!" He watched Nancy's behind disappear below deck. "You don't have to get dressed; there's no need to hurry. The damage is done. We've got the name, now we might as well play the game." He followed her below, watching her trying to fasten her garter belt. He pulled her to him fiercely, one hand on her back, one urgently pressing her buttocks. His erect penis was between her legs.

Desperately she pushed him away. "For God's sake, leave me alone. This is disgusting!"

Peter shrugged. Disappointment cut deep into his face, he stumbled back to the deck. She heard him pulling the anchor and then the throb of the engine as it responded to the starter. Hopelessly, she finished dressing. Her hair was wet and plastered against her head, but the boat was pitching too wildly for her to comb it. Oh, God, God, what will I do? *What will I do?* What will I say to David when he sees those pictures? She suddenly realized how very much she loved him and how absolutely hopeless it would be to try to explain. What would happen to their family now? To Sue and Jimmy?

Unable to stop crying, she climbed out of the cabin. Peter, guiding the wheel with one hand and drinking from an open bottle of Scotch with the other, smiled at her forlornly. To Nancy he was no longer the sophisticated, suave man of the world. She noticed the heavy lines on his face, and thought of her father back in Massachusetts. She had nearly made love to a man as old as her father. Why? What in the name of God possessed her today?

"You need a slug?" Grinning wearily, Peter handed the bottle to her. "Stop blubbering. Fritzi won't do anything too scandalous. She'll have the pictures enlarged to about the size of a billboard. Then in a month or two when, presumably, I've forgotten all about it, some night when we're having guests for dinner, I'll find us beautifully framed on the wall. A cynosure for my guests' admiring eyes."

"You mean she lets you get away with it? I'd divorce you!"

"No, you wouldn't. Not if I had as much on you as I have on Fritzi. Besides, she doesn't really give a damn. It's just her female vanity that's wounded. We'll never get divorced; community property laws make it too expensive. Only the lawyers and the State would benefit."

They were approaching the yacht club. Peter patted her behind. "It's too bad, Nancy Herndon. I had a feeling for a minute or two you would have enjoyed our lovemaking. Is tomorrow another day?"

Nancy scowled.

Peter shrugged. "There *is* another thing. Knowing Fritzi, she already knows more about you than I do, and she probably blames you more than me. She would be delighted to screw up your marriage."

"What will she do?"

"I'm not sure, but whatever she does I'll be happy to tell your husband the truth."

"Which is?"

"That nothing happened."

"Something happened, all right," Nancy said. "It's not your fault, but today Nancy Herndon drowned. You thought you saved her, but it's just an illusion."

Chapter 10

David didn't mind the drive from San Pedro to his small factory; after three years he drove the twenty-six miles to Los Angeles mechanically. He had become just one more combination of man matched with machine among the millions of others pursuing their destinies. As he merged into the traffic on the Harbor Freeway, he reflected that for two years he and Nancy had spent at least two, and often three nights a week with the Sheas, playing bridge, going to movies and parties together. The families were so involved in many facets of each other's lives that they had come to depend a little on each other. Now Nancy's sudden refusal to have Horace and Tanya over last Friday was ominous, and he felt sure she suspected.

"I'm getting my period, I guess," he heard Nancy tell Tanya on the telephone. "I just feel miserable and mean. I wouldn't be nice to have around." But Nancy wasn't about to menstruate, and Tanya knew it. In the past year, to David's annoyance, Tanya always knew when Nancy's period was due.

Horace had yelled to him from his front lawn last night, "How's Nancy?" Even he seemed worried. Here it was nearly a week since they had seen the Sheas. Nancy's only reaction had been that she was sick of seeing people and particularly peeved at Horace Shea.

"I heard him ask you if I had recovered from my fall," she said angrily. "He's a damned old biddy."

"What's this about you falling down? What does Horace know about it that you didn't tell me?" Almost hopefully he wondered if lightning had struck; maybe Nancy and Horace were finally a little interested in each other.

Tanya had mentioned the possibility many times. "They're always so distant and circumspect when we're together," she said one day. "Life would be simpler if they liked each other the way we do. It would make us seem more legitimate."

"What do you mean?" David had demanded. That was last Wednesday, really the last time that he had been able to talk with Tanya since this estrangement.

Tanya had snuggled in his arms and murmured into his chest. "Oh, I don't know, David. If Horace and Nancy were as involved as deeply as you and I, then maybe they wouldn't be shocked at us." There were tears in her eyes as they made love. "Sometimes I'm shocked at myself. Why can't I give us up? Why can't we just go back to being friends? But I love you, too." She smiled at him sadly. "It's hopeless."

David had no answers. For two years now he had succumbed to that necessity of the American middle-class male, the other woman. No, that wasn't essentially true. Tanya was more than just another woman, much more than a sexual spree. He had acquired a deep need for the brightness and vivacity of her. She offered a necessary counterpoint to his New England stodginess.

But Nancy's reply to his questioning about her bruise squelched any hope that she and Horace might be involved, at least a little, with each other. She told him, for the second time, that she had tripped on the front step and that Horace, on his way to work, saw her fall and rushed to help her. "I caught my heel on the sidewalk," Nancy said, and even showed him the broken spike on her shoe.

But it didn't explain last Monday night, and that package from Carrollton Furriers. David smiled. When you were guilty yourself, you tried to find justification in someone else's potential guilt. Still, Nancy had been acting very oddly ever since that mink coat was missent to their house. They had been eating dinner when the doorbell rang. Jimmy answered it. "It's a package for Nancy—Mummy, I mean!"

They watched Nancy sign for it and then examine the box before opening it. "It can't be for me," she said, nervously slitting the tape that sealed it, "I never go to Carrollton's. They're much too expensive." And then, shrieking with delight while Sue enthusiastically buried her face in the fur, Nancy held up a mink coat. "My God, David, it's an Autumn Haze!" She hugged him. "Oh darling, whatever made you so crazy? It must have cost at least four thousand dollars. Oh, I love you for being so silly. But where would I ever wear it?"

Feeling as if he were welching, David confessed that while he would like to have bought her a mink coat, he simply couldn't afford such lovely extravagance. "Maybe Horace sent it to you," David tried to be jovial. "Or maybe you have a wealthy lover who spends afternoons in bed with you." He thought he noticed a swift expression of panic and fright on Nancy's face, but in a second it was gone.

"You can be sure that Horace didn't send it," Nancy folded the mink back in the box. "It must be a mistake. I'll call Carrollton in the morning so they can pick it up. Finish your supper. I'm glad you haven't gone that crazy."

"You were pretty happy when you thought I sent it." He sighed and examined the label. "Damned funny; it *is* addressed to you."

Nancy had refused to discuss the mink further. When he came home Tuesday the mink was gone. "Carrollton got us mixed up. "Look." She insisted that he look at the "H's" in the telephone directory. "See, there's another Herndon family in Rolling Hills."

"Another Nancy Herndon?"

"No, well, the listing is for Frank Herndon. He's wealthy, I bet. Carrollton's shipper couldn't read the sales girl's order, and when he checked it in the phone book he got the wrong Herndon."

David didn't pursue it, but they both knew she hadn't explained the Nancy part of the label. Nancy had continued to alternate between moodiness and an advanced case of the jitters. As soon as the kids were in bed, instead of reading or knitting, she went to bed herself. Sunday night when he made love to her she lay beneath him with a minimum of response. "I can't reach a climax," she sobbed finally. "I took some phenobarbital. Doctor Westly prescribed it for my nervousness."

When he insisted that she tell him what was troubling her, Nancy just looked at him strangely. "If you really love me, David, please, please don't let me go! Hold me to you. Hard! No matter what you may think, I need you!"

David felt as if he had been kicked in the stomach. Had Nancy discovered the truth? Why didn't he have the nerve to admit the whole business? But what was the truth anyway? Did he want to divorce Nancy and marry Tanya? What would that accomplish? He wasn't even sure that Tanya wanted to marry him. The truth, which he might not admit to Nancy or Tanya, was that he wanted to have his cake and eat it too. But society demanded a choice. Either he and Tanya would have to stop seeing each other, at least in bed, or they must divorce their present mates and marry each other. In the United States, in the twentieth century, there was no middle ground.

As David eased his car into the lane for the Santa Monica Boulevard exit he knew he had been ignoring the root of his problems. There was no longer any doubt that Tanya was pregnant; she had passed the time of her second period. "I'm certain it's our child, David," she had said, "And I can't say I'm really sorry. I hope it's a girl." But despite Tanya's determination to accept fate, their stolen Wednesdays had now taken on a quality of subtle recrimination.

"I thought you always took pills," David said. "Anyway, I was careful."

"Not too careful." Tanya grinned. "It happened the day we went swimming near Mendocino. You weren't too careful that day!"

David remembered that he had flown up to San Francisco in August, for a week. The story he told Nancy concerned an important contract in the offing for a new chain of jewelry stores. At the same time Horace went off to a conference of sociology professors and to teach summer school in Chicago; Tanya had left the week before, presumably to visit her mother in New Mexico. Actually, she met David at the International Airport, and they rented a car and drove north. For four glorious days they stayed at Mountain House. Tanya wanted him to see the art colony at Mendocino, because it reminded her of New England.

As they paused in their wandering through the town of weathered clapboard houses to examine a painting, Tanya expressed what David was thinking. "Oh, it's too bad," she said. "Nancy would love this place. Do you feel guilty, David?"

He shook his head. "I love you, Tanya. These few days are a very tiny but important part of our lives. I'm simply closing off the moralizing part of my brain. We aren't really hurting either Horace or Nancy."

They discovered a lonely cove where the redwoods grew close to the ocean. Naked, they reveled in each other's flesh and the joy of discovering the wondrous physical differences of each other. Momentarily neither Horace nor Nancy existed. Tanya's response to his touch was magically quick. She enjoyed his tongue searching in the crisp blond hairs of her labia; she floated deliriously as his tongue gently explored the bright thread of her clitoris. She fondled and kissed his wonderfully engorged penis with a delicacy and a joy of discovery that he laughingly assured her could only result in permanent priapism. And then, in shallow water, the caress of the waves rolling over them, they were gently cradled in a newfound rhythm of love. They lay joined, responding like helpless sea creatures to the recurrent push and pull of the tide. So uncontained was the peak of their love that they came close to drowning each other. Then, in helpless laughter, they sprawled on the sand. They lay entwined, and the sun dried their bodies, until Tanya reawoke him to her need while he lay helplessly entranced by her touch.

She held his salty, limp instrument in her long fingers. As she brushed her lips and tongue over it, she suddenly remembered. "Oh, God, love, I've been so carefree with you, I forgot!" She shook his now completely revived penis. "You devil, I love you, but you just better not have, or I'll eat you up!"

She had forgotten her pills. "I'm not the responsible type, David, and you'd better get used to it. I'm not like Nancy. Tuesday when I realized that I hadn't taken them for a week, I figured, so it's nearly time for my period anyhow." David, only half hearing her words, was deep inside her again. She sat on him, her hair marvelously askew, her breasts dangling in his face. "The pills are dangerous, anyway," She giggled. "They make you put on weight. If I were too fat, I couldn't do this."

David might have wanted to tell her that he thought it was very damned stupid for two educated adults who knew where babies came from to get caught with an unwanted pregnancy, but how could he think? Not when his hunger to lose himself in her was matched by her own desire.

"I think you really wanted to get pregnant," David told her later, captivated, in spite of himself, by her easy acceptance of what she called "fate." She was not like him or Nancy; she didn't try to force life to conform to some private vision of her own. "At least," Tanya had comforted him, "if I'm pregnant, I'm not an unwed mother. Horace wouldn't mind being a father again, especially if I'm lucky and we have a daughter."

But her words were a kind of bravado. Later, at supper, the candlelight casting warm shadows on the planes of her square Scandinavian face, the flames enhancing the amazing circumference of her eyes, her natural fears surfaced. "The only thing that frightens me, David, is what will happen to us? After a while we mustn't see each other any more." She stroked his fingers tenderly. "We'd certainly look kind of silly sneaking into a motel with me in a maternity dress."

Now, weeks later, when the pregnancy was confirmed, David couldn't help himself; he had to probe deeper. "How can you really be sure it's our child?" he demanded. "I've never asked you too much about your sex life with Horace."

Tanya looked at him strangely. Finally she said, "I never asked you to make our child legitimate, David. But it *is* ours. Horace was in Chicago nearly five weeks. While I didn't keep score, you and I did keep rather busy on our trip north."

"I suppose when Horace returned you made love with him." David wondered why his tone was bitter. Of course, Tanya would have made love with Horace, maybe even more passionately than she did with him. After all, he had been to bed with Nancy, and not under duress. To demand exclusive possession, at this late date, was ridiculous.

Tanya maintained her sense of humor. "If I screwed with Horace, sweet, and I guess I did, it still was too late. I'm more than two months overdue and, oh, David, stop analyzing it all. We needed each other. But all right—in New England you might say that, since we were already married, we should have maintained restraint and that, because we didn't, we're now adulterers. But I don't feel that way. I find you very lovable, even when you're acting like a bad kid and rejecting me. We've made love at least a hundred times in the past two years. I love you, and I no longer have to ask why."

David stared at her glumly. "Don't forget that Horace can count as well as you. Also, you have blue eyes, and so does Horace. It's going to be damned peculiar when you have a brown-eyed baby!"

"Good God!" Tanya marveled. "Such attention to details! I can see why you're a successful businessman. Maybe Horace or I had a brown-eyed grandfather or grandmother. Anything can happen in this best of all possible worlds."

David remembered that he had pulled her on top of him. His penis pushed gently at her labia. Shivering pleasantly, Tanya's fingers guided him into her vagina. She looked at him through tears. "I'm not being flippant or brave, David. I'm scared, too. Everything we've been saying skips the main point. Why, when we have perfectly good mates—nice families—why didn't we resist? Why did we let us go this far? Why wasn't one man enough for me? What was missing, that I could respond to you? Why do I love you and still care very much for Horace? Do you love Nancy? Do you love me enough to divorce Nancy and marry me? If your answer is yes, then what happens to our kids? Oh, David, we've a thousand questions to ask ourselves, haven't we?"

Chapter 11

~~~~~~~~~~

Turning off Santa Monica Boulevard, waiting for a traffic light, David reflected. As he had a thousand times, he tried to reach back into his past, to rediscover the man he once was. If he had never moved his business to California, he would never have known Tanya. But if he had stayed in Boston, might he not have met some other woman, another Tanya, and become just as involved? Was it his environment or his marriage to Nancy that was at fault? Weren't he and Tanya merely creatures of their time? They lived in a world that sanctified monogamy but was humorously permissive in its attitude toward adultery. Of course, what was comedy when it concerned someone else became tragedy when you yourself were involved. Could there be any doubt, furthermore, that the seeming lack of purpose or meaning in the average man's life made absolute fidelity unrealistic? Didn't many marriages collapse because a lifetime of monogamy was too big a burden for any human to bear in a society where the danger of starvation was only a quaint fact of history and people were conditioned to indulge their appetites?

Most lives were narrowly circumscribed by the daily task of making a living, paying taxes, saving money for the children's education, and scrimping to buy insurance to protect the family. Whatever time was left over was devoted to becoming good citizens, good spending-buying-consuming units. For what purpose? Because the economists and the men who ran the government were conditioned by a nineteenth-century belief that the history of man's progress was a line moving steadily upward from the bottom, or hell to the achievable top, which was heaven. To maintain his sanity, man was handed adventure as a prepackaged commodity. Planned vacations, paid for through credit cards, created the illusion if not the fact of adventure. Television and the movies provided him with some shadowy, presumably cathartic, substitute for dull reality. Mass entertainments such as football and baseball and the glamour of the space race were the refined, modern substitutes for the mayhem and mass orgies of the Roman circuses. And then there was the automobile, that

64

Nancy and he agreed was the greatest illusion of all. What had been adventure on wheels for her father, what had given an earlier generation a feeling of new worlds to conquer, as their wonderful horseless carriages responded with a roar of power to the gas pedal, had become a monotonous necessity. Where muddy roads leading into the wilderness once challenged man to venture forth, now a network of indistinguishable highways joined cities that were tall stone and glass copies of each other. Perhaps the only real adventure left was the form of Russian roulette played on the highways, where each day at least a hundred out of the millions of speeding cars utterly demolished themselves and their occupants.

Was there any real rebellion left? Or was man content to tighten his knuckles on the steering wheel and spend a large percentage of his time on this earth breathing the gas fumes of the temporary "enemies" he encountered on the highways of life?

David edged his car into the lane that would, a few miles farther, let him turn off to the Herndon Showcase and Fixture Corporation. There was one other dangerous adventure left in a world where everything was cut and died and prepackaged and pronounced good for human consumption. The adventure of discovering another human being was a great deal more than the urge to pursue the female that had first impelled him to ask Tanya to lunch. The adventure was both sexual and mental. Who was Tanya, really? How did she think? What was important to her? In the long run would her flesh be more compelling to him, more of a refuge, than the flesh of Nancy? The first adventure a male and female had with each other was supposed to culminate in marriage, but did the first adventure also have to be the last?

With Nancy he was one person, with Tanya another, and yet both persons were essentially himself. He believed the adventure with Tanya actually opened the possibility of a different adventure in his relationship with Nancy, if only Nancy would understand, which she would never do. Once she knew about Tanya, she would insist that his behavior toward herself was less than was required of marriage. Comparison and criticism, the dread spoilers of man's relationship to his fellow man, would set in. Without his saying a word, or no matter what he said, Nancy would be convinced that Tanya was a better partner than she was. But that wasn't the explanation. They were very different women. Though they both had the same female equipment, the minds that set it in motion made each of them unique.

David turned his car into the parking lot in front of the Herndon Show Case. As he turned off the ignition he was

65

suddenly aware that he had no memory of his drive from San Pedro. He smiled grimly; his conscious mind kept escaping from Tanya's pregnancy. What were they going to do? Would Horace divorce Tanya? If the situation were reversed, would he divorce Nancy? He guessed he would. How could two families live next door to each other when everybody knew that one wife had screwed with the man next door and was carrying his child? The situation would scarcely create a congenial environment for married life.

Thank God it was Wednesday! After a week apart, with only unsatisfactory telephone calls spent discussing Nancy's odd behavior and agreement that an abortion was out, since she didn't want one and it would let the cat of the bag anyway, at last they could be together again. He remembered Tanya's last words on the telephone. "Our Wednesday afternoons are kind of sad, aren't they? The second we meet, we know that within a few hours the long wait will begin all over again." And this Wednesday they must reach a decision so difficult that already it cast a long shadow over their precious time together.

As he walked in the front door, Bill Sapolio, his general manager, greeted him. "Before you get involved with other things, Dave, I'd like to go over these figures with you on the Marshall Stores bid." David walked into his private office, and his manager followed. "We could take the interior work on their Pasadena store and meet their February deadline," Sapolio said. "If we could get the contract within the next ten days, we could hire a few more men and start prefabricating immediately."

Pleased with his ability to concentrate on the problem at hand, David worked his way through pages of typed estimates. "It looks good," he said at last. "Get us an appointment with Snowden and the Marshall building committee. See if you can make it for Friday. If we capture this one we should hit a two-million gross next year. Should make for some damned good bonuses."

Sapolio folded up his papers. "I'll let you get at your mail," he said. David glanced at him and wondered if Bill resented his taking Wednesday afternoons off. As an executive, Sapolio probably figured he should have an afternoon a week off, too, and before long even the woodworkers, through their union, would be insisting on their right to equal treatment. David smiled, and his manager smiled back with a look of complicity as he rose to leave. "Good luck this afternoon, Dave," he said. "Get a hole in one, but don't do anything I wouldn't do." All the employees understood that the boss played golf Wednesday afternoons. Occasionally David felt guilty at the subterfuge. He wondered if Sapolio or Betty Vinson, his secretary, ever suspected that he spent his few hours of leisure at more enjoyable endeavors than swinging at a golf ball. Of course, Betty could easily check with the club; some day she might even feel that she had to reach him there. But so what? If she discovered that Mr. Herndon rarely played golf on Wednesdays at the Canyon Club, what could she do about it?

As David strolled into the outer office he noticed that the wall clock showed nine thirty. Betty smiled. "No important mail today, Mr. Herndon, mostly circulars." She handed him a letter. "This is from John Crail of Crail Industries. He's hoping you will serve on a committee for the Display Man's Convention in January and, oh, this came by messenger. Looks as if it might be photographs."

David looked at the large manila envelope curiously. It was carefully taped at the flap and was boldly marked, "Personal. Do not bend." There was no return address. He tucked the envelope under his arm and slowly walked through the factory, greeting workmen here and there. The Herndon display islands which he and Jay Johnson, his store engineer, had designed after a careful study of the gift and stationery retail market were being assembled both for inventory and to fill an order from the Sanderson Greeting Corporation for their chain of card stores. The hum of machinery, the look of crisp efficiency, pleased him.

As he returned to his office he remembered the envelope still under his arm. He ripped the tape. Betty was right; they were photographs, maybe a half-dozen standard eight-by-ten glossy prints. He stared at them in amazement. First, not recognizing Nancy, he assumed someone had played a trick on him and sent him a set of pornographic pictures. California was full of this kind of stuff. There was a man, stark naked, standing in what was obviously the cockpit of the boat. The bastard had a full-blown erection, and he was grinning at whoever had taken the picture. Opposite him, on her knees, evidently trying to crawl out of sight, was a woman. Her buttocks were full and round as she cringed from the camera. He looked at the next photograph. Impossible! He grunted his stupefaction aloud. Betty Vinson appeared at the door of his office.

"Did you call, Mr. Herndon?"

Hastily David flipped the photographs over. "No, it's nothing, Betty," he said hoarsely. "Go back to work and close the door after you."

David examined the photographs carefully. There was no doubt that the naked woman was Nancy! Over and over in his mind as he stared at the pictures the thought kept returning. How little we really know the people we love! Nancy! Nancy, the cool one, was really a hot little bitch. He stared at his nude wife, trying to contain his bitterness and anger. In three photographs Nancy's face was fully visible. Was her face contorted in fright, or anger, or sexual tension? Startled, he realized he was examining this woman, not as his wife, but as he might look at undressed females in a girlie magazine. This stranger, this Nancy with full breasts, erect nipples, flat stomach, her hair in disarray, was a very sexy-looking woman. He picked up a magnifying glass and examined her pubic hairs. God almighty! It wasn't only the hairs on her head that were mussed up!

He studied the pictures of the man. The bastard's penis was enormous. Who was this man who had plowed his wife, or was about to do so? Nancy! Nancy! My God, how long has this been going on? Nancy, with all her damned Puritan manners and her passive waiting for him in bed. Nancy, who never took the first step toward fucking. Was she really nothing but a sexy tramp? David wiped the tears of anger out of his eyes. Christ! Why did she do this to him after fifteen years of marriage? While he was working his balls off to get this business off the ground, Nancy was playing the field. While he was driving himself to an early grave providing comfort and security for Nancy and the kids, his wife was playing the role of whore of suburbia.

And who in hell had taken the pictures? David's stomach felt queasy. How many times had he gone to bed with Nancy when her vagina was still overflowing with the gyzym from a previous fucking? He wiped the perspiration from his forehead. Carefully, he reexamined the envelope that had held the pictures. It had been addressed with one of those thick-stroke lettering pens. Just his name and the Herndon Showcase address. Tearing open the envelope, he discovered a sheet of paper that had become attached to the glue on the flap. On it was a message printed with the same pen: "Please tell your wife since she enjoys playing with fire she better light one of her own. This fire went out years ago." There was nothing else.

Chapter 12

～～～～

Driving toward the Dairy Valley Motel a few miles south of Anaheim, the envelope with Nancy's pictures on the seat beside him, David tried to think coherently. At a stoplight he pulled the pictures out of the envelope and looked at them for the hundredth time. It was fantastic, incredible. He could swear that if the man were Don Juan himself, Nancy was still too damned prudish to get caught stark naked and in broad daylight with him. How could it have happened? The really shocking thing was that he had never considered the possibility of Nancy seeking another bed-mate. When he and Tanya had discussed it, hoping that it might occur with Horace, well Horace was Horace, and somehow that was different, and both he and Tanya could have accepted him. But a total stranger!

Still, this couldn't be a complete stranger. Nancy wouldn't have been in a boat with him if she didn't know him at least a little. From the pictures, David guessed that the boat was an expensive Chris-Craft in the thirty-thousand-dollar category. That meant whoever owned it was either wealthy or a fourflusher; In Los Angeles it was easy to accept either possibility. Whoever he was, he wasn't young; maybe forty-five to fifty-five. Rugged-looking, the type that attracted females. But not Nancy! While Nancy often seemed indefinably seductive, it was strictly an illusion. Over the years, when acquaintances had occasionally tried to warm her up, David watched, pleased with her cool, stand-offish indifference. His wife had the aura of a happily married female who was engrossed with her husband and children. Amazing, utterly amazing! He had lived with the woman fifteen years, gone to bed with her practically every night, and now suddenly he discovered he scarcely knew her.

For a second David felt sorry for Nancy. Obviously it was the man's wife who had sent him the pictures. God, what a mess! A divorce-suit based on adultery; Nancy caught red-handed. Her everyday life was shaped by a conviction that what the neighbors thought was important. David was certain she couldn't take scandal, and that she must be in a state of shock. As he drove into the motel entrance David grinned with a sudden inspiration. Why hadn't he thought of it before? Those damned pictures could solve all his problems.

Pleased to see Tanya's car already parked in front, he turned in beside a cottage numbered eighteen. For sixty dollars a month, paid three months in advance, this was his and Tanya's Wednesday afternoon home, their retreat from suburbia, a small indulgence, a tiny detour on the inevitable road to the grave.

David opened the door with his own key. The shower was running. He poked his head behind the curtain and was greeted by a squeal of delight. Soapy and dripping, Tanya snuggled her wet face against his. "Come on in," she said. "Let me wash away your cares."

"Later," David said. "I need a drink first. Hurry up, I've got something to show you."

"There's Scotch and ice on the dresser. Make me one." Tanya walked into the bedroom holding a pink towel that spanned her behind. She snapped the towel and shook her breasts and hips in a provocative invitation. "Is what you are going to show me better than this?" She arched her mound toward him and then giggled at his lack of interest. "My God, David, you *are* serious today. I thought you might enjoy something different, like maybe a hungry female."

"What's in this envelope isn't so damned different," David scowled as she tried to kiss him.

Tanya shrugged. "After two years I'm just as old-hat as Nancy." She bit his neck. "Come on, unwind. Because I'm going to be the mother of one of your children doesn't mean I've forgotten the delight of having you inside me." She lay down on the bed, her legs negligently open, and looked expectantly at David.

Unable to stop himself, he leaned over and kissed her breasts. "My God," he groaned, "why couldn't I have been like most men and be satisfied with male playmates? Women bewilder the hell out of me. Here you are, pregnant, but you refuse to fret about such a trifle. All you want to do is make love."

"Seems only sensible," Tanya chuckled. "At least we don't have to worry about contraceptives."

David tossed the envelope on her belly. "We don't have to worry about anything anymore. Take a look at these; fate has intervened."

He grinned as he watched Tanya's face. She examined the pictures with oh's of disgust. "My God, David, poor Nancy! These are awful; what rat took them? I could cry for her. She must be in shock."

"Poor Nancy!" David exclaimed. "What about poor David?"

On her elbow, her breasts dangling, Tanya's eyes danced with laughter. Her broad smile expanded into a gale of laughter that grew louder and louder as David's look became more and more puzzled. "David, David," she gasped, "you can't mean it. Be careful. You're not really poor David, are you? Suppose whoever took the pictures of Nancy pointed his camera *at you*. Just in case, you better undress and join your paramour. But I'll bet that man Nancy was with has a more effective-looking weapon than yours is right now."

"I don't think you see the opportunity this gives us," David said, trying to conceal his irritation. "With these pictures I can get a divorce fast, and then marry you."

"But aren't you, we, just as bad as Nancy and whoever she was with?"

"I'm not comparing Nancy's morals with mine. I'm just smarter. I didn't get caught."

"David, take off your clothes. I can talk to you better when we're both naked."

David undressed slowly. "Believe me, Tanya; what I want to do right now is talk. Business before pleasure. We're in a serious mess. I want to know what you propose to do about being pregnant."

He lay down beside her. Tears in her eyes, she stared at him a second and then kissed him fiercely. "Why in hell did I ever get mixed up with you?"

"We fell in love. It's that simple."

"Maybe Nancy is in love with this man." Tanya looked at one of the pictures. "It's silly when you stop to think about it. Why did you want me? Nancy has a better figure than I. My breasts are smaller. Nancy is a very feminine-looking woman. Who's the man? Where did you get these pictures?"

David explained that he had never seen the man before in his life. The bastard's wife had obviously decided to cook his goose.

"He's very handsome," Tanya sat up in the bed. Her eyes were liquid with tears and love. "David, I think you ought to go home. Nancy must know you have these, and if she does she must be half out of her mind."

"You must be out of your mind," David responded angrily. "Why this big love for Nancy? She got caught with her pants down. It was pretty stupid, if you ask me."

Tanya sighed. "David, I like Nancy. I refuse to justify my love for you by hating her."

"I know," David said morosely. "You like Horace, too. If

71

you like him so much, why are you so eager to make love with me?"

Tanya sensed an argument brewing, but couldn't stop herself. "Damn it, David, you're a grown man, and you should act like one. You know I still sleep with Horace. I have never pried into your sex life, but I'm sure you take care of Nancy occasionally."

"I still don't like it."

"Like what?"

"You sleeping with Horace."

"But it's all right for you to go to bed with Nancy?"

"For God's sakes, Tanya, this is ridiculous," David pulled her into his arms. "I'm only trying to find a solution for us. I want to marry you."

"So your solution is to divorce Nancy. What about Susan and Jimmy?"

"Nancy won't get custody of them, *now*," David said grimly. "That's obvious. Believe me, she's in pretty deep. This guy must be the character who sent her a mink coat."

Tanya grinned. "She must be pretty good in the sack. No one ever gave me a mink."

David scowled as Tanya pulled his head against her breasts. "Oh, David," she whispered. "Your world is so black and white. If you divorced Nancy, despite the mink coat and the pictures, the courts would give her custody of the kids." Tanya gasped as David's penis, hovering on the edge of her vagina, was sucked in. She kissed him wildly. "You can plant the seed, but that doesn't mean you know how to tend the garden."

David silently enjoyed his loss of identity. At last he murmured, "So where does that leave us?"

"In the same mess. If Horace decides to divorce me, you will end up stepfather to two boys and the father of this one." Tanya rotated her stomach against his. "You know I always feel much more content in the first few months of pregnancy. I'm nothing, really, but a hpapy, copulating, gestating female. I don't believe Horace would divorce me. When I finally tell him, he'll probably telephone you or, if we're still family friends, he'll put his arm around you and say, 'David, old man, if I'm willing to play father to this poor bastard, the least you can do is contribute to its support.'"

David sensed Tanya was whistling in the dark, and he refused to respond to her gaiety. "To hell with all this good fellowship. It's my child too," he said. "Nancy and I could bring it up."

"Nancy and you! That's great! You just divorced her, remember? Anyway, this child in my belly is a love child; I'll never give it up."

David held the curve of Tanya's cheeks in his hands. "Are we quarreling?"

"I guess maybe," Tanya smiled through her tears. "David, you can't divorce Nancy. If she loves this man and wants to divorce you, that's different. I don't believe she does. Anyway, if he is married, he probably has no intention of divorcing his wife. If you divorced Nancy, or she you, what would she do? Live alone with her kids? You'd have to support them. And I'd worry so much about Nancy and Horace, you would never be happy with me."

David knew they both were searching for the impossible. They wanted a painless answer, but they weren't going to find it. "You may be able to hypnotize Horace," David said, "but when Nancy knows that you're pregnant by me, that we've been going to bed with each other for two years, you'll hear the screams of wrath all over San Pedro. Nancy is the kind of female who'll hate you because society tells her she should. To her, deep down, you'll be nothing but the rotten bitch who seduced her husband. There's only one solution. While I have the offensive, I'm going to keep it."

"One thing you are going to do." Tanya was moving her buttocks slowly. "You are going to give me those pictures. Aren't you?"

"Don't delude yourself, Tanya. Whoever sent them would have sent a duplicate set to Nancy. By now, Nancy knows I know. Anyway, what would you do with them?"

"Burn them!" Tanya said firmly. "They're disgraceful." She kissed David's eyes and sucked his tongue against her teeth.

They made love, but their orgasms were mechanical. Neither of them could surrender their minds. They were joined, but their peaks of emotion were separate experiences. They did not participate in each other's joy. When it was over they were more withdrawn and lonely than before.

Chapter 13

Driving home from California Institute of Sociology, Horace Shea calmly appraised his conference with Frank Kitman, President of the Institute. Sylvia Mai had been there, listening imperturbably.

"In fact, Horace," Kitman said between puffs on his pipe, "if the Institute did permit you and Sylvia to offer such a course, and the newspapers got wind of it, it wouldn't be Professor Horace Shea and Sylvia Mai, his assistant, who would get the unpleasant notoriety. It would be me and the Institute itself. I've read your proposal in the *North American Journal of Sociology*. What did you call it, 'Pornography, Censorship and the Teen-ager'? You have an interesting concept, and of course in a technical publication you are a professional talking to professionals. That's fine. But while I might agree, and mind you I don't say I do, from the viewpoint of the public there's only one answer; keep the lid on. Can you imagine the nationwide reaction to your course? I can see the story now, in *Life*, in *Look*, on TV. Boys and girls in a mixed class are being taught a course of literature devoted to hard-core pornography." Kitman smiled. "Next step, visual demonstrations."

"It would *not* be a literature course," Horace had said, trying to control the anger in his voice. He opened a suitcase and dumped fifty paperbacks on the conference table. "Just look at these, Frank. They're available almost anywhere for a dollar or less. They've *all* been reviewed in major media such as *The New York Times* and *Time*. Look at these titles: *The Story of O; The Tropic of Cancer,* by Miller; *Candy; Glover; My Secret Life; The Pearl; The Complete Marquis de Sade.* This edition has been abridged slightly, leaving de Sade's theories out but the degradation in." Horace flipped the pages of *Juliette.* "Listen to this; the teen-agers can buy and read this stuff. A Monsieur Noirceuil, previously identified by de Sade as a 'shit lover,' discusses his sexual problems. 'My child,' he says, 'as you can see, I remain unaroused. What I am going to ask you now is to perform an act . . .'"

"Dr. Shea!" Kitman snapped. "That will be enough. If you are not embarrassed, then I'm sure Dr. Mai must be."

"I am not shocked at all, Dr. Kitman," Sylvia said coolly. "I agree wholeheartedly with Professor Shea. To ignore this literature and the values it purveys, to permit the younger generation to discover it and attempt to evaluate it independently in a society in which the home and church do not know how to cope with it is to contribute to the devaluation of the human being."

Kitman had shrugged. "Everything you say may be true, but I'm not seeking martyrdom. You may have heard Frank Lloyd Wright's statement, that if the United States were tilted, everything loose would tumble into Southern California. I do not intend to contribute further to that image. There are other ways of combatting these things, and as one of the proponents of Proposition Sixteen, I can assure you that, though we were defeated at the polls, eventually we will succeed. A moral revulsion will some day seize the country, and the works of the Marquis de Sade and his like will once again be consigned to the flames."

Horace tried to explain his belief that censorship was simply not the answer. The battle against it had been won. But there was still a religious contest between those who believed that man was ultimately evil and those who would attempt, against all odds, to help man realize his potential. "I never want to see de Sade or his portrayal of degraded men driven underground again. Now that we have let this stuff come into the light of day, let's examine it for what it is. The family or the church can't do this. In the family environment the entire subject is loaded with pruriency, disgust, shame, and the simple inability of parents educated in the old traditions to measure the true values of their own lives or to frankly discuss the mystical wonder of sex and love."

Dismissing him and Sylvia, Kitman had patted Horace's shoulder in a fatherly way. "Really, Horace, the prospect of calmly discussing sexual intercourse and defecation as four-letter words with youngsters in their first year in college, even using the words before Professor Mai, is too far out for California Institute of Sociology. Maybe you should transfer to that university in the midwest where they study human beings copulating."

As he drove in the slow lane, Horace was aware that he was thinking on several levels at once. Was he morally capable of teaching the course he and Sylvia had planned? When he had written the article for the *Journal*, he had not yet strayed into adultery. Now that he had risked his marriage by going to bed with Sylvia Mai it was obvious that he must redefine his own moral beliefs. Amazingly, when he had implied his indecision to Sylvia, she had said, "Oh, Horace, you're *so* rooted in middle class concepts. Sure, we've enjoyed each other sexually, but that doesn't mean I have any designs on your life. It has simply been a pleasant experience; and don't you agree it has cleared the air between us, and made it possible for us to understand each other on a deeper plane?"

But Horace had not been able to absorb the idea of free love so easily. To his own surprise his attitude toward Sylvia had acquired a subtle tinge of possessiveness. He smiled at his thought. Of course, monogamy was a male concept. It was a one-way street of fidelity imposed by the male on one female or, if society permitted it, a whole harem.

In the twelve years of marriage, up until these two episodes with Sylvia, he had been faithful to Tanya. There it was, the old cliché again. Even he couldn't escape it. What did it really mean to be faithful or unfaithful to another person? Joining his sexual organs with those of Sylvia was no more an act of faithlessness than the pursuit of his career was. In neither of them could Tanya share whatever made him the man he was. For Tanya, sociology was equivalent to social work and hence in her words "a socially approved form of meddling in other people's lives." During the early years Horace had often wondered whether he would have been more deeply involved in marriage with a woman who could identify with his intellectual interests. But he had made his choice of Tanya consciously. A man needed a woman who loved him enthusiastically, boisteriously, warmly, affectionately, proudly. Tanya had given him this kind of love. Wasn't that sufficient for any marriage? Whether Tanya read the books he read or thought the thoughts he thought, or whether he was vitally interested in Tanya's field of art and fashion advertising was of little relevance. And, of course, if he had married a woman like Sylvia the day-to-day challenge might have been too great. They might have spent their lives trying to excel each other.

Strangely, the need to determine whether Sylvia would go to bed with him had developed almost simultaneously with the Herndons moving next door. Was Nancy responsible? Prudish, unavailable Nancy with her New England austerity was in striking contrast to happy, bubbling, uninhibited Tanya, and even more so to beautiful Sylvia who, ten years younger than either of them, was the product of a Negro father and a Chinese mother, and had a doctorate in sociology from the University of Hawaii.

Whatever had motivated him, his only reasonable excuse was the inevitable curiosity of the male who had made a lifetime commitment to one woman. What would day-to-day life and sex be like with another, a different female? If men or women never asked that question, never speculated about or fantasied the other paths open to them, they denied an essential part of the nature of human beings.

Intellectually at least, he could consider the worth of a female like Nancy Herndon, willing and ready to be molded by the man she believed in, or a woman like Sylvia, who was already formed in a mold more like his own. He was certain that Nancy was available. Not lie-down-and-open-your-legs available, but subtly available, as in a room with the door closed but the key left in the lock. A week ago when he had rushed into Nancy's bedroom and found her naked on the floor, he sensed that their curiosity about each other was finally stripped of its polite suburban veil. Friendship was at the flashpoint of passion. A week ago he could have penetrated her flesh. She might have protested a little, but hers would have been the kind of protest that admitted surrender was inevitable. After three years of friendship, they both wanted to know what the other was like in bed.

It wasn't love, though perhaps it could be love. But mature men and women were conditioned not to capitulate to curiosity. It was simple logistics. Tanya loved him; Tanya was his wife. Nancy loved David; Nancy was David's wife. A man's own wife should be sufficient for any man. Even if she weren't, men and women made commitments. For its own protection, society created the laws and the environment that forced compliance.

Grinning a little at his thoughts, Horace turned into the driveway of his house. In an hour or so Tanya would be home and the little womb of domesticity that he and she had created in an alien world would bathe him in its warmth. Why did men even consider relationships that would destroy the solidity and permanence that were a vital need of the psyche? Had the Greek philosopher Plotinus summed it up in the words, "Out of conflict comes harmony?" But pure, continuous harmony would be as intolerable as permanent conflict.

Horace wondered whether the Herndons would come over later this evening, or if he and Tanya would visit with them. Maybe tonight they could skip the cards and television and talk about this problem with Frank Kitman. Usually he and David did not discuss their work. He noticed that, like most wage earners, David assumed that work was the means, not the end, of existence. Well, what really *was* the end of existence? Horace wasn't sure he knew. Why was he here and where was he going? Ah, immediate events, the here and

77

now, were more interesting! Like, why was Nancy acting so peculiarly? She had avoided him and Tanya for the past week. Had she been spying on him, and why had she stood on a chair, stark naked, to watch him do his business in the bathroom? He felt sure her nakedness was no accident. Maybe he had become an erotic stimulant to her, and the fact that she was an unseen voyeur aroused her sexually. She must have been interested in him, but was she aware of her own purpose? Would she have masturbated later? If she had, was it because David was inadequate to her sexual demands? Was it the reverse of the usual story of marriage, with the woman growing more sexually released as the man became less and less interested?

As he walked up the path to the front door he was surprised to see Nancy open it for him. She was wearing a brown woolen dress and a rather prim flowered hat. When she spoke he knew that she had been crying. "Oh, Horace, I'm glad you finally got home. I've been waiting for you." Her voice was tight and trembly. "I hope you won't mind, but I need a favor."

"Sure," Horace grinned. "You look as if you are all dressed up for a P.T.A. meeting. Do you want me to go with you?"

Nancy didn't respond to his joviality. "I'm going home, Horace. I have reservations on the eight o'clock plane to Boston. Would you drive me and Susan and Jimmy to the airport?"

Not fully comprehending, Horace took her arm and guided her back into the living room. Mitch, Sam, and Jimmy were watching a cowboy story on television. Susan grabbed his sleeve.

"Mommy's taking us to New England to our grandfather's house. We're going to play in the snow and go sliding."

Nancy smiled at him uncertaintly. "They've almost forgotten what winter is like."

"Isn't this kind of sudden, Nancy?" She was obviously distraught. Horace was wondering how he was going to calm her down. David and she must have quarreled. This going home was a typically impulsive, female way of striking back. If he could keep her here awhile, David would come home and they could thrash it out. "Does David know about this?" he asked.

Nancy shook her head. Her eyes were too bright, her voice a bit too high. "Horace, don't probe! I know what you're thinking, but you can't stop me. It's too late. Besides, the children and I need a change. David never gets home on

78

Wednesdays until seven thirty or later. If you're busy, I'll drive *my* car to the airport. David can pick it up later."

Horace shrugged. Nancy was his friend, not his wife. He couldn't lock her in a closet until she cooled off. With Mitch and Sam lugging Nancy's suitcases to the car, asking innumerable questions about Boston and New England, and demanding to know when they could fly to Boston, it was impossible to talk. The boys sat in the back seat. Susan, in the front seat, sitting between them, snuggled against Nancy.

On the freeway Horace tried again. "I have a feeling this is a female way of clawing back. You are wounded. Why don't you wait a day; tomorrow you may not feel so grim. You can always make new reservations." Nancy didn't answer. "You're putting me on the spot. What am I supposed to tell David—that I aided and abetted you?"

Nancy shrugged. Her voice was a sigh.

"He'll probably be glad you did. You won't have to tell him anything. Unless I'm mistaken, he knows. He'll tell *you*." Silently she watched the automobiles they were passing. "It's so warm today. It's hard to believe it's December seventh."

"Pearl Harbor Day."

"I was about Susan's age." Nancy's voice seemed distant. "And I wore pigtails."

"The world's still a mess." Horace smiled at her in the mirror. "Little people should cling together. What other defense do we have? Boys should hug little girls with big brown eyes who wear pigtails."

He watched her rueful expression in his rear-view mirror. She shrugged. "They don't, though. If you make a mistake, even a trivial one, the little people will brand you with it."

"I made a mistake today," Susan said. "I erased it!"

Nancy hugged her. "Did you smudge the paper?"

"I wore a hole in it," Susan admitted, "but the teacher didn't care."

"She's a very unusual teacher." Nancy stroked Susan's hair softly.

Horace asked Nancy about school. Christmas vacations didn't start for ten days.

"They're not in college, Horace. A few missed classes won't harm them. I talked to the principal, and she was very understanding."

Horace grasped at the straw. "You'll be back after New Year's, then?"

Nancy didn't answer, but she squeezed his arm as he drove in front of the passenger terminal. "I appreciate this, Horace. Don't park your car. Just leave us off here. I hate good-byes."

A porter took her suitcases. Standing on the sidewalk, with

the motor of his car still running and Mitch and Sam yelling, "Come on, Dad, let's go home," Horace saw that Nancy's eyes were bright with tears. He hugged her awkwardly. "Whatever it is, Nancy, come back."

She opened her satchel handbag and held out a large brown envelope to him.

"Remember last week?" she asked.

Horace nodded.

"I guess I really was a maiden in distress. I should have let you save me. It might have been more excusable."

Horace stared at her in bewilderment.

"Don't look at what's in that envelope now. When you do . . ." Nancy shrugged, "I guess you'll find even old friends can be a surprise. Those pictures were taken the same day." With Susan and Jimmy clinging to her hands, Nancy quickly followed the porter into the terminal.

"Hey, buddy," a policeman yelled just as Horace slipped the top photograph out of the envelope. Horace looked, and hastily jammed the picture back. "Your girl friend is gone. This ain't no parking area. Look at her pictures somewhere else."

Chapter 14

~~~~~~~

As the time approached when she must leave the motel Tanya knew, much as she had tried to prevent it, that her own feeling of hopelessness had communicated itself to David. Their affair was over; all that remained was a renunciation of each other. Lying together, their passion spent, they watched the afternoon shadows gather in the room. Words between them had dwindled, yet in the pressure of his hand on her back, the brush of his lips on her neck and breasts, Tanya knew that David was denying the possibility that they might ever have to give each other up.

She crushed her body hard against him and tried to prevent him from seeing her tears. I love you, David, she thought. I love Horace. If love for one man is good, can it be evil when it is multiplied? Why had she taken a chance on David? Her marriage was good. As a sociologist, Horace himself had defined it as beautifully average. She rarely fought with Horace over anything fundamental. They loved their boys. While they didn't identify with their house in do-it-yourself projects the way a lot of families did, they enjoyed the comfort of their home. Evenings when they didn't see the Herndons or other friends they pursued their own different interests. Separate, but comfortably together, she at a drawing board, working on new fashion layouts for Bayberry's, while Horace prepared a lecture or was deep in some book on sociology or psychology. Maybe neither of them was too much interested in the other's occupation, but how many husbands and wives were? In bed they were still able to release many of their deeper thoughts without embarrassment. Maybe their lovemaking had settled into inevitable routines. But was that sufficient excuse for a childish pursuit of romance? Why had she needed David? She and Horace really leaned on each other. With David she had to fall back on her own strengths; he gave her no feeling that he was protecting her from the world, as Horace did. He accepted her as very much his equal. Figuratively, marriage with Horace meant walking one step behind the warm shelter of his masculinity. With David, you fought the demons together and marched side by side. Tanya's thoughts amused her, though only briefly. She knew she lacked no freedom in her marriage with Horace. The truth was that both David and Horace had become necessary to her; in combination they extended the boundaries of her life.

To avert the suspicions that might be aroused if they both arrived home at the same time, Tanya left the motel an hour ahead of David. As she drove toward home, David's words, "I love you, Tanya," were echoing in her mind; she could still feel his hungry, fearful, bruising kisses on her lips. She felt both a compulsive need to apologize to Horace and a dreadful longing for David. Could she ever explain to either of them separately, or both together, the fact that she was a passionate female? Not that she would lie down with a total stranger, but that, so long as she was secure in their love, she was perfectly capable of wholeheartedly loving both Horace and David?

What would David think if he knew? Perhaps he had guessed. Tonight, if Horace felt affectionate with her, she would accept his love warmly and hungrily. Any feeling of guilt would come only from her inability to explain to either of her men how this was possible. And could a society that insisted a female love one man exclusively ever accept the possibility that a woman could love two men as loyally as one?

As she entered the driveway, Tanya noticed that Horace's car was in the garage. The first movement of bridging the gap, completing the metamorphosis from lover to wife, always unnerved her. It seemed to Tanya that her answers to Horace's questions about her day seemed hollow and insincere, that her lies sprawled naked between them. She was happy to see Mitch and Sam racing across the lawn to meet her.

"Ma, Daddy took us to the airport!" Sam jumped into her arms. "We watched the 707 Jet take off for Boston. It was great!"

Mitch was behind Sam clutching a worn teddy bear that he still took to bed with him. "Susan and Jimmy are going to play in the snow," he said. "Did you ever make a snowman, Ma? Can we go to Boston with Mrs. Herndon sometime?"

Tanya swept Mitch off his feet and carried him up to the house. Horace, waiting at the front door, kissed her cheek. "For heaven's sake, what's going on?" she demanded. "Has Nancy really gone home? Why didn't she wait for David?" Following Horace into the living room, Tanya shivered. Would Horace ask how she knew that David hadn't gone to Boston, too? Feeling cold perspiration spreading from her toes to her cheeks, she tried not to stare at a large brown clasp envelope Horace held in his hand. Deep in her satchel bag, swinging at her knees, was an identical envelope with these horrible, naked pictures of Nancy. Did Horace have a duplicate set? If he did, who had given them to him? Nancy, of course; but why? Timidly she asked, "Why, *why* did Nancy leave so suddenly?"

"We'll talk about it later." Horace gestured toward Mitch and Sam, "When the big ears aren't listening. For the record, Nancy has gone home for the Christmas holidays. She asked me to drive her to the airport."

"Why didn't she wait for David? We all could have driven her to the airport and had a farewell drink with her." Tanya's thoughts were racing. If David had known about this he would have told her. Nancy must know Horace better than they thought; otherwise why would she have given him a set of those pictures? As David said, Nancy must have been playing around. What if Nancy were actually in love with that other man? If Nancy fled to Boston, certain that David would want to divorce her, where would that leave David and her? Unaccountably, she wanted to hug Horace. Somehow she must make him understand she loved him.

She saw Horace put the envelope on the top shelf of the bookcase. If it did contain a duplicate set of pictures, why had Nancy given them to him? Were Nancy and Horace more than just friends? Bewildered by a hundred questions, not daring to reveal what she knew, she decided to busy herself in the kitchen. She told Horace she would make a simple meal, just scrambled eggs and toast if that was all right with him. Yes, he could fix her a Scotch to sip while she was getting supper ready.

From her kitchen window she could see the Herndon driveway. Soon David would arrive, and then he would look toward her house and smile. Had Nancy left him a note? If there was no note, he would think Nancy and the kids were at the Sheas. Tanya dropped the spoon she was whipping the eggs with and ran into the bathroom. All the water in her system seemed to be gushing out at once. She dried herself and looked hastily at her belly. It seemed quite flat. My God, I'm pregnant, she thought. Slowly she washed her hands and face. She looked at herself in the mirror and saw that she was pale. How could she face David? Now that Nancy was gone, he would confront her, and Horace would immediately sense the awkwardness between them.

The front doorbell tinkled. She heard David's voice, and then Horace was cordially inviting David to break bread with them. As David came into the kitchen, she saw that there were tears in his eyes. He looked past Horace at her; his brown eyes seemed to burn into her brain. "Nancy's gone home with the kids," he said. His hand touched hers as he gave her a note. "Go ahead, read it. You might as well know."

Embarrassed, Tanya mumbled Nancy's note aloud: "David, I'm sorry. Today, in your office, you will have discovered the truth. I'm sure that you must be horrified. I am not the wife or mother you thought I was. How could you ever want to live with me again? I love you, and I never meant to hurt you. You have the evidence to file for divorce. I won't contest it. Please, David, leave the children with me. Nancy."

Horace put his arm around David. "I drove her to the airport. She wouldn't wait. But I'm certain Nancy doesn't want a divorce. She loves you."

"What did she tell you?" David demanded. Tanya wondered if David was going to blurt out the truth about them.

"Nothing, really," Horace replied. Tanya could tell he was being evasive. "David, don't do anything foolish. Whatever she has done, or whatever you may have quarreled about, Nancy loves you. I'm sure of it. My advice is for you to go to her. If you get a twelve o'clock plane, you can have breakfast in Boston together."

David shrugged, and his eyes sought Tanya's. "I don't think so, Horace. Maybe it's time for a showdown."

Tanya's eyes pleaded with him. Not now, David, please. Give Nancy a chance. Give us all a chance! Seeing David's look of despair, Tanya was certain he was going to reveal everything.

"Horace and I don't want you to wreck your marriage," she said. "We're friends to *both* you and Nancy." Tanya's thoughts rushed to bridge the physical gap between them. Please, she begged silently. Not now. No showdown. I'm the one who must tell Horace, when we're alone. Tonight.

"Okay, the hell with it," David's hopeless smile wrenched at her throat; his look was palpable as an actual touch. She swallowed unhappily. "Thanks for the invitation to supper," he said, "but I've lost my appetite. See you good people later." They watched him cross their lawn. He slammed his car door, backed into the street with a roar, and raced toward the freeway.

Horace sighed. "What a mess. Now he'll get drunk or kill himself. The cuckolded American male's way of venting his anger."

"You wouldn't react that way?" Tanya tried to keep the tears out of her eyes.

"I'd probably be worse." Horace hugged her. "Come on, scramble the eggs. I'll separate Sam and Mitch from the television set. There's more to the story. We'll talk about it after the kids are in bed."

Tanya couldn't eat. She watched Horace buttering his toast, eating his eggs, slowly sipping his coffee. With an agonizing deliberateness, he explained to Mitch and Sam that Uncle David couldn't go to Boston because he had to work to support his children and buy them food to eat. Mitch quickly trapped him in a discussion as to why Mommy had to work and Mrs. Herndon didn't.

"Your mommy likes to work," Horace said. "From the looks of things, it's not a bad idea. Ladies get lonesome when their children are in school."

Only half listening to the conversation, Tanya wondered how you tell your husband you've slept with another man, not once but many times. How do you tell him that another man's child will soon be stirring in your womb? It was impossible, but tonight she had to do the impossible. If she procrastinated, David might take the initiative. That would be wrong; she must be the one to tell Horace.

After the boys were tucked in bed he still didn't want to talk about the Herndons. Tanya tried to keep her eyes off the envelope, and she warned herself that any question about it would be too obvious and might reveal more than she was supposed to know. Yet she could not be perfectly sure the envelope was the same as hers.

She looked at her watch; it was only eight, and the night was hot and dry. Horace decided to take a swim in the pool, and suggested they bring the portable television outside and watch it. Tanya guessed that this was Horace's roundabout way of asking if she wanted to make love. They had done it before, on air-filled mattresses under the stars, but she hadn't particularly enjoyed making love less than a hundred feet from David's bedroom window. Though the Herndons couldn't see the pool too easily from their house, her imagination vividly portrayed herself naked, her legs in the air, copulating with Horace while David watched.

Tanya could hardly refuse Horace's invitation, but first she douched herself with warm water and, in the shower, scrubbed the touch of David and his kisses from her flesh. She had long since made up her mind she would always come to each of her men as if the other did not exist. A man had a right to demand of his woman that for their time together she be uniquely his. Ordinarily Tanya didn't find this difficult. Though Horace and David were quite different in their lovemaking, she had adjusted to their separate qualities, and she was certain that good love and sex made no comparisons. In the act she abandoned the world. Tanya sighed as she walked toward the pool, wearing a white transparent housecoat. She knew tonight was not going to be easy.

Horace was sitting in a beach chair near the swimming pool watching the television he had set up on a small redwood table. There was no moon. The pool, rippled by the warm wind, was deep in shadows. A small outdoor reading light was hooked over Horace's chaise. With a hollow feeling in her stomach, Tanya recognized the eight-by-ten glossy photographs of Nancy.

"The world's a conundrum," he said quietly. "It's too bad, but it looks as if the Herndons' marriage is about to rip apart." He held the pictures out to her.

When she was showering, Tanya had thought, I'll wait. I won't even ask him about the envelope. We'll make love first, and then, somehow, I'll try to tell him. She pictured Horace as first a little shocked, and then warm, affectionate, and understanding, as he finally realized that she loved him, too, and not a bit less. But now the gradual approach was no longer possible. She couldn't feign any longer.

"I've seen those pictures, Horace," she said softly. She sat down beside him. "They're awful! Poor Nancy!"

"You've seen them?" Horace's voice was quizzical. "Don't tell me Nancy showed them to you, too? What in the hell is going on? Is she in love with this joker with the big jamoke?" Horace chuckled. "He looks a lot older than Nancy, but he can still get it up."

"Nancy didn't show me the pictures," Tanya's voice was flat. She brushed, ineffectually, at the tears flooding her eyes. "David showed them to me this afternoon—in bed, in a motel a few miles from here."

She became frightened as she watched him stare at her in silence. She could tell he was trying to absorb the meaning of her words. The television sputtered and danced with shadows telling an equally improbable story, but the contrived problem in that electronic box was contained within the bounds set by scriptwriters who had kicked it around in air-conditioned comfort as they puffed on cigars and applauded their perfect solutions. Tanya was aware of the night air, a hot, dry caress against her body. She put her arms around Horace.

"Honey, honey, I know it's insane," she sobbed, "I know it. But I love you, too!"

His words were measured, frighteningly remote. "You mean that you have gone to bed with David?" There were tears in his eyes. "Why?"

86

"My God, Horace, I don't know why." Tanya looked at him pathetically. "I like David, and he likes me. A long time ago he invited me to lunch," Tanya gasped. "I don't know why. He wanted to make love to me. I guess I wanted to make love with him."

"A long time ago?" Horace's words were frigid. He seemed as unemotional as a courtroom lawyer. "How long ago?"

"I don't remember. Nearly two years."

"You mean David has been screwing you for two years?"

Tanya shivered. The word "screwing" seemed too mechanical. "I guess you might say so."

Horace pushed her back on the chaise. His face contorted, he ripped her housecoat open. His hands were harsh, they were bruising the soft flesh of her breasts, his fingers dug into her. Kissing her roughly, he crushed her mouth against her teeth. She cried out in pain, sure that her lips were bleeding. His only defense seemed to be to level her, to reduce her to her animal essence, to fuck her in the full degraded sense of the word, and then walk away from her. Disgusted with the foulness and depravity of his desire, he would discard her with a shudder. Her scream of fear was muffled by his mouth on hers. His steely fingers were searching her mound, bruising her labia. Then, suddenly, he stopped. He shoved her back on the chaise.

"What in hell are you, anyway, a nymphomaniac? You spent the afternoon fucking with David. Now you come home and try to seduce me." His voice was a snarl of frustration. "When I was a young man, I refused to go to whorehouses because I'd heard it's pretty sloppy in a wet cunt."

Naked, her breasts and cheeks burning from Horace's wild attack, Tanya tried to sit erect on the reclining chaise. "I never forced myself on you, Horace." Desperately she tried to control her gasping sobs. "I've always been scrupulously clean. I've been *your* female when we've made love. I don't blame you for hating me. Go ahead, rape me; fuck me if it will make you feel better. I can't apologize or say I'm sorry. I can't even explain but, believe me, it wasn't just sex with David. I like him; I love him." She sighed, "But I love you, too."

Her eyes were wide, swimming in tears. She stared at him hopelessly. Horace was suddenly aware of a female in need of protection, hunched over in despair, her breasts drooping, her shoulders curved, her body wracked and shaking with emotion. Her suffering and sheer fragility as a human being pierced through the wall of his anger. Suddenly he asked himself, why not? What was the matter with him? If he could accept Sylvia Mai's amorality, why should he condemn

87

Tanya? Marriage vows didn't essentially change the female character. Whorish? No; females like Tanya and Sylvia were simply alive to their primordial drives; perhaps they couldn't deny the primal, maternal necessity to preserve the race. It was a proud need, that the male, despite the religious and social taboos of ten thousand years, shouldn't question. Instead, he should immerse himself happily in the warm vaginal juices that flowed continuously not only for him as an individual, but for all men.

Horace put his arm around her. Her face against his chest, Tanya clutched his back as she tried to quell her hysteria. For a moment, while Horace's fingers, tender and affectionate now, traced the curve of her back and the cheeks of her buttocks—for a moment they were husband and wife again, a unity against a dispassionate world. Tanya kissed him fervently as his unspoken words of understanding increased her confidence and overwhelmed her with a feeling of love for him. She had to make a complete confession *now,* and she knew it. Later it would be a sad anticlimax.

"There's something else, Horace . . ." She sat up in the chaise. "Please, my God, please understand. I love you, but I'm pregnant. It's David's child."

"You rotten little bitch!" Springing to his feet, Horace pulled her with him. She recoiled at the sharp sting of his hand across her face. "You fucking bitch!" Horace's face was contorted and ugly. Terrified, she screamed. His fingers bit into her shoulders; he shook her and then shoved her violently away from him. She stumbled backward, vaguely aware that she was on the edge of the pool. Tottering for a moment, she tried to regain her balance and then, with a scream of terror, hit the water flat on her back.

Horace watched her sink to the bottom as chlorinated water filled her nostrils and mouth. Thrashing wildly, she rose to the surface, her dark blond hair plastered tight over her skull. Horace grabbed her roughly under the arms. Protesting feebly, she felt herself being dragged across the cement coping of the pool. He dropped her sagging body on the flagstones.

"Good-bye," he said. "It's over."

Unable to move, she heard the slam of the downstairs door. A light from the bedroom carved jagged shadows across the backyard. Bruised and shivering, her knees, belly, and breasts lacerated, she lay with her face against the wet cement. She tried to vomit, but only a nasty bile came into her throat. She raised herself slowly to her knees and was horrified to see Mitch at the back door, watching her.

"Mommy, Mommy!" He screamed, and ran to her.

"Oh, Mitchell!" She hugged his small face against her wet breasts. "Oh my, honey, I'm so very, very sorry." Frantically, she kissed the fragrance of sleep on his head. She heard the starter of Horace's car, saw the flash of his headlights, and then heard the furious roar of the engine, a symbol of his anger, as it faded into the night.

Chapter 15

With a feeling of loneliness and a need for David that made her mind ache, Nancy huddled in her reclining seat and fought to contain her tears. Jimmy and Susan, entranced with their ear plugs, sat beside her and watched the in-flight movie flicker across the screen at the end of the cabin. Nancy shuddered at the title; it was called *Not With My Wife You Don't*, and it was a sophisticated comedy of near-adultery. Could either of them know what the title meant? She had tried to tell them not to watch such a silly movie. "But we can't sleep now," Jimmy explained patiently to her. "The Captain just said we're thirty thousand feet in the air over St. Louis, Missouri." There was a certain logic to that.

In less than three hours she would be home. It would be five in the morning in Boston, and Dad, fretting a little because he would be late for work at his office, would be waiting with Mom at Logan Airport, worried by the suddenness of her return after a three-year absence. Home. But in fact it was no longer her home; it was only her father's and mother's home. After fifteen years of not living there she thought of herself as being reduced to little more than a picture leaning on the mantelpiece. "That's my daughter with her husband and two children," her mother might tell a guest. "She lives in California, you know."

Momentarily, when Nancy arrived home, her mother would be just as ecstatic as she had been over the telephone. "Oh, darling, you've answered my prayers. I was just telling your father last night, if only you and David and the children would come home for Christmas, it would be all I could ask."

But would Mother be so enthusiastic when she discovered that David wasn't with her? What would she think when she finally realized that her daughter might become a permanent guest? But that was impossible; the house wasn't big enough for her to move in with Jimmy and Susan. Any arrangements would have to be temporary. Susan could sleep with her in the spare room, and Jimmy could bunk on the convertible sofa in Dad's den. Had she been coming home normally,

David would have insisted that they stay in a motel, because he couldn't stand being cooped up with strangers. Her mother and father were strangers, now; they loved her for the past, for the child she had once been. And, of course, they were proud that she had given them two grandchildren to talk about. Still, they wouldn't relish a dependent daughter with youngsters being thrust upon them. Today females might have more freedom, more chances to function as full human beings, but once they had children they had no choice but to swap independence for security. Wise women accepted the inevitable; there was no double standard for them. They must be faithful.

Would David follow her to Boston? What if he decided that he just didn't care? What if he decided that he had had his fill, that she had given him the perfect way out? In the past few years she hadn't been the easiest person to live with; David had a right to expect more warmth and affection. Sick with fear at the thoughts cascading through her mind, Nancy could only pick at the dinner the stewardess put before her. Oh, God, please, please let him need me, she thought. Let him come after me, not with anger nor with recriminations, but just with the words, "I love you, Nancy." With the right words she could release the floodgates of her misery. She needed to love him with a torrent of words and passion, and in his response he could convince her that he understood her infidelity. She could never beg for forgiveness. And could he ever believe that she had never actually made love with Peter Alberti? What difference would it make if she had? Would she be any the less Nancy who loved David and would spend the rest of her life quietly proving it to him?

If he didn't pursue her to Boston, then she must expect to spend the rest of her life trying desperately to make ends meet. Even with alimony, she would be a drain on Mother and Dad. Someone would have to mind the children while she went back to work. It was all so stupid, really. I love you, David. The words trembled on her lips. But no matter what, she would never telephone him and beg his forgiveness. Somehow, without her making the first move, he must understand, must care for her so much that even after seeing those disgusting pictures he would still love her.

Nancy smiled through her tears at the stewardess who removed her tray. "I'm not hungry," she apologized. Oh David, David, I love you so much.

David stared at the dial on his watch and decided his eyes were too blurry to read it. What difference did the time make? Right now, Nancy was in an airplane flying over the middle of the United States and Tanya was home in bed in Horace's arms. Had she finally convinced Horace that he would be overjoyed to have a new baby in the family? David ordered a fourth Scotch from the topless waitress. He tried to keep his eyes off her G-string, which was in danger of being sucked between her slightly parted labia. When she brought the drink back to his table she purposely brushed a naked breast and erect nipple against his ear. He smiled at her feebly. "Sorry, sister, my wife has gone to her mother, and my girl friend is convincing her husband she never should have strayed."

The waitress leaned over him. He could smell the perfume and powder and flesh of her pendulous breasts. "The band is playing 'Marching to Jerusalem,'" she said. "When it stops, run for a chair, or you'll be out."

A little befuddled, David stared around the smoky barroom. What in hell was he doing in this dive? Getting plastered, obviously. Why? It was childish. The spurned lover reaching for the bottle. He remembered once telling Nancy that all movie writers relied on this gesture, because they couldn't conceive of any other reaction to failure.

Vaguely David watched two naked females on a tiny stage in back of the bar who were gyrating mindlessly to the jukebox, bumping their pelvises half-heartedly at the men who watched them. The males, drinking their beer, escaping for an hour or two from the old lady, probably didn't feel cheated. Did the dancers confirm that there was still life in these men—life stirring uneasily between their legs? Was this all that man knew about love? The thrust of helplessly bloated flesh, soothed at last by warm vaginal fluids. The hungry clitoris pleading for soft friction.

Nancy, his wife, with her legs open, helpless to the demands of her body. Her face softened with her desires; Nancy, pleading, enraptured by these new hands molding her breasts, these new lips sucking her nipples. Sobbing as she guided this new flesh into hers, and then exploding, her eyes closed tight as she was momentarily overwhelmed by the wonder of herself. And now her eyes open and liquid with joy as she smiled her appreciation, her fingers a delicate touch of approval as they trickled over this stranger's back and dug into his buttocks, apprehensive lest he leave her too soon.

Was he really thinking of Nancy? Yes. No. It was Tanya. Tanya, but it could have been Nancy. What had Nancy needed that he hadn't given to her? More sex. Not really. She never seemed to have the urgent need for it that Tanya did. Why had she fled? Was she afraid of his wrath, or was she in love with this man? Would Nancy have run away if she had the missing piece to the jigsaw puzzle, the piece that pictured Tanya in a maternity dress? Would their shock at each other's behavior have canceled out their hatred and ended in forgiveness? Could he forgive Nancy? It was an academic question. If Nancy had a man, he had Tanya. When the music stopped playing Horace would be the man without a chair. No problem. A hundred women would want Horace. Too bad in a way that Horace wasn't in love with Nancy; he had heard of things like that happening. Next-door neighbors divorcing and remarrying each other's spouses, and everybody living happily ever after. But the Herndons and the Sheas didn't add up smoothly. The truth was apparent. Tanya never had said otherwise. Horace loved her and she loved Horace.

David had a sudden recollection of Tanya in bed with him, only this afternoon. God, this day was a hundred years long. Tanya was leaning over him, dangling her breast lightly over his lips while her hand feathered his penis. A big smile extended the lushness of her lips. "You know, David," she said, "I think you love Nancy, too."

It was true enough. He certainly had had no reason not to love Nancy, at least, not until today. When he had voiced the thought to Tanya she sighed. "Oh David, David, I'm afraid that Horace won't believe I love him either."

"What's good for the goose," David said.

"Are you feeling okay?" The naked waitress had returned, leaning over him solicitously. David smiled sadly at the brownish pink aureola with its soft, sleeping nipple, looking into his face. For a dizzy moment he felt an urge to bury his face in her breasts, which somehow seemed independent of her person—soft retreats for little boys whose problems were too much for them.

He stood up and put five dollars in her hands. "The only damned trouble with the world is that men and women need each other and are afraid to admit it." He grinned at her amazement. "Unless you're serving tits for a late evening snack, I think I'd better go."

In his car, behind the wheel, he tried to clear the alcohol from his mind. Home was where Nancy and the kids were. He couldn't return to an empty house. Home was where a woman was. And Tanya would be only a few hundred feet away from his bedroom. What had Horace said when they had moved into their house? Nancy and his bed separated by two walls and a few feet of land were so close that Horace could keep score of their orgasms. It was a vivid exaggeration that David had often tried not to think about, but tonight he wouldn't be able to sleep in his empty bed, because thoughts of what Tanya was doing would keep him awake. Was Horace's face lost in the warm sensuous odor of Tanya's breasts? David didn't doubt that she might actually convince Horace that she still loved him. Under similar circumstances, could Nancy have convinced him? No; but why? Because Nancy had broken her marriage vows to him? But so had Tanya to Horace.

David was a little smashed; his mind was a muddy pool. As he drove slowly to the factory he thought the only way to clear his head was to work. Tonight he would sleep on the couch in his office. At least, the Herndon Showcase and Fixture Corporation was emotionally stable. Competition was fierce, but it didn't involve sex. Work was a man's salvation. Work and duty. Not sex. Not love for another human. Work to find reality. Love wasn't reality. Love was expectant, demanding, wrathful, disappointing.

Inside, the factory was illuminated by a few night lights. David wandered unsteadily past the woodworking machinery. The bright country smell of newly sawed wood mingled with the sharp excitement of new enamel, proclaiming the birth of the finished Herndon Showcase. But the pride he usually felt at his accomplishment was only a hollow feeling in his stomach. What was it all about? Why had all this effort been expended? Did it really have any meaning in and of itself, without the reference point of a woman, children, love, yes, damn it, love! The delight of the female for the male. The caution of Nancy. The vivacity of Tanya. Why did he have to give up either?

In his office he slid back the panel that opened the refrigerator of his built-in coffee-table bar. Another Herndon product that he had designed himself. Next year he would allocate a promotion budget to the Herndon Office Bar. No executive should be without one. The H.O.B., BY . . . . The executive hobby that every wife would approve. Better than women, and tax deductible, too!

He poured a full glass of Cutty Sark over ice cubes, slumped in a leather chair and stared at the picture of Nancy, Susan, and Jimmy hanging on the paneled wall. Nancy had given it to him for his birthday. His family—a certainty amidst the confusion and uncertainty of life. He opened Nancy's crumpled note, decided that he was too bleary to read it again, and tossed it on the carpet. Nancy said she loved him. Tanya said Nancy loved him. Horace said Nancy loved him. He drained half the glass of Scotch. The damnable truth was that he wasn't at all sure he was capable of accepting either Nancy or Tanya, for that matter, other than in the role of adoring, monogamous wives fathful to himself. The Nancy he had never known, his wife, had given safe harbor to that enormous prick. How long had he suffered with Nancy's comparisons? Had Nancy suffered by comparison with Tanya? Maybe. Yes, at the beginning. But later, no. Nancy simply didn't seem to care for sex as much as he. No. That wasn't strictly true. But perhaps she didn't like men as much as he liked women.

David sipped his drink. Maybe she did, maybe she did. It was really impossible to think anymore. He closed his eyes. Damn, he was going to have a pounding headache. Too much liquor. Just when he needed to think clearly. The alcohol released hundreds of unrelated images across the screen of his mind. Nancy, sitting at the breakfast table, tears in her eyes as she demanded to know why she couldn't come to work with him; Nancy, departing somewhere on a boat, waving good-bye to him sadly; Tanya, naked on the docks beside him, comforting him; Horace moving in beside Tanya, telling her it was time to go home; Nancy, leaning over him solicitously (How had she come back from her sea voyage so quickly?) undoing his tie, brushing her lips against his, unloosening his belt, her hand warm on his belly.

David woke up with a start. He was lying on the broadloom rug of his office. Nancy was sitting on the floor beside him. No, Christ almighty, it wasn't Nancy. It was Betty, his secretary.

She grinned at his groggy expression. "I think you're hung up, Mr. Herndon. I've been trying to rouse you for the past twenty minutes."

"I must have conked out," David groaned. As he propped himself on his elbow, he was dimly aware that his shirt had been unbuttoned and that the zipper of his trousers was loose. The light hurt his eyes, making the demons in his head angrier. Before he closed them he stared at Betty Vinson suspiciously. "Why in hell are you working so late? It's against the law."

Betty laughed. "To tell you the truth, I'm glad you're alive. Ever since I came into this office and found you on the floor slumped against that chair, I was sure you were breathing your last."

David closed his eyes and slid full-length on the floor. "Go home," he muttered. Dimly, he was aware of a cold damp towel on his forehead; the light touch of fingers on his face. Betty's voice was a whisper from a long distance. "You can't stay here, David. You've got to pull yourself together."

His first name being spoken like a caress by his secretary cut through the murkiness of his mind. "Miss Vinson, I appreciate your solicitude. Go home. I'm Mr. Herndon." He opened his eyes and found himself looking between the naked calves of his secretary. She was crouched on the floor beside him, her dress high on her knees, her cleft and the soft hairiness of her crotch clearly visible. She intercepted his gaze but made no effort to close her legs.

"I'm not Miss Vinson," she said nervously. "I'm Mrs. Betty Vinson. You don't read your personnel information very carefully. I read the note your wife wrote you, and I'm sorry, David."

He closed his eyes again. Somehow, he needed the determination to struggle to his feet, tell this dame thanks for your trouble, and dismiss her with all the majesty of David Herndon, President of the Herndon Showcase and Fixture Corporation. It was bad business to be caught by an employee with your pants down, especially when the employee was obviously the one who had undone your pants. But it was impossible to rise; he could will the thought, but he couldn't execute it. Worse, he had to expend all his effort not to get damned sick. Betty, holding his head while he vomited, would be the last straw. He tried concentration. With his eyes grimly closed, he asked her what time it was.

"It's one thirty. I was driving home from my brother's house and saw the light in your office." She bent over him. He felt her lips on his and then her voice in his ear. "David, my husband left me two years ago. I have two kids. My sister-in-law takes care of them. If you can get on your feet, you can sleep it off in my apartment. It's not far."

David didn't answer, but Betty's veiled plea wriggled insidiously into his mind. In plain language, Betty Vinson wanted to be fucked. No. That was a male concept. Everyone in this damned state was either divorced or about to get divorced. And every last one of them, male or female, after one ride on the merry-go-round, couldn't wait to climb aboard again. He had read it in some damned book or other. What was it? "Cock seeking cunt, neither able to escape?" But was that yearning only a small manifestation of the loneliness existing in every marriage? Was Nancy smiling at him for a second?

"Sorry," he said finally. "I can't help you, Betty. I've got troubles of my own." He noticed for the first time that her face was thin, ravaged, that her cheekbones were too pronounced. There were tears in her eyes, she was a skinny waif that needed male protection. "What in hell are you crying about?" he asked.

"I hate myself. Why do I need you to love me?"

David forced himself to his knees and smiled wanly at her. "Okay, chum, you stayed too long. I'm going to puke."

She held his head while he retched into the toilet. Bewildered, not giving a damn what happened, he let her slide off his shirt and trousers lest they get soiled. When there was nothing left but dry heaves, the man reduced momentarily to the lost helplessness of the child he once had been, she guided him back to the couch in his office, took off her dress and lay beside him naked. Her fingers were cool icicles gliding across his chest and stomach, weaving in the soft hairs around his limp penis.

"Look," he said weakly, his eyes closed. "You're a nice kid. I'm a male. First thing you know, even though my pounding head says it is impossible, I'll be screwing you. If I did, tomorrow we'd both regret it, and I'd give you your notice. So please go home."

He felt Betty's fingers grip his penis, her short-cut, tousled hair caress his belly. Through half-closed eyes he saw her kneel over him. A smile on her face, she sucked his penis until it rose hard and full in her mouth. She held him erect, her tongue a warm tickle over the glans, a mischievous grin on her face.

"Competent secretaries are hard to find," she said. She got off the couch and slid into her dress. She shook his engorged penis playfully. "One pain drives out another. You can't have a headache and an erection like that simultaneously. If you're going to fire me tomorrow, the least you can do is take me home tonight."

An hour later, breathing the springlike smell of Betty's hair, her face burrowed into his chest and her legs woven between his, David, his mind bouncingly clear of alcohol, could reach only one conclusion: every human being was condemned to his own driving need for the love and comfort of another human being. The trouble was that somewhere along the way, the need for love, much stronger than the small gift of sex given along the way, got equated with sin. He wished Betty were Nancy, in his arms. Somehow they both might care for each other enough to listen.

Chapter 16

Like a canary whose owner has accidentally left the door of
the cage open, Horace flung himself into furious flight without any clear idea of where he was going Years of marriage
and responsibility to another person had gradually diminished
the narrow circle of his freedom His rush of wild anger at
Tanya subsided to a dull bewildered realization that without
Tanya or Mitch and Sam, his teaching career, even the pursuit of knowledge and social understanding, was meaningless.
How did any man, alone, sustain himself? Remove the props
of marriage from those who were married, and the very
structure of their existence collapsed. Yet marriage with one
person for a lifetime was a challenge that more and more
people seemed unable to cope with.

Had Tanya needed David to give a meaning to her life that
he, with his academic background, had been unable to provide? If they had had more friends would she have been less
likely to take up with David? Except for the Herndons, they
had few friends. There were his colleagues at the Institute,
but Horace had never made any effort to become involved
socially with them. The reason he had made no effort had
something to do with Tanya's lack of academic background,
her too-purposeful ingenuity in social gatherings and the fact
that after a day of teaching, Horace preferred the escape to
home or to the different world of the Herndons, that scarcely
acknowledged a need for teachers.

Horace was driving toward Santa Monica and Sylvia Mai.
Finding refuge with her was scarcely an adult way to face the
problem of Tanya, but he couldn't go back. Accepting that
your wife had made love with another man was one thing;
adultery was a fact of life. But to watch your wife grow fat
with another man's child in her belly while she told you she
loved you was impossible. How could Tanya have been so
careless? There was only one answer. Her love for David had
been so great that she didn't give a damn.

Sylvia, on pills, never would take chances. Three times
they had enjoyed each other sexually as an outgrowth of their
day-to-day companionship. He had told Sylvia that she would

like Tanya, and she had told him that, despite appearances, she was not promiscuous. She said she found it "kind of sweet" to discuss common interests, without tension, with a man she admired intellectually. Their love-making was a pleasant counterpoint to their working relationship. Someday she might marry, especially if she found a man who would understand that an occasional afternoon of dalliance with a colleague didn't threaten their marriage. Was Sylvia's reaction so different from Tanya's? Did all of them, Nancy, David, Tanya, Sylvia and himself, in their reaching out for a special love relationship, point to a larger driving force, to man's deep need to find identification, to merge his own mind with the mind of all mankind? Was the blending of flesh simply a necessary point of departure?

As he pushed the floor number in the automatic elevator at Sylvia's apartment, Horace had a sudden ridiculous glimpse of himself. It was a vision of the cuckolded husband, disheveled and miserable, running to another woman. What did he expect from Sylvia, balm for his punctured ego? Right now she might be in bed with another man; he really knew very little about her private life, and had not asked about it, because he sensed that his lack of commitment to her gave him no right to probe. But he knew she had once been in love, and had wanted to marry. "But not at the expense of my individuality," she had said. "In a way, I suppose I'm like your wife. I want children, a home, but not as ends in themselves. The reason Tanya is so valuable to you is that she hasn't tried to become a carbon copy of her husband."

In his marriage with Tanya and in this brief affair with Sylvia both women had given him a feeling of deep involvement. Here was their strength; it grew out of a seemingly defenseless giving of themselves as individuals. Yet it was now painfully apparent that Tanya had been able to maintain a segment of her emotional life completely independent and apart from him. It was the shock of this discovery, perhaps more than the physical aspects of her sexual relations with David, that dismayed him. Yet, hadn't he duplicated Tanya's performance? Not quite. He had had intercourse with Sylvia only three times, and after each time he had felt guilty toward Tanya. How many times had Tanya made love with David in two years? And was his child stirring in Sylvia's womb? It was not!

Horace rang Sylvia's doorbell. Finally she opened the door a crack and peered at him. In the gap left by the hooked night chain, with the light behind her, Horace could see the clearly naked outline of her body under a sheer nylon housecoat.

"Are you alone?"

"Fortunately." Laughing, Sylvia unhooked the night chain. "I won't always guarantee it. What gives? Tanya away and Horace has the night out? You might have telephoned."

Horace leaned awkwardly against a sofa. "I've got problems, and I thought you wouldn't mind if I bunked here tonight, though not necessarily in your bed."

Sylvia was amused. "Why not? I've invited you before, but you said it would be impossible to arrange Even so, it would be nicer to plan in advance. Would you like a drink or a snack?"

"I'm not hungry." Aware that his marital problems were suddenly canceled out by the serious, questing look in Sylvia's eyes, Horace groped for words. "I came here to talk, but now nothing seems as urgent as the need to hold you in my arms."

"Just hold me in your arms? My God, Horace, you *are* devious." He followed her into the bedroom A light on the night table and a pile of books beside it indicated that she had been reading in bed. Smiling she dropped her housecoat beside the bed and lay on the sheets naked, watching him undress. He lay beside her for a moment, not speaking kissing her neck, tasting the warm sleepy smell of her breasts. She shivered and wound herself sinuously against him, inviting his penis with a slow, unhurried movement of her buttocks. The hairs on her mound, as they penetrated his pubic hair, felt like tiny shots of electricity against his flesh. "Sleeping is much better with a man," she whispered. She rubbed her face against his chest. "Especially a nice hairy man like you."

Horace was embarrassed by his response; a stiff prick has no conscience, he had once heard someone say. Yet Sylvia, by accepting his need for her, uncomplicatedly without wiles or a demand for commitment, puzzled him. The act of love demanded responsibility; he couldn't accept the gift without feeling obligated to the giver. Sylvia's fingers trembled happily over his penis. He pressed against her parted legs felt the dry resistance as her labia, at first refusing admission, slowly parted and then engulfed him into the warm liquid world of her vagina.

"An hour ago I was about to make love to Tanya."

Sylvia kissed his nose. "But you didn't succeed."

"How did you know?"

"Your little friend wouldn't be so eager, or feel so enormously good."

"Tanya is in love with someone else, David Herndon, a friend of ours who lives next door. I may have mentioned him. We've known the Herndons for some time."

"So you ran to Sylvia to soothe your wounds."

"You're doing a remarkably good job."

Sylvia pulled away from him, leaned on her elbow and looked into his face. Her hair was a beautiful tangle, her seriousness magnetic. Horace wanted to kiss her wildly. Whatever "I love you, Sylvia" meant, he wanted to say it.

"Wait a minute, sweetie," she said. "First we talk. I like you, Horace, very much; I may even love you a little. I know you may not believe it, but I'm very choosy about the men I have coitus with. I may even want to sleep with you occasionally for the rest of my life. But I don't ever plan to be a refuge from your marital problems."

"I don't understand."

Sylvia smiled. "The other-woman syndrome is too easy. My breasts only seem to be an escape. Ultimately we all face life alone. You have to be realistic."

Horace shrugged. "I am. Tanya has not only been sleeping with David Herndon, she's pregnant by him." He lifted Sylvia's free hand and kissed her fingers. She watched him and waited. "Something ugly and repulsive to myself surfaced tonight. For a moment I was furious with jealousy, blind with rage. I struck Tanya, and then I left." Slowly, still holding her hand, Horace pieced the story together. Sylvia listened with her face snuggled against his neck.

"Sounds like one of those soap operas," she said. "I feel sorry for Tanya. She tried to tell you she loved you, despite everything."

Horace stared at the ceiling. "For Christ's sake, what is that supposed to mean? All of us bandy the word love around. I could accept the fact that she might want to try another man in bed, but to get pregnant in this day and age . . . You know, Sylvia, the truth is that I can't understand why she wants to have David's baby. Without my even knowing it, she could have had an abortion."

"Maybe she wanted another child."

Horace snorted. "Not Tanya. She's been happy as hell to get Mitch and Sam in school so that she could work."

"There's one thing you don't know about the female psyche, Horace. I believe every female who surrenders herself to a man entertains a primitive drive to have his child."

"Do you want to get pregnant by me?"

Sylvia laughed. "Suppose I told you right now that I *am* pregnant, and that *you're* the father."

Horace stared at her. It was difficult to tell when Sylvia was kidding.

She laughed and squeezed his penis tenderly. "I may forget occasionally where babies come from, but not for long. Remember, I'm a practical *single* girl. Not a wife of fifteen years, starved for the romantic aspects of love. But let's explore my proposition. Here you are, a stalwart citizen, Professor of Sociology at California Institute of Sociology, with a wife and two children Then out of the blue your assistant gives you an eye-popping announcement. Inadvertently, you got her pregnant."

"Inadvertently?"

"You can bet on it."

Horace was amused. The difference of ten years was showing. Sylvia's generation seemed more able to cope with reality. "I suppose I'd have three choices I could see if we could get you an abortion, or I could divorce Tanya and marry you, or you could have the baby and we could put it out for adoption."

Sylvia shook her head. "If I were pregnant I might want to keep our baby and *not* marry you. Having a child is no disgrace."

"Impractical. You'd make your chance for marriage more difficult, and you couldn't bring a child up by yourself."

"You'd have to support me, at least for the first years." Sylvia kissed him. "Poor Horace your real problem wouldn't be me. It would be Tanya. I don't know Tanya, but I do know you. You'd have a guilt-feeling toward Tanya for the rest of your life. And Tanya would resent your apparent lack of love for her. A fine basis for companionship in your declining years. Reminds me of *Ethan Frome*."

Horace sighed. "You know, there's a certain kind of insanity to this conversation. I can't assimilate the reality. Tanya is home in bed, probably sobbing her heart out, David is somewhere drinking himself into oblivion, and Nancy has gone home to Boston—I'll bet she's crying herself to sleep—and I'm here discussing the whole mess with you. It seems unreal."

"Progress always seems unreal to conservatives like you." Sylvia hugged him for a moment. "I like you, Horace. Maybe I should take you away from Tanya. But let's not leave our problem. There's another solution. You could bring me home to Tanya and tell her you love me, too. Why couldn't we all live together?"

Sylvia was looking at him wistfully, her oval face and slightly tipped eyes the dream of medieval painters of madonnas. He knew she was forcing him to reevaluate his thinking, to somehow accept the fact that Tanya could love David and still love him. But the role she was playing was neither his nor hers. "Bigamy is against the law," Horace pointed out. "Even if it weren't, two females couldn't live under the same roof with one man," he said ponderously. "They'd never adjust to each other."

"Oh, Horace, you are stuffy. Tanya and I have at least one thing in common; we both find you companionable. Bed arrangements are only a small fraction of marriage."

In spite of himself, Horace smiled. "Well, don't get carried away. By now David has probably staggered home, and he and Tanya are deciding that divorce is the only solution."

"And somewhere Nancy is in an airplane flying to Boston. My God, humans make their lives complicated." Sylvia put her arms around him, shivering a little as he entered her body. "It's too bad I'm not Nancy," she said. "David and you could simply have switched spouses." Her pelvis became a swaying bridge, her fingers grasped his buttocks, splaying them against her. Identity was lost. Deliberately they both floated dangerously near the climax, delaying as long as they dared before they tumbled into orgasm. Then, in a rush and scream of delight they lay together, panting and laughing at the silly joy of their passion.

"Tonight must be the last night," Sylvia whispered in his ear. "At least for a while. It's getting much too good. If I don't stop us, I'll get caught up in a need for you."

Horace watched her snuggle in his arms. Her even breathing completed the surrender. She slept. In the dim light of the bedroom, his face buried in her hair, he thought Sylvia could be Tanya or Nancy. Any of the three women, with a touch, a smile, the locking of their fingers in his, their faces and their breasts against his body, could make him aware of the simplicity that was happiness.

In the morning Horace shaved with Sylvia's razor. They dawdled silently over a breakfast of oranges, toast, and coffee. "You're pensive this morning," Sylvia smiled at him. "Post-coital depression?"

Horace squeezed her hand. "A silly notion. No, but I was wondering whether Tanya is calmly driving the kids to school, or is on her way to work at Bayberry's."

"Do you want her to stay home and do penance for her sins?"

Horace shook his head. "Actually, I'm worried about her. The simple thing would be to hate her and David, but I can't sustain the first shocked reaction. She's a human being, and she loved me once."

"Since you're a male, it probably hasn't occurred to you that if Tanya knew about me, she wouldn't be very pleased with you either."

Horace smiled. "It's different with us; we're ships passing in the night. You made that clear the first time. Probably, if

103

you hadn't, I'd have repressed my natural curiosity. Sooner or later you'll find a nice young man, and maybe, occasionally, remember old Horace. 'What's the old boy doing now,' you'll ask. 'Still teaching at Cal Institute, I suppose. Poor soul. He'll die there espousing lost causes.'"

"Supposing I wanted to marry you?"

"Do you?"

She laughed. "Don't rise to the bait so fast; I can hear your wheels grinding. The dreamer's solution David marries Tanya, and they have five children Nancy finds a childhood sweetheart in Boston, and Horace starts like all over again with a young bride." Sylvia sipped her coffee "A few nights ago I saw an interesting movie. A Swedish film, *My Sister, My Love*. Did you see it?"

Horace shook his head, aware that Sylvia was trying to channel his thinking.

"A brother and sister, whose family is dead, have clung to each other in their early years When the picture opens he has returned to their village after an absence of four years. Their dormant need makes them recognize that they are in love with each other. She tries to pursue 'normality' by being betrothed to a wealthy landowner with whom she is not in love. Both the brother and sister are aware of the consequences of their love, and the horror of incest, in their village environment. But their desire is so strong they make love anyway. She becomes pregnant marries the landowner, who knows that it is not his child, but accepts the situation with her promise never to reveal who the father is. Even when he discovers that the father is her brother, he abjectly tells her that his need for love, or possibly power, is so great that he is willing 'to lie beside them and share their love.' The story ends with the sister, who is about to have her child, being shot to death by a young woman who thinks the brother is in love with her." Sylvia smiled at the quizzical expression on Horace's face. "The ending seemed wrong."

"Why? It's the accepted norm. Sin must be punished."

"But life isn't like that. The sister had suggested to the brother that when their child was born they could run away to another place and live together as man and wife. But in deference to a popular opinion the story stressed the possibility that the child would be deformed. But an old lady, who has an imbecile son, presumably because her father had lain with her, slashes the child free from the dead sister's womb and, proudly holding the baby up as it squalls, says with tears in her eyes, 'It's a healthy child.'"

Horace shrugged. "The genetic problems of incest are

grossly exaggerated by ancient taboos whose roots are else-where."

"That's not the point. I would have ended the picture dif-ferently, or perhaps given it no ending. The murder of the sister is the easy way out, the pat solution. Man, the perfec-tionist, always tries to wrap his problems into nice little pack-ages, but mostly they won't be contained. Life is too fluid, it spills over. The murder would have been much more accepta-ble if the brother and sister had had no recourse other than marriage to each other. If they had married, would they have been able to sustain their love against a disapproving society or their own embedded fears of sinfulness?"

Horace was silent for a moment. "You're trying to tell me something. What?"

"Sweetie, I don't know. Only one thing. Ultimately *you* have to make a decision for better or worse."

"You think I should go home to Tanya." Horace's voice was bitter. "Bring up David's child as my own and live hap-pily ever after." He looked into Sylvia's eyes and noticed they were bright with tears.

"If you and I were characters in a movie, I'd press my ad-vantage by convincing you that Tanya is the wicked one, while I'm perfect. Triumphantly we'd walk into the sunset to-gether." Sylvia smiled. "But to come back to reality, you can stay here tonight. Tomorrow, you'll have to move into the *Y.M.C.A.* I have a Japanese friend coming tomorrow." Syl-via kissed his cheek. "Did you ever stop to think that if we had a child, it could be quite black. In that event you wouldn't be welcome in Palos Verdes, or at Cal Institute, for that matter."

"You're cynical." Horace wondered if Sylvia wanted him to ask about her Oriental friend.

"No, honest. I love you, but love isn't marriage. You and I teach this to our classes every day. Marriage is society's pro-tection for the children. You and Tanya and David and Nancy have a commitment, not to yourselves, but to your children." Sylvia put the dishes in the sink. "Come on, lover, I have only one commitment—to my nine-o'clock class in Marriage and the Family."

They drove to the Institute in their own cars. Horace lec-tured a class in Max Weber's theories of the development of Household Economics, but half his mind was occupied with a vision of Tanya and the innumerable Wednesday afternoons she had spent with David. How many times, separated only by a few hours, had she later climbed in the sack with him and blissfully made love? How could she have done it with equanimity? How could he have lived with her for the past two years and not detected a subtle difference in their relationship? As a lover, how did he compare with David? The answer was obvious. With David the sex must be better; but why?

Sylvia found him in his office at noon. She was bubbling with laughter. "You'll never believe it. Remember our symposium on Marriage and the Family? A woman named Fritzi Alberti just telephoned. She attended the sessions and has been reading Masters and Johnson's *Human Sexual Response*. In her opinion, the authors, with their subjects hooked up to electrodes and copulating machines, were scarcely scratching the surface. She says if I'm interested and can bring a suitable companion, we can join them tonight as participating voyeurs at a spouse-exchange party."

Horace snorted. "Wife-swapping. Jesus Christ, that's all I need!"

"Not wife-swapping. Fritz's group doesn't like that word; she's learned the sociological lingo. She says their group is called S.O.S., for Save Our Spouses, and is carefully structured." Sylvia giggled. "They have a special modus vivendi with a unique set of overtones. Why not go with me? We owe it to our professional curiosity. I told her I'd call her back."

Horace tried unsuccessfully to keep the look of disapproval off his face. "My God, Sylvia, you can't be serious," he said. It occurred to him that while he was fully aware of Sylvia's capabilities as a sociologist, and the joy of an orgasm with her, he had never really wanted to know too much about her past sex life. He had a sudden momentary vision of Sylvia naked, a creature of her sexual drives, abandoning herself in slobbering ecstasy to a swarm of erect penises.

Sylvia was amused. "Your silent condemnation is frightening, Horace. Whatever you may be thinking, you're not in a position to judge. After all, you did subject me to a stiff campaign of invitations to bed. What did you keep repeating? 'Since we're in close daily contact with each other, my going to bed with you might ease the strain.' " She grinned. "Personally, at the time, I wasn't aware of any strain."

"Have you any idea what a shallow, orgiastic business wife-swapping is?"

"I'm not a wife. Remember?" Sylvia said coolly. She patted his cheek. "I'm ten years younger than you. My generation has passed beyond that phase. We gave up sex for the psychedelic kick."

Chapter 17

~~~~~~~

With his seat belt fastened and his chair tilted back, Horace closed his eyes and waited for the jet to take off to Boston. It seemed impossible it was only Friday. The even flow of his life had turned into a churning river; he was shooting the rapids with no certainty of quiet water below. Flying to Boston to talk with Nancy, for purposes he could only vaguely imagine, was as incredible as the hilarious sexuality of Fritzi and Peter Alberti's Save Our Spouses party. Was there a common meeting ground between them, a faint thread of Ariadne that might lead Theseus out of the labyrinth? Horace grinned at his thoughts. Whatever form the Minotaur had taken in their lives, he had no confidence in his ability to slay it.

Relaxing from the first tension that always gripped him as an airplane sought its flying altitude, Horace let his mind merge with the torrent of air streaming by his window. In the ceaseless drone he fumbled for correlation.

After reluctantly agreeing to accompany Sylvia on her mad venture to the Albertis' party (Had he been fearful that otherwise she would consider him a part of the past-thirty, and hence untrustworthy, generation?), and promising to pick her up at her apartment at seven o'clock, he had telephoned Tanya at Bayberry's. Her voice was soft, subdued with tears, when he told her he would be home at four to get his clothes. "Horace, it's your home, too," she said. "Nothing is going to be solved by your leaving. The boys need you, even if you think I don't."

"I'm not blaming you, Tanya," he told her, and he was aware that his tone was brusque; he was the unemotional teacher lecturing his pupil. "I can't help but assume that somewhere in the past two years you must have weighed the alternatives. You were aware of what could happen, and you made your decision."

He heard her sigh. "Honey, not everything in life is an equation. I'm sorry. I didn't premeditate anything; I don't think David or I ever considered hurting you or Nancy. Can we at least talk?"

"With you telling me to take it calmly?" Horace couldn't keep the bitterness out of his voice. "And David putting a friendly arm around my shoulder and saying, 'Buck up, old man, I didn't mean to fertilize your honey pot.' "

He could hear Tanya sobbing. "There's no sense in trying to discuss it on the telephone," he said. "I'll be home long enough to get a few suits and shirts. Maybe then you can tell me just one thing. Why, if our life together is so damned important to you, why didn't you have an abortion?"

Thinking about it now, Horace could only feel that his attitude represented the greater logic. He was also being a damned sight more permissive than most men would be toward their wives. He could accept the human need for Tanya and David to want to experience each other sexually. But to blithely accept a continuation of marriage, with David's child in his house as a constant reminder of her infidelity, to live next door and accept David both as his friend and his wife's lover was impossible.

Tanya was waiting at the front door when he turned in the driveway. She looked defeated and humble as he walked toward her. He noticed her eyes were swollen from crying, and he was disturbed at his own reaction. Could she be conscious of the desire stirring in his loins? Did she know his need, born of long companionship, to put his arms around her and comfort her?

"Sam knows you're angry with me," she said, "but not Mitch. I told Sam that sometimes mommies were bad, like kids are, and daddies had to spank them. Sam agreed to play with Mitch outside for a little while so we could talk."

Horace sat in the chair in the living room. He felt like a visitor, seeing his pipes and books, the accouterments of stability, as if they belonged to a stranger.

"Where's David?"

She shrugged. "At work, I suppose."

"I thought the two of you would have spent the night together planning our future."

"David didn't come home. He telephoned me this morning. Last night he fucked his secretary, Betty Vinson."

Horace shivered. Tanya's crude bluntness, and the possibility that, in a subtle way, she was asking him what he had been doing last night, stunned him. "You mean he actually told you?" Horace asked.

Tanya grinned ruefully. "Not in so many words, but the meaning was clear. I'm not married to him."

"You don't even give a damn?" Horace stared at her incredulously.

Tanya didn't answer for a moment. "I suppose he needed

108

someone. Don't we all? He got drunk, she took care of him. I would guess he was in a frame of mind to be easily seduced."

Horace was bewildered and admitted it. "You two must really have something going for you, if you can accept that so easily. You still want to have his child?"

Tanya's deep blue eyes enveloped his. He knew it was because she was nearsighted, but she gave him the feeling that she was trying to open her soul to him "Even if I didn't want David's baby, it's too late now. I guess I thought it would be nice to have another child. I bore Mitch and Sam easily." She looked at him desperately. "Oh, God, Horace, I don't love you less. Just seeing you like this, knowing that I'm responsible, makes me want to hug you and tell you how sorry I am."

Horace scowled. "But you're not so repentant that you resent David. He's at least partially responsible for the jam you're in. What does he plan to do?"

"I told him to go to Boston and bring Nancy home. She *is* his wife. He doesn't have to tell her about me, and I won't tell her." Tanya shrugged. "Since he has strayed from the paths of virtue himself he can afford to be magnanimous and forgive her minor sin."

Horace shook his head grimly. "For Christ's sake, you're balmy. The truth is that you're counting on me to accept this mess. After I get over my indigestion you're hoping I'll adjust to necessity. Do you really expect me to maintain the illusion that we have a happy marriage, even to pass out the cigars when the new child is born?"

"No, God damn it, I'm not expecting anything. I don't need to live the rest of my life with a martyr for a husband. I'm perfectly capable of supporting my children."

"How does David feel about that?"

Tanya shook her head. "Men are so nice and fawning when they need a woman, and so damned pompous when they think a woman needs them. David refuses to go after Nancy or even telephone her. He feels that when she knows the whole story, she'll divorce him. According to David, Nancy could do penance for her own sins but, with her New England upbringing, could never live with him knowing that he had had sexual intercourse with me."

"It's not Nancy's background," Horace said stiffly. "Damned few men or women would tolerate it. Poor Nancy! She's the type that will take sleeping pills when she knows the whole damned story. Then you and David will have that cross to bear."

Tanya was crying. "I'm not so crass as you may think. I wish I could talk with Nancy face to face. I know she's not very tough."

"And you are?"

Tanya smiled sadly. "Not really, Horace. I just try not to let too many people see how easily I get hurt."

Sam ran in from the yard and leaped into Horace's arms; he was followed by Mitch, who clambered aboard Horace's lap. For all practical purposes, that was the end of the conversation. Sam looked at Horace solemnly. "Mommy isn't going to be a bad kid any more. You aren't mad at her, are you?"

Hugging them, he knew that Tanya could see the tears in his eyes. He avoided the supplication of her glance. "I'm not angry with Mommy, but right now your dad has a big problem to solve." Desperately he sought for a way to explain without explaining. "You know, Sam, when Mitch and I play chess against you, sometimes you don't want to move anything for a long time. You want to think out all the possibilities. Well, that's the way it is with me. I've got to go away for a few days, to think what the right move is." He grinned feebly. "Maybe I can't win the game, but maybe I can figure out a stalemate. Do you understand?"

Mitch nodded enthusiastically. Sam brightened. "Will you bring us back a surprise?"

Horace kissed his cheek. "You bet. Better ones than I brought you when I went to Chicago."

"I remember," Mitch said. "We had fun at Grandma's. Is Mommy going with you, like she did that time?"

Horace was suddenly aware that his trip to Chicago last summer had given Tanya the opportunity for a rendezvous with David. He smiled sourly at her.

She blushed. "This time, honey, Mommy will stay right here. In a few days we'll be having a Christmas tree. Maybe Daddy will read you all about Bob Cratchit and Mr. Scrooge." She didn't dare ask him if they really would spend Christmas together.

While the boys watched, Tanya insisted on packing his bag. He nodded without interest at her choice of two suits for him. Watching her brush the tears from her cheek, Horace felt as if he had just gone ten rounds in a heavyweight fight and was hanging on the ropes waiting for the knockout blow. As he drove toward Santa Monica, the freeway was a blurred mist of smog, but the smarting in his eyes was from his own tears. God damn it, why couldn't he just hate Tanya? It would make the whole stupid mess that much easier to solve.

In Sylvia's apartment, with a second Scotch in his hand, he tried to explain his feelings to her. "Tanya just stood in the doorway when I left. Those damned eyes of hers, so big and innocent, make her look like a lost and bewildered child. I could tell she was half forming the words, but not daring to say, 'I love you.' " He shrugged. "What am I supposed to be, Jesus Christ?"

Sylvia smiled at him. "In a way, Horace, you look the part. You have the ravaged type of face. All you need is a slight beard to accentuate the martyred expression."

"I'm not in the mood for humor."

"Or for a wife-swapping party?"

"Amen! For God's sake, even if my life was going smoothly, I don't think I'd be interested in the spectacle of man reduced to his rutting instinct Why do we have to go?"

Sylvia stood up from the couch and straightened her dress. "Because first, I am not going to spend the evening commiserating with you, or watching you get drunk, or helping you to forget your miseries, momentarily, in sexual games with me. And second, perhaps you need some perspective. The four of you and your domestic tribulations have little significance. To prove that, all you have to do is stand above the fray for a moment; the party may help you do that. And tomorrow, if you want my opinion, I think you should fly to Boston and talk with Nancy. There's only a few more days of classes before Christmas vacation, so I can cover for you. One of the three of you *has* to tell Nancy the other half of the story." Briefly, as she sat in his lap and rubbed her warm face against his, she seemed more like a daughter than a lover. Her deep brown eyes looked into his. "I would guess you're better equipped to do it than David or Tanya. Who knows? Once all the fat's in the fire you may discover you have no choice but to accept things as they are."

As he argued with her the impossibility of any solution except divorce and the impracticality of his going to Boston to tell Nancy the part she didn't know Horace gradually began to wonder if Sylvia wasn't right. Actually, Nancy and he were the most aggrieved ones Talking together, and thinking rationally, could they forgive and, just possibly, preserve their marriages? "I don't know, Sylvia," he sighed, aware that her tiny kisses on his neck were designed to overcome his resistance to the Alberti party. "I suppose that Nancy might forgive David. Right now, thinking she's wholly to blame, she's probably considering how hard it will be to bring up her children alone. You never can tell, but it's my guess she'd never marry again. Who knows? Maybe she'll accept what David has done. As for me, I'm not at all sure how I feel about Tanya."

Sylvia ruffled his hair. "Tell her about me; maybe that'll balance the equation."

Horace accepted two miniature bottles of bourbon from the stewardess. Yielding at last to Sylvia's urging, he had racked his brain for Nancy's maiden name. He remembered her telling them that she lived in Graniteville, a suburb of Boston, and then it came to him that her father owned an insurance agency called Neleh and Ross. Martin Ross had died, and Harry Neleh inherited the partnership. She was Nancy Neleh Herndon.

The long-distance operator located the telephone number, gave him the area code, and told him he could dial it direct. A woman answered; it was Nancy's mother. He told her that he was Horace Shea, a neighbor of Nancy's, calling from California. Shaking his head at the insanity of what he was doing, he could hear a female voice, high-pitched and excited. "Nancy! Nancy! It's California," and finally Nancy's voice, disappointed when she recognized him. "Oh God, Horace, what's the matter? Is David all right?" Confused at first by his forced chuckle and his insistence that David was fine, she finally murmured assent: "I don't know why you'd want to leave Tanya and the boys at this time of the year, but if you're coming to Boston anyway (He had told her he had to talk with some professors at Harvard.), all right, I'll meet you at Logan Airport." Her tone made it obvious that they must talk *alone*, before he met her family. "Of course," she said before she hung up, "you'd be too busy to come to Graniteville, anyway."

Under pressure from Sylvia, he confirmed that airline reservations were available, though he was disappointed to learn that the flight scheduled to leave at nine the next morning wasn't sold out. He still fantasied how easy it would be simply to telephone Nancy again and tell her he was sorry all flights were booked.

"You've got your hand in now," Sylvia said happily. "Even if you treat it as an academic problem, Horace, and I'm afraid you may, someday you'll be glad you took the initiative."

While he waited at the phone for the girl at the Sherilton chain to confirm reservations at their Boston hotel, he kept repeating to Sylvia that she was responsible. "It's a damned fool idea. When I'm away from your influence I'll probably regret it as an even greater madness than going to a wife-swapping party."

"I'm not your wife, sweetie," Sylvia choked with laughter. "But don't worry; tonight I'll assure the Albertis I'm too young to be swapped."

Horace switched on the sound of the movie, but was unable to concentrate on it. He had to stand aside from his problems before they drove him berserk, but for the moment it was even impossible to assimilate the Alberti night of madness during much of which one part of his mind worried about Tanya and another part wondered what he could possibly say to Nancy.

Exactly ten days ago the Sheas and the Herndons had been, at least on the surface, reasonably contented middle-class citizens, with reasonably happy marriages, nice children, and comfortable homes. They were simply good neighbors who had become good friends. What had happened? He wondered if the trouble was that man no longer paid heed to an authoritarian religion or to a God who helped him control his natural instincts. Or was what they had all done symptomatic of a deeper, more basic risk-taking that led some people to climb mountains or dive deep in the sea or explore space, and others, perhaps even braver, to seek their adventure in the wonder and diversity of other human beings? He could ask himself whether the need to have intercourse with Sylvia was because of Tanya's inability to satisfy him sexually, but he knew the answer. Tanya was as capable as any female in the erotics of sex. While Tanya and Sylvia were different, the difference that reflected itself in bed was not in the physical act, but rather in their widely varied capitulation. And that *really* was the adventure. In the surrender of the mind, with their defenses down, each couple set the limits of their physical merger and with it the potential of expanding the horizons of each other's lives. In a mechanized society the only true unknown was the never-to-be-discovered mystery of another human being. Monogamous marriage, because it limited the opportunity to know even one other person or have one other friend, came a cropper on the natural yearning of the human soul.

Chapter 18

～～～～～

A few minutes before the plane landed in Boston the pilot announced with a chuckle that the flight had nearly been diverted to Miami because of a howling northeaster that covered the Eastern Seaboard from Bangor, Maine, to Philadelphia. He reported that before it would end, late Saturday night, the major cities were expected to be buried in fifteen to twenty inches of new snow.

As the aircraft lost altitude and the landing gear jarred into position, Horace watched the snow, an unbroken torrent, as it sped past the plane. If there was a city below them, it had disappeared in the fierce storm. Horace shivered Wearing a light topcoat, and without rubbers or overshoes, he was ill-prepared for the New England weather or, he thought grimly, the Puritan mind Would Nancy be waiting? Whatever his approach to their common problem might be, it had been impossible to rehearse it. What had T. S. Eliot once said? "Between the emotion and the response Falls the Shadow . . . for Thine is the Kingdom." No, and Horace smiled at his thought, he would not accept the role of the hollow man.

The ground lights flashed past his window, and then the plane shuddered and skidded to a halt. Protected from the storm by a portable corridor connected to the terminal, Horace followed the other passengers to the waiting room. Nancy, in a beaver jacket, ski pants, and a tiny knit cap with a red tassel perched on top, greeted him with a fierce hug of delight.

"Oh, God, Horace I've been so worried. It's a wild night. I drove to town in Daddy's old Buick three hours ago when it was just beginning to snow. All the broadcasts have been telling commuters to go home early. Daddy was furious. He insisted that I didn't need to meet you, and that you would telephone." Nancy looked at him earnestly. "But I couldn't do that to an old friend from sunny California."

She clung to him as they walked to the baggage room, and Horace was aware that he was seeing Nancy differently. Her cheeks were glowing with natural color, her brown eyes were alive with questions. She looked much younger and childishly vulnerable. How was he ever going to tell her about David and Tanya? Could she ever resign herself to the truth? As far as she knew, David had strayed even farther beyond the fences of matrimony than she had. Really, how could *he* give advice when he had no counsel for his own predicament?

"David isn't coming, is he?" she asked, as they waited in the baggage room. Her eyes were awash with tears. "I was so excited when you telephoned that I thought for a second you were David. My heart was pounding so crazily and I felt so faint, I'm afraid I couldn't talk intelligibly." She forced a smile. "So good friend Horace has come to soften the blow. Oh God, Horace, what am I to do?"

"You're to get a grip on yourself. David doesn't even know I'm here, but we'll talk later. Right now I feel like Admiral Byrd at the South Pole. I've never been to Boston before; I came to see the charming New England weather you've been so homesick for."

Nancy brushed away her tears. "I was a bore, wasn't I? When you see what it's like in the streets, you'll be certain I was quite mad. This has already been the worst December on record, and winter hasn't even officially started."

With his suitcase in his hand, Horace let Nancy lead him through the terminal. "I thought at first you might come to dinner with us in Graniteville," she said. "Normally, it's only a half-hour ride on the expressway."

Horace looked in disbelief at the snow whipping against the windows of the terminal. Outside, a long line of taxis, their headlights and windshields encrusted with ice, inched forward to accept the more aggressive and daring who scurried through the blast of snow to reach them first.

"I'm never going to hear the end of this," Nancy said. "Daddy's car must be half buried in the parking lot. All the covered spaces were full, and I had to park way out in the middle of nowhere. Even if we could get it out, it has no snow tires, and you have no overshoes. Oh dear, I think we'd better take a taxi to your hotel and figure it out from there."

Finally in possession of a taxi, but unable to see out of the fogged window, they watched silently as the driver plowed and skidded through the drifts as he drove toward the Sumner Tunnel. "It's a stinking night," he said. "I just heard on the radio that the Southeast Expressway is jammed all the way from Graniteville back to Boston. They won't untangle it for hours." He appraised them in his mirror. "A good night to snuggle in the sack and watch television. After I drop you at the Sherilton, that's what I'm going to do. It's a hell of a lot easier to listen to my old lady yak than sweat this out."

115

Horace glanced uncomfortably at Nancy. "It looks as if you're going to spend the night in Boston," he said. He kept wondering how Nancy would react when she learned what he had to tell her. Would she be hysterical, or would she simply withdraw?

Now she was attempting to be sociable. "Poor Horace, I guess you're stuck with me. Never mind, I'm sure that it'll clear up later. Then I can take a taxi home." And, she thought, listen to Daddy while he complains and demotes me from a married woman with two children to a wayward adolescent who should have known better than to get his car buried at the airport.

Despite Nancy's insistence that she couldn't possibly stay in town overnight, Horace asked the room clerk at his hotel if they had another room. The clerk gestured at the crowded lobby. "Impossible, Mr. Shea. The house is sold out. We've got a heating and ventilating men's convention, and from the looks of things a lot of people have decided to shack up here tonight and dig their way home tomorrow. But we held your reservation." He smiled at Nancy. "Some people are bunking together. There's twin beds in your room, Mr. Shea." Nancy avoided Horace's questioning glance as the clerk grinned at her. "Under the circumstances there would be no extra charge."

In the room, after the bellboy left, they stared at each other with a what-do-we-do-now expression. "Really," Nancy said, as she fidgeted with the telephone dial, "I can't stay here all night. How could I ever explain to Mother and Daddy? Anyway, I have to phone them."

Horace sat on the bed nearest the door and listened while Nancy nervously dialed home. She assured her mother that she was quite all right. "I'm with Horace Shea. Yes, he arrived okay." Nancy listened patiently for a minute. "I know it's silly, but we can get Daddy's car dug out tomorrow. I really think the best thing is for me to rent a room here at the Sherilton." Her eyes flickered; she was embarrassed by her lie. "Yes, tomorrow, as soon as it lets up I'll take a taxi home. Are the kids all right?" She grinned uncertainly at Horace, waiting for Susan and Jimmy to say good night on the telephone. "Yes, Mommy is snowbound in Boston. You be good. Do what Gram and Grampy tell you, and tomorrow we'll go sliding and build a snowman." After she hung up she held her hand on the phone as if she were afraid to lose contact with her children. "I'm sorry, Horace," she said. "I don't mean to compromise you. But they haven't even started to plow the streets in Graniteville, and there's no way for me to get home. I'll sleep very quietly. I don't snore or anything."

Horace exploded with laughter. "For God's sake, Nancy, you're not a college girl about to lose her virginity. As for me, I snore occasionally. You'll have to do what Tanya does, reach across the bed and give me a shove."

Nancy sat primly on the other bed. "Well, you have to admit it does look kind of funny. David and Tanya would be sure we planned it this way."

Horace shrugged, as he took off his jacket and tie. His mind was involved in the problems of the evening ahead. It was only seven thirty, and for the hundredth time he wondered why he had ever come to Boston. What could he possibly say to this woman? When he told her the truth, that her husband was in love with his wife, that she was pregnant by him, would the roof cave in? And what about Nancy, right now? Was she being a little too resigned to the situation? Was she expecting him to take the initiative? The possibility of their making love had existed ever since the night they swam together naked in his pool. What would it accomplish if they did? He liked Nancy, but beyond that, what?

"Let's not beat around the bush, Horace," Nancy said. She slid out of her coat and knit sweater and sat in the only chair in the room, her feet on the bed, her breasts full and rounded under a red jersey that matched her ski pants. She looked at him speculatively. "I gave you those pictures. David has his own collection. Three days have gone by, and David hasn't called me." She suppressed a sob. "You might as well tell me the truth. David's going to divorce me, isn't he?"

Horace tried to parry her question. He hoped his expression conveyed the ridiculousness of such a thought. He telephoned room service and asked for a bottle of Scotch, soda, and ice. "It's early, Nancy. We need a drink or two. Then we'll find a restaurant in the hotel."

"Why are you avoiding the issue?"

"I'm not." He patted her hand. "The truth is, I know more about those pictures than you think I do. Last night I was invited to Peter Alberti's home."

"Oh, my God, no!" Nancy gasped.

"My God, yes!" Horace laughed. "But the pictures and the Alberti party were quite funny in an insane kind of way."

Nancy began to cry. Horace stood beside her awkwardly, patting her bent shoulders. "Tears aren't going to solve anything," he said. "I'm going to shave and take a shower. When the bellboy brings the Scotch pour us both a good one." Horace calmly undressed to his shorts. As he dropped his shirt and pants on the bed he noticed that Nancy was being careful not to look at him. While he was lathering his face he heard somebody deliver the Scotch and then the tinkle of ice

117

as Nancy poured the drinks. She appeared at the bathroom door, tiny paths left by her tears still on her cheeks. "Do you want it now?"

Horace took the glass and pointed at the toilet bowl. "Sit down. You might as well watch me shave in comfort." He noticed she was gulping her drink. "This beats standing on a chair."

"Please." She frowned. "How much do you think I can take? I wasn't really spying on you. God, that was only two weeks ago." She glared at him angrily. "You don't believe me, do you? You think I'm some kind of a nymphomaniac."

"Scarcely." Horace resumed shaving, enjoying his facial contortions in the mirror. "I think you're a normal female with average repressions. I think if I had ever attempted to have intercourse with you, and you had yielded, you would spend the rest of your life regretting it." He smiled at her. "Over the past years, after all, I've become pretty well acquainted with the mechanisms that make Nancy tick."

Nancy scowled at him. "Since you're so damn certain that I was purposely watching you, I suppose you even know what motivated me? I suppose you know why, the very same day, I went with that horrible man on his boat. I suppose you think I'm quite promiscuous always ready to go to bed with anybody. I suppose you even think I planned this, and that I want to seduce you." Her lips trembled as she waited for his answer. When he didn't reply, she went to the bedroom and made herself another drink. While she drank it, she watched him rinsing his face. "I'm a secret lush, too. You didn't know that, did you?"

Horace smiled. "I know if Nancy drinks too much she'll get sick; then old Horace will have to put ice packs on her head. I know you didn't actually have sex with Peter Alberti, though you might have. If you had, I think you might have contemplated suicide afterward. What's more, I'll be willing to wager the only man you have ever been to bed with is David."

"God damn it, I hate you!"

Horace swallowed the remainder of his drink. "That's better. I enjoy angry females. I'm going to shower. Go into the bedroom, take off your clothes and join me."

"You are insane. Do you really think I'd do that?"

"To tell you the truth I don't, and if you did I wouldn't know what to do with you anyway." He turned on the shower faucets. "I'm going to take my shorts off. You better leave before I offend you."

As he soaped himself he wondered how he could ever save Nancy from the wound he was about to inflict on her ego.

118

He had one hunch. The trick, he guessed, was somehow to turn Nancy's flaring temper into laughter. No matter how he felt personally about Tanya and David, mutual remorse wouldn't solve their problems. He grinned as he washed his genitals. What if Nancy had taken his dare? After two nights of making love to Sylvia, he doubted that the old boy had any stamina left. After all, he wasn't nineteen or twenty any more. There was only one way to approach the evening: Treat Nancy as a friend and stay remote from the sexual overtones of their being snowbound together.

He was about to turn the water off when the shower curtain was pulled back. Nancy, naked, a frightened child in a lush female body, looked at him apologetically.

"For God's sake, Horace, don't make any remarks," she gasped. "Just invite me in. If you say anything, I think I'll go to pieces."

Chapter 19

~~~~~~

Soaping Nancy's back timidly at first, Horace speculated that she had probably bathed only a few hours before, and scarcely needed a shower. Then, as his soapy hands slid gently between her buttocks and legs, he knew she was nervously using the bath as an excuse to grant him an intimate exploration of her body.

"You have a very nice body." He tried to keep his voice casual. Water streamed from his face. "Aren't you afraid of getting your hair wet?"

"Nope." She avoided his glance. "David likes it short." She blushed; the mention of David's name while Horace was soaping her breasts seemed inappropriate "I mean that short hair dries easily, though I'll need some hair spray before I can face the world again Want me to wash your back?"

Nancy brushed against his penis and jumped back with embarrassment at its obvious enthusiasm; Horace was happy to turn away from her startled expression.

"How do I compare with Tanya?" Nancy blurted the words. She was being careful that her hands didn't stray below his shoulder blades. "Oh dear, I'm not very subtle, am I? I'm really sorry about mentioning David."

Horace took the soap from her hands and placed it in the receptacle. "Come on; we're clean enough. I haven't been comparing you with Tanya—or Sylvia." He emphasized Sylvia's name, and was amused at the startled expression on Nancy's face as he patted her breasts and stomach dry with a bath towel.

"Sylvia—" she whispered, trying to comprehend. "For God's sake, who is Sylvia?"

Horace led her out of the bathroom toward one of the beds. He pulled the covers down, ignoring her doubtful look. "Get in; I won't bite you. It's big enough for two. I'll make you another drink and we'll talk. What better way to get acquainted with your neighbor than bundling on a snowy New England night?"

Beside her, lying on his back, Horace stared at the ceiling.

For a long time he avoided the questions he knew she had on her mind.

"Maybe you better not tell me," she said with a sigh. "I guess I really have a small-town mentality Lying here, I can only think of you as Horace who belongs to Tanya. Somehow it's not right; we both know it. I'm in bed naked with Tanya's husband, and Tanya is my friend." Nancy's eyes were wet. "I really haven't many friends."

Horace shrugged. "I have a feeling that Tanya wouldn't mind. As for Sylvia, she's my assistant at Cal Institute. Sylvia is a very charming mixture of Chinese and Negro Last night I was in bed with her." He smiled at Nancy's sharp intake of breath. "All night she kept insisting that I mustn't change my mind. that I must come to Boston and talk with you."

Nancy's face was an opaque combination of disgust and astonishment. She moved closer to her edge of the bed. "Just *why* are you in bed with me?" she asked. "I think I'd better go home."

Horace looked at her grimly. "Nancy, tonight, perhaps unwillingly and for reasons that aren't wholly your fault, you are going to grow up. I'm not going to make any advances to you. You can forget how sinful we might look to others, since no others will see us, and *you can listen.*"

As he groped for words to explain his relationship with Sylvia, he wondered how Nancy, a married female, who was naturally protective toward the ties of monogamy, was reacting. And how, ultimately, would she respond to his more bitter revelations about David and Tanya?

"Let me put it this way, Nancy. Like you, I'm not really promiscuous. The few times I've slept with Sylvia have merely expressed our friendship One day Sylvia will get married. Neither of us has related our bodily pleasure. our mutual search for companionship the bodily penetration, or our defenseless acceptance of each other to the institution of marriage. For Sylvia, as well as for me, it has been a way of saying, 'I like you, you are my friend.'"

Nancy was weeping silently. "What I nearly did with Peter Alberti was worse, I guess. I didn't even like him. I was being an adventuress. Does Tanya know?"

Horace shook his head. "I'm telling you about Sylvia for a reason. and it's important that you know more about Peter Alberti and his way of life, which I don't pretend to understand. I haven't really had time to rationalize it myself. But it may be important that we puzzle it out together."

As Horace explained why Fritzi Alberti had contacted Sylvia, he noticed that Nancy had stopped crying. She was curled on her side of the bed, the sheet pulled up to her chin,

121

her body not touching his, listening with a rapt expression on her face. "We drove over to the Sherman Oaks area in my car. I had never asked Sylvia about her sex life. A wise man accepts the moment with the woman in his arms. Her past or future can add nothing but fears or misery. But to be honest, a sexual orgy involving her, or any woman I cared for, ran counter to what has always seemed to me to be the natural possessiveness of the male. As for the female psyche, I'm not too certain, but I would never assume that an evening of 'wham-bang' was a normal female desire."

"You're right," Nancy said emphatically. "Only a neurotic female would let herself be used by a lot of men."

Horace laughed softly. "I don't think the females in the Albertis' group are neurotic. I wonder what marriage will be like fifty years from now. Females will have shaken off all areas of inhibition. Freed of the fears of pregnancy I'll wager the female will be no more monogamously inclined than the average male, or maybe she'll demand a form of monogamy that permits other sexual interests. Anyway, I asked Sylvia if she had any idea of what we were getting into. Well, she kept her cool and said she thought that as observers we might reach some interesting conclusions. The phenomenon of spouse exchange presumably involves a very large subculture in the U.S."

" 'Don't worry,' Sylvia insisted. 'The maximum that can happen is you may have to belly-bump with six women. Fritzi told me that is the average female turnout from their group of twenty couples who meet every four or five weeks.' "

Horace couldn't help grinning at Nancy's grim expression. "I asked Sylvia if she could possibly enjoy sexual relations with six different men in one evening."

" 'Not enjoy,' she told me. 'Experience.' Sylvia's reaction was that since she was protected from conception and, by what she assumed was the nature of group sex, from brutality, the only thing she had to fear was a male's bad breath; but I knew she was teasing me. A competent wiggle of her torso and she wouldn't have to put up with that problem too long."

Nancy gasped her disapproval. "I don't like your Sylvia."

Horace grinned. "Well, I have to admit that she was making me feel like a senior citizen." He didn't tell Nancy that his own bleak marital problems had left him with a what-the-hell-does-it-matter attitude. "As you know, Peter Alberti is a very wealthy contractor. We drove through Coldwater Canyon and finally found the road leading to the top of the Santa Monica Mountains, where the Albertis live. As we

122

climbed, passing homes with more than an acre of grounds, we knew we were penetrating a different world. Even the smog of Los Angeles was left behind. Sylvia was nervous but enchanted. I remember her saying, 'The rich seem so different. I wonder what it's like to have a million dollars.' "

"But money doesn't solve the problems of the rich, either," Nancy observed.

Horace touched her hand, which was now outside the sheet. "We've all lost our moral underpinnings. The old rules don't seem valid any longer."

"Perhaps people don't really know enough." Nancy was aware that she was conversing with Horace on a level she rarely achieved with David. "It seems to me that the whole world is in a mad flight from reality. Like a trip on LSD or marijuana or alcohol, a sex orgy certainly doesn't add up to anything meaningful."

"What is reality? What is meaningful?"

Nancy looked at him strangely. "I don't know, Horace, maybe us, now, talking, trying to find answers; maybe the only reality is the striving to understand another person." She was embarrassed at her inability to find the words she wanted. "Oh dear, I wish I could convey what this moment means for me, just to listen and watch your serious face—and what it means to me that you think me intelligent enough not to simply condemn you and everything you're telling me. Please, what happened?"

"By the time we arrived at the Albertis' and I had parked my car with a Mercedes, two Cadillacs, a Jaguar, and a Rolls Royce in a tree-lined turnaround, I was beginning to feel like a Crusader about to scale the castle walls of some heathen baron. The grounds are protected by a semicircular stone wall about ten feet high and covered with vines. Where there's no wall, a sheer cliff drops off for maybe a hundred feet or so. All that's missing is a moat and a drawbridge. We couldn't see the house from the driveway, but we finally located an arched door, gothic style, strapped with black iron. Over it hung an ancient ship's lantern We rang the bell and waited Finally a metal window in the gate was slid back and Fritzi Alberti's eyes twinkled as us 'Miss Mail' she said. 'Wonderful. You're just in time.' She let us in." Horace took a long swallow of his drink. "She was quite naked. Between thirty-five and forty, rather too-big breasts for her height, but otherwise in good proportion."

"So that's Peter Alberti's bitch wife!" Nancy said sourly. "If she has such good merchandise, why did she have to screw up my life? If these people are all so damned promiscuous, why did she have to send those pictures to David? One

123

more female, more or less, in her husband's life, what could it matter?" Nancy was angry. "Oh, I know what you're thinking. It doesn't excuse what I did."

Horace grinned. "If you *had* gotten away with an afternoon of dalliance, you really wouldn't feel so grim about yourself, would you?"

"Damn you, Horace, I'm not one of your students. Don't preach. And don't try to tell me that I'm basically immoral. I'm not like the Albertis, or like you—with a lover on the side." Nancy looked at him bitterly. "I don't really think it's any of my business, and I don't want to hear any more."

Horace held her cheeks in his hands and solemnly kissed her lips. "Of course you do. You want to know every gory detail."

In spite of herself Nancy gave him a little grin.

"In fact," Horace said, "I don't think it ever occurred to Fritzi that she might be creating a problem between you and David. In her group, such an escapade would have been treated with a boisterous laugh. In this case, because Peter didn't get away with it, he was made to pay for his sins.

" 'You'll have to undress' Fritzi told us. 'We have ten cabanas each with toilets, showers, a large bed and even a television. The damned place is a regular motel.'

"We followed her undulating behind as she led us through an enormous flower garden. In the shadows created by diffused lighting we could see the second story of the house almost at ground level on the near side of a pool. The house was nearly four hundred feet long, bisecting the rectangle of the enclosure. Frank Lloyd Wright style, the first floor conformed to the slope of the mountain, facing into twin, kidney-shaped swimming pools and a patio lighted by flaming torches. Far in the distance the billion lights of Los Angeles were a shimmering backdrop for the Alberti stage.

"Fritzi explained that the maids, the chauffeur and the cook had been given a four-day holiday. 'We have the joint to ourselves until Sunday afternoon,' she said. 'At all our Save Our Spouse parties, the men do the cooking' she grimaced. 'Open charcoal steaks, of course. Do men ever think of cooking anything else?'

"We could see men and women swimming in one of the pools or sitting around the edges. They were all naked. Fritzi took us to a cabana, found a room and told us to hurry, because the Inquisition of Peter Alberti was ready to commence.

"Sylvia and I stared at each other, both of us ready to admit while we were undressing that the better part of valor

124

would be to run for the car, and hightail it back to our little world."

Horace smiled at Nancy. "Beyond our own harmless pool party, and our half-cockeyed excursion into nude bathing, I had never been naked in a mixed group before. I felt like a novice entering a nudist camp. It didn't help any to have Sylvia whisper, as we walked naked onto the patio, 'Now admit it, Horace, if you could screw all these naked ladies with impunity, without obligation, wouldn't you want to try it?' "

"Would you?" Nancy demanded. Leaning on her elbow, staring at him intently, she was heedless that her breasts were dangling a few inches from Horace's face. "Did you actually get in a daisy chain?"

Horace roared with laughter. "How do you know about such things?"

Nancy was embarassed. "Oh, I read about them in a paperback. You've seen them; this one told all about wife-swapping. It was so ugly I burned it."

"Well, don't anticipate," Horace said. "This was a bit different. As I think about it now, the whole arrangement was matriarchal. You might call it a new form of female permissiveness. This group believes in giving their husbands sexual variety within their group but controlled by a strict code of rules and regulations. That's where Peter Alberti got into trouble. He violated the tribal mores in an attempt at exogamy, and Fritzi caught him."

"I don't understand," Nancy said.

"You will. Fritzi introduced us to the group by first names. She identified us, amid much guffawing and happy approval, as two sociologists who were going to observe the evening's fun, and who would participate only if we wished."

"What were the women like?" Nancy demanded. "Who were they?"

"They were just average females wearing no clothes to identify them or give them status. The age-range was from the late twenties to the early forties, with the men averaging about forty, and Peter himself being the admitted granddaddy of the group." Horace shrugged. "To tell the truth, I was a little stunned by such an array of tits, pussies and penises. It was some time before I could adjust to conversation in which the whole body of the person became a related entity. There was an Alice, pretty plump; two girls named Sandra, one with cupcake breasts, the other built like a Greek statue; and there was a Mary and a Catherine. I think Fritzi also introduced us to Peter Alberti, who has a very handsome body for a man of his age, tanned all over."

"You don't have to describe him to me," Nancy said. She

got out of bed and, having decided that her own nakedness was of small concern, poured herself another drink. "You probably were fed on the plane, but if I don't eat pretty soon I'm going to be tipsy." She looked out the window and announced that it was still snowing.

Horace suggested that they get dressed. "I'm too lazy," Nancy replied, and slid back into bed. "Call room service. Can't we order some chicken sandwiches? I want to hear the rest of your insane story, and I want to find out what it has to do with my problem."

As he dialed room service Horace reflected uncomfortably that he was still dodging the real issue of Tanya and David. Did the Alberti evening really relate? He was sure it did somehow, but he still couldn't put the thought in words. "Well," he continued, "the half-dozen or so pictures that Fritzi took of you and Peter were on tables around the pool. At least five or six sets of them. Peter pointed to them with a grin. 'I've been a bad boy, as you can see,' he said, 'but unless you know the whys and wherefores of our S.O.S. parties you can't possibly understand what's going on here tonight.' Peter asked that somebody explain the house rules to us.

"The woman named Catherine offered us a drink. While one of the men poured them, and we sat in the middle of the group on chaises, she explained. 'There's nothing written down,' she said. 'You might say our rules and customs have evolved through experience, some of it sad, some of it quite ugly. Take drinking. We've found that liquor and good fucking don't mix very well, and since our prime purpose is to have sexual fun, none of us drinks more than one or two, largely to get rid of our inhibitions, of which there aren't many left. Basically, the females are in command. We make the arrangements. If we have any philosophy, it shakes down to the idea that we want to stay married. With all our various marital faults and disagreements, we feel that divorce is no answer, though some of us have come pretty close to it. We've seen friends go through numerous divorces and remarriages, and still they come apart at the seams. While we don't think sex is all there is to life, we think that there's a natural male drive and probably a female one to experience sex, and through it friendship and communication with more than one person of the opposite sex. Monogamy has created an unnecessary and artificial barrier to that need. For example, a few years ago I was becoming rather stodgy, and Jack, my husband, was ready to divorce me. Bed had become a place to sleep or argue. Somehow or other, because of this group, we've learned how to laugh at ourselves, and we've grown psychologically younger, or at least I have.'

126

"One of the men, who identified himself as Harry, agreed. 'But there are areas of control on which we have a common accord,' he told us. 'You may have read about wife-swapping and the degraded, sleazy business it usually degenerates into. We've limited our group very carefully to exclude anyone interested in sexual deviations. Peter calls us HOPE, for Happy Orgies People Enjoy. Hence there is no interest in homosexualism, lesbianism, sadism, or fetishism, or in wearing clothes or in being partially clothed merely to titillate each other. Since we always approach each other early in the evening as naked human beings, and play together for hours before any actual lovemaking you might say that we're a logical extension of the nudist philosophy though I doubt if any dedicated nudists would agree Basically we think we're eliminating the neuroticism that society has created by prohibiting or making sinful the natural joy of the human animal in its fondling, caressing, and flesh-seeking contacts. We've been taught that men and women outgrow their childhood drive to tumble and curl up together in the identity-need of each other's warmth and affection The truth is that we never do and that, in our mechanized world, with the inevitable depersonalization of human contacts, our day-to-day human problems are tremendously magnified, and we grow more apart and lonely each day of our lives.' "

Horace smiled at Nancy. "I must admit that Sylvia and I were impressed by their apparent sincerity Right or not, their rationalizations were well thought out. We were naturally interested in how they restrained jealousy and to learn why particular males or females in their little society didn't become so enamored of other partners that they might create tensions or disrupt their existing marriages.

"It seemed to shake down to this. During their extended weekends over the past two years each person in the group had at one time or another slept with each member of the other sex at least three or four times, for several nights in a row. They approach each other in the act of coitus and before, not only for sexual enjoyment, but as friends, willing to make allowances for what they once considered as odd or obnoxious qualities in each other. In essence they make a supreme human effort. By consciously submerging their egos, they pour oil on the waves of aggression. In the process they have come to know and to like each other.

"All the women use contraceptive pills. Vasectomies for the men are considered unnecessary, though one man had the operation long before the group came into existence. He explained that after bearing four children in the first years of

127

their marriage, he felt his wife had exceeded her duty to continue the race.

"They agreed that, with interesting exceptions, pornographic movies, group sex, or situations where members of the group copulated before each other were a decided bore. The females decide who their bed partners for a particular weekend would be, and they have devised a number of humorous ways of accomplishing the final choice. Currently popular is the auction."

Nancy was intrigued. "You said there were exceptions, and, for heaven's sakes, do you actually mean they auctioned off the males?" She giggled, realizing suddenly that she was lying with her head on Horace's shoulder. Embarrassed, she transferred her weight to her elbow. Horace's reply was interrupted by a muffled knock on the door.

"Oh, my God," Nancy squealed. "It must be our sandwiches!" She pulled the sheets over her head. "I can't get dressed. You'll have to open the door. Don't let him in!"

Grinning at her, Horace yelled to the room-service boy to have patience. He fumbled in the closet for his topcoat. After he had at last opened the door a crack, he accepted the tray. Muttering to the boy to keep the change, and certain that the ten dollars he gave him was too much, he kicked the door shut with his bare foot.

Nancy watched him with delight, knowing that in his momentary confusion Horace was as rattled as she had been. Crossing her legs Indian-fashion, she sat naked on the bed, the tray of sandwiches between them. Horace watched her eat her sandwich ravenously. She was oblivious for the moment of her lack of clothing; her face was alive and vibrant, and it occurred to him that she looked a little like a teen-ager fearful of being caught at something forbidden. He was conscious, too, of her nipples—slightly engorged, tilted, smiling at him with a warm grin from the lush breasts of a woman. Her brown eyes widened into embarrassment as she became conscious of his erection. Blushing, she quickly looked away and tried to concentrate on his face. "Oh, Lord," she said, "if David or Tanya or my mother and father could see us now, what would they think?"

Horace kissed the tiny hairs curling at the base of her neck. "That we were lovers. What else?"

"But we won't be, will we?" she asked him nervously. She stared at him for a moment, trying to interpret the expression of wonder and affection on his face. "Oh, Horace, why not? Yes, I want you, too!"

Chapter 20

~~~~~~~~~

Long before she opened her eyes, Nancy was awake and dimly aware that it was morning. The subdued dressing-table lamp was still lighted, but the room had lost its deep night shadows. The light that filtered through the drawn curtains was that of another gray, sunless day. Floating between reality and her dreams, she was momentarily in her bed at Palos Verdes. The muffled footsteps on the floor of the room above were Jimmy and Susan, who were playing in the living room while they waited for her and David to come upstairs. They would all have Sunday breakfast together; she would make scrambled eggs and bacon. But it wasn't Sunday, it was Saturday. David was beside her. As he stirred, touching her hip and leg, her brain cleared, and she realized with a flash of fright that this man next to her wasn't David; it was Horace. Startled that she had been holding his penis in a sleepy embrace, she gently withdrew her hand.

She had done it; she, a married woman, had slept with another man. My God, that was a euphemism. She had made love with an insatiable need and fury. What did Horace think? That she was love-starved, of course, or a nymphomaniac. It couldn't have been later than nine o'clock, forgetting their unfinished sandwiches, that they had tumbled together into the bed. Wild passion had merged into deep fulfillment. Amazingly, Horace responded over and over again to the involuntary rhythm of her vagina. They had drifted together in a communication beyond words.

Thank God she hadn't stopped taking her pills; the night's adventure would leave no physical trace. But mental traces, ah, they were something else again! No matter what happened from now on, she had already surrendered the marital complacency of being faithful and the security that went with it. Why had she succumbed so easily? Why, even at the airport, had a sixth sense told her that tonight she would sleep with Horace? Why, in the short period of two weeks, defying everything she had believed, had she almost hypnotically abandoned the sanctity of marriage? Even now, with a compulsive desire to kiss Horace awake, wasn't she tacitly accepting that her marriage to David was finished? If there had been any hope at all of finding her way back, hadn't she now destroyed it?

If last night had never happened, she might have convinced David that the day with Peter Alberti had really only been a madcap kind of adventure and that, when the chips were down, she had withdrawn from the game. But last night with Horace she had willingly capitulated. Why? Was it because she was certain that Horace had come to Boston to tell her the cold truth, that David, the cuckolded husband, was accepting those nasty photographs as a simple way out of a marriage gone sour? But why had Horace come all this way to tell her? If he had hoped as a friend to affect a reconciliation, making love to her was an odd way to achieve it.

Had Horace shown the photographs to Tanya? Nancy shuddered. Tanya moralizing over Nancy's failure as a wife was unpleasant to contemplate. After all, who knew what Tanya did during her supposed working hours? Horace had probably told Tanya that he was coming to Boston to meet with sociologists at Harvard. Certainly he hadn't told her he was traveling three thousand miles for the purpose of seducing Nancy. Seduce! That was a laugh. The truth, even though she hated to admit it, was that she had wondered often in the past year if Horace would ever dare approach her as more than a friend. Once she had even caught his eyes searching her face, and she was certain that his thoughts were in tune with hers. The morning he had picked her off the floor naked, even while she prudishly protested that he must leave, she had been willing. If she had let him make love to her, the Alberti nastiness never would have happened. But what would their adultery have achieved? Nothing. For her it could only have been a dead end, with tears and recriminations.

Even while they were making love, she had actually asked Horace some of the questions that were churning through her mind. Between wondrous climaxes she had tried to interject reality, to divert his attention from the Alberti insanity back to the real problem of David and Tanya. But Horace was insistently on one track. Deep inside her, his penis expanded to the embracing fullness of her vagina; in happy possession, he assured her he might remain there permanently. But then he had talked. "I hope you won't think I'm not fully aware of how warm you are, but for a moment my thoughts were wandering. Since you were to blame, you really should know how they made Peter's punishment fit his crime."

"I was to blame!" Nancy gasped. "That's not true! I know you won't believe me, but I've always been naive. Can't a

130

man sincerely enjoy the companionship of a female without immediately wanting to spear her?"

Horace smiled. "In an odd sort of way Fritzi and the females in the S.O.S. group would agree with you. Peter violated the taboo of the tribe. Within their group there is presumably enough sexual diversity without seducing Nancys, whoever they might be. No member, male or female, is permitted to seek other outlets. When they court-martialed Peter and demanded to know why he took you on his boat, why he tried to make love to you, he couldn't explain it himself." Horace chuckled. "His only excuse was that you looked as if you needed servicing."

"I suppose you think that's funny!" Nancy exclaimed. "Damn males, anyhow, I'd like to get my hands on him!" Tears of anger trickled down her cheeks: she wiggled out of Horace's arms.

Grinning, he rejoined her, and she didn't protest as he kissed her salty lips. "You don't have to take the law into your own hands, Sea. Six ladies did it for you."

Aware that it was the first time he had ever used David's diminutive name for her, Nancy listened quietly.

His eyes had twinkled as he watched her growing astonishment. "While the rest of us watched, Fritzi produced two sets of handcuffs. Giggling, one of the women snapped them around his ankles, while another, holding Peter's arms behind his back, secured them on his wrists. On the patio they used air cushions to create a combat area about fifteen feet square. The procedure was devilishly simple. They stretched Peter out prone as a sacrificial offering. The six women, eager to scrub away his sins, sprinkled him throughly with a garden hose and then, completely naked and armed with glycerin soap, they buried him in lather. In a few minutes, laughing so hard he was gasping, Peter had all but disappeared beneath the suds and the mass of naked females. They slithered over him, poked at him, squatted on him and tortured him with complete abandon. Most of the time it was impossible to see the victim. After about twenty minutes, when all of them were breathless from laughter, one of the Sandras, herself covered with soap from head to foot, announced that they had punished him not once, but twice or possibly three times —they had lost count—and that he was now purged of his guilt. But, she said, whoever was silly enough to bid for Peter in the auction could expect a complete lack of interest in the female sex, at least for the night."

Nancy knew she was listening in shocked silence, yet she was unable to restrain a grin of satisfaction as Horace described Peter's scourging. It served Peter right, but she was

131

puzzled. Why did Horace keep hinting that such madness had any possible relation to her problem or, for that matter, to their being in bed together?

Enjoying the half-serious expression on his face as he talked to her, Nancy encouraged him to forget the Albertis. For long hours David and Tanya receded into another world; reality was here and now.

Their lovemaking became a counterpoint and temporary safe harbor from the storm. Outside, the snow, whipped by a furious northeast wind, slashed against the window of their bedroom. His lips on her breasts, she surrendered to the unfamiliar touch of his long fingers exploring the curve of her stomach, making her nerve-endings tingle as they flitted through her pubic hairs and parted her labia in a light caress. And then his penis found the depth of her vagina. She smiled at his certainty that they could delay their climax and float together for hours if they wanted to. And then came her chagrin as the hours became minutes and she burst into sobbing release and appreciation of him and of her own surrender while she lay beneath him, warm and tender, absorbing his happy laughter as he managed almost impossibly to survive her weaving, throbbing onslaught. And later, the salty taste of his penis as she gaspingly tried, *needed* to contain him within her mouth, while his tongue traced her clitoris and finally again, his penis urgingly, necessarily, safely resheathed in her body, once again she .gasped her breath into his mouth. It was a never-ending orgasm, a joyous, helpless writhing that merged into his wondrous explosion and yell of sheer delight. She knew that his fingers were bruising her shoulders, but they felt good. She raked her nails across his buttocks and the length of his back until their passion burst into hysterical laughter and they regained the saner perspective that they must be both sex-mad. And finally they had finished the sandwiches they had abandoned. Grinning and shy with each other, they both were aware that their passion and coupling were good, because they held within them something over and above sex. They were friends.

As she recalled the evening of love, Nancy could only think, I am not ashamed. Horace was nice, he was affectionate, though she made no effort to compare him with David. She could no longer feel sinful—not with Horace. If there was any possibility that David still cared for her, she hadn't divided her love for him. She had multiplied it.

"And so what happened at the auction?" She had grinned weakly at him. Her breasts had finally stopped heaving, her heart was beating evenly again, her breathing back to normal. "Oh, honey, I feel you oozing out of me, but I'm too pooped to stand up. Besides," and she snuggled into his shoulder, "I'm beginning to realize that you *have* to finish the Alberti story and make some kind of moral out of it. I'm listening."

"It's not that I think the Albertis have discovered the great panacea for human misery," Horace assured her. "But I do feel that in their madcap joie de vivre they've eliminated jealousy and neurotic behavior and have found a way of relieving tensions for themselves, at least. I told you they don't copulate publicly. But it's quite approved behavior for a male to touch any female in a friendly caress while they're swimming together or dancing. For the females, the male is constantly fair game. No male can spend an entire evening without all of the females having, at least once, teased him into an erection by a quick touch or a purposeful brushing of her body against him. It's a test by fire, an auto-da-fé, evidently designed to make certain that the male will approach the female who has chosen him with uncontained fervor.

"The auction is a good example of uninhibited behavior. Nearly a year ago each female was given one hundred Russian roubles that Peter had bought from a dealer in foreign money; ever since, these roubles have been the only money used in the auctions. Thus no female could easily replenish her bidding funds, and each must buy her male from the funds that she has available. The privilege of being auctioneer for a particular evening is rotated, and the auctioneer is permitted to bid. Obviously, the auctioneer has the highest purchasing power and the first choice is therefore hers. When she bids high for a particular male, the money she bids is immediately divided equally among all the other females. Thus the money is kept in circulation, but the current auctioneer, if she isn't careful, is often left with little money for a future evening."

Horace laughed. "Last night the tall Sandra was auctioneer, and the men were lined up on a platform near the pool. Enjoying herself thoroughly, Sandra commented on their hairiness, their muscles, and their weight, and she chided them if they seemed too plump or didn't properly pull in their stomachs or throw out their chests. She even commented on their penises and advertised their length and circumference. The men, except Peter, were in an alarming state of readiness and were not a bit loath to touch or goose the auctioneer as she sold them to the highest bidder."

Horace smiled at Nancy, who lay in his arms with her eyes closed. "Peter was finally sold to Catherine for ten roubles. She said she didn't really mind, because she was pooped herself from shopping all day in Beverly Hills. Peter hugged her

133

and told her not to worry because, he said, 'Bears often turn into bulls. It depends on market conditions.' "

"Are you asleep?" Horace kissed Nancy softly.

"No. I'm listening to every silly word. What woman bought you?"

"None. Sylvia and I were only observers; remember?"

"And you slept with Sylvia last night?"

Horace nodded. Nancy was piqued, but she couldn't have said exactly why. After all, Horace wasn't *her* husband. Feeling decidedly immoral, she edged slightly away from him. "My God!" she exclaimed, "Does Tanya suspect that her husband has satyriasis?"

Horace choked with laughter. "While I know you won't believe it, Sylvia and I slept in one of the cabanas, and I mean *slept*, we were so exhausted. After the auction the men finally broiled steaks and, while we ate, Peter told us he had recently rigged one of the downstairs rooms, at a cost of several thousand dollars, with psychedelic lighting. He said that later we would dance to music that activated continuously changing patterns of light. 'We've had fun body-painting and decorating each other in designs from head to foot with washable paints,' he told us. 'Now we can experience a totally new environment. The lighting in this room consists of light panels operating in three light channels with five colors and a variety of patterns. It's synchronized to turn the beat of the music into light in terms of color and intensity, so we'll both see and hear the music. I've also installed three electronically controlled strobe lights that produce intense flashes of light from various locations in the room. These lights, also activated by the music, flash thirty times a second. When we're exposed to them we'll seem to have the detached motion you've seen in the old-time movies.' "

Horace grinned at Nancy. "It was out of this world. We were changed from a group of naked human beings who had some familiarity with each other into a number of weird creatures floating, shifting, dancing in an environment of thousand-hued colors. Individuality vanished: we became erotic musical flesh. As we danced with naked partners who from second to second changed color and motion, our individual identities merged into a composite identity. It was the ultimate eroticism. One by one the couples melted away to their various beds, having merged mentally even before the ultimate joining."

Nancy looked at her wristwatch on the night table; it was six fifteen. As Horace had told her the final details of the Alberti party, his words had become softer and wider-spaced.

"Dear Nancy," he sighed, "I'm asleep and still talking. Have you been listening?"

"With one ear, half a mind, and a thousand unanswered questions," she had told him. "But not questions about the Albertis—really about us. I have a feeling that all this conversation has been a gigantic red herring to avoid the real issue. When are you going to tell me the truth?"

He fell asleep even while she was speaking. Quietly, lest she wake Horace, Nancy got out of bed. She peered beyond the drapes, and saw that it was still snowing; the mean, defiant New England blizzard had lost none of its intensity. Far below she could see the deserted paths that had once been Boylston Street and Commonwealth Avenue. Plows that had been through hours before had buried the parked automobiles, and still the streets were deep in snow. The city seemed deserted. Even at this height she could feel its wintery silence.

Sitting on the toilet, half asleep, feeling the unaccustomed ache of her body from so much lovemaking, she wondered if the splash of her urine would wake Horace. Afterward, relieved to find him still asleep, she slid back into bed and welcomed his face against her breasts. I can't possibly go home today, she thought; we're snowbound. Suddenly, with a flash of intuition, she knew that her old life with David was finished.

Chapter 21

~~~~~~~~~~

The reality of a new day slowly erased the ecstasy of the moment. The fragile web of their lovemaking dissolved into constrained silence as they dressed for breakfast. Horace, subdued and efficient-looking in a dark blue business suit, his slightly receding hairline accentuating the height of his forehead, seemed the epitome of a Boston banker. Waiting for Nancy, he grinned as he surveyed himself in the mirror. He could be a visiting corporation executive who had had his fling with a purchased partner of the evening. Now he was waiting with some impatience to round out the amenities. He'd buy her breakfast, make promises for some distant future, and be off to more lucrative pursuits. Waiting for Nancy, he turned on the television. Thinking more realistically, it occurred to him that Nancy, his friend, could be his wife.

Only half listening to the weather forecast, he barely grasped the words; the heaviest snowfall on record would continue through Saturday. If there were a possibility he might have to spend another night with Nancy, the denouement couldn't be postponed. The contained and febrile atmosphere of this room, still heavy with the sultry odor of their coupling, was not the environment to tell her the truth. Could he be calmly honest at breakfast? Would Nancy, in the hotel dining room, summon up her New England heritage and keep a stiff upper lip while she absorbed the painful news that her life with David could never again have the calm certainty and security of their early years? Could he keep her from drowning in her own misery while he attempted to explain the "solution" which he had slowly been piecing together?

Fully dressed in her ski clothes, her fur jacket over her shoulders, Nancy waited until the weather report was finished. She smiled apologetically. "It doesn't look as if I'll be able to get home today, either. Poor Horace, you didn't expect to get stuck with me." She really wanted to say, this is madness isn't it? What can we possibly do all day? Even newlyweds can't make love continuously. And we *aren't* lovers,

are we, and scarcely newlyweds! Then she thought, this man
guiding me to the elevators, this man I permitted to explore
my body so thoroughly, who even delights in the mole near
the bend of my knee and the one tiny hair growing near the
nipple on my left breast, this man is a stranger. We have no
resources to draw us together. With David and Tanya we
were a unity, but alone we have no experience, no understanding of how to function together.

They passed a newsstand in the lobby. Nancy glanced at
the paperbacks. For a silly, flitting moment she wondered if
they could buy a book and read it together. Really, it
shouldn't be that difficult. She had known Horace for three
years. Isolated by the storm, perhaps they could really break
the artificial barriers. His flesh had united with hers. Could it
become a prelude? Could they discover each other in a way
that most males and females never achieve? Hadn't she often
wished that one day Horace might really reach out, talk to
her on a level they had never realized as a foursome?

Nancy draped her coat around her chair at a table near the
window in the Caravan Room. She sat opposite Horace, her
knit cap perched on her head. While they waited for the
waitress, she studied him with a wide-eyed innocence that
both unnerved and startled him as he recalled the violence of
her surrender. Afraid to express their thoughts, they watched
the heavy snow swirling in wild cross-currents through the
mall of Prudential Plaza as the top floors of the Tower
probed and vanished in thick, ominous clouds. A gray monument to man's superior strength against the elements, the
building seemed detached, remotely disdainful of the storm
lashing against it in a futile fury. The snow landing on the
heated walks of the concourse quickly melted, but beyond, on
Boylston Street and Huntington Avenue, the roads were buried in constantly shifting drifts that were temporarily beyond
the efforts of man and plow to restore normal functioning.

Nancy finally dared to look directly at him. "If I can't get
home today, I don't think we should be together again."

"Are you regretting last night?"

Nancy sighed. "Oh, Horace, I'm sorry. I can't help it."

She voiced a tiny sob. "Sitting here, seeing myself objec-
tively, through your eyes, the picture seems ugly. Without
being in love with you, I used you in retaliation for David's
indifference." Her lips trembled. "David doesn't love me,
does he? It's all over with us. I know that. Why did you come
to Boston, anyway? Don't you think it's about time you were
honest with me?"

Deliberately, Horace stirred the heat from his coffee with a
teaspoon. He had decided the only way was to be mercifully

137

blunt, and now he took the plunge. "The truth is," he said, "that for the past two years David and Tanya have been lovers." Conscious for a moment of her stupefied silence and of its contrast with the commotion of the crowded breakfast room, Horace watched the impact of his words register on Nancy's face.

Next to them, two men heatedly discussed foreign policy; their weirdly irrelevant talk added to Nancy's bewilderment. Everyone at breakfast was the prisoner of his own tiny world. With tears obscuring her vision, Nancy stared at Horace without seeing him. Her mind strove to reconstruct the past two years. When? How? David and she were presumably Horace and Tanya's friends. She knew David liked Tanya, whose gaiety contrasted to her own stodginess. But lovers—laughing at her naivety? She shuddered.

"I guess I've been pretty stupid," she said. Though she had lost the desire to eat, she tried to extract a section from the grapefruit in front of her. "Maybe I really guessed it all the time." I'm smiling bravely, she thought; I won't come apart. "That clears the air for you, doesn't it? You still have Sylvia." But now she couldn't hold back the tears, "Oh God, my God, Horace! Why have you done this to me? Did you have to come three thousand miles to humble me even more?"

Horace's fingers encircled her wrist. "Nancy, we didn't make love casually. I care for you. Maybe that means I love you." He grinned feebly. "Who can really define love? Strangely, after the initial shock, I'm not angry with David. Perhaps he and Tanya found something in each other that you and I were unable to provide." He shrugged. "On the other hand, Tanya and I have lived together fifteen years. The fact that she and David have made love doesn't erase the lives we've both shared. I'm beginning to believe that Tanya is quite honest when she says she still loves me, and I'm certain that David still loves you."

Angrily, Nancy pulled out of his grasp. "*You* can have that kind of love. In my family we get married to one person, and we don't go around screwing the whole world even if we feel like it!"

"You're not being honest. You enjoyed last night. With a new lover, perhaps you even released a Nancy you've always held in check with David."

"I was a whore," Nancy said scornfully. "It was a cheap business. You tumbled into bed with me after an orgy at the Albertis. What kind of person are you, anyway? Go back to Tanya, who loves you, too. You and David can share her." She shuddered. "My God, what I did with Peter Alberti was harmless by comparison."

Horace noticed the two men nearest them were eating silently as they eavesdropped; he had a momentary urge to grab Nancy's arm and lead her out of the dining room. Yet, he thought, maybe her anger is a necessary catharsis. "We aren't going to solve anything by recriminations," he said mildly. "You might as well learn to roll with the punches. Tanya is pregnant."

"That's just great." Her false laughter echoed her disgust. She stared at him bitterly. "So Horace is the martyr, Tanya had her fling, and now she can come home to hatch."

"The nest is not really mine." Horace decided not to mince words. "David is the father."

Nancy knew that her loud gasp of dismay and her tears were attracting the attention of everyone in the dining room. Trying to control the shudders that were wracking her body, she slid into her fur jacket. "I'm sorry, Horace, but I think I'm going to be sick. I've got to go to the ladies room."

Somehow she threaded her way through the blurry maze of people and tables. Searching frantically, her eyes caught the exit doors. As she fled out of the lobby of the hotel into the Prudential Mall she was dimly aware that she had left her pocketbook at the table, but it didn't matter. Icy snow, caught in a fierce downdraft from the Tower, congealed the warm perspiration on her face. The shock of Horace's words churned the juices in her stomach; her brassiere and panties clung to her, clammy with sweat. It was insane to run. The wind, rippling through her ski clothes, turned her flesh to goose bumps. Despair and hopelessness grasped at her bowels. Fearful that Horace would follow her, beyond words and even tears, she ran across the concourse toward Boylston Street. After sliding and skidding down the stairs, she stumbled into the street, knee-deep in wind-whipped snow.

It's over, she thought wildly, it's over. There is nothing left. Oh God, please God, let me die! Let me die!

Breathless, she ran toward Massachusetts Avenue, struggled through a waist-high drift and fell face down in the middle of it. A lone man, dressed in a hunting cap, mackinaw and hip boots, plowing down the center of the street, yelled at her, yanked her to her feet and held her against him. Bewildered, she let him guide her into an area where the snow was only a few inches deep. "Rough going, lady." He stared curiously at her tearstained face. "Nothing in the world worth freezing to death for. Want me to help you to the hotel?"

Nancy pulled out of his grasp. "Leave me alone. I'm all right. Thank you for your trouble." In the tracks left by a snow plow she staggered away from him, heedless of his warning that Massachusetts Avenue was in worse shape than Boylston Street. Suddenly she knew clearly what she must do. The bridge over the Charles River. Harvard Bridge. Suicide Bridge. The icy waters had often given refuge to the lost and bewildered. There would be no one to stop her, no one who cared. Even Horace couldn't bring himself to say, "I love you, Nancy." And David! David! *David!* "Why, oh God, why?" she sobbed. David, in a passionate naked embrace with Tanya, writhed in her mind, or was it herself, Nancy, abandoned in her lust for Horace, or for Peter?

A strange calmness possessed her as she trudged blindly toward the bridge. Unmindful of the snow, freezing on her face and stinging her eyes almost closed, she exulted in the silence of the snow-whipped city. She was alone. There was no love, no need, no caring. Just fuck. Ugly fuck. The mindless voice screaming in her brain was the monster at the fun house, laughing insanely, dissolving into a naked, glistening skull of death. Hurry, hurry, hurry! The scream became a silent, urgent whisper. The bridge swept clean of snow by the howling wind was only a few hundred feet ahead of her. Not far now, she told her exhausted shuddering body. Not far. Oh David, Susan, Jimmy, I love you. But I'm so sorry I can't face it alone, oh so sorry!

PART TWO

The Commitment

~~~~~~~~~~

Chapter 1

~~~~~~~~~~

I suppose it's somewhat disconcerting to discover that a novel you've been reading suddenly changes perspective and assumes a first-person reality. Any one of us, Tanya, David, or Horace, could continue our story. That I elected to do the entire job, first as a third-person observer, and now more intimately, like an actor who temporarily drops his part and harangues his audience, is perhaps one of the necessities of Nancy. As Horace put it, "We were four characters in search of an author. But inadvertently, like Dr. Frankenstein, we have now created our own monster."

I realize there is both laughter and gentle reproof in that remark. None of the others is wholly in agreement with me in my role as recording secretary. Nevertheless, the strength of our commitment is the recognition that we love each other, not as reflections of each other's ego, but as intensely individual human beings with our own specific drives.

As I think back now, many months later, the Nancy who came close to freezing to death in that December blizzard,

141

the Nancy who was so self-centered that she could contemplate suicide, is no longer comprehensible to me. Yet I suppose I was not different from many females. I believed that David *should* love me, or at least, if I could replace his lost love with a new love from Horace, that I should continue to pursue the folly of expecting love as a requirement for giving it.

Yes, I have changed, but so have the four of us. Like pilgrims, we have plowed through the sloughs of despond and slowly discovered whatever godliness there may be in our own joyously ridiculous and wondrous humanity.

If you are completely despondent and seem to have lost the reason for living, I guess freezing is a simple death. A city snow crew, high in the cab of a huge plow, discovered me late Saturday afternoon. I vaguely remember two men arguing whether to take me to a police station or directly to a hospital. Evidently they decided I was in pretty bad shape. Nearly numb, with a dull indifference to what was happening, I let them hoist me into their truck. Even with my eyes open I could scarcely see them. They ignored my suggestion that it was my privilege to die if I wanted to, and plowed their way directly down Massachusetts Avenue to Boston City Hospital.

In the process of being unthawed by two nurses, who stripped off my soaking clothes, fed me hot tea, and massaged me while a doctor watched—he seemed rather grim, and demanded to know why I was "sleeping it off" in a snow drift—I kept floating in and out of consciousness. They wrapped my face in cool towels. I was aware that my feeble protests were being ignored. My pulse was good, and I heard someone say that I had only mild frostbite. And then the doctor was asking my name and where I lived. But I couldn't answer. How could I? If I told them, I would have to put up with visits from Mother (hysterical) and Daddy (proclaiming that he always suspected the worst about David). As for Horace, I had drifted in and out of memories of my joyous surrender to him and finally yielded to the nagging conviction that he too had simply been caught in the whirlpool. Perhaps he was sympathetic, but as far as I was concerned he was just an innocent bystander who wanted to help, but had no desire to become involved.

Sunday morning, half drugged from whatever the doctor had fed me, I gradually became aware that someone was sitting beside my bed. I grinned feebly, certain I was dreaming. It couldn't be Horace.

"How did you ever find me?" I muttered, and started to

cry. "Oh, my God, why are you torturing me? Why don't you get out of my life?"

Horace sat on the edge of the bed; he leaned over and kissed my cheek. "The torturing has been mutual," he said. "If you don't think so, just try playing hide and seek in a strange city."

"Am I dying, or just sick?" I moaned. "I feel terrible."

"You had a pretty bad exposure, and right now you're loaded up with penicillin and tranquillizers. But you're all right. The doctor is releasing you tomorrow afternoon. He wouldn't give you this private room until I told him I was your husband and that we had had a family quarrel."

"Thanks, but you're not your brother's keeper." I opened my eyes, startled by a sudden thought. "What about Mother and Daddy? I suppose you told them about the whole miserable mess." I half expected Mother to dash into the room and start to yell about her "poor baby."

Horace grinned. "You can stop worrying. It wasn't easy, but things are under control. I've been through six hours of hell. When the waitress pointed out that it was unlikely you would have gone to the ladies' room without your pocketbook, I rushed back to the room and waited there until two o'clock. By noon, thinking you might have gone home, I phoned your mother. Posing as an airline reservations clerk trying to reconfirm your reservations to Los Angeles, I discovered you weren't home. Then I really began to worry. After all, I was responsible for you."

"I don't see how. You told me what I would have discovered eventually. It's not your fault." I shrugged, feeling hopelessly resigned. Whatever Horace's motives were for coming to Boston, they scarcely seemed important now. My life was at a dead end.

"You implied that I had come to Boston to humble you," Horace said quietly. "You assumed that our lovemaking was a retaliation against David and Tanya. I was fearful of what you might do. Finally, about three o'clock, I telephoned police headquarters. I told them you were without identification and that you were so upset you had run off and left your pocketbook. I described your clothes and appearance, and then for two more miserable hours I waited. At six they telephoned the room and said you were probably at the City Hospital." Horace smiled, "I held your hand for an hour last night, but you didn't wake up."

"Nothing is solved." I squeezed my eyes shut, trying to hold back the tears that wouldn't stop. "I've just made the mess messier. Mother and Daddy must be frantic."

"They're all right. The children are fine. When I finally located you, I telephoned them and covered for you. I told your mother that you were going to the airport to meet David, but that you weren't certain, because of the weather, which plane he would make."

I squeezed his hand. "Oh, thank you. At least, I don't have to explain this."

Horace ruffled my hair. "With tears in your eyes, you're a very desirable-looking woman. Don't sell yourself short. Your hospital nightie becomes you. Are you naked below the waist?"

I knew that Horace was trying to change the subject, and it irked me a little. His hand beneath the sheet, calmly exploring my hip, was slowly moving toward my middle. "Either you're a satyr," I told him, "or you have necrophiliac tendencies." I pushed his hand away. "I'm sorry about last night; we never should have made love. It was stupid."

"I didn't think so," he said, "but I'm not going to probe why you lost faith in yourself. In a way I understand, and yet I don't. You never exactly impressed me as being so dependent on David that he could pull the rug out from under you."

I didn't answer him. I wasn't sure, then, that any person could explain to another the fright and sheer loneliness that grips you when you suddenly realize that all the meanings and values you have built into your life are dependent on the love and existence of another person. But even wanting to die, I wasn't blaming David. I simply knew that I didn't have the stamina of those people who are wiped out in a hurricane or a tornado and who try to build again.

"Can't you understand," I said finally. "Everyone would be better off if I were dead. When the doctor kept asking who I was, I knew, all right. Nancy. Nancy Nothing. David loves Susan and Jimmy. If I were dead, he would marry Tanya. You have Sylvia. Living, what do I have to look forward to? Alimony from David, working for Daddy in his insurance office, bringing up two children without a father. Ultimately, a middle-aged old lady who is a drag on her children's lives."

"No doubt you visualized David weeping beside your coffin."

"You're a beast," I sobbed. "I don't know why you didn't tell the whole gory business to Mother and Daddy. They would have phoned David and told him to take me back."

Horace sat wearily in the chair, and didn't answer until I was forced to look at him. "Do you want David to 'take you back,' as you put it?"

"No! God damn it! Let him fuck Tanya the rest of his life and have a million kids by her."

"You sound like Tanya," Horace said mildly. "I never realized you knew such words."

"I don't. I'm sorry. Can't you see I'm confused."

Horace sat on the bed beside me. "As a matter of fact, *I* telephoned David!"

My heart jumped wildly; I wanted to hug Horace, and then I didn't. He was meddling. The last thing in the world I wanted was that David should feel obligated to me. "I suppose you told him I tried to commit suicide?"

Horace calmly pulled back the sheet and kissed my exposed stomach. "Of course not. I told him how much I enjoyed you in bed and that after three years I had acquired an entirely new perspective on Nancy's erotic abilities."

"You're not funny," I gasped, as he calmly kissed my breast. "For God's sake, be your age. What if a nurse walked in here." I grabbed his hair. "Damn you! Stop it! I'm not interested in my unwilling sex potential. Did you really telephone David?"

Horace reluctantly placed the sheet over me. "I didn't tell him anything. I simply asked if he and Tanya would trust me and if they would get the eight o'clock plane Monday morning, and fly here with Mitch and Sam."

"You must be insane." I couldn't believe he was telling the truth. "That's all you told him?" Our night of lovemaking at the Sherilton, with me reaching unending climaxes, doing things with Horace that made me blush to think about, flashed through my mind. What would David think if he knew?

"I told David that I thought the four of us should talk in some place other than San Pedro. You see, Nancy, my making love to you was not entirely unpremeditated. I came to Boston with a vague purpose that I'm still trying to clarify."

"What can the four of us talk about? Horace, you *are* crazy! Where can we talk?" I was so flustered that I didn't ask about his purpose. The whole business sounded like a sophisticated comedy by Noel Coward. "Are we going to talk about fucking in Graniteville? Maybe in Daddy's playroom, with the four kids and Mother and Daddy offering advice? Oh God, *NO!* I don't want to see David or talk with him ever again. What could it accomplish?"

Horace looked at me with a grim expression. "I really don't know. Maybe nothing. But David agreed to come. The four of us are going to make an effort, and somehow suppress our petty little egos while we try to rediscover each other." He grinned. "Let's not try to probe the future. You'll be released at noon, and David and Tanya will arrive at about four. The nurse told me I shouldn't stay more than an hour, so after I leave you can telephone your mother and prepare her. We'll have to pick up Susan and Jimmy before we meet them at the airport."

"Just what do I tell Mother?"

"I've been thinking about that. When I talked with her last night I set the stage for you. There's no need for your father or mother to know what happened. For the time being, at least, it's our secret. I don't think even David or Tanya should know, unless you want some irrational sympathy from him."

I was astonished by his cool dismissal of what I had been through. "Sometimes, I don't know whether I like you or not, Horace. I'm not trying to hold David with the threat of suicide." Again I was crying. "The whole idea is stupid. Why don't you just go? Nothing I can tell Mother will convince her that I couldn't have telephoned her myself yesterday. She'll suspect something."

Horace shrugged. "All you have to do is be a good actress. Tell her you waited half the night at the airport. Tell her it was way past midnight when you discovered that David's plane had to lay over in Chicago because of the storm. Tell her you talked with David, that he will arrive tomorrow. Tell her you and David and the children, together with the Sheas and their children, are going north for a winter vacation." Horace laughed at the amazement on my face. "A second honeymoon. Tell her we won't be in Graniteville for Christmas, but we'll all come back for New Year's Eve before we fly home."

"You *are* crazy," I gasped.

"Families always enjoy togetherness on New Year's Eve." Horace smiled, ignoring my consternation. "You ought to be able to sell your mother that idea, especially if you hint how important it is that David and you be reunited in a new environment. Finally, tell her Horace Shea has rented a Volkswagen bus. Tell her you and Horace will pick up Susan and Jimmy about one thirty. If you sound enthusiastic, she'll buy your story."

"And where in the world are we going in your Volkswagen?" The whole idea seemed so ridiculous that I began to laugh hysterically. "Some fun! The four of us with our four kids, trapped together."

"We'll drive to New Hampshire," Horace said coolly. "I've been looking at some travel folders. All the motels are open, and the skiing is great."

I knew I was only half comprehending the magnitude of Horace's dream. "My mother won't believe a word of it," I objected.

"You're not a child." Horace said impatiently. "You're thirty-six years old. Anyway, your mother must suspect that David and you are having marital difficulties. If you're properly jubilant, she'll want to help you."

"But Daddy's car is still at the airport."

"Tell him you'll drive it out tomorrow. The major roads are all cleared. I'll follow you in the bus."

"Have you actually rented it? Honestly, Horace, the whole idea is absolutely mad. What are the four of us going to do for ten days? When we get wherever we're going, am I supposed to sleep with David and forgive him, while you welcome Tanya back to marital bliss with Horace, the forgiving Jesus?"

Horace leaned over me and kissed my lips. "For heaven's sake, Nancy," he said crossly, "let's not plan everything. Let's play it by ear." He handed me a piece of folded hotel stationery. "I've got to leave. After you telephone your mother read this. It's from a poem by W. H. Auden. I wrote it down for you because it'll give you a refreshing thought to sleep with. Get a good night's sleep. I'll be back at noon tomorrow."

Horace was right about Mother. After an interminable conversation, during which I listened to a long description of the catastrophes that she and Daddy had imagined and of her shock when she telephoned the Sherilton and discovered that I wasn't even registered there (I told her I had moved to the Copley because they had no rooms Saturday when I returned from the airport), I finally managed to make her listen to Horace's plans. Her complaints slowly turned to enthusiastic approval. It was splendid! All of us young people together with our children. A lovely vacation, and we would be back for New Year's Eve; that was lovely. I heard her relay the news to Daddy, who immediately started making plans to invite us all to the Graniteville Neighborhood Club.

"Your father says he has the keys to the Chesley's lodge at Lake Sunapee." Mother was bubbling by this time. "We were up there last fall. It's a lovely place, with four bedrooms, and it's completely furnished. Dad will telephone Henry Chesley, and I'm sure he'll want you to use it."

My God, no, not a house, I thought grimly. Too much togetherness. Better a motel. "We won't need it," I tried to tell her. "Besides, I'm not sure where we're going."

"It won't cost you anything," Mother insisted. "Henry is going to Europe next week, and Bob Chesley is on his third honeymoon in Italy. At least, you can let your father ask. I'm sure David would like it. Henry came to your wedding, you know. He'll be delighted."

It was futile to object; I could do that tomorrow. After I finally hung up, telling her please not to call me back, since I would be in and out of the room, I tried to stop the insanity of Horace's junket from whirling in my brain. We were four people who had slept with each other's spouses, four people who had broken their marriage vows, and one of us pregnant by the other's husband. Horace must be cracking up. If we didn't hate each other now, just give us ten days together. Even if David and Horace could take it in stride, I was sure Tanya and I would tear each other's hair out. Before I fell asleep, I read the poem Horace had written out for me.

> For the error bred in the bone
> Of each woman and each man
> Craves what it cannot have,
> Not universal love,
> But to be loved alone.

I didn't know whether to laugh or cry.

~~~~~~~~

Chapter 2

Driving to the airport to rescue Daddy's car, I couldn't respond to Horace's enthusiasm over the Volkswagen bus he had rented. The temperature had dropped below zero and the main roads had been reduced to tiny lanes girded by soot-covered mountains of snow. The bleakness of the day penetrated and heightened my gloomy depression. I tried to erase a vision of Nancy, frozen solid, her legs protruding from a frozen pile of snow on Massachusetts Avenue. I knew I hadn't convinced the doctor who signed my release that I was quite all right or that I never really had any intention of taking my life. My words had sounded hollow to me. Horace's blithe assumption that we could all go away together and rationally discuss our problems seemed naive and Pollyanna-ish. I dreaded meeting David; I could never explain those disgusting pictures to him, and I couldn't forgive him. As for Tanya, I didn't hate her, but I certainly didn't like her, either.

I told Horace he had been right about Mother's reaction. "She is *so* pleased," I told him bitterly, "that we're going to have a little vacation with our *best* friends. Daddy is asking a family friend to loan us his lodge at Lake Sunapee. I've never been there, but Mother and Daddy think it quite natural that four friends could share it." I tried to explain my fears to Horace. "It's too idyllic," I said. "You're creating an impossible situation." Later, after we had located Daddy's Buick, and with the help of a parking-lot attendant were jockeying it clear of a snow drift, I told Horace that even if Henry Chesley did offer his ski lodge, I wasn't going there, because the four of us under one roof were bound to stir up trouble.

Horace's answer was oblique. "Do you ever want to sleep with me again?"

The tears came to my eyes. "What kind of answer is that? I wish the other night had never happened. I'm not proud of myself. I feel as if I've jettisoned every moral belief I ever had. You may think that wife-swapping is the answer to our problems, but I don't. One thing for sure, I'm not going to bed with you in the same house with David or Tanya, no matter what crazy ideas you may have absorbed from the Albertis."

Horace was amused. "You can sleep with Tanya. Really, I'm not interested in sleeping arrangements, but I am interested in discussion, lots of it. Maybe we can find what makes us all tick. The Chesley lodge seems ideal to me."

It was useless to tell him that I wasn't about to sleep with his wife, either, or that while he might be able to have a non-emotional discussion in a classroom, none of the rest of us was going to accept Horace as the all-wise and loving father-image.

I gestured at a cardboard box overflowing with books on one of the rear seats of the Volkswagen. "You didn't bring those with you from California. What did you do, rob the Boston Public Library? I hope you don't have some insane idea we're all going to read to each other?"

Horace chuckled. "On cold winter nights, when the kids are all in bed, and things get dull, they'll help keep our minds off sex."

With Horace following me in the Volkswagen to Graniteville, I could only smile. I wondered if he had picked some nice novels of undying love for us to read. It wasn't until several days later that I realized the extent of the Utopian scheme he had been hatching.

There was no way I could reject the loan of the Chesley lodge. Henry Chesley, who was delighted to have us use it, had known me since I was fifteen years old; I was the daughter he had never had. Once he thought I might marry one of his boys, but that was before David appeared on the scene.

Horace hugged mother and told her David would be very happy at the lodge. It was much better than trying to find a motel. Mother had baked two cakes, and had filled a box with special goodies for the children. "You'll have to buy groceries," she said. "Be sure and keep the children away from the lake; the ice may be thin. Daddy says you can rent skis, but for heaven's sakes watch the children on that ski lift at Mt. Sunapee, and remember you haven't been skiing for years. Don't break any legs." She rattled on, dispensing advice, while I packed Susan's and Jimmy's clothes. Horace had disappeared into the cellar playroom with Daddy. "Oh, Nancy," Mother said, "I do hope everything will be all right with you and David. Mr. Shea seems like such a nice man, not at all like some of those people you hear about in California. I'm sure that the four of you vacationing together will be more fun than you and David going alone. Do you and Mrs. Shea get along?" I tried to avoid a direct answer. Then she asked what kind of woman Mrs. Shea was. "She works doesn't she? It's difficult to work and have time for your home." Nervously, I assured her that Tanya and I liked each other and that Tanya was a good mother. "Well, that's nice," she said, but I knew she was trying to wring a confession from me. "It's unusual when two women can be friends. Does David like her?"

I felt like shouting, "David *loves* her," but somehow I managed to assure Mother that everything was quite all right with David and me. Feeling as if I had been through the Inquisition, I finally climbed into the Volkswagen beside Horace; Susan and Jimmy were already in the back seat impatiently urging us to leave. I noticed that Horace and Daddy seemed rather jovial, and guessed that Daddy had used the opportunity for a snifter or two in the name of friendship. Horace assured Daddy that we would be back the day before New Year's, and told him we would stay at a motel nearby.

"I'm not coming back here with David and Tanya," I told Horace angrily, as he drove us toward Boston. "You must be out of your mind. If Mother meets Tanya, and gets on her ear, she'll ferret the whole business out of her."

Horace beamed. I refrained from commenting on his driving ability under the influence of alcohol. "Your father feels that you have led a very sheltered life," he said. "Since you're an only child, he's sure your mother had made you believe that only men enjoy sex, and that for women it's a necessary accommodation. He suspects that you caught David playing around. After a third drink, he became very confidential. 'I hope Nancy isn't rocking the boat,' he told me. 'Trouble with women is that they don't understand. Eventually roosters come home to roost.' "

"I suppose he told you about the affair with his secretary."

"You knew about it?" Horace seemed surprised.

"Oh, I was never told directly. Laura was a friend of Mother's. Her husband died when he was very young; then Daddy gave her a job in his real estate office. She often came to dinner, and I called her Aunt Laura. She seemed to have a more bubbly and joyous philosophy of life than Mother. Then, after a couple of years, I remember that Mother seemed very cool toward her. Aunt Laura suddenly went away, and after that, Mother decided to have her own bedroom."

"You mean that she never had intercourse with your father again?"

"How would I know?" I said unhappily. "Sometimes I wonder why men get married, anyway. Every male in suburbia, when he gets to a certain age level, thinks he has to find love all over again in some other female's bed."

As we approached Logan Airport, I began to feel queasy.

151

Did a normal female rush up and kiss her arriving husband while his pregnant mistress was hanging on his arm? Obviously not. I was lost, sick at heart; Horace, humming softly, and exhilarated by his drinks, was no comfort.

When David and Tanya and the boys came through the door at the airport, I had a feeling that all of us, except the children, were reassessing each other, not as husbands and wives, but as strangers. David kissed me awkwardly on my cheek; Horace seemed cool in Tanya's embrace. Hundreds of questions none of us dared to ask hung between us.

I noticed that David stood near Tanya while we waited for their baggage; they seemed to have a bond between them that wiped away our fifteen years of marriage. Tanya was his wife. I was the interloper. Conversation about the dreadful New England weather, and how smooth the flight was, drifted into silence as we watched the luggage come down the unloading chutes.

David, grinning self-consciously, finally plunged into the gap. "We'll have to talk eventually, but what are your plans, Horace? You said to leave everything to you. Have you made reservations somewhere? With this gang we'll need four rooms." David seemed embarrassed. Unsaid but obvious was the question, would I sleep with him?

Horace didn't seem disturbed. "I'm hoping that we continue to be as adventurous as we all seem to have been in the past." He grinned at Sam, who had climbed into his arms. "Outside in the parking lot is a rented Volkswagen bus. As soon as we corral your bags, we're driving to Lake Sunapee." He shrugged at David's surprised expression. "As far as I'm concerned, we might just as well be astronauts on the way to the moon, though Nancy's father gave me a map and we have the keys to a lodge. I'm hoping you won't mind driving, David, at least until we get out of the city. From now until New Year's, the Herndons and the Sheas are going on vacation together. Maybe we can discover whether we hate or love each other, separately, or . . ." Horace seemed to lose his train of thought as he noticed David's growing amazement.

Tanya filled in the uncomfortable silence. "My God, Horace," she gasped, "how can we talk with a house full of kids listening?"

"It's Horace's idea all the way," I told her grimly. "I'm not sure that all we have to talk about couldn't be said in front of lawyers in about ten minutes. Horace seems to think we should prolong the misery."

Horace couldn't keep a trace of sarcasm out of his voice. "If nothing else comes of it, we owe it to the kids to give them a good final vacation with their loving parents." He hugged Susan and Sam, who were listening, while Jimmy and Mitch were rescuing the baggage. "In case you've forgotten, we do have four other lives to think about, besides our own. For their sakes, I'm sure we can put up with each other for ten days. After that we'll let the chips fall where they may. Right now, I'd like to suggest that from this point on we don't discuss 'us' in front of the children. Every night they'll be in bed by ten at the latest. Then we can either play the games people play or discover that it may be more fun to use our brains." Horace admitted later that, though he seemed quite confident, he was a little unnerved by the atmosphere of hostility and gloom that had settled over the rest of us.

"Okay," David said finally. "I'm fascinated. What other rules are you propounding, Professor?"

Horace laughed. "Some of them I'm not even certain of. Anyway, it'll be more intriguing if we formulate them together."

We all piled into the Volkswagen. Horace sat in front with David. In the seat behind them Tanya and I gingerly avoided each other. The kids and the baggage filled the rear seats. As David finally located the route north, Tanya complained that Horace or David should have warned her to be ready for snow and cold. She pointed out that while I was wearing a ski suit and was obviously ready for the worst, she had no outdoor clothes. She could have picked them up at Bayberry's. But since she didn't, how could she be expected to tramp around in the woods in high heels or go skiing in a cocktail dress? I was tempted to suggest that, since she was pregnant, a maternity gown might be more appropriate. But damn it, I had to admit that Tanya didn't look pregnant, and that with a halo scarf framing her face she even looked remarkably virginal. If it had been me, I would have blown up by this time; my breasts would be fuller and my cheeks plump, "advertising the coming event," as David once had put it.

After David had finally groped our way out of the early evening traffic and we had listened for twenty minutes as Horace and David extolled the merits of the Volkswagen (they were obviously trying to fill the silence with inanities) David pointed out that it would take us at least three hours to get to Sunapee. He wanted to know what I knew about the Chesley lodge.

"Nothing. Had I married Bob Chesley, I might be living there," I said sarcastically. "Horace is our tour guide. He worked it out with Daddy."

David was in a tit-for-tat mood. "I heard Bob Chesley just took on his third wife. You would have been a displaced per-

153

son by this time." I scowled at the reflection of his grin in the windshield. "How did you ever convince your mother to put her blessing on this trip?" he asked.

Horace broke it up. "We told her we were all going on a little holiday. What else?" he asked calmly.

"Happy holiday for eight," Tanya sighed. "Sounds like a convention. Just how big is this place? Most ski lodges I've been to, everyone sleeps in bunks like in a big dormitory."

"If you're subtly asking how many bedrooms, Tanya, there are four, all with walls between them." Horace didn't turn in his seat, but I could see a flicker of a smile on his profile.

We drove the next few miles in silence as I tried to imagine our separate, bewildered thoughts. Were we going to attempt a surface show of being contented married couples? While the children wouldn't understand all the nuances of our behavior, they were old enough to expect, on the basis of past performance, that Mommy and Daddy would sleep in the same bed together.

Horace penetrated the gloom. "While we're all contemplating our sins, I'll break my rule about discussion of us. I'm sure it will go over our audience's heads anyway, and it may give us all something to think about for the rest of the trip. As you might have heard on television, the storm here last Friday was the worst on record. Nancy met me at the airport, but the weather was so bad she couldn't get home." I gasped at the suddenness of Horace's revelation. I knew he was using our night together as a challenge to David and Tanya, but I had no sense of triumph, only a feeling of being used.

Tanya's soft "Oh" was both a question and an exclamation of surprise. In the dim light I noticed she was looking at me with a half-smile on her face.

"Why not?" I shrugged, trying to conceal my anger. "Everybody else is doing it." It seemed to me that David's concentration on the road became more intense.

"What is everybody else doing?" Susan's voice rang loud and clear from the back seat.

"Nothing, honey," I told her quickly. "Uncle Horace and I were snowed in. We had to shovel snow all night."

"So," Horace chuckled, "since we're all well acquainted with the overtones of snow shoveling, at least until we come to some further conclusions, I can give you a second proposal. Nancy's father gave me a pretty good idea of the floor plan of the lodge. Two rooms have double beds, and two have four bunks each. The kids can have the bunks, and I think it might be nice if the daddies slept together in one room and the mothers slept together in another, at least to-night, unless someone has a better idea."

"Jesus!" David was laughing. "I think Horace wants us all to go back to school. He even has sex-segregated dormitories. You won't mind if we throw spitballs at the teacher?"

"I'm not going to be a teacher," Horace said equably. "Just director of traffic."

I think we were all aware of the sudden silence of Sam and Jimmy, who had decided to sleep so they could go skiing at the crack of dawn. Mitch had beat them to it. Dead to the world, he snuggled against Susan, while she, in the role of the obviously superior female, remained wide awake in order to study the passing roadstands, billboards and filling stations.

I asked Tanya a few days later how she had felt during our trip to Sunapee. "I was terrified," Tanya told me. "I wanted somehow to say, Nancy, I'm deeply terribly sorry to be involved with David, to be stupidly pregnant. I kept thinking, I didn't make love with David to hurt Nancy. Yet I knew, inevitably, we would hurt you. I kept wondering, why did human beings, who have such a fragile hold on life anyway, mess up their few hours on earth so badly. If we skidded on the icy road and crashed, we could all be dead in a second. And then what would all our petty problems amount to? Who would care? I wondered if maybe somehow we could all learn to like each other again, yet I knew how impossible that was. We couldn't be friends anymore; we had had sexual intercourse with one another's spouses and, under the rules of monogamous marriage, we had made our marriages and our friendships untenable. But I was happy with Horace's sleeping arrangements, and I hoped we might somehow be able to talk."

At the moment I scarcely felt so charitable and pleased. Horace was putting me on the spot and, of the four of us, I was the most injured and the least guilty party. If he walked out on Tanya, he would still have Sylvia. David and Tanya had each other. I was a mother with responsibility to her children. It was pushing the Jesus-factor too far to expect me to sleep in a double bed with my husband's mistress, who was carrying his fertilized sperm in her womb. Not even the craziest modern novelist could conceive of such an impossible relationship, unless the denouement was to be murder. I searched my mind for a milder but not less conclusive solution.

Chapter 3

After several urination stops we arrived in Henniker, New Hampshire, ate dinner in a Howard Johnson's and, at Horace's suggestion, while he and David were having gasoline put in the Volkswagen, Tanya and I found a small market that the owner impatiently kept open while we surveyed his limited stock. Somehow Tanya seemed more in the spirit of things than I did. "Whatever happens to the four of us," she said cheerfully, "the kids have to eat."

She ignored my insinuation that she was already feeding two. We finally accumulated coffee, cereals, milk and a dozen overripe bananas; and we agreed that in the morning we would have to find a supermarket. I think we both felt we could tolerate each other better in the company of Horace and David. We hurried back to the car.

Our safari continued with David still driving. By ten o'clock, after several extended disagreements over Daddy's directions and a wrong turn which took us twenty miles in the wrong direction (David's fault, though he refused to admit it), we finally located the road that circled Lake Sunapee. It was a narrow, country road that had been plowed only halfheartedly. Weaving like a driver with one too many drinks, David tried to hold the Volkswagen in the frozen ruts left by other travelers. Fortunately there were no oncoming cars.

We were alone in a frozen northland. Tall black pines and spruces, their needles frozen and aloof, hung over the road like ominous sentinels. Glistening and shimmering in our momentary light, they receded in a mournful procession into the black night.

We couldn't see the lake from the road, and it occurred to Tanya and me simultaneously that we might have to turn off the road and go some distance into the driveway to reach the lodge, which was next to the lake. "Since there's no one living there," I pointed out, "it's unlikely the drive will be plowed." Horace, obviously surprised that he hadn't anticipated everything, was silent. David slowed down and stopped before a rural mailbox that suddenly appeared next to two fieldstone entrance posts guarding an unplowed road that led into the woods. Our headlights caught the name Chesley on a luminous marker. How far would we have to struggle through hip-deep snow to find the lodge?

"What do we do now, Professor?" David sounded grumpy. "Got a rule for this?"

"No. And you can damn well drop the professor bit and come up with an idea yourself for a change." David shrugged, and I couldn't help laughing at the thought that Horace's love-thy-neighbor attitude was cracking under the strain.

While Horace and I were wearing high boots and were well prepared, David had only a pair of rubbers, and Tanya was dressed for an evening in suburbia; she would have to wait in the car. David edged the car as far off the road as possible without getting it hopelessly stuck in the snow. He rolled up his trousers and volunteered to carry Susan. Horace could carry Mitch. By this time Jimmy and Sam, enthusiastically plowing around in snow almost up to their armpits, were ready to tackle the Himalayas. "I'm not staying here alone," Tanya wailed. "You might have to walk miles, I'm coming."

"Don't be insane." David sounded more like her husband than her lover. "You can run the engine and keep the heater going. Horace and I'll come back as soon as we can and carry you in."

But Tanya was adamant. She slid out of the car, knee-deep in snow, and squealed as she felt the sudden cold against her legs.

"You'll freeze your pussy," I told her; I couldn't restrain the words. "But that's probably not such a bad idea."

Sulkily peeved with each other, three of us united against Horace and his mad acceptance of the Chesley lodge, we trudged along after Jimmy and Sam, who kept urging us on through the untrodden snow. The boys' flashlights revealed the outlines of the road which was edged by a black pine forest. The damp cold penetrated my ski suit, and I knew that Tanya, plodding beside me in a cloth coat, must be frozen to the marrow. In a few minutes I was actually feeling sorry for her when, with a sob, she took off her high heels and informed us that she might as well go barefoot. "I'm only a dumb Swede among all you brains," she moaned. "Tomorrow you can saw off my frozen feet."

I told David to carry her, but Horace put Mitch on David's back and, despite her screams of indignity, tossed Tanya over his shoulder, fireman's style. David now carried Susan in his arms and Mitch piggyback. After we had floundered nearly a quarter mile through the deep snow, the boys' flashlights picked up the outline of a building nearly a hundred and fifty feet long. Built with pine siding and stained black, the roof heavy with snow, it huddled remote and lonely near the shore of the windswept and desolate lake.

Horace unlocked the door of the lodge and we cautiously entered what felt like a damp, pitch-black subterranean cave. The lights didn't respond to the switches, so we puttered around uneasily as David coaxed a fire to life in a huge fieldstone fireplace on the lakeside wall. Jimmy and Sam said they were hungry. "You ate only two hours ago," Horace told them. "You can wait for breakfast. The best thing now is to climb into bed and keep warm. We'll find the fuse box tomorrow."

With flashlights and some candles I found on the mantel we explored the bedrooms. There was a pile of white woolen blankets at the foot of each bed, but no sheets. Sam and Jimmy dragged mattresses in front of the fireplace and undressed to their underwear. Rolled up in blankets, they gleefully insisted on camping near the hearth. Susan wanted to sleep with me. Horace suggested that, since the bunks were big enough, she and Mitch could sleep together.

"He's a boy!" Susan said indignantly. "Girls don't sleep with boys until they're married."

Mitch, who could scarcely keep his eyes open, started to cry.

"Oh, all right." Susan smiled like a good mother. "I'll sleep with him."

David, who was still looking for the fuse box, ignored us all. I found Tanya in one of the double beds rolled up in a blanket. She was shuddering as if she was about to shake apart.

She peered at me pathetically. The candlelight cast deep shadows on her face. "My dress was wet through, so I took it off. I'm so cold I feel sick, and I'd just as soon die."

"I know the feeling." I hesitated, wondering if I would ever tell her just how well I was acquainted with freezing. Hurriedly I took off my clothes and grabbed another blanket. "Come on, unwind." I told her. "Two bodies under a blanket will heat up faster than one." For a second, as she welcomed me into her blanket, I saw her naked body. She clung to me, her teeth chattering. "My God," she sobbed, "you feel so nice and warm."

I rubbed her legs and ankles. "I nearly froze to death once," I told her, as I wondered why I was being so damned accommodating. "I guess it's nice to have someone to hold onto." I didn't tell her that I felt like crying too. This woman

158

I was lying with naked, our breasts touching, had slept with David. While she passionately made love to him, what had she thought about her naive friend, Nancy? Why didn't I hate her?

When David and Horace came to the doorway of the bedroom and shone their flashlights on us, both of them grinning their approval, as if they were saying good night to their daughters instead of their wives. I didn't hate them either, though I certainly wanted to chuck something at them.

In the morning Tanya and I woke to the hum of an oil burner and the cheering smell of percolating coffee. Somewhere outside I could hear Sam and Jimmy yelling enthusiastically as they played in the snow. I looked into Tanya's face and found her staring at me with her eyes wide open.

"I feel ghastly," she murmured.

"Maybe it's morning sickness," I told her sourly.

She jumped out of bed, evidently deciding, no matter what, she wasn't going to be ill in front of me. "I think I'll live," she said shakily, and tried to smile. "Thanks to your good massage, my legs seem to belong to me again." I watched her fumble with her dress, which was still damp. Her body was lithe, with only a slight trace of curvature in her belly. As I looked at her blond bush I wondered whether David had kissed her there. Had Horace? Well, they had both kissed me between the legs, so why not Tanya, too? What kind of madness were we all involved in? I tried to suppress my thoughts.

Tanya wrapped herself in her blanket. "Maybe you have something I can borrow? David didn't give me time to shop, but he unearthed some old winter clothes for himself. Mitch and Sam and I are prepared for Miami, not New Hampshire. How do New Englanders survive in this climate?"

David peered into the room. "The hot-blooded ones don't. They move to California." He blushed in recognition of the accidental ambiguity.

"Some of us never thaw out," I said sarcastically.

David tried a new tack. "Horace and I have been up for two hours. We found the fuse box. The lights are on, the oil burner is going, and everything is cozy. We even found a complete stock of winter equipment, including skis, toboggans, snowshoes. We've been back to the car and unloaded the stuff on a toboggan."

Horace appeared with suitcases; he was followed by Susan and Sam. "Get dressed, you two," he said gaily. "Susan and Sam helped make breakfast. Our vacation has begun."

I stood up with my blanket around me. "If the males will leave the harem, I'll find Tanya something to wear."

Susan watched me shuffle through my suitcase. "You slept

without any clothes on," she said disapprovingly. "Why can't I sleep without pajamas? Why couldn't Uncle Horace and Daddy see you naked? Are women naked in a harem?"

Tanya smiled weakly. "There's no harems anymore, honey. The females didn't like them. Today, men aren't supposed to see ladies naked unless they're married to them. Maybe when you grow up things will be different."

I gave Tanya an extra set of ski clothes, but warned her they would seem baggy because my behind was bigger than hers. At least they would keep her warm.

By daylight it was apparent that the Chesley's had designed their lodge for a maximum in winter sports luxury. The ceiling of the main room and the walls were completely paneled in pine. Four huge beams supported the roof. The highly polished floor, with three very large orientals seeming like scatter rugs, was arranged into separate areas around clusters of couches, chairs, and lamps. In effect we had acquired a magnificent hotel lobby as a setting for our fun and games. The kitchen was completely equipped with an electric stove, freezer, and hotel-size refrigerator. Evidently the Chesleys were accustomed to having a full house on ski weekends.

"Everything is here but food," David said as we ate our meager breakfast. "I've a feeling that the Chesley's aren't planning to use the place this year."

"Bob Chesley is on the Riviera at the moment with his third wife." I shrugged. "He'll be back, no doubt."

"Cheer up," David said sarcastically. "Even if he had divorced you, you'd have collected a lot of alimony."

"I didn't marry him, remember? But, since I seem to be going the same route, it's obvious I wouldn't have been any worse off. Have you seen your lawyer?"

"You're forgetting our agreement," Horace said calmly. "Let's leave discussion for tonight. Right now we have to go shopping."

Horace and David invited me to sit on the toboggan with Tanya, Susan, and Mitch, but I declined and plowed through the snow with them to the highway. We drove to Sunapee Harbor, and in less than an hour spent two hundred dollars on food, ski clothes, ski boots and sheets. Before we drove back we found a State liquor store. With encouragement from Tanya, I increased David's order of three bottles of Scotch to six Scotch, six gin and a case of champagne.

"Looks as if the girls are planning to get crocked." David was amused. Horace tried to split the bill with him, but David insisted on paying it all. "By the time we hear the rest of your rules, we may want to come back and replenish our supply. Then you can pay."

Back at the lodge, as if in conspiracy, Horace and David insisted there was time before dark to show the children the ski lift at Mt. Sunapee. Tanya and I could prepare supper. I didn't want any heart-to-heart talks with Tanya, and told them so.

"You go with them," Tanya said. "I'm a little pooped anyway."

I was cornered, I couldn't leave Tanya to prepare supper alone. After they left, Tanya wandered through the lodge as I examined the box of books that Horace had lugged with us. I couldn't help smiling at the titles he had chosen: *Education and Living,* by Ralph Borsodi; *On Being Human,* by Ashley Montagu; *Kibbutz,* by Melford Spiro; *Society with Tears,* by Irving Sarnoff, and a dozen others. What was Horace planning? Did he really think the rest of us were suddenly going to take up reading?

Tanya reappeared with a happy look on her face. "There's a sauna back there," she said excitedly. "Have you ever tried a sauna? It's great; you'll love it. Maybe we can all use it tomorrow and play in the snow naked afterward." Her smile vanished as she noticed my grim look. "That's what they do in Sweden," she added lamely.

"And then we can have a wife-swapping party," I said sarcastically. "Won't that be fun! Horace is an expert. Has he told you about the Albertis?"

Tanya was startled. "Wasn't it Peter Alberti that you were mixed up with?"

"How did you know?"

"Maybe you don't want to talk about it." Tanya smiled at me, embarrassed.

I shrugged. "David has no doubt shown you the pictures. Despite appearances, I know a lot less about Peter Alberti than Horace does. I suggest you discuss it with him." I walked toward the kitchen. "In the meantime I suppose we might as well get dinner."

Tanya followed me. "If we sleep together again tonight, maybe we should talk."

"You mean compare notes on David's and Horace's virility? No thanks."

Chapter 4

While Tanya and I tucked the children into their bunks and promised that tomorrow we would all go skiing and build snow forts and snowmen and, yes, we would try the toboggans and snowshoes, David and Horace built up the fire with six-foot logs. They brought Scotch, ice, glasses, and water into the living room, and then they waited while Tanya put on a housecoat. I kept on the dress I had changed into earlier.

David poured the drinks for all of us. "Well, here we are, alone at last. Three days before Christmas. Peace on earth, good will to men. All good pals and jolly good company." He grinned nervously at Tanya's sour look. "Okay, Horace, it's your party. No big ears listening. Just four adults marooned in the north woods. What do we do now?"

"Something we've never done before," Horace said coolly. "See if we can slice beneath the superficial friendship we have had for nearly three years and stop playing roles with each other. A kind of group therapy, perhaps, to see if we can find any common denominator or basis for a lasting relationship."

I slumped in a chair near the fire. "You said once you had a solution for us. Why don't you start with that?"

Horace shook his head. "If there are any solutions, we'll have to discover them together. Besides, you've all made it clear that I'll have to stop sounding like a pedantic schoolteacher. While David has never told me so, I know I can be especially irritating to him."

"As a matter of fact, Horace," David said, "I've got kind of used to your professor talk. I know you think I'm a dumb slob who is only interested in making a buck, but occasionally I do have other thoughts."

"I could say, *obviously*." Horace smiled. "If I left that as a finished statement, I'd have implied that you had plenty of time to make love with Tanya. It's a good example of the kind of useless remark we have to avoid if we're going to get anywhere."

"You still sound like a schoolteacher," Tanya said with a

162

faint smile. "But I'm used to you, Horace. And after all, I'm the only stupid one here. All the rest of you graduated from college."

I took a long swallow of my drink. "The only thing you've been stupid about is getting pregnant, and then not having an abortion. If you had, you and David might have continued your little affair indefinitely."

"No one took *my* picture with my pants down." Tanya smiled, but the inflection of her words was incendiary.

I glared. "Okay, so the fat's in the fire. What am I supposed to say now, Horace?"

"That you hate Tanya because she stole your husband's affections," David said.

I knew Horace wanted me to say, No, I don't really hate Tanya. But watching her sitting on the couch with her arms wrapped around her knees, unaware, or perhaps fully aware, that her short housecoat hung away from her undercalves so that the curve of her behind and the dark area of her crotch were visible to David and Horace, I could feel the anger churning in me.

"You're damned right I do," I said to David, "I don't like flagrant women. Look at her; she has that wide-eyed, innocent look. But the innocence is just an act. She knows damn well the way she's sitting, she'd advertising her wares. Tanya, why don't you just open your legs wide and give David and Horace a good look?"

Tanya banged her feet on the floor and pulled the housecoat around her. "Some day, Nancy, maybe you'll grow up! You think you have such a treasure chest that men should adore you for it, but most men get bored with your kind of female."

I was so angry that as I bounced out of my chair I was determined to leave the room. "I don't see any sense in the whole business. My suggestion, Horace, is that you and David take Tanya into the bedroom. She's the type that could screw the whole Army and have enough left over for the Air Force."

Before I could get out of the way, Tanya snatched a water pitcher off the coffee table and threw the contents at me. "That'll cool you off," she snarled. She stared at me defiantly, her arms flexed, ready to fend off a counterattack.

Neither David, who was watching in a state of shock, nor Horace, who had a supercilious smile on his face, had made any attempt to enter the fray. Shaking with anger, I stood up and ripped off my soaking dress, bra, and panties.

"There," I said, shivering not from cold, but from wrath. "If we're going to compete for sexual interest, let's do it right. There's nothing the boys haven't seen anyway. I've screwed both of them." I poured a refill of my Scotch; then I slumped back in the chair with my feet on the coffee table and my legs wide open; I looked into their shocked faces. "If you think I'm going to lower myself to Tanya's level and fight with her, you can forget it. Now what do we do?" I was dimly aware that poor Horace must feel he had bitten off more than he could chew. The drink I had consumed so rapidly was making me feel weepy.

Tanya, still standing, took off her housecoat. "So now you have one common denominator, Horace," she said calmly. "Two naked females who hate each other. Why don't you and David both undress. Like in the Marquis de Sade, we can have an orgy and end up murdering each other."

David's only comment was, "For God's sake, why don't the two of you act your age?" He turned on Horace. "It looks as if it's up to you and me to see if we can stay unemotional and decide rationally what to do. First, I want you to know that I didn't intend that Tanya and I should foul up our lives or yours. I don't think she did, either. And though I was shocked that she let herself go so long, when she knew she was pregnant, I'm not irresponsible and I'm not pinning all the blame on her. I know I'm at fault, not only for seducing Tanya, but for failing as a husband to Nancy."

I clapped my hands. "Hurray for the big hero!"

David ignored my sarcasm as he sat down on the arm of the chair beside me. "You know, it's a funny thing. Last night, huddled in bed, and now sitting naked here by the fire, both you and Tanya look kind of lost and pathetic, like little girls ready to cry." He took an afghan off the top of the sofa, pulled me to my feet and then pushed me down beside Tanya. "If you sit together, it'll cover both of you." He tossed the knitted blanket over us. "At least it'll keep the drafts off."

"And keep our minds from wandering," Horace said with a grin.

I felt Tanya's shoulder and leg touching mine. "We could get dressed," I said to Tanya, who was sobbing. "I think the two of them are trying to make us lesbians."

"One thing you have to understand," Tanya said through her tears, "is that I want this baby and that I'm not the least bit ashamed of anything I've done. If it hadn't been for those pictures of you with Peter Alberti, and my being afraid that if I didn't, David would tell Horace, I would have convinced Horace that it was his child. Then I would have broken off with David and you would never have known anything except that Tanya was having another baby. That would have been the best way."

"I'm sorry I fouled things up," I told her sarcastically. "I guess you don't love David very much. You just wanted a stud."

"Nancy, please don't be so quick with words," Tanya pleaded. "I love David, and I don't want to destroy his life."

"So you'd continue to live with Horace even though you don't love him. You're quite a martyr."

"I didn't say that." Tanya's voice was cold. "I presume you still love David, despite your fucking party with Peter Alberti."

Horace intervened. "Somewhere we're going to have to define love." He seemed a little bewildered. "Can the two of you restrain the fireworks and display of temperament? Perhaps we can make progress. You say you aren't irresponsible, David. What do you propose we do?"

David shrugged. "It seems to me the only sensible thing is for Nancy and me to get out of your lives. If you don't want a child that's not yours, Nancy and I could adopt it and move away."

"Do you love Tanya?" Horace demanded.

Both Tanya and I stared at David while he pondered his answer, but it was Tanya who broke the silence. "You don't have to say you love me. It was just a hot-sheet business at a motel once a week. You don't have to be responsible to me."

"Whether he loves you or not, David is responsible," I said. I felt drawn to Tanya because she seemed so defeated and hopeless.

"Oh, Nancy," Tanya sighed, "I'm sure that neither you nor I could live with that kind of responsibility."

"Maybe Horace is right," David said slowly. "Maybe we should define what love means to each of us. How do we begin? I know I like both you and Nancy. The liking is so great that it has become a need." David smiled fleetingly. "My God, how inadequate words are. I enjoy your companionship, your very different but equally female outlooks on life. I guess somehow, Nancy, when I was with Tanya, I felt I wasn't hurting anything essential in our marriage. Tanya and I discussed all of us often, trying somehow to equate our joy with our guilt. I know she feels the way I do. If it's difficult for you or Horace to understand that we could be in love and still find no fault with either of you, I'm sorry. I'm not sure that I understand myself."

"Maybe you want to be a bigamist," I said. "And have us both for adoring wives?"

"Don't be so caustic, Nancy," Horace chided me. "If we

can keep love, until we define it for ourselves, and all the rest of the Christian-Judaistic overtones of romance and sexual possessiveness out of this, and just think about ourselves as four people who have the possibility of liking each other, we may find we have more in common than we suspect. During the past few days I've been trying to unearth the roots of our friendship. Perhaps I discovered them in a book by Irving Sarnoff called *Society with Tears*. Sarnoff is a professor of psychology at New York University. I brought a copy of his book along. Maybe you all can read it, and we can discuss it together. It comes to this. In three areas of contact we all have with the world: religion, our political feelings and our lack of desire for self-aggrandizement, we are very much in accord in our basic feelings. In religion, only Nancy has made some halfhearted attempts to expose the children to modern theology. But basically our approach to life has been humanistic rather than God-oriented. Hence, as four people, we're not conditioned by the inanities of most religious dogma. In addition, I think we have a common world outlook. If the chips were down we would fight for our country, but we have a feeling that democracy is not exportable, that other political systems may have validity for other countries. And finally, while David works hard at his business, just as I work at teaching, I'm sure that neither of us feels that materialistic rewards are the end-all of existence. Simply, we both tend to enjoy the elusive pursuit of perfection, and I doubt any of us has a great drive for material wealth."

Horace smiled at our attentiveness as he reached for his drink. "I know this relatively calm appraisal may seem like ducking the issue, but if you think about it, the fact that we all see eye to eye on these three aspects of living probably makes us members of a fairly small minority group. Actually, I suspect it's lack of conflict in these areas as much as our living next to each other that has made us more comfortable with each other than with other friends. Since David has committed himself, I'll join him and say to Nancy and Tanya that I like you both. In addition," and here Horace chuckled and glanced at Tanya and me, "you're both very different and enjoyable bed companions."

I think Tanya blushed, and I knew I did. David laughed as Horace poured himself another drink. "I'll have to say one thing, Horace, this isn't the kind of conversation Martha and George had in *Who's Afraid of Virginia Woolf*."

"Thank God for that," I said, "but we still have a long way to go if we want to understand what motivates us. For instance I have a feeling this insistence on 'liking' is not very particularized. Both of you would 'like' any female who

166

would climb into the sack with you, so we'll all understand each other a little better if we dare to be honest about our sexual drives."

Horace shrugged. "Nancy wants me to muddy up the waters by telling you about Sylvia Mai." I noticed that Tanya was looking at Horace, and as he spoke I realized that while he had been quite honest with me, Tanya had never guessed that he had ever embraced another woman. Horace fidgeted his pipe. "The way you're all staring at me, I've a feeling you consider me some kind of Casanova, or possibly a Don Juan."

Sipping our drinks, we listened to Horace while the logs in the fireplace collapsed into a molten glow of red and yellow flame. The dimly lighted room was immersed in a thousand dancing shadows. As he told us about Sylvia Mai and tried to make us appreciate her quality as a person, Tanya and I, feeling the warmth of the fire, and heedless of our nudity, let the afghan slide to the floor. Since we had both enjoyed Horace in the act of love, perhaps as completely as any females could enjoy a male, I suppose we were both comparing ourselves to this unknown woman. Not that Horace was descriptive. He sought words that might explain Sylvia as a human being, not a sex object. "I suppose," he said, and paused, obviously a little embarrassed, "Nancy is right. The concept of liking can be spread too thin. On the other hand, I haven't been promiscuous. Despite the Albertis and their group, I don't think flagrant sexual congress with many women or many men is the answer to the loneliness that besets every human being. In fact, Tanya, I have had intercourse five times outside our marriage: Four times with Sylvia and the other night with you, Nancy. With Nancy it was premeditated and purposeful." Horace shrugged at my gasp of disgust. "Leave the reason alone for a moment, Nancy. With Sylvia my motives were perhaps quite similar to your escapade with Peter Alberti; perhaps the same drives, Tanya, that made you and David seek each other. After many years of marriage, two people erect barriers between themselves that become impenetrable.

"While Tanya and I enjoy intercourse together, we stay clear of talk about areas of our lives that we think the other is not interested in. I think this is true of most marriages. If the man's work is remote from the wife's interest, and the male is necessarily absorbed in his work, a gulf comes into existence that is not easily bridged. Because we are human, the simple penetration of the penis into the vagina, or the acceptance of the vagina, is only a partial response. We all want a nakedness with another person that is over and beyond bodily nakedness." Horace relighted his pipe. "You've never met Sylvia, Tanya, but I think you'd like her. She's unassuming, devoted to teaching, and certainly not possessive of me. I would miss her friendship and the stimulation of her thinking, but I have always encouraged her to find a full life of her own."

Horace looked into the fire. We were all silent and contemplative, thinking God knows what thoughts. I noticed that Tanya's eyes were awash with tears; she was obviously more stunned by the discovery that Horace had made love with Sylvia than by the revelation that he had been to bed with me.

Tanya sighed. "God knows I've failed as a wife in more ways than one. I guess we never should have married, Horace. I never had anything to offer you, really, except sex." A smile trembled on her lips. "I wasn't shocked about you and Horace, Nancy. I guess my biggest surprise was that it hadn't happened a long time ago. You and Horace have a great deal in common."

"You've given me a great deal more than a roll in the hay, Tanya," Horace said quietly. "You've given me security, warmth, abundant affection, love. There's that word again. I'll take a shot at defining it. Between a male and a female it is the discovery of the amazing interacting delight of being the other, the Jesus-joy of pure altruism. At its height it washes out loneliness. It would be a neat trick if we could develop the ability to live that way for a lifetime." Horace smiled. "I may be putting words in your mouths, but I have a feeling that the four of us, searching for answers together, momentarily at least, love each other."

"What about you and Betty Vinson," Tanya asked David. "Was that episode love?"

It was my turn to be shocked. "Don't tell me you slept with your secretary?" I asked coldly. David no longer seemed a husband to me. "Maybe you need psychoanalysis. They say that promiscuous males are really covering up a basic fear of impotency."

"Don't you believe it," David said with a grin. I listened while a new and strangely different David, one who had rarely discussed sex and the act of love with me, calmly gave the details of his evening with Betty Vinson. "Of course," he continued, "it was a mistake, and if I had been sober I would have resisted. Not because I wouldn't enjoy the adventure, but because I would have feared that Betty wanted a good deal more than hit-and-run. But, let's face it, the average married man constantly considers what it would be like to go to bed with somebody other than his wife. If the male wasn't fascinated with the female mammaries and genital equipment, he probably wouldn't have the original stimulus to marry."

"You mean if sex were easily available, the male would *never* marry." I was determined to pin him down.

David laughed. "Nancy, honey, you were available before marriage, and still I married you. I said original stimulus. I don't think the average female realizes it, but early in life most males become nest builders, too. Perhaps the difference is that if another bird flies by, the male whistles. He's perfectly willing to enlarge the nest. It isn't premeditated; it's in his genes."

Horace had been shuffling through his box of books. "Here's something I'd like to read to you," he said. "It's from a speech by Abraham Maslow that he delivered at Synanon. Maybe it sums up what we've been saying:

"The process here basically poses the question of what people need universally. It seems to me that there is a fair amount of evidence that the things people need as basic human beings are few in number. It is not very complicated. They need a feeling of protection and safety, to be taken care of when they are young so that they feel safe. Second, they need a feeling of belongingness, some kind of family, clan or group, something that they feel they are in and belong to by right. Third, they have to have a feeling that people have affection for them, that they are worth being loved. And fourth, they must experience respect and esteem. And that's about it. You can talk about psychological health, about being mature and strong, adult and creative, mostly as a consequence of this psychological medicine, like vitamins. Now, if this is true, most of the American population suffers from lack of these vitamins. There are all sorts of games cooked up to cover the truth, but the truth is that the average American citizen does not have a real friend in the world. Very few people have what psychologists would call real friendships. Their marriages are mostly no good in that ideal sense as well."

Horace tossed the book on the coffee table and looked at us while the words sank in. "I hope I'm not boring you, but I see an equivalent need in all of us. It might be the reason we're here."

David chuckled. "Whether it comes to anything, it's a hell of a lot more interesting than looking at television." He poured himself another drink. "The girls have been following you so intently they've forgotten they're naked."

"It's hot," Tanya and I said almost simultaneously. Neither of us made any attempt to capture the afghan piled at our feet.

"It's damned erotic," David stared at us coolly. "And I don't know whether I'm addressing myself to your faces or your tits. While all this discussion is very fascinating, I don't see that we're any closer to the answers for ourselves. This is a fluid situation. One thing is certain, the four of us are beautifully inhibiting to each other. I'm sure, Horace, if you or I were alone here with either Tanya or Nancy, we would certainly be interspersing our conversation with lovemaking. It comes down to this, and I think we should come up with an answer before anyone has another drink: Is this a vacation from sex, or do we occasionally sleep with each other?" David smiled, obviously enjoying our consternation at his bluntness. "And I don't mean males with males," he added.

"Are you sure we aren't all too tipsy to resolve that problem?" Tanya grinned at David and Horace. "Anyway, what else can Nancy and I do besides listen? Do you want us to reverse the roles and attack?"

David shrugged. "Since Horace and I are gentlemen of the old school, we'll obviously have to decide who gets whom on a logical basis. Perhaps we should toss for you."

Horace shook his head. "The winner of the toss would have to make a choice, and I refuse to stick my neck out. If either Nancy or Tanya has made a decision, I suggest they give us the word."

"Damn it," I exclaimed, "I can get along without either of you. I'm not a doll someone wins at a carnival. You can both go to hell."

"Second the motion," Tanya said. "Let's you and I go to bed, Nancy, while the males ponder a solution."

Horace, an amused expression on his face, seemed to be watching us with the fatherly expression of a psychologist enjoying his rats as they whirl around a maze. "I don't want to pontificate," he said with a twinkle, "but there's a very obvious moral here. Our separate transgressions against the normal codes of married behavior have severed the sense of ownership or possessiveness that we could normally demand from each other. In a sense, we're creatures of a brand-new environment, though we haven't yet learned how to cope with it. If you and Tanya wish, Nancy, David and I could undress. Then we could all have a few more drinks together and all fornicate communally. We can even try the daisy chain that Nancy told me she read about. Finally, when David and I have passed into a state of euphoria, we can all hobble into bed with each other."

Tanya giggled. "You mean we can substitute passion for brains, and when the heat's off we'll be back where we started."

"Exactly!" David surveyed us quite coldly. "Shall we start now?"

"NO!" Tanya and I couldn't help laughing at the spontaneity of our reaction.

I shivered. "We'd be like animals—as if we didn't like each other."

"Or as if we were all trying to degrade each other," Tanya said.

"We must be making progress," Horace mused. "We seem to like one another a little, or it wouldn't make a damned bit of difference. The other night at the Albertis I learned that matriarchy is the only sensible solution. It's obvious that the females have to decide."

Tanya looked curiously at me. "It has to be your decision, Nancy."

"Why?"

"I may be wrong, but Horace seems more forgiving than you are." She grinned. "At least on a short-term basis."

"Maybe you and Horace deserve each other," I said. I really didn't want to argue, but the truth was that I wasn't very enthusiastic about either Horace's or David's approach. I was convinced that no decision I might make could solve anything. Even though I knew that I couldn't have them, and that they would only make everything stickier, I wanted straight New England answers that covered not only tonight, but tomorrow and the weeks and months ahead. "I'm not so sophisticated as you all seem to be," I said. "Horace has evidently forgotten that you're pregnant and you can obviously swallow Sylvia Mai, so it looks to me as if you have given each other carte blanche to screw the world. Why should I choose Horace? He doesn't love me. David and you must be in love. I think the best solution for you and David is to go to bed. I'll sleep alone in one of the bunks."

Aware that I shouldn't have had so many drinks, but not giving a damn that I was naked, I tried to walk past David to the bedroom. I'm sure he tripped me, though he swore he didn't. In any case he caught me and swung me into his lap.

"You damned little fool," he murmured.

While I struggled to get free, yanked at his hair and ripped at his back, right in front of Tanya and Horace he kissed my breasts, my neck, my lips and cheeks. "I'm not your wife and property anymore," I yelled as he stood up and staggered with me toward the bedroom. "Let me down!"

"I'm making the decision," he said coolly. "Good night, Tanya and Horace. Damn it, Nancy, shut up before we're invaded by four kids!"

Chapter 5

Perhaps I was a little tipsy from the Scotch, but not enough so as to dull my awareness. In the confines of the bedroom, alone with David only a day short of a week since I had flown to Boston, I lay on the bed silent and naked while he quickly undressed. I had the odd feeling that years of marriage had been erased and that we had become strangers. This man quietly taking me in his arms, tears of emotion in his eyes, whispering, "I love you, Sea," was not the David I thought I knew so well. The familiarity and the dull certainty of our responses had vanished. He loved Tanya, and I had surrendered to Horace. Was he thinking of her as he kissed me? Did my vagina feel as different to him as his penis did to me as he slipped inside me? We were not the same David or Nancy, and never could be. Perhaps the truth was that we were approaching each other for the first time as equals, knowing that something (dependency, faithfulness?) had vanished. The mental environment we were floundering in created its own eroticism. Our need for a climax and then our gaspingly wild orgasms were an inadequate attempt to say something to each other that was beyond words.

As we lay entwined I somehow held back the bitter words that hovered on my lips. Why, when we could make love like that, did he need Tanya? How could it be any better with her? As I had the thought, the image of myself with Horace flowed through my mind. I wondered if the truth was that the amazing joy of a male and female for each other was not really the blinding need for an orgasm, which was selfish, but rather the happy trust, the driving need to be defenseless with another human being in a return to the wonder of childhood and the child's bubbling love affair with life, in which the inexpressible and infinite possibilities of existence seemed once more to be within your grasp.

Tonight, for the first time with David, and the other night with Horace, I had experienced this absolute empathy.

"I'm sorry, Sea." David, lightly tasting my nipples, was still immersed in his own ecstasy.

"I'm sorry, too." I pulled him closer to my breasts and

trickled my fingers over his back. "But maybe we shouldn't be sorry. Regret doesn't really change anything." Slowly, I tried to explain about Peter Alberti. "It wasn't deliberate, though I suppose if his wife hadn't interrupted us I would have had intercourse with him. I might even have been drawn into an affair that would have had ugly overtones."

"The moth attracted to the flame?" David seemed reluctant to let me go.

"Not really. Maybe a need to be the kind of devil-may-care, reckless person I have never dared to be with you."

"Maybe that's not even it," David mused. "Maybe nobody can ever wholly release himself to all the aspects of another person."

"Meaning that you are David with Nancy, and David with Tanya, and neither Nancy or Tanya could ever know the complete David."

"It sounds complicated," David said, "and I'm not sure I completely understand my own motivations. All I know is that, whether or not the four of us ever define love, I have my own understanding of it. Because I feel completely protective toward both you and Tanya, I must love you both. That's not playing the game according to the old rules, but it's true."

"Why aren't you jealous? Right this minute Tanya is probably making love with Horace as violently as I have with you."

David smiled, "One thing I am sure of. The act of love is a gift, not a possession. I enjoy the gift both you and Tanya have given me. As a male, I accept the trust of the surrender. It's the most wonderful commitment a female can give a male. It's the reason why prostitutes and the casual affair are always inadequate. Yet, it would be no good if the male couldn't accept the gifts without an equal commitment." David sighed. "My God, I'm getting as involved in words as Horace. All I'm sure of is, that a trade-off won't solve anything."

Snuggled with my behind curved against David's stomach, his hand cupping my breast, I thought about Horace. Somewhere I had read that the inability of a male and female to make a final commitment was a sign of immaturity, and I wondered if it were true. Could the four of us expand our lives together? I liked Horace; I enjoyed his searching approach to life. I knew, now, that we could both surrender to each other in the act of love. But tomorrow, after he had been with Tanya, could I casually go to bed with him? If I could, I'd still have to love Tanya, and that seemed impossible. That damned word love again!

At quarter of seven in the morning the four children, still in their pajamas, tiptoed into our room, but when David invited them into bed with us their silence turned into an uproar.

"We woke Uncle Horace and Tanya," Susan said as David tousled them. "They went to bed without any clothes on, too!"

"If it's Uncle Horace," I said, trying to divert her from our nudity, "it should be Aunt Tanya."

Mitch thought that was funny. "That sounds silly. Tanya doesn't go with aunt."

"Neither does Nancy," said Jimmy. "Anyway, Tanya's not my aunt."

Horace, dressed in a sweatshirt and chino pants, appeared in the doorway with Tanya. "Maybe they should call us all Mommy and Daddy," he said, and grinned, obviously enjoying my disheveled appearance.

Jimmy shook his head. "Daddy said I could call him Dave. I know a kid in school named Horace. They call him Ace."

"Ace it is," Horace laughed. "I like it. Enhances my ego. Makes me feel like a Las Vegas gambler."

"Daddy calls Mommy Sea." Susan said. "I like that."

"Poor me," Tanya sighed, "I'm stuck with my Hollywood name."

"Tan's a good name," Sam volunteered.

David chuckled. "Sea and Tan. It's settled. Sounds like a lotion to soothe Ace and Dave."

"Why don't you get in bed with us?" Susan asked Horace and Tanya, who were hovering near the foot of the bed.

"With four kids, plus Sea and Dave, I don't think there's room."

"Dave and Sea have no clothes on," Jimmy announced. "Ace and Tan can't see them without clothes on."

"Why?" Sam demanded.

"Because they're not married, stupid," Mitch said.

"I think you all better leave," I told them. "We'll get dressed."

At breakfast Susan speculated on a new idea. If the four of us slept in the other bedroom where there were four more bunks, we could talk in bed instead of staying up all night arguing. Tanya smiled at me. "Did you listen to us?" she asked Susan.

Susan shrugged. "For a while, but it sounded kind of noisy and dull. We were listening to Sam tell ghost stories. They were scary. Maybe Ace and Daddy, I mean Dave, could tell you and Sea some good stories."

"Grown-ups don't tell stories to each other." Mitch looked at all of us coolly. "When they go to bed they kiss and hug."

David changed the subject by proposing that today we could all go skiing.

"You and Horace and the kids can break your necks," I told him. "And Tanya too, if she's up to it. I never was any good on skis, and it's too late to start now. Besides, in case you've all forgotten, the day after tomorrow is Christmas. Is Santa Claus going to come? Are we going to give each other presents?"

Tanya quickly demurred on skiing. "By myself I'd take a chance, but my friend inside me might get dizzy," she said. She suggested that we all go shopping for Christmas presents and that later, when we got back, the girls should find a spruce tree which the men should chop down before they went skiing.

On the way to Newport, where David said we could find stores, we got into an extended discussion of who should buy presents for whom. The kids for the kids, and the four of us for each other? Or should everybody buy presents for everyone else? But that would be too costly. After all, Christmas was for the children. What did the four of us need? Why not just buy presents for the kids?

"My God, why can't we make it fun?" David asked. "I'd be happier buying a present for everyone."

"It would be too expensive," Tanya said. "What could Nancy and I buy for you and Horace under twenty dollars?"

"We bought really expensive presents last year," David said. "It seemed like a contest. Rather than spend a lot of money, let's use our imagination. First, we'll set a time limit. We can't spend the whole day shopping. We'll be in Newport by ten o'clock. By one thirty all Christmas presents will be bought. That will give us three and a half hours. Each of us will buy seven presents. The kids can have three dollars for each present they have to buy. The rest of us can have five dollars per present."

Envisioning four packages of shaving lotion and shaving cream for Horace and David, Tanya and I groaned.

David read our thoughts. "Oh, shut up," he said. "You can exert yourselves and find something interesting. If it's all right with Horace, he and I'll each contribute a hundred and twelve dollars. Then we'll spread it around so each of the kids gets twenty-one dollars and we get thirty-five apiece. The kids can go together while the rest of us separate, and we'll meet back at the car with the loot. One rule: Nobody tells anyone else what he bought. Everything is a surprise, not to be opened until Christmas morning."

"My God," Horace marveled. "I can see why you're a successful businessman. I vote for it."

When we climbed out of the car in the parking lot of a huge shopping center, Tanya wanted to know if David was about to fire a starting gun. David laughed. "No, but I'll get an extra present as a surprise for the one who buys the most unusual gift."

We finally got our money allowances divided up and left the children, almost hysterically enthusiastic, in a toy store. Tanya and I walked off together, while David and Horace seemed slightly bewildered as they wondered which direction to take. "Don't you like the idea?" Tanya asked, noticing the tears in my eyes.

"I guess I'm a little overwhelmed," I told her. "I'm discovering a fun-David; I guess I really never knew him. It must be your influence. He's as buoyant as the kids." I smiled at her through a haze. "I don't know why, but for the moment I don't even feel jealous of you."

She squeezed my arm. "Well, I'm a little fearful of you. Whether you realize it or not, Horace thinks you're the sleeping beauty who never found the prince to awaken you. He thinks you have a vast unexplored potential."

I was suddenly angry. Had Horace calmly discussed my sexual performances with Tanya? I felt like Olympia, the mechanical doll in *Tales of Hoffman*. Wind me up, and "all the birds in the trees speak to me of love."

Tanya must have read my mind. "I don't mean sex potential, Nancy. In that area we're only competing with our bodies." She smiled at my rueful expression. "You're on your own, just don't buy Horace a Jaguar with your five dollars."

Chapter 6

As I write this I realize that in those first days together we were slowly discovering that ultimate happiness lies in the deep intimacy of human beings interrelating in a common warmth and friendliness with each other. At the Chesley lodge, isolated from any kind of entertainment except what we could provide for ourselves, we were forced into a kind of unity that escapes most suburban families. The radio in the main room didn't work, yet none of us seemed interested in tinkering with it. Without television and even newspapers, which we failed to buy on our shopping expeditions, we were briefly cut off from the world. One day I mentioned all this to Horace.

"Temporarily, we're positively synergistic," he said happily. "Ruth Benedict described some primitive societies with high synergy and others with low synergy. 'Societies where non-aggression is conspicuous,' she wrote, 'have social orders in which the individual by the same act and at the same time serves his own advantage and that of the group.' She spoke of societies or groups 'with high social synergy, where their institutions insure mutual advantage from their undertakings.' In our case we have a hostile environment. It's going to snow again. The eight of us are mutually dependent. 'Those societies,' in Abraham Maslow's words, 'have a high synergy in which social institutions are set up to transcend the polarity between selfishness and unselfishness, between self-interest and altruism, in which the person who is simply being selfish necessarily reaps rewards for himself.'" Horace lifted his eyebrows and smirked at me. "'The Society with high synergy is one in which virtue pays.'"

Susan was listening without comprehending. She and Jimmy were dealing cards for an eight-handed game of hearts and were trying to persuade us to play with them. Wistfully, she stated it all more simply. "I wish this vacation would never end," she said. "We're all having such fun together."

Maybe joy was a better word than fun. The joy of our

shopping adventure as we bought gifts for each other (probably chosen because we liked them ourselves) and the ultimate paper bags and boxes piled high in the rear of the Volkswagen (with all of us giggling infectiously, determined not to reveal our surprises, but letting hints fall on eager ears) culminated in a sauna bath for the three females and a skiing expedition for the men and boys.

When the skiers had gone, Tanya immediately started the heater in the redwood-lined sauna. She urged Susan and me to join her. "It'll take about twenty minutes to heat up. All you'll need is a towel." Urged on by Susan, who, in the space of five minutes of questioning Tanya, had become an expert on the value of sauna bathing, I stripped down and then found Susan already flitting around the huge living room, waving her towel like a flag over her skinny body. "It's such fun," she yelled, her whole body trembling with enthusiasm. "Jimmy and Mitch and Sam are going to be sorry they didn't stay here."

I cautiously followed her into the sauna. Tanya, lying naked on one of the shelves, grinned at my sharp intake of breath. "The temperature is about a hundred and seventy, but the dehumidifier takes the water out of the air; otherwise you couldn't stand the heat. Lie down and relax. You'll enjoy it."

"That's what you think," I gasped. In a few seconds I was perspiring copiously. "My God, after ten minutes of this I'll be five pounds lighter."

"You'll gain it back fast. In about twenty minutes we'll run out and throw snow on each other. Some people use a shower, and then do it over again. Playing in the snow will be a lark. You'll see. It'll recharge you!"

"Do we play in the snow naked?" Susan demanded. Tanya twinkled a yes at her. I noticed that Susan was staring at Tanya's blond and my brunette delta with considerable interest. Her question startled us. "Why don't women shave down there like they do under their arms?"

Tanya grinned at me. "Lord, I hope I have a daughter," she said. I felt a twinge of bitterness as I watched Tanya give Susan a brief hug; if you have a daughter, I thought, it'll be David's daughter. How could I ever accept that? It occurred to me that Susan's own crotch hair, barely visible now, would make a nice tickly cushion for her husband when she got married.

"Oh," Susan exclaimed. "I didn't tell you. Sam wanted to lie on top of me."

Tanya and I stared at each other as we wondered how to respond.

"Did he?" I finally asked.

179

"He had his clothes on," said Susan primly. "But he showed me his thing; it looks bigger than Jimmy's. When are we going to play in the snow? I'm hot."

"Should we pursue the subject at hand?" Tanya grinned at me.

I shook my head. "It may amount to little more than sugar, spice, snails, and puppy dog tails. Anyhow, I doubt if there's any immediate likelihood of a Shea impregnating a Herndon." I looked her in the eye. "Young or old!"

We followed Tanya into the deep snow that surrounded the lodge. The crust broke under our weight, and we plunged in hip-deep, screaming at the shock, tossing the snow wildly about us, rubbing it on our heated bodies. I felt a sudden vast aliveness as the three of us tumbled together. Tanya briskly rubbed the powdery snow over my breasts and belly; half embarrassed, I did the same for her. Massaging each other, glorying in the joy of just being human animals frolicking together, I hugged them both, and reveled in the warm need and compulsion to express my happiness. Momentarily my mind and body blended with theirs. Somehow I understood that in our hugging and touching of each other's flesh we were expressing feelings deep within us that were beyond words.

Just as we were about to run back to the house, Horace and David, tugging the boys on a toboggan, greeted us with a yell of delight. Screaming, we ran for the lodge, but not before Horace had grabbed me around the waist and tumbled with me into a snowdrift.

"You're insane," I hissed. "What will the children think?"

"That you're naked, that Susan's naked, that Tanya's naked, that we like each other, that you're all having such fun we should join you."

"We're not waiting," Tanya tried to catch her breath and withhold her laughter. David, following Horace's example, tumbled with her in the snow, then pulled her erect. "Our snow bath is over," Tanya said. "You men can use the sauna. Try it by yourselves, but don't freeze your dinguses off afterward."

Horace and David had brought back a twelve-foot spruce that Tanya and I had picked out, and they promised to erect it tomorrow in the living room so we could all decorate it together. After dinner, self-consciously waiting until it was bedtime for the kids while Horace and David played chess with the boys, Susan, Tanya and I listed all the Christmas tree decorations we could make ourselves; we had decided against any commercial decorations. Susan suggested paper loops. Tanya offered to teach us all origami, so we could create folded paper stars, Santa Clauses, toy boats and bells. Susan wanted to string together cranberries and walnuts. Sam pointed out that in school they had peppermint candy canes and stockings with candy. It was obvious that Tanya and I would have more than enough to do the next day.

"It's a female project," said David, who had been listening. "On the far end of the lake, where the snow's all blown off, they have ice boats for rent. Horace and I are going to race with Jimmy and Sam for crew." Mitch immediately started to cry; he wanted to sail a boat, too. Tanya and I listened, amazed, while Susan convinced him that he'd have more fun making things for the Christmas tree. She bet him that she could make longer paper loops than he could. Grinning through his tears, Mitch accepted the challenge.

While Horace and Sam were getting ready to checkmate Jimmy and David, I put snow in a pail and cooled four bottles of champagne. Finally, alone again, with a tiptoe feeling of four strangers who hadn't found a common ground of discussion, we stared at the fire.

"It looks as if we've survived our second day," Horace gave the impression of a man about to move his first pawn. "No casualties yet."

David twisted the wire on one of the bottles of champagne. "The daytime truce has its merits." He grinned at Horace. "In fairness, and for auld lang syne, I should aim this cork at your head."

"Truce is over," Tanya said, smiling at me nervously. "Let's start the war."

"I don't feel belligerent," I sighed. "Just damned confused."

Horace sipped the champagne David had poured. "Judging from our poor performance on skis today, I'd say David and I were a little preoccupied, too."

David slouched in his chair; Horace sat between me and Tanya on a sofa.

"I think it's time you laid your cards on the table, Horace," David said. "It's obvious you think we can forget the past and that maybe we can continue along somehow. The question is, how? Even if you have a formula, it has to be based on some new kind of idealism. Are all of us able to eliminate suspicion, hatred, jealousy? Maybe we can do it here in New Hampshire, but for the long haul . . ." David shrugged, at a loss for words.

"If you'll be patient with me for about an hour I'd like to ramble through a series of what may seem to be unrelated ideas, and try to head them up in a proposal. It may give us something to think about." Horace grinned, but he seemed very serious. "Or to argue about, anyway. First, I want to give you my reaction to the Albertis and their Save Our Spouse parties."

We listened, sometimes looking at each other, trying to gauge our reactions to Horace's words, but mostly following him rather intently as he calmly detailed his evening with the Albertis. I felt oddly happy. I guessed that all of us were discovering in these evenings of probing discussion an indefinable identity with each other. We were something new in the world, four people who were trying to catalyze the impossible into a workable reality. In the process, we were creating a bold concept of a new super-individual, *us!*

"Frankly," Horace was saying, "I think that wife-swapping as a way of life not only devalues the individual but ultimately creates a sex contact that is simply an emotional jolt. It's completely independent of the thousands of emotional relationships that can—and that should always—transform the sex act into a kind of deep communication. By their various rules and regulations, in a slap-happy way, the Albertis recognize this, but the infrequency of contact and the multiplicity of exchanges obviously means that no temporary sex partner can know, or probably really wants to know, the deeper human aspects of the other person. In a sense, if you have read pornography, it's pornography acted out with live subjects." Horace laughed. "I've always thought a real craftsman could write much more exciting pornography. He'd simply have to have the brains to make it at least fifty percent subjective. The whole history of man using sex for a temporary thrill, as a shot in the arm, shows that it works like any other form of drug. In the proposal I made to Frank Kitman to teach a pornography course, one of the aspects I wanted to develop was the inevitable progression in much modern writing, including pornography, of devalued sex going by stages to sadism, brutality, and murder. Similar, in a way, to the use of marijuana, which can lead toward heroin for a bigger emotional kick.

"But to get back to the point. While I'm sure the Albertis' group will eventually fall apart, two things struck me vividly. First, their matriarchal approach to spouse exchange, which has given them a limited form of control. The males defer to the females without question. This has had the effect of releasing the females to express their natural eroticism, normally held in check by male domination. Second, at least on the surface, their happy, laughing enjoyment of each other's sex drives, which has created an environment where sexual intercourse with somebody other than your spouse doesn't seem to be equated with infidelity in marriage. Their marriages and responsibilities to each other in other areas are not jeopardized. They simply do not conceive of adultery in their controlled environment as a divisive factor. On the other hand, the *unknown* person on the fringes of monogamy, as in the case of Nancy with Peter, with the possibly destructive overtones of romantic concentration, is considered quite as dangerous as in the normal one-to-one relationship of monogamous marriage."

Horace opened another bottle of champagne and filled our glasses. "I know I'm lecturing you, but if you'll have patience, you'll see that I'm trying to give the possibilities open to the four of us a philosophical framework; any lasting social change needs guideposts for action. Here's a couple of short things I want to read to you. The first is from a book by Ashley Montagu, *On Being Human.* He says:

"The biological basis of love consists in the organism's drive to satisfy its basic needs in a manner which causes it to feel secure. Love *is* security. Mere satisfaction of basic needs is not enough. Needs must be satisfied in a particular manner, in a manner which is emotionally as well as physically satisfying. . . . It is a discovery of the greatest possible significance for mankind that the ethical conception of love independently arrived at by almost all existing peoples is no mere creation of man, but is grounded in the biological structure of the functioning organism. . . . It means that man's organic potentialities are so organized as to demand but one kind of satisfaction alone, a satisfaction which ministers to man's need for love which registers love, which is given in terms of love—a satisfaction which is defined by the one word, *security*."

Horace picked up another book. "This is titled *Environment for Man, the Next Fifty Years.* In a chapter called, *The City as a Mechanism for Sustaining Human Contact,* Christopher Alexander writes:

"Modern urban society has more contact and communication in it than any other society in human history. . . . But as the individual world expands, and the number of his contacts increases, the quality of the contact goes down. A person only has twenty-four hours in a day . . . as his contacts increase his contacts with any one given person become shorter, less frequent, and less deep. In the end from the human point of view they become altogether trivial . . . People who live in cities may think that they have a lot of friends, but the word friend has changed its meaning. Compared with friendships of the past, most of these friendships are trivial. Intimate contact in the deepest sense is rare. *Intimate contact is that close contact between two individuals in which they reveal themselves in all their weaknesses, without fear,* in which the barriers that normally surround the self are down. It is the relationship which characterizes the best marriages and all true friendships. We often call it love . . . we can make it reasonably concrete by naming two essential preconditions without which it can't mature. These conditions are (1) The people concerned must see each other very often, almost every day, though not necessarily for a very long time. (2) They must see each other under informal conditions without the special overlay of role or situation which they usually wear in public . . . It may help to keep in mind an even more concrete criterion of intimacy. If two people are in intimate contact, then we can be sure that they sometimes talk about the ultimate meanings of their lives. . . . If they do not talk about these things then they are not really reaching each other, and their contact is superficial. By this definition it is clear that most 'friendly' contacts are not intimate . . . Friends who come to dinner once a month ('Honey, why don't we have them around to dinner sometime?') or the acquaintances who meet for an occasional drink together, clearly do not satisfy the two conditions which I have defined . . . What social mechanism is required to make contact intimate? In preindustrial society, intimate contacts were sustained by primary groups. A primary group is a small group of people characterized by intimate face-to-face association and cooperation. The three most universal primary groups were the family, the neighborhood groups of elders, and the children's play group. Many anthropologists and sociologists have taken the view that man *cannot live* without primary groups. Many architects and planners have tried to recreate the local primary group artificially, by means of the neighborhood idea. They have hoped that if people would live in small physical groups, round modern village greens, the social groups would follow the same pattern (of the preindustrial society) and these artificial groups would then once more provide the intimate contact which is in such short supply in urban areas today. But this idea of recreating primary groups by artificial means is unrealistic and reactionary; it fails to recognize the truth about the open society. The open society is no longer centered around place-based groups; and the very slight acquaintances that do form around an artificial neighborhood are once again trivial; they are not based on genuine desire."

Horace paused and grinned at our bewildered silence. "You can read this in detail later. Now we come to the point that I believe is vital for us." He continued to read:

"The only vestige of the primary group which still remains is the nuclear family. The family still functions as a mechanism for sustaining intimate contact. But where the extended family of preindustrial society contained many adults, and gave them many opportunities for intimate contact, the modern nuclear family contains two adults. This means that each of these adults has at most *one* intimate contact within his family."

Horace sipped his champagne. "Alexander goes on to exclude children as adequate intimate contacts because the adult-child relationship is essentially one-sided in this area. Now he adds what is to me the most interesting statement in the chapter:

"I believe that intimate contacts are essential for human survival, and, indeed, that each person requires not one, but several given intimate contacts at any one time. I believe that the primary groups which sustained intimate contacts were an essential functional part of traditional social systems, and that since they are now obsolete,"

"The emphasis is mine," Horace said,

"it is essential that we invent new social mechanisms, consistent with the direction that society is taking, and yet able to sustain the intimate contacts which we need."

Tanya finished her third glass of champagne and smiled at me weakly. "I've lived through fifteen years of this, and tonight I'm glad you're here to take some of the brunt of Horace's wild ideas." She kissed his cheek. "I'm not sure I know what in hell you're driving at. Do you, David?"

David grinned. "I think Horace is saying that inadvertently we may have something going for us, but I'm not sure what."

I guess I was stunned. I knew what Horace was driving at, all right, but the impossibility of it made me want to argue the details before I even guessed their full scope.

185

In his enthusiasm, Horace mounted the hearth and jiggled the fire into a roaring flame with a poker. "Leaving Nancy's escapade with Peter Alberti aside, and if my interest in Sylvia had never been discovered, and assuming David's brief fling with his secretary was only a reactive phenomenon, we have just one thing to contend with that makes our marital problems difficult to resolve. Tanya is pregnant and David is the father. I think we've all considered the normal, approved avenues open to us. My contention is that all these harsh solutions are condoned in the framework of a social and religious setup that is more interested in preserving outmoded values than in individuals. We're conditioned to believe that unless life proceeds along a certain narrow track, individuals must collide in tragedy. At the very least, this concept is open to question. If we have the courage, we can build switching points that keep the machinery of living in motion. Up to the time we discovered one another's infidelities, we were reasonably good friends. I'm not going to pretend that we loved one another. In the past we may have had moments when we actually disliked one another as individuals or as composite married couples." Horace smiled. "Without probing, I'll wager, David, that you and Nancy have united against us many times, just as Tanya and I have against you two. You don't have to answer. But, to put it in a nutshell, I think we could learn to love one another. We could minimize the antagonisms that are bound to occur, and do it as a united group of four people with four . . ." Horace laughed at my frown ". . . five children, just as we can as two separate, monogamous couples. Furthermore, since we've reached this impasse, I'm not too sure, if we could approach our problem properly, that we might not discover some by-product benefits that escape most monogamous marriages." Horace looked at us with an amused expression on his face. "For one thing, we could enjoy sexual variety within the home."

For a second we all started to talk at once. "Wait," Horace pleaded. "We'll get back to sex later. There's one potential in this idea that may be even more important than the joy of having two different wives to take to bed, or two different husbands to nag." He picked up a pamphlet that was among the books on the coffee table. "This is called *Population Characteristics*. It's published by the United States Department of Commerce, and between the lines it reveals some frightening facts. I think it'll make you vividly aware of the transience of man. Maybe it points up what I'm trying to say, that we can't afford to make tragedies and hatred out of our problems. Listen to this: 'In the United States in 1966 there were 58 million households. The average number of people in a household was 3.30. The average number of persons per family was 3.72. Twenty percent, or 11.6 million households in the United States, had a female head. One half of these were widows, another one fourth had disrupted marriages.'

"In the obvious interpretation of these statistics, these homes were run by women who were divorced or separated from their husbands. Now add the rest of the picture: 'In 1966, 26.9 million families, or about half the households, had no children.' " Horace paused. "Obviously, half the households in the United States are here-today-gone-tomorrow affairs. Of the households that had children under eighteen years of age, 8.3 million had one child, 5.2 million had two children, and 5.3 million had three or more children. If you think of these figures in terms of family stability, only a small proportion of the families or households in the United States have any roots or any reason to hang together. The rest of us have a very tenuous hold even on the space we occupy. In the normal course of things the temporary phenomena called the Herndon family and the Shea family will quickly disappear from the earth. How long do we have? Maybe fifteen or twenty years more? And long before you'd expect either family to break up, David or I could drop dead, or any of us may disappear as a statistic on the freeway. Should this happen, we have left behind a condition that's not unlike the result of divorce." Horace smiled. "If you really think about it, all this gives us a damned good reason for joining together and loving one another."

To my surprise David seemed nearly as excited as Horace. He slapped the arm of the sofa enthusiastically. "Whether you realize it or not, Horace, you're throwing an interesting sidelight on another phenomenon. If you think of the family as an organization with its specific purposes, it has many similarities to a business firm. The way the world is moving, the individual is caught between two disintegrating forces. He no longer has strong family roots. He's got to earn his living in an increasingly depersonalized environment with all the trivial contacts you mentioned that are part of the big-business

187

setup," David opened the third bottle of champagne and filled our glasses. "This country was built on a strong family system as well as a strong entrepreneurial system. Most of us are still influenced by the Horatio Alger dream, that any man with ambition can start a business from scratch and build it into a substantial enterprise. The politicians still give lip-service to the idea. They start bureaus like the Small Business Administration, which lends money to aggressive young men. But they mortgage them up to their ears to protect their investment. We're told that there are more than three million small businesses in the United States. The truth is they're nearly all Mom and Pop businesses. The majority lead their owners into debtors' court or at best provide a meager living. Most don't last as long as your transient family structure. Four fifths of all the business transacted last year in the United States was in the hands of less than a thousand top companies." David looked at us grimly. "Even so these top companies and those slightly below them in dollar volume, are in a mad merger scramble. There were twenty-five hundred mergers or acquisitions last year, and most of them involved very large companies." David shrugged. "It may interest you to know where Herndon Showcase fits into the picture. It can't grow fast enough, or ever be profitable enough, to finance further growth through its own earnings. It can't borrow on the same terms as the big industries, yet it's taxed on the same basis as General Motors."

"Maybe I'm getting drunk," I said, "but you seem to be saying that the big are getting bigger while Horace is saying the small are getting smaller. So what can we do about it?"

David laughed. "Horace's suggestion is that we should reverse the trend. Damned if I don't think it may be logical. The only defense the individual has left is to fight back, not alone, but by merger. As a family of four adults and four children."

"Five children," I said.

"Five children, six, who knows? Together we could be a hell of a lot stronger financially. As mortal human beings we could maintain a continuity that is impossible any other way."

"I'm a little slow to catch the full drift," Tanya said, raising her eyebrows at me. "But it seems to me you're both saying we should live together communally. It would seem, Nancy, that we married a couple of daydreamers." Tanya smiled at Horace and David like a tolerant mother listening to the youthful enthusiasm of her children. "If couples get into marital difficulties and can't adjust to each other, just what would happen if the four of us tried to be married together?"

Tanya asked. "Reminds me of that poem by Robert Frost. Which is the best way for the world to end, fire or ice? I'll add, divorce or murder? We'd never make it."

"We're getting along remarkably well tonight," Horace said.

"That's because we're stuck here in the backwoods," Tanya replied. "We've been playing ring-around-a-rosy temporarily. For all you know, a little green man called Jealousy may jump on our backs as soon as we get home. Even if we were all angels when we are back in San Pedro, in our separate houses, surrounded by middle class neighbors, we'd be asked to vacate the neighborhood. We'd be accused of destroying the morals of the community." Tanya downed her glass of champagne. "Maybe they'd never hear about it at Cal Institute, but, good God, if Tom Bayberry found out he'd have a heart attack. He's a strict Baptist. He may tell dirty jokes about fucking, but he definitely would not approve of a Utopia, where four people fucked communally."

Laughing, feeling quite giddy from the champagne, I was both repelled and attracted by the idea. "You can intellectualize all you want, but the little business of who goes to bed with whom will knock the props out from under your paradise even before it starts."

"Nancy surprises me," David kidded. "She has sex on the brain."

"Not at all," Tanya said. "Let's accept your proposition as possible. What you should have said is, *your wives* have sex on the brain. What are you going to do about it?"

Horace and David stared at the fire, neither one of them daring to take the initiative. It was Horace who finally broke the silence. "I'll solve the problem. We have eight more days in our Utopia. For the next four nights Nancy and I will sleep together. For the last nights Tanya and I will sleep together. After that we can take it from there." He took my hand. "Come on, Nancy; if Tanya and David want to drink the last bottle of champagne, let them. I think you and I should go to bed with reasonably clear heads."

We all looked at each other seriously for a moment; then we exploded in laughter. Maybe it was the champagne, but for the moment everything seemed quite simple.

Chapter 8

How do I capture the strangely idyllic quality of those eight days in New Hampshire? We were four human beings exploring a new world of our own making. Somehow we sensed, without daring to express it, that if we could overcome our hostilities and get at the root of our jealousies, we held within our hands the possibility of creating a unity that would be more vital than any of us as a separate human being. If we could find the cement to add to the sand, we could mold the components into an exciting new structure. Obviously, it wasn't going to be easy. Surrendering old prejudices, carving new paths through the jungle of individual emotions and years of conditioning, we were two husbands and two wives enjoying one another's spouses. What we were doing broke the Seventh Commandment and, to an outsider, might even seem orgiastic. The theologians might say, here commenced the downfall of Sodom and Gomorrah. More realistically, I think all of us were voyagers on uncharted seas, with very little in the history of love to guide us.

In bed with Horace that night, still wearing my bra and panties, because I didn't want to be naked with him, I wrapped myself in my miserable thoughts and sobbed.

"If you're not happy, why did you come in here with me?" Horace asked quietly.

"It should be obvious," I sopped up my tears with the edge of the sheet. "Neither of us had a choice. Since you're advancing the idea, you had to be gallant. But the truth is that David and Tanya are in love, and you love Tanya. I'm just a problem—your problem. Keep Nancy happy and maybe something will work out."

Horace unhooked my bra and lifted it off my shoulders. "Dear Nancy," he sighed. "If you will unclutch your hand and touch the middle part of me, you'll discover that I'm far from uninterested."

I smiled at him weakly. "That isn't love. Any male reacts the same with any female." I slipped off my panties. "Go ahead, you might just as well get it over with. That's what's expected."

Horace kissed my face with tiny kisses. Gently, he pulled me into his arms. "Nancy, curl your body against mine. Sleep for a while. I want you, but only if you want me, joyously, unafraid."

I grinned at him. "I'm not afraid of you."

"Well, that's a good beginning."

"Beginning for what?"

"For falling in love."

"You don't have to . . ." I sighed. "I don't know what love is. But I know I like you."

Horace's fingers trickled down my back; he pressed my behind so that I could feel his penis against my stomach. I arched my leg over his body and felt him slowly, unhurriedly enter my vagina. "My God," I gasped, "you do feel nice!"

And we slept that way. As if Horace, in a long embrace that left me floating and bodiless, was trying to communicate with me not through words but in the simple joy of a man and a woman who could surrender to each other. Somewhere, before morning, I awoke, missing the fullness of him, and kissed his cheek. In a sleepy embrace the urgency of our need culminated. I lay half asleep in his arms. "I wasn't me," I murmured. "I was you."

"Do you think you can make love that way without loving" he whispered.

"No, I guess not." I smiled a little, embarrassed as Nancy became Nancy again.

"Well then, without constraint, and not because I'm intellectualizing our situation, will you marry me? I love you."

"My God, you're insane!"

"Maybe not." Horace snuggled his face against my breasts. "Maybe some day the world will consider we were quite sane. Go to sleep, Sea. You're not alone."

But my conscience slept with me. I awoke again in the gray light of morning with a vivid picture of the children suddenly opening the door and discovering their mother in bed with Ace, who belonged to Tan. Jimmy might decide he had named him rightly. And me, too! Ace Shea! Ace of Hearts! I groped on the dresser and found Horace's wristwatch. He opened one eye, reached out, grasped me around the waist and tumbled me back in bed on top of him.

"It's five o'clock," I said. "The kids will wake up soon. We can't stay like this."

Horace stopped kissing me. "I guess we'd better get in bed with David and Tanya."

"You're mad," I gasped. "What would the children think? Go tell David to come here with me."

"What if they're making love?"

191

"That's your embarrassment." I grinned at him. "Slap him on the behind and tell him he has to hurry."

Grumbling, Horace tiptoed out of the room naked. In a few minutes David crawled in beside me. "Ye gods," he sighed. "Is this supposed to be a vacation? I'm not getting enough sleep."

"You'll have to start taking vitamin pills." I looked at him with a sarcastic expression, but he only smiled back with his eyes closed. Contentedly, he tried to snuggle against me. My God! Wasn't one woman a night enough? I was tempted to push him away, but then he opened his eyes, sensing my withdrawal, and looked at me like an innocent boy. I was refusing him the maternal breast. "Don't you like me anymore?" he asked.

Somehow, even though I hugged him briefly, I couldn't answer the question. I liked him; he had been my friend for fifteen years; I even loved him. But at the moment, knowing he had just come from Tanya, I didn't feel affectionate toward him. Then he had the nerve to taste my nipples and try to arouse me. I pushed him away, but I couldn't help laughing.

"No thanks, chum," I said. "For the next three days I'm remaining faithful to Horace. He just offered to marry me."

Christmas morning David and Horace took turns passing out the gifts. Amazingly, among the ties, shaving cream, bottles of bubble bath, toilet water, at least six different games, books, and paint sets there were no serious duplications. Tanya had concentrated on art supplies for the kids, and offered to teach them all how to draw and paint. Horace had shown a predilection for books slanted at his thesis that we could "make it together." He gave David *Eupsychian Management*, by Abraham Maslow, me a book called *Romantic Marriage—The Twentieth Century Illusion*, and Tanya a book by William Schutz with the simple title, *Joy*. David bought black leotards for Tanya, Susan, and me (we accused him of spending more than his five dollar allotment) and insisted that we immediately put them on. I gave David and Horace boxer shorts with hearts on them, and turtleneck sweaters. To the kids' delight the men stripped and wore them, to the exclusion of other clothes, for the rest of the morning. Tanya gave David and Horace identical Banlon shirts and red-and-green, hand-knitted penis protectors with a sack for their balls. "I knitted them myself last fall," she said. "I never thought we'd be in a climate where they might be practical."

The kids were fascinated, but the men refused to model their penis protectors. I wondered if we were being too brazenly sexual in front of the children. It also occurred to me that Tanya had coolly packed them and brought them along with her. If we had been in the same stage of friendship that we were in six months ago, they would have been typical Tanya gifts that would have been received with good-natured innuendos. I wondered how, at the moment of leaving California, she had had the nerve to think she would be in an environment where she would dare to give them. Obviously Tanya was accepting the situation with more equanimity than I was.

Tanya and I had conspired on our gifts and gave each other simulated pearl necklaces and drop earrings. Wearing them with our black leotards, we looked surprisingly sophisticated. We promised to buy Susan a set so all the females would look alike. David gave the prize, a Frankenstein monster rubber mask, to Sam for his gift to Susan of a bird's-egg hatcher, all equipped with three eggs, and for an ant farm he gave Mitch, who immediately wanted to dig under the snow for ants.

But David and Horace admitted later, when the kids were in bed, that Tanya's special present to them deserved the prize for originality. It was a box of twelve bottles of watercolor paints, with a special invitation to develop their creativity by painting themselves two new wives.

The men were bewildered at first. "Have another drink," Tanya told them. "We're two loving wives who are giving you a chance to release your inhibitions. In Greenwich Village and Haight-Ashbury, the privilege we're going to give you costs twenty dollars a half hour. There, for your money, you get the paint and a nude female model. You can paint her any colors or designs you wish. Here, there's no special time limit, though Nancy and I insist that the artists be naked too, and that we get equal opportunities to refurbish our husbands."

Horace protested. "Not me, not on your life; I'm not being painted naked. For God's sakes, how do you know the stuff will come off?"

"Don't worry," Tanya laughed. "I may not know much about sociology or group marriage, but I do know watercolors. We can wash them off in a shower afterward."

Nearly collapsing from laughter, we watched Horace take the first dabs. Timidly he painted an orange circle around one of my nipples and then painted the nipple purple. With more courage, he matched the color scheme on my other breast. Then he looked at himself and announced that this business was too damned erotic; he couldn't go on. He hastily gulped his drink. Tanya, laughing loudly, grabbed a brush and

193

daubed his penis a flaming red. In less than an hour, as we plunged into the joyous craziness of painting each other all colors of the rainbow, Tanya and I had been transformed into creatures with winking eyes to replace our breasts, grinning mouths at our navels, and appropriate painted beards below. My behind became the pouting cheeks of a zany creature whose eyes were in the middle of my back, and Tanya's rump became profiles of two plump-faced men winking at each other.

Tanya and I were finally much more thoroughly decorated than either Horace or David, though we occasionally dabbed at them, and Tanya managed, to David's annoyance, since he was so enthusiastic with his own efforts that he didn't want to be distracted, to paint a hairy face on his stomach so that his penis looked like a lighted cigar clutched in the mouth of a popeyed man. When we had no more flesh to paint, and the colors were beginning to get muddy from too much overpainting, Horace suggested that we take a shower and start over again, but Tanya and I called a curfew and ran for the bathroom. We milled around in the shower cabinet, two at a time, until we were all soft pink flesh again.

"I like you both better this way," Horace said as he dried our backs while David merrily swabbed the front of us. "Before we all sober up and stare at each other and wonder whether we're sinful, I suggest we all go to bed together and talk."

And we did. We tumbled into one of the big double beds, Tanya and I were squeezed into the middle, and Horace flopped down beside me, insisting that he still had three nights left with his new wife.

"What do we do now?" David laughed. "Make love and watch each other?"

"Not on your life!" Tanya shrieked.

I murmured my agreement. "I think that would be sleazy. Even animals don't copulate in groups. Making love is a subjective experience. If four of us made love together, it would become objective. We'd be voyeurs; it would be ugly."

Horace squeezed my hand. "So we've got one problem solved. Personally, I feel very comfortable. It's snowing again. We don't have to have intercourse every night. Why not just enjoy the warm cocoon the four of us have made together? We could just sleep."

"Before we do, I'll offer a challenge." David, leaning on his elbows, smiled across the bed at us. "We've tried to define love. Now I'll ask a question about sex that may be just as hard to handle. What do you feel at the height of intercourse, and what do you feel afterward?" We pondered on that silently for a while. Outside, the snow snapped against the window.

"Are there any words for it, really?" Tanya asked. "The moment is too short to hold. Maybe the real delight is in the surrender, and the wonder that you can surrender and want to."

There were no words, of course, but we tried. As we lay together in the dimly lighted bedroom, and slowly exposed our feelings, we were more completely naked than we had ever been in the act of love itself.

Chapter 9

Sometime before morning, David sleepily took my hands and we tottered off to the other bedroom, because we still didn't have any explanation for the children. I knew this was a reflection of the larger problem we would face if we tried to convince the world that we weren't entirely mad.

We spent the days with the children in a warm little island of our own making, but while we slept together according to Horace's plan, sex was not the keynote of our existence. Rather, as in an oil painting whose undercoating gives the final colors their vibrancy, the delight in our sexuality became a warm undercurrent between us. We had plunged into a new world where the intimacy of our private surrender to each other pierced the smog that people ordinarily exude in their daily contacts; we had colored all of our actions with a warm, understanding laughter.

I suddenly realized that I no longer felt jealous of Tanya or possessive of David. I had discovered myself to be a hungrily responsive person quite willing to share the easy affection that had become quite natural between all of us. The children, sensing the unity we had created, responded in an undifferentiated way that embraced Tanya and me as friends and equally valid mothers. Susan and Sam were entranced with Tanya's art lessons and spent hours drawing pictures and unrecognizable portraits of all of us. Mitch and Jimmy built an igloo with Horace. David, who had become intrigued with a book by Ralph Borsodi called *Education and Living,* occasionally went outdoors and supervised, but mostly he lay on the sofa reading excerpts to anyone who would listen. After one of our daily saunas, which we all took together naked, all eight of us, shivering, crawled into the kid's snow house. Mitch and Jimmy crumbled the roof on top of us. Thrashing and laughing, we disappeared in a huge pile of snow.

While our evening discussions continued, we spent more time reading separately, each of us engrossed in one or another of the books that Horace had brought. Without admitting as much, we were searching for guideposts in books like Milford Spiro's analysis of the Kibbutz, John Noyes's *History* of American Socialisms, and Hine's *California's Utopian Colonies.* Was it possible that now, or somewhere in the past, men had envisioned a way of life that encompassed two families? Could two families, without the blood-ties of marriage, weave a communal life together with common goals and without serious interpersonal difficulties that would disrupt them? The ideas motivating the kibbutzim were interesting, but they were religiously and politically oriented. The Kibbutz was a necessary response in a harsh land and a hostile environment. It embraced too large a group; by its very size it tended to deny the free expression of individuality. The basic needs of the community seeking the fundamentals of food, clothing, and shelter were considerably different goals from what would be necessary in our suburban environment. It was apparent too, from John Noyes, that all the abortive attempts at communal living had been organized in a striving toward religious or agrarian goals. Could we find some goal or principle that would keep us together?

David, who identified with Borsodi's disillusionment with the advertising and business environment, read to us from *Education and Living.* "If we have any raison d'être," he said, "it has to be in Horace's analysis of the disintegration of the family. Here's what Borsodi says:

"But the idea of the family is three dimensional; it conceives of a family with a past, present and future. This continuum is a corporate entity; with a corporate name, corporate value, corporate history and traditions, corporate customs and habits, corporate reputation and goodwill with a corporate estate, real and personal, composed, not only of its present membership, but a membership in the past, and a membership in the future, of which the members in being and in occupation—the living family group—are representatives, entitled to the usufruct of the family's corporate heritage, but obligated, as trustees for their posterity, to the conservation of that heritage; and finally conscious of the institution of which they are members. *Anything substantially different from this or omitting any essential element in it, is not a normal but an abnormal idea of the family.*"

David read the passage with a glow of interest. Many weeks later we recognized it as the inspiration for the startling idea he proposed for us. His enthusiasm was captivating. "Borsodi quotes from Bertrand Russell's book, *Education and the Social Order,*" David continued:

197

"If any young readers take up this book, I beg them merely to contemplate the facts of human experience now revealed to us in fuller measure than ever before. There is one supreme human relationship which has created the home and made the family fireside the source out of which man's highest qualities have grown up to transform the world. As a historical fact, it is to family life that we owe the greatest debt which the mind of man can conceive."

David grinned. "I'm not going to read to you all night, but here's one more from Borsodi himself:

'The family was not only a corporate existence but the be-all and end-all of life. It was an entity to be dealt with, not as a means to that other end which I believe to be more truly human—the end of individual self-realization and self-expression—but as a self-sufficient end in itself. To this the humanist can make only one answer: the family—like any other institution—is a means. *Not the family but living is the end.* Individual life should not be organized primarily for the benefit of the family; *family life should be organized so that the individual may live as nearly like a normal human being as possible.*"

David smiled. "So there's a dream for you. If the Herndons and the Sheas could create that kind of family and erect it on the shaky foundations we have started with, some day someone will build a monument to us!"

I pointed out that most Utopian communities eventually foundered in personal disagreements among their members; I still couldn't resist the role of Cassandra.

Horace insisted there was no need for us to fall into the Utopian trap. "We shouldn't try to create a Utopia. Most visionaries of the perfect society have created dropout societies. They try to embrace too much of the world. Ultimately the only social situation they can posit must exist in isolated circumstances protected from the main currents of life, or they must assume that the whole world is ensnared in their dream, which leads to a ruthless dictatorship that aims to exterminate those who don't agree with them.

"There are hundreds of active, intentional communities in the United States today. Most of them, including Borsodi's Schools of Living, can't make a realistic truce between the spurious values they're rejecting and the very real achievements of our industrialized, computerized society. They're on

198

the horns of a dilemma. Whether it's the Borsodi theory of homesteading, or a complete return to fundamentals in the Thoreau tradition, the baby is thrown out with the bath water. It amuses me to read some of the writings of the homesteaders who insist on milling their own flour, baking their own bread, building their own houses, but who're still willing to accept the gasoline tractor to till their fields, or the power saw to cut their wood, or the main power lines or gasoline generators to light their houses."

Horace grinned. "I don't think we'll find the specific answers in any book. If we dared to try communal marriage, the trick would be to succeed within our present environment, using all the artifacts of our culture, bending them to our needs, and not vice-versa. We would only reject values which didn't contribute to our basic need as a group family . . ."

"Corporate family," David said. "A corporate marriage seems more plausible and more contemporary than a group marriage."

While we continued to discuss the idea, we agreed with Horace that we were not trying to predicate Utopias as a solution for our personal problems. But, of course, the truth was that four adults, attempting to work together toward a common goal for themselves and their children, were delving deep into the basic reason that large-scale Utopias had never worked—*People!*

"There's another reason why Utopias fail," Tanya pointed out. "Any perfect society, with no problems, would be damned boring. If the four of us could merge our families, I don't think we could act like saints. Maybe it's necessary in the contained environment of the Chesley lodge, but back in San Pedro, Nancy and I would inevitably be in much closer contact with each other than with either of you. If we needed to have a slam-bang argument or to hate each other for a while, I think we should."

We had been sitting around our favorite evening gathering place, the huge coffee table in front of the fireplace. The words were scarcely uttered than a slam-bang argument erupted from the children's bedroom. Susan emerged, tears running down her cheeks, followed by Jimmy, Mitch, and Sam, who flatly insisted that *she* couldn't sleep in their room anymore. It was impossible to find any sense in their argument; Susan must have been aggravating them in some obscure way.

Tanya and I, grinning a little at each other, tried to pacify them as Susan insisted that she didn't care. "Why can't Dave and Sea move into the other room with me? Let the boys have their nasty own bunks together."

David finally entered the fray. "I think we all need an escape valve for our aggressive feelings," he said with a broad smile. "How about an old-fashioned pillow fight? Ace, Sea, Mitch, and Susan can be on one side. Tan and I, Jimmy and Sam on the other."

Whatever the tearful argument had been, it was dispelled in a minute. With a roar of glee we all ran for the bedrooms, grabbed pillows and started hurling them at each other. Susan concentrated on Jimmy who, for some reason, seemed to have incurred her wrath more than the other boys. Tanya bounced one off me that knocked me to the floor. I was about to hurl a pillow at her when Mitch, with a whoop, slugged her with one that tumbled her to the floor. Horace clobbered David with a pillow that split on contact and deluged him in feathers. In a few minutes the room was in shambles and we were all puffing and weak with laughter. Then, to my amazement, David suggested that we all sit around the fireplace; he said maybe Horace could be persuaded to read something to us. Like an embarrassed actor who was only too willing to display his talents, but needed encouragement, Horace let us tease him.

"As a matter of fact," he said, "when we were in Newport I bought a copy of Dylan Thomas's *A Child's Christmas in Wales*." He looked at us in embarrassment. "I always enjoy rereading it on Christmas."

"You don't have to apologize." Tanya smiled. "Horace doesn't have to read it; he knows it by heart."

With the slight overtone of a Welsh accent in his voice, Horace embraced all of us in the warm, friendly Christmas of time past. Uncles and aunts, fathers and mothers, spinsters and old bachelors, grandfathers and grandmothers joined us around the fireplace as Horace brought Dylan Thomas's world alive. When he finished, Jimmy who was half sitting in his lap, snuggled against his neck. "I like that story, Ace. Will you read it again?"

We voted that tomorrow Horace would, and that he deserved a hug. David pointed out that *he* needed a hug, too, for having suggested the idea.

That night, after four nights with Horace, I slept with David. I guess Tanya felt as nervous as I did at the switch back. Out of hearing of either David or Horace, she suggested that immediately, just before we went to bed, we make excuses to leave them. "Quickly—not for more than three minutes," she giggled. "Then we'll jump in bed naked together, first with Horace, then with David." I thought it was kind of daffy, but the men, responding to our hilarious ministrations, lay like naked caliphs and protested loudly when we told them the treatment was over.

Minutes later, as soon as we were alone in bed with each other, David, with a big grin on his face, hugged me hard. "I wish I had a movie of the two of you," he said. "You were like bad little girls, amazed at your lasciviousness." He kissed me. "Sea, I don't know whether you're aware of it, but suddenly both you and Tanya have a new youthfulness and girlishness about you that transforms you. Do you know what I mean?"

I snuggled against him, knowing he was right. The interacting magic of the four of us wasn't affecting only Tanya and me; David and Horace had become bright, sparkling lovers. Yet I could not get rid of the nagging worry that what we were doing was immoral. It couldn't work. If there was no law against it, and I was sure there must be, and even if we could ignore our heritage, what we were doing was wrong. We still lacked the legal marriage commitment that one man and one woman could make to each other. Could we ever overcome that? David my husband, making love to me, last night had slept with Tanya. I asked David why I wasn't jealous; then I laughed softly as he rejected my attempts to probe the impossible. It didn't matter. Eventually I could keep Horace awake all night with my worries.

Chapter 10

Most marriages that have lasted fifteen years might be compared to a novel that two people have been reading together. Midway through, perhaps still dimly hoping for a few unexpected climaxes and surprises, they adjust themselves to the slower pace of the second half. A few readers may get bored and try to discover a new story, but most plod quietly along, finding it easier and more comfortable to read through to the predictable ending.

Returning to San Pedro, to the same houses, we soon discovered that it wasn't easy to close the old book and concentrate on the new one. The new book didn't follow the formulas most people live by; it had no standard of social behavior to guide us. The accepted routines of monogamous living had vanished. Our combined intimacy, if it were to continue, forced us to reevaluate every detail of our lives. Even the impersonal aspects of our environment acquired a new coloring and sheen as we slowly substituted the group consciousness of the eight of us for our separate individualities. In some subtle way the exchange of our bodies depersonalized our possessions. Within a few weeks Tanya's dishes had moved into my house; the Herndons' phonograph records and books moved into hers. Carelessly discarded clothing ended up in one washing under an agreement that at least once a week we would tackle the whole mess together.

Tanya decided to continue working until April, and she convinced Tom Bayberry that after the baby was born she could still do fashion layouts at home. And the formal, priggish Nancy Herndon of less than a month ago, lonely and at our wit's end, came alive. I was caught up in a world of family living—bubbling, confused, messy, argumentative, but excitingly demanding and roaringly vital.

Tanya had stumbled on a book called, *Thank You, Doctor Lamaze*, a delightful, factual account of childbirth. I read it with her, identifying with both the author and Tanya. I became the pregnant mother, as well as the mother-in-law, anxious that her daughter should have a healthy child. Based on Pavlov's theories, and widely used in Russia and France, the book extolled natural childbirth without pain for the female who could master the technique. Tanya became so enthusiastic that she decided to have our baby (we told her she couldn't call it hers anymore) at home, suggesting, since we were all involved, that there was no good reason why we all couldn't watch and assist her.

"Even the children, why not?" she demanded hotly. "It'll be very valuable education for them." I don't know who was more shocked at the idea, myself, Horace, or David.

"Even in primitive tribes accouchement is a spectacle for women only," Horace protested. But he had to admit that the traditional practice excluded the father from a rather crucial marital experience.

"If you're referring to me as the particular father," David said, "then revise your statement to coincide with your principles. This is a family affair. We should all be involved."

In most of our talk we skirted the whole business of whether the children should watch, since we hadn't been able to agree on a proper explanation, for them, of our involved marital relations. Tanya, meanwhile, engaged in a frustrating telephone search for a doctor willing to deliver a child at home, using the Lamaze techniques. She insisted she was a tough Swede, and that even if things didn't go according to plan, this time, at the birth of her third and last baby, she was damned if she was going to be asleep or even half-asleep. She said she was going to find out for herself if the final push is the thrill they say it is. But at first she had no luck in finding a doctor sympathetic to her idea.

We spent most of our first evenings back in California discussing our sleeping arrangements. It was obvious that unless we explained to the children, we had no choice but to attempt involved and clandestine bedtime meetings while maintaining the surface appearances of monogamous parents. Unless we came to grips with the problem, the habits of the old nuclear family arrangements of our two separate houses would overwhelm our daydream of a corporate family.

David summarized it for us a few days after we returned home. "Eating and fornicating under separate roofs," he said, and grinned at my displeasure at his choice of words, "splits us apart at the two vital centers of contact."

"Eating together is simple," I said sarcastically. "We could very easily eat together." I blushed as Horace smiled at the double meaning, and lamely added, "Food!"

Strangely, we all seemed to be embarrassed to face the sexual problem head on. "We can't sneak between bedrooms every night," Horace said.

"Even if we could," Tanya added, "I'm not sleeping with

203

David one night and Horace the next. It's too confusing; there's no continuity."

"Not to mention that it's demoralizing," David chuckled. "Some nights I just need to sleep. So where do we go from here, Horace? After the relative simplicity of New Hampshire, isn't it time we faced the facts?"

"Stating it without innuendo," I said coldly, "David hasn't slept with Tanya since we left the Chesley lodge." As I looked at Horace I tried to search his mind. "Probably the truth is that you've made your truce with conformity and would prefer to continue monogamously with Tanya."

Horace wasn't perturbed. "On the contrary, Nancy, the only reason I proposed the idea in the first place was to insure a future with *two* wives. Seriously, I miss our nightly arguments about the impossibility of the four of us working it out. Tanya is a more complacent bed-fellow."

"They weren't arguments; call them discussions," I said. "If that's all you miss, I'm sure I can accommodate you."

Tanya insisted we come out of the clouds. "Like tonight, for instance. If we agreed, how do we accomplish it? Mitch and Sam's bedrooms are right next to ours. You have the same problem in your house. They're going to be very surprised and confused kids if they wake up in the night and discover a strange mommy or daddy in the bedroom."

"We'll have to tell them," Horace said calmly.

"Tell them what?" I demanded. "That it's all right, because their daddies and mommies love each other? If I were Susan or the boys, I'd feel uneasy, sort of as if the rug were pulled out from under me. They may not be old enough to understand everything, but they're well aware that their friends' mothers and fathers don't exchange bed-mates, that a family has two parents, not four."

"I think we can gradually recondition them." Horace shrugged. "But before we get in too deep, we better be damned sure that we're in basic agreement. It would be disastrous to end up squabbling among ourselves."

"If you're asking that Nancy and I never become jealous of each other," Tanya said, "it's contrary to all female behavior. In a few months Nancy is going to be a more desirable sex partner than I will, with my bloated belly."

I scowled. "But after the baby is born, that's something else again."

"What do you mean?"

"You and David will have a stronger tie than Horace and I have."

Horace laughed. "Do you want me to get you pregnant? We could even things out."

"God, no! Five children to explain us to are enough," I sighed. "What we really need is something overriding, something equal to the commitment of monogamous marriage. When two people get married they soon discover that marriage is not all hearts and flowers, but the social and legal arrangements hold together the cracks in the walls."

While the others seemed more pragmatic than I, and appeared content to develop our future off the cuff, I was plagued with the fear that the whole business of calmly sleeping with each other's spouses was immoral. Our sleeping arrangements had now become haphazard; there was no predetermined pattern. Horace and David sneaked into each other's bedrooms late at night, but retreated to their own rooms by early morning.

In some way I was unable to define, I cared deeply for both David and Horace. Tanya and I discussed it together often. "I think they feel the same way," she told me. "When you think about the four of us, it's more amazing in reverse. I'll wager that if we could take a poll of females, we'd find that the typical female is much less jealous and possessive than her spouse. Females are basically amoral. Yet, as males, David and Horace think you and I are too subjective. We probe too much." Tanya looked at me with mild embarrassment. "At first, when David was in my arms, I couldn't stop thinking about you. I'd ask myself, did David respond in the same way to you as he was responding to me? I'd close my eyes and see him with you, and I wondered if there was a real distinction in his mind. Was there in mine? Or were we both just mechanical robots on whom someone had pushed the fuck button? Still, I was certain that with Horace I was a quite different female. Not quantitatively." Tanya grinned at my laughter. "Oh dear, I don't know if there are any words to pin any of us down. I think I discovered that my duality wasn't entirely real, or if it existed at all, was only partial. I was happy with both of them." Tanya shrugged. "Equally important, Sea, is to *dare* to explore my feelings with you."

I couldn't stop myself; I hugged her quickly. "That's the magic, really," I said. "We're friends. The wild passion, the blending with Horace wouldn't be possible for me with a stranger, or in a situation that didn't encompass the four of us. I'm female, and I've been naked with Horace in a way that I had never dared to be with David. Now, slowly, after years of marriage, I'm learning how to be an individual with David, too. I'm no longer just a wife; I'm Nancy, and I'm in love with us all. When I was shopping today, I couldn't help an inward smile. I was the only female among all those harried women who had two men in love with her. I left like

205

dancing and singing my soy, like shouting, 'Dull, stodgy world, wake up and love!' "

I suppose that explained my fears, too. We were not immoral in a sexual sense. I could no longer think of us as adulterers, as breaking the Seventh Commandment. As Horace pointed out, there was a better commandment in Leviticus: "Thou shalt love thy neighbor as thyself." To adulterate meant make corrupt, impure; to debase. We were adding to, purifying, cleansing, creating a new vital entity that enlarged us all.

When we returned to Graniteville for New Year's Eve with my family we took rooms as proper families at a nearby motel. Later, when we discussed the celebration and the New Year's Eve need for people to rediscover their emotional dependence on each other, we concluded that our dual relationship in New Hampshire was more basically honest than the sexual sparrings of suburbia. Even Mother had to admit it was a good thing Tanya and I were not relocating in Graniteville. Two new females, in the contained atmosphere of the Neighborhood Club, could fatally disturb an environment already shaken by numerous deviations from idealistic monogamy. By contrast, our immorality was simply against a morality that made it impossible for us to declare ourselves.

While we couldn't agree how to involve the children in the deeper aspects of our relationship, we decided that as a start toward reconditioning them we could blend our family meals by eating breakfast and dinner together. Neither the kitchen nor dining room in our twin houses was adequate to accommodate eight at a sitting, so we bought a large round table with center-leaf extensions, and turned the Herndon living room into a dining room. The kids were ecstatic. Slowly we evolved a dining ritual which encompassed them in all our conversations. Whether it was discussing school, homework, David's business problems, Horace's teaching, Tanya's breathing exercises as she prepared for the baby, television, or what any of us had been reading, we purposely encouraged the children to participate and voice their opinions. After dinner, at Susan's suggestion, the table became a joint homework table. On weekday evenings while we read or answered questions or, later, played games with them before the children's bedtime, the television remained silent and happily neglected.

Since Tanya arrived home an hour or two before David and Horace, she and I decided to do our food shopping jointly. To eliminate argument over money, David and Horace contributed one hundred dollars each to our joint food fund and replenished it equally when it was gone.

Perhaps it was the food fund; perhaps it was David's continued reading of Ralph Borsodi; or perhaps it was our growing relatedness as a family of eight. Possibly it was our decision to bring the television out near the Sheas' swimming pool on Saturday night and watch the movies with the kids, while all of us, comfortably naked, swam, talked, and good-naturedly exchanged acrid comments about the drama we were only half watching. But who knows really what all the various origins and inspirations were for David's bombshell idea?

In the late evening, as he smiled and kissed and hugged each one of the kids good night, I intercepted a far-off, amused expression on his face. Tanya ruffled his hair. He ran his fingers lightly across the new curve of her belly as she passed by his chair and snapped off the television. I sat beside Horace, dangling my feet in the pool. For a moment we didn't say anything, but simply enjoyed the welcome silence of the television. The nervous throb of an automobile engine on the street in front of our houses seemed too near. Slowly it faded away; then it became pleasantly distant; soon there was a moment of absolute quiet.

"David seems lost in his thoughts." I smiled at him. "I think he should take us along with him into outer space."

He twinkled at me. "The truth is that I'm happy, and I'm surprised at the simplicity of happiness. It's the four of us, together here, indolent, content with the fact of each other's existence." He laughed and waved toward the top of the hill. "I don't know who the neighbors two streets above us are, but they've been watching us down here, either in awe or shock, for the past two hours."

"My God!" Tanya scowled at him. "You should have told us. I didn't realize they could look into this yard. One of these days we're going to be raided."

I agreed with her, though the men seemed unconcerned about our casual family nudity. Tanya and I had carefully cautioned the children not to make it a subject of discussion among their friends in the neighborhood or at school.

"We know," Susan had told us haughtily. "We're not stupid!"

"Do you think we are?" Tanya had asked.

Jimmy shook his head. "I think it's fun," he said. Mitch agreed. "The Materi kids never saw old lady Materi in her birthday suit." He laughed. "I think Sea and Tan are kind of interesting to look at."

I still had my doubts, but Horace insisted it was healthy for the children to grow up with a calm acceptance of us all as quite human beings who sometimes found it convenient to be naked.

"Forget the neighbors for a minute," David picked up the thread of his thoughts. "Since we've arrived at a point where we can discuss and solve most of our problems, except how to explain our sleeping arrangements to the kids, I'd like to propose an idea that's been flitting around in my mind for the past few weeks. It might be the step, if we dared to take it, that Nancy feels is so necessary. It would be a larger commitment to the belief that what we're doing is sound. I propose that we sell these two houses, pool all our resources, and incorporate as a joint family. If we did, we could build a home that made more sense for all of us. In the process we'd have to explain to the kids exactly what we hope to achieve."

Horace, stretched out on an air cushion, stared into the star-pricked sky. "How do you propose to do it?" he asked. He leaned on his elbow to examine my face and breasts, which were right-angled to his belly. "Nancy looks startled."

David shrugged. "Not with the idea. It's just that she can't believe the rugged Republican individualist she married could accept communal property sharing. It's an interesting fact that most middle class families, at least among themselves, have a greater reluctance to discuss their financial strength or lack of it than they do their sexual relations."

"Or lack of sex," Tanya grinned. "It's one problem we've overcome."

Horace trickled his fingers across my shoulders. "I'm not so rich that I care."

"I've known you three years," David said. "I could only guess at your earnings."

"Seventeen-five from Cal Institute." Horace laughed. "I'm in the ranks of the poorly paid pedagogues. Tanya has been earning seventy-five hundred. My father left an estate of seventy thousand, mostly in blue-chip stocks, which earn about thirty-five hundred in dividends. All told, discounting Tanya's salary for the long haul, about twenty-two to twenty-three thousand."

We spent the rest of the evening in an excited money discussion. David was earning twenty-four thousand from Herndon Showcase. If the company had a good year he could take a few thousand more, but more likely he should plow the money back into inventory and new machinery.

"My God," Tanya marveled. "Together we're filthy rich. We have a total income of nearly fifty thousand dollars."

As we explored in detail our total assets, we discovered that our combined savings totaled twenty-six thousand dollars, the equity in our houses came to thirty thousand dollars, and the paid-up value of our insurance policies was about eighteen thousand.

David estimated the Herndon Showcase Corporation was worth about two hundred fifty thousand dollars, and Horace pointed out that the Herndon assets were greater than his inheritance. David didn't think that was important. "We can't measure this merger by money values. We're four people in reasonably good health. The question is, do we have the nerve to love and cherish each other until death do us part?" David explained in detail Sub-Chapter S of the Internal Revenue Code, under which he thought we could legally form the Herndon-Shea Corporation. All of our assets would be transferred to the corporation. Our combined income would be funneled through the corporation without double taxation, with one corporate tax on our earnings. Moreover, we would have the numerous advantages of corporate deductions and provisions such as the pension plans permitted to corporations. "You have to understand this is a special type of partnership corporation. It's permitted under the laws as long as there are no more than ten stockholders." David laughed. "We're under the wire with nine of us; one to go!"

Tanya and I were slightly bewildered with the details. "Do we understand you right? All of us including the kids would be equal stockholders?"

"It's the only practical way, because it would minimize taxes. If we issued one thousand shares, each of us and each child would immediately be given one hundred shares while a hundred unissued shares would be left for contingencies."

"If you're grinning at me, forget it," I said. "No contingencies. I take my pills religiously. Nine under one roof is enough."

We tossed the idea around for several days. The potential for us as a united family was fascinating and intriguing to contemplate. Our corporation would have sufficient income and assets to swing a mortgage on a unique house designed for a unified family. The corporation could not only be planned for so that we would have ample financial security for the four of us, but it could become a continuing source of income for the children as they grew older. If we designed our new home correctly, it could become a living thing, expanding to meet the needs of the entire family. Later, if any or all of the kids wanted to live with us, our corporate home could become a true family compound.

Tanya immediately got us involved in drawing plans for the kind of home we would need. Horace wanted to gamble. Could we immediately create what he called a "three-generation home"? He grinned at David. "You and I are without living parents, but Sea and Tanya each have a mother and father who are alive."

"You mean build a house large enough so that my mother and father could move in?" Tanya was stunned. "Jesus, NO!"

I agreed. "My mother and father would drive us insane. But you don't have to worry, the immorality of the whole business would give mother a fatal heart attack. She'd never come in with us."

Horace wanted to know what Tanya and I would do if our father or mother died. Put the survivor in a senior citizen center? I shrugged. It was something I didn't like to think about.

"I agree with Horace," David admitted. "After all, do we or don't we believe in what we're doing? If we don't, we should split up. If we do, then the purpose is to create stability for an entire family. If you think ahead, in thirty years, if we all live, we're going to be outcasts. The kids will have to decide what to do with us."

Tanya suggested we might begin to dislike each other after just a few years. What if we couldn't tolerate each other? Jokingly, Horace suggested that we design the house with hate-each-other apartments. David's intriguing contribution was, if someone should die or we couldn't get along, to have a prior agreement to sell the individual shares in our corporation to an outsider of the same sex. "That way," he said, "if Horace and I got bored, we could sell out to some impotent old man who might get a charge out of having two young wives."

Tanya and I, hysterical with laughter, vetoed the idea. If Horace and David got bored servicing two women, the only alternative would be for them to sleep together.

"What if one of us dies?" I asked.

"That's just the point," Horace said. "Let's say I die first. You and Tanya and the kids would have the kind of security with David that he and I are both trying to achieve for you independently."

"David would be a bigamist." Tanya wiped the tears of laughter from her eyes. "That would be illegal."

"Somehow, I think we're illegal right now." I was convinced of it. "I wish one of us dared ask a lawyer. Could we be put in jail for immoral conduct?"

"The hell with the legality of our private, married lives." David frowned. "We aren't hurting anyone. What we do together is nobody's damned business but our own!"

Chapter 11

~~~~~~~~~~

David and Horace, hell-bent to unite our activities as a family, began searching for an auxiliary sloop so that we could sail together and perhaps spend weekends on Catalina. Sundays, while they explored boatyards and marinas with the kids, Tanya and I caught up on our housework, which had become an increasingly co-operative effort.

While Tanya and Horace were enthusiastic over David's plan of incorporating as a joint family, and we finally agreed that David should ask his lawyer to form our corporation, I still had lingering doubts.

"It isn't only that you and I may one day come to blows over systems and methods of housekeeping," I told Tanya, as we tried to organize the accumulated week's confusion of the Shea house. "But there are other things that bother me. David's assumption that we can make a commitment by pooling our income and resources is all right, so far as it goes, but, damn it, we still lack social legitimacy."

I tried to find the words to express the daydream shaping in my mind. "If we're going to survive the social upheaval we're creating, there should be some way we could get married in a civil ceremony as two couples." Tanya was piling clothes in the washing machine as I continued. "If there were such a form of marriage, approved by the state, I think a lot of people would find it a solution for their problems. At least, those who didn't agree could only say we were insane, not immoral or illegal."

Tanya whistled. "You've been reading too many of Horace's books. Most females wouldn't take the risk of sharing their husbands."

"You and I have."

"Maybe we're crazy. I've noticed, though, in the past four weeks since we've been eating meals together, that you're getting a little sloppier and I'm getting a little neater. That's a marriage I never thought we'd achieve!"

I laughed. "Since we aren't in competition for the males, we're becoming happier females. While I don't see eye to eye with you on many things, and I know I'm more of a worrier

211

than you are, somehow I actually love you." I blushed. "I suppose that's a dumb thing to say to another female."

Tanya's eyes glistened. "Oh, Nancy!" She hugged me quickly. "I need you, too. It's strange. Sometimes I feel like an older sister, protective toward you, and yet I know it's mutual. I'm the dopey one who leans on you."

"Still," I persisted, "if there was such a legal marriage arrangement, it would give us protection against the Sylvia Mais and Betty Vinsons. Betty is still working for David. How do you know Horace isn't continuing his afternoons with Sylvia?"

"My God!" Tanya beamed at me. "Maybe, but I doubt it. I suppose as a last recourse we could compare notes. But my hunch is neither David nor Horace has enough stamina to keep three women satisfied, even if they wanted to try. Anyway, they're so ecstatically happy with the whole adventure of their new family that I don't think it's a problem. At the moment, I think the children should be our only major concern. It's obvious that Sam and Susan, if not Jimmy and Mitch, know that the four of us act differently toward each other than other families do toward their friends." Tanya shrugged. "Since I doubt if the four of us will live to see the day when we're legal, I think we should face the problem of the kids head on. We have to tell them; they have to understand that the details of our family, even playing around naked together, are not for publication."

Of course Tanya was right, though the challenge was not only to make them understand, but also to create an environment that would give them a strength and security, a way of life they could believe in should we ever be exposed to public controversy, as I was sure we must be. Tanya and I agreed that spontaneous affection expressed with bodily contacts would help in the reconditioning process. All four of us had been raised in an atmosphere where overt emotions were rarely revealed. Just plain happy hugging, face rubbing, or tears of joy in our eyes because we liked each other were considered embarrassing or unfashionable.

At first the children thought we were silly when we snuggled them good-bye in the morning. They watched curiously when we embraced Horace and David, urging them to hurry home because we would be lonesome. Tanya and I pecked them all on the lips and cheeks, while we ranted with any joyous nonsense that crossed our minds. Within a few weeks even Susan, who at first starchily withdrew from the confusion of good-byes and hellos, joined the fray, hugging Tanya and Horace as cheerfully as she did David and me. The men complained that it was taking as much as ten minutes to leave and even longer to be welcomed home, yet they had to admit that our first constrained attempts at affection had passed into a spontaneous nuttiness they looked forward to. While the warm feeling of belonging may not have been intellectualized by the children, it was obvious they were responding enthusiastically to the communal atmosphere.

In the crazy-quilt pattern of the life we were stitching together, Tanya's pregnancy and the coming baby became a continuing subject of dinner-time discussion. Tanya had reluctantly gone to a local doctor for prenatal care, but he had tried to make her give up her determination to have a natural childbirth. One night late in February when David arrived home, he seemed unusually effervescent. Having kissed me good-bye first in the morning, he reversed the order—hugged Tanya, felt her belly and pulled us both down on the floor while he tumbled with the kids. I smelled his breath and told Tanya he hadn't been drinking. Horace arrived in the middle of the confusion and joined us, remarking to David that he must have sold a new account.

"Nope, business was just its dull self," David said as we sat down to eat. "I've a surprise for Tanya, though, but I'll tell you all about it later." He sipped a glass of tomato juice and grinned at the kids. "I was wondering on the way home if you all knew where Tan's baby really came from."

Tanya and I looked at each other in shocked silence. Was David going to tackle the impossible without consulting with us? He glanced at us indulgently, as if to say the time had come to let a business tycoon handle the problem.

"Sure," Sam grinned back at him. "Ace planted a seed in her belly."

I couldn't help laughing. Let the big boss wiggle out of that one.

"Do you know how a female gets pregnant?"

Susan smiled knowingly at Jimmy, but didn't say anything. Then to my surprise, Jimmy answered. "Sure, when people get married they go to bed and make love."

Tanya gasped at the next question. "Do you know *how* a man and woman make love?"

"They kiss each other," Mitch suggested.

"That's not all," Susan said, showing her superiority. "A man puts his penis inside the woman. He has seed there, and a woman has an egg inside her." She smiled at me. "Sea told me all about it. It happens when they get married, and that's why people get married."

"They don't have to get married to do that," Sam said, "but I guess they should."

213

I was getting increasingly nervous. Where was David going? How far?

Horace, quite fascinated, joined the discussion. "Why do you think they should get married?"

Sam shrugged. "I don't know, and I don't think I'll get married. Girls are a pain in the neck."

Horace laughed. "You'll probably change your mind. In the next few years you'll slowly discover you need a girl as much as she needs you to complete yourselves as human beings. You both may want to make love. When Tan and I were about twenty-two, we made love. Eventually you and Mitch came to life in her belly. So marriage is a kind of agreement between a man and woman who are willing to work together and love the babies they make together and take care of them. It would be a very bad world if men just pushed their seed inside a woman's belly and after a while a baby was born, and then neither the man nor the woman wanted to love their baby or take care of it."

"I don't understand why a man wants to put his penis inside a girl, anyway." Jimmy said this as if the answer wasn't important one way or the other.

David smiled. "Nobody really knows the answer to that. All we know is everything male in life wondrously wants to merge with everything female. Someday, when a girl says, 'I love you, too, Jimmy,' it will be the most joyous thing that ever happened to you. That's why Ace and I are both so happy. We discovered that Sea and Tan love us both, and we both love them."

I could see that Sam and Susan were a little bewildered now that the fat was in the fire. "It doesn't happen in every family, honey," I said. "You know that we've been friends for a long time. Gradually, we discovered that Ace loved me, and that Dave loved Tan. Not only did we all love each other, but we loved you kids, too." I couldn't help blushing at the simplicity of this statement that explained everything and nothing.

Mitch grinned. "On television, when the daddy loves somebody else, the mother cries and gets pretty mad."

I silently applauded Mitch for his perspicacity; nine-year-olds certainly knew the score. For a moment David seemed unsure of himself. "In this family," he finally said, "we believe that a father can love another mother and father. I love Tan and I love Sea. Sometimes Ace makes love with Sea. The baby that Tan is going to have came to life because my seed fertilized the egg in Tan's belly."

Tanya and I both gasped at David's sudden revelation, and I noticed that Tanya's face was flushed. "It's kind of compli-

214

cated." She stumbled trying to find words. "I don't think you kids have to understand it, just that in our family, with all of us together, it's a very nice thing."

I was watching the children's faces. They continued to eat and didn't seem perturbed or alarmed. How much did they really understand?

Horace took another tack. "We've decided to build a new home, a great big one for all of us so that we can all live together. How would you like that?"

"Can Sam and I have a room together?" Jimmy asked excitedly. "That would be a lot more fun."

"You boys could have a big bedroom together." Tanya smiled. "And a couple of other rooms for hobbies and junk."

"I hope Tan has a girl," Susan stated emphatically. "There's too many boys in this family." She stared at me with sudden interest. "Did Ace or Daddy make me inside of you?"

I blushed. "Daddy did. He helped make you and Jimmy."

"Why did he make another baby inside Tan? Why didn't he make it inside you?"

We were hoist by our own petard, and Susan, by reverting to calling David "Daddy," had revealed her own uncertainty and confusion. Now I was sure David had carried the discussion too far. Shocked, not knowing how to answer, I looked querulously at David and Tanya.

"Daddy loves Tan, too," I said lamely.

"Could Ace make a baby inside you?" Sam demanded.

I ignored Horace's huge grin. "I suppose so, honey, if we all decide we need another baby."

"Then you should marry Ace," Susan said very matter-of-factly. "And Dave should marry Tan. Is there any ice cream for dessert?"

Horace, Tanya, David, and I burst into laughter; we had crossed over the chasm. The demons, frothing smoke and fire in the gorge below, would have to wait for the next adventurers.

We were so happily self-assured as we cleared the dishes that David felt in the mood for challenging dragons. "I've solved another problem, today," he told us coolly. "I found out that Betty Vinson had her baby using the Lamaze technique, and a Doctor Harry Schacht in Beverly Hills knows the method inside out. He's going to telephone tomorrow."

Tanya intercepted my startled glance. Was there some substance in my fears? "For God's sake, David," she said angrily. "Do you discuss your family business with your secretary?"

"Of course not. I just mentioned that my wife was pregnant and was interested in natural childbirth."

"It seems a damned odd thing to discuss with a female you claim that you're not really interested in," I said coldly. "Now that you've pinned Tanya and me down, I suppose you're looking for new fields to conquer."

David refused to be rebuked. "I made love with Betty once in a hopeless mood and because of circumstances I hope never to experience again. I explained to her weeks ago that she had been a good friend and that I didn't regret the evening, but that on the other hand I didn't need a mistress or a new wife. I told her my marital problems had been solved, that my wife was pregnant and I was delighted." David grinned at Tanya and me. "Good God, I have two women to take care of my sexual needs now. What do you think I am, a satyr?"

"Am I the pregnant wife?" I demanded.

David looked puzzled.

"Obviously, Doctor Schacht is going to telephone Mrs. Herndon."

David chuckled. "I never gave it a thought. You can make the appointment for Tanya."

Horace joined the discussion. "I suppose eventually Tanya will have to tell him her surname, fill out forms and what not." He tugged his ear reflectively. "In any event, what name will the poor waif have on the birth certificate?"

"Let's not make it complicated," Tanya said. "The baby's last name has to be Herndon, unless we decide to combine our family names. I'll tell the doctor the truth. He has to know it anyway; otherwise why should you all be in attendance?"

My protests that we hadn't fully warned the children about what they could or couldn't say about their family, and my surprise at David's and Horace's calm acceptance that Tanya's baby would have to carry the Herndon name got lost in David and Horace's worry about the propriety of having the children watch Tanya give birth. Horace doubted that any doctor would permit an audience. Even if he would, watching could be a traumatic experience for the children.

David suggested we feel our way along and that, for a starter, it would certainly do no harm to study the whole birth process with them. Horace had numerous books showing the successive stages as the baby moved through the womb during labor. Tanya had recently purchased a book by Dr. Pierre Velay entitled *Childbirth without Pain* that had numerous detailed photographs of all stages of labor. As she pointed out, "If they see pictures like these, and we discuss the amazing mystery of birth, and they see the expressions of joy and wonder of these mothers in labor, I think they'll identify with me." Tanya grinned. "Most people think a woman in stirrups, with her legs spread, and the baby emerging from her womb is ugly, or is somehow related to nasty sex. I don't think we should bring our children up that way. This is maybe our last opportunity, unless Sea changes her mind, and we have another kid."

We couldn't come to an agreement. The children lived in the world as it was; how far could we go toward a greater sanity? As Horace pointed out, like it or not, most adults never witnessed birth. If anything went wrong, it could be quite grueling.

Tanya laughed. "All four kids and the entire Materi brood sat with the Materis' female cat last year. The cat went into labor about three in the afternoon, and she had a hell of a time. According to Mitch and Sam, she even ate a bite between stages. Two kittens, a lot of meowing and wandering around—Mrs. Materi even told the kids that the second litter was probably the product of a second father—and then three more kittens!"

I remembered. Susan and Jimmy were ecstatic. We still had Spook, one of the black angora males. Really, wasn't Tanya right? Why shouldn't the child, maturing in a society where the facts of life were happily more honest, see the birth of a fellow human being? One day these same kids would be involved in the end of the amazement—death!

Tanya hugged Horace and David, and squeezed my hand. "Please go along with me; I'm not inviting you to an execution. Every damned step of the way, even if I'm groaning, I'll be entranced at the miracle of me and us."

Chapter 12

In March we were all arrested for immoral behavior, adultery, wife-swapping and generally subverting the morals of the community. As I try to sort out the kaleidoscopic confusion that whirled me onto television, launched Proposition Thirty-One, made a cause célèbre out of the Herndon-Shea ménage, got Horace and Sylvia suspended from California Institute of Sociology, and enraged Peter and Fritzi Alberti so thoroughly that they became champions of corporate marriage, I'm still amazed that we managed to survive the buffetings of the tempest we created.

In a way, the spectacle of eight of us, wrapped in Tanya's blankets and sheets, stark naked and barefoot, being herded by irate policemen through a crowd of grinning neighbors to a paddy wagon parked in front, had a kind of insane humor. As David insisted sarcastically to Peter, the wheel had come full turn. It was only poetic justice that the Albertis had to suffer from the follies of the Herndons and Sheas. Peter and Jun Makura, a new acquaintance, both of them flushed and angry, ignored him. Naked and sadly ineffectual against the uniformed representatives of the law, while the rest of us were still too dismayed except to shuffle in open-mouthed embarrassment, they argued in vain with the police. They claimed that the officers, by bursting into our home without cause, had flagrantly invaded our privacy. Peter's flat statement that he'd put the ass of the entire Police Department in a sling was no appeal to sanity. One of the police coolly retorted, "Brother, when we're through with the fucking lot of you, you won't have an ass to sit on."

They wouldn't let us put on our clothes. A policewoman, who had come with them, emerged from Tanya's bedroom. "We want you the way we found you," she said as she thrust blankets and sheets at us. She was obviously horrified at our nudity, though she coldly accepted the lascivious grins of the male supporters of the law. Her arms protectively around Susan, Jimmy, Mitch, and Sam, she watched in gothic anger as, to the wailing of sirens, we were taken off to jail.

I suppose it's my New England upbringing. I've always

been a "private" person. Even in college, when I often agreed wholeheartedly with some of the radical ideas of the fringe groups, I couldn't join them vocally. I often imagined myself as an active feminist, espousing unpopular causes, nationally famous because of my dynamic leadership; but this was Nancy the dreamer, not the real Nancy. In reality, like most females, I found it easier to conform. I kept my unpopular thoughts to myself and rationalized that it wasn't the female's job to change the world. She had a difficult enough time maintaining equilibrium in a world governed by men whose optical nerves were conditioned to recognize only black and white. It wasn't the female prerogative to see gray.

Of course I was quite certain that the idea of corporate marriage and the sexual exchange the four of us were practicing would attract wide interest, much of it prurient, if it were known. We all realized that if we overcautioned the children we would put them in the defensive position that their family was not quite normal. Tanya and I had quietly tried to make them aware that our neighbors might not understand our group nudity or our marital exchange. Yet, with David, Horace, and Tanya, I seemed to be fighting a losing battle. Their bland belief that we shouldn't live our lives shrouded in a veil of secrecy was in direct contrast to my own feelings. The less known about us the better, I thought. It's amusing that when the top blew off we reversed our roles. Somewhere, unknown to me, there was a snarling tigress buried deep in the old Nancy. Now our family was threatened. Our only hope was to come out snarling, claws bared.

The week before I was still on the defensive. When Horace coolly told us that Sylvia and a friend of hers, Jun Makura, a young lawyer, were fascinated by our corporate marriage and wanted to meet Tanya and me, he awoke all the dragons that had been nagging me. I accused Horace and the others of not giving a damn who they told about us. I even suggested they were adopting the typical self-justification of the criminal, that we were right and the world was all wrong.

"Why don't you take an advertisement in the Los Angeles Times," I demanded, amazingly predicting something I would be doing myself in less than three months. "Why not let the whole world know the delights of communal fornication?"

Horace poured us each a Scotch. "It's Friday night. You might as well relax, Sea, and listen to the whole story." He calmly explained that Sylvia had become a day-to-day confidante (and advisor?) to the Herndon-Shea household, and he said we had to understand that she was his colleague. Also, Frank Kitman had finally given approval for an experimental course on pornography.

219

"We'll work with a small group of seniors in the final quarter," Horace said. "It occurred to me all of us might enjoy an evening discussing our approaches. Sylvia feels, since we all have children, we may be able to project the reaction of older students and their families. We want to interpolate the readings into the whole structure of their lives and value experiences."

I had no sooner made a mental concession to the logic of knowing Sylvia, so that I could survey our potential competition in person, than David lighted the fuse in the next bomb. "You'll like Sylvia and Jun; I met them today," he said. David slouched in his chair, looking at me speculatively over the rim of the glass. He was obviously preparing for a return barrage. "Horace and I went to lunch with them. Peter Alberti came along. He was so fascinated he finally insisted on paying the check."

Even Tanya shivered a little at that revelation.

"Peter Alberti!" I yelled. "For God's sake, I mean what the hell are the two of you mixed up with him for?" I glared at them. "You must be absolutely insane!"

David gave me a condescending and aggravating smile. I felt like pummeling him. "Really, Sea, for a former English major your question lacks a certain formal structure. I hope the book you are writing about us has better grammatical construction." I restrained myself and didn't throw my drink at him. "It's really quite simple," he continued. "Jun Makura is one of Alberti's lawyers. Neither Horace nor I knew this until a few days ago. Wednesday, after a few minutes' conversation with Henry Cavers, who has handled legal work for Herndon Showcase, I decided the whole concept of the Herndon-Shea Corporation was too much for him. His ideas of property, and its relation to love and marriage, are Victorian. He suggested the four of us see a psychiatrist and divorce lawyer, in that order."

I'm sure I only partially grasped David's words. The image of Peter and his blatant wife loomed like a huge red danger signal in my mind. At the moment, all I could comprehend was that the privacy of our lives really existed only in my mind. Sylvia was not only fully informed, but she had obviously told everything to her boyfriend, who had told his boss, Peter Alberti. It was the beginning of a mathematical progression that would quickly embrace all of Southern California.

"I think you are both out of your minds," I said, frightened to the point of tears. "Everything we're attempting depends on privacy. The first thing you know, reporters will be ringing our doorbells. I can see us now, sophisticated wife-swappers, splashed all over the Sunday supplements."

Horace tried to soothe me. "Really, Sea, you're making mountains out of molehills. When David told me we needed a young lawyer who would enjoy twisting the law slightly to make room for us in this changing world, I mentioned it to Sylvia, who suggested Jun. Jun is about thirty and has a keen mind. You can absolutely stop worrying about Sylvia. First, I'm sure she's in love with Jun. Second, like David, I haven't the desire or energy to attempt a liaison with a third female. I'm quite happy and preoccupied with the fascinating problem of two women and the interplay between all four of us. What we've already got is complicated enough to last a lifetime. Third, Sylvia's attitude toward us is that of a mother who is responsible for her brood. She's not only intrigued with us as a unique sociological experiment, but she feels partially involved."

"I know," I interrupted angrily. "She made you go to Boston to seduce me. Next thing you'll be asking Alberti to be godfather. You won't think it's so damned funny when he tries to go to bed with Tanya or me."

David was amused. "According to your story, when you demurred, Alberti acted quite the gentleman. I can't say I blame him for trying, but if you have a hankering for Peter, maybe Horace and I can arrange it."

For a second I couldn't help smiling. "I'm glad I'm sleeping with you this week. You'll pay for that!"

Horace was choking with laughter. "You didn't let David finish. He was about to say, we'd arrange it next Friday. Peter, Fritzi, Sylvia, and Jun are coming to a backyard barbecue." Horace's words faded to a whisper as he saw my astonished expression. "David and I'll do the cooking," he said uneasily.

"You can eat without me. I won't be there." I was more than shocked; I was appalled. Even though both men hastened to explain that Peter was quite interested in our ideas for a new kind of group-family home and might even be persuaded to finance and build it, and that Friday would simply be an evening of discussion, I had a queasy feeling that David and Horace, having broken down the sexual barriers between the four of us, might feel, what the hell, a further enlargement of our group would be harmless. I voiced my feelings in no uncertain terms.

"Do you really approve of this, Tanya?" I demanded. "The first thing you know, you'll be in the sack with this lawyer, Horace will be curled up with Sylvia Mai, Fritzi Alberti will be seducing David, and Peter will be chasing me around your

221

swimming pool. Later we'll be expected to play group grope while we all fuck together."

Tanya only grinned at me. "Really, Sea, I think you're exaggerating a little. This is our joint house. We can keep things under control. Anyway," she laughed, "I don't have to worry. At the moment I'm not particularly glamourous. Anyone who wants me would have to be content with rear entry position. 'Please be careful; don't disturb the baby, and please hurry!' Kidding aside, I do agree with you, wholeheartedly. What we're involved in definitely isn't monogamy. Any extracurricular sexual activity affects three other people, not just one. I think it would devalue us all." She smiled at Horace and David, who were listening closely. "You've both traded philandering for the absolute security and certain delights of two different bed-mates. Any more are out!"

Gradually, after David's opening gambit with the children, we had arranged a Sunday-through Saturday alternation of bed partners. Tanya and I were the queen bees of our own bedrooms. While this created some inconvenience for the men, who once a week shifted their clothing from house to house, mostly they complained about our combined washing program, which often ended up with their discovering they were wearing each other's underwear or socks. The children took naturally to the changing bed scene. Saturdays and Sundays, when we often slept later than they did, they ran courier service between the houses, indiscriminately, and without waiting for invitations, bursting into our bedrooms and tumbling in bed with us in groups of two or four. On weekends, all eight of us reunited for a naked plunge in the Shea pool.

The week before our marital dream erupted in a nightmare was my Horace week. Since I had been unable to alarm David or Tanya about our coming Friday evening, I took the opportunity to harass Horace with my doubts.

His patience was formidable. "Sea, we've taken a giant step. David knows it. I know it. You and Tanya have nothing to fear. While the four of us, interacting on each other, have severed the chains of monogamous marriage, I think we're all constantly aware of each other, not as owned husbands and wives, but as individuals. The we-are-alone atmosphere of two married people trying to forge a life together in this madly confused world has vanished. I think the idea of the four of us is giving us a unique strength and confidence. something we've never had before. What's more, I have no doubt, because every day we *dare* a little more to be the individuals we really are, that David and Tanya and you feel exactly the same way. In the process, sex and love have blended into a new component. You love me and I love you, but our surrender is enlarged and magnified in the larger cohesive factor of the four of us united as a meaningful family. No outsider could possibly give David or me the sexual satisfaction we have with you and Tanya." Horace kissed me, silently tracing with his fingers the curves of my breasts, back, and behind. He looked at me with tears in his eyes. "Sea, are you aware how you've changed? How Tanya has changed? Not competitively, but each realizing yourselves? Yet you have one wondrous thing in common—a lovely, warm, laughing affection. David and I've discussed it. We're not such Utopians that we'd be willing to blend our economic lives if we didn't believe we were doubly lucky in having two women who love us. Most men scarcely have one."

While Horace played the devil's advocate for Peter Alberti, my fingers fluttered lightly over his penis, though I was careful not to excite him too much. "I told Peter I wasn't for or against his S.O.S. parties," he said. "I simply doubt their validity for any human being, just as I doubt the value of licensing prostitution. Any individual, even of low intelligence, ultimately is disgusted with himself by mechanical surrender. God, the human spirit, call it what you will, whatever drives us, comes to life and demands a deeper interaction. You can't use sex as a mad kick to fend off boredom. When I suggested that to Peter at lunch the other day, he agreed with me. On the other hand, he can't believe we're quite sane, either."

Horace tasted my nipples, and his words drifted into a whisper. "Next Friday will be an interesting experience. As our intense self-involvement diminishes, the four of us really have to join the world again." His tongue traced my clitoris in a featherlike touch. A warm murmur expressed his delight at my reciprocal kisses. If we had to join the world, it was good to retreat from it, too. Maybe it was even nicer to float forever, walk on tiptoes along a precipice, sway dizzily over the sheer drop below; fascinated, holding back and yet unable to delay the inevitable plunge. Oh, my God! Hold on! I raked his back, clutched his behind hard against me; shrieking, sobbing my joy, I sailed with him over the cliff. YES! YES! All for love and the world well lost!

Chapter 13

~~~~~~~~~~

While Horace looked forward to Friday as an opportunity to test our defenses, David and Tanya were scarcely so subjective.

"It's a business deal, Sea," David insisted. "Alberti is one of the biggest contractors in Los Angeles, and he owns a half-dozen high rise apartment buildings. What's more, he's very much involved in one of these new-city projects. With his interest in the changing concepts of community housing, I think he'll be intrigued with the design of our corporate home."

Caught up in the enthusiastic hope that Jun Makura might solve the problems of incorporation, and might even entice Peter into financing and constructing our new home, I shoved my fears into a remote corner of my brain and worked with Tanya on a final draft of the floor plans for our two-generation home.

Even though with our combined resources we could afford a substantial mortgage, I was against creating a house that was financially beyond most middle-class income levels. It wasn't only that I felt we could use the mortgage money and interest we saved more constructively, but that, without saying so, I was obsessed with the feeling that many other couples might actually believe in what we were doing and want to follow in our footsteps. I had no real idea how this might happen. I scarcely foresaw that the invitation of the Albertis, Sylvia, and Jun Makura would end up in a mad party that would transform my daydream into a frightening reality.

Our final plan for a Living Home * that could expand or contract to meet our needs called for a one-story, approximately half-circular structure set about twenty feet off center on the bisecting diagonals on a minimum twenty-thousand-square-foot lot. The outside wall would have a radius of sixty feet, and the inside wall a radius of forty feet. This half-circular structure could ultimately embrace the entire rear of

* A floor plan and perspective drawings of the Living Home may be found in the back of this book.

the lot, enclosing about six thousand square feet of outdoor space. At the beginning, the amount of floor space in this area would give us more than adequate bedroom and extra playroom space for the children, as well as two master bedrooms of about five hundred square feet apiece, each with a bath. All bedrooms would have sliding glass-window walls facing into an outdoor center with gardens, a large swimming pool, and a jungle play area, on the outer perimeter, heavily planted with trees. If we ever needed additional rooms, they could be added on the ends of the half circle, finally enclosing it into a full circle, if desired.

Nearly tangent to this half circle would be a similar fifth-circle, flanking the corner of the lot. This partial circle, based on a radius of fifty-five feet for the inner wall and thirty feet for the outer wall, would leave room for a circular drive in the front of the house. Facing onto this circular drive, on one end of the smaller circle, would be the kitchen, with its own entrance off the drive, and a window-wall living-room area. The kitchen area would be approximately five hundred square feet, and the living-room area, which we planned for a general family and entertainment area, would be twelve hundred square feet. On the kitchen side, where the smaller circle abutted the half circle, there would be a dining room of approximately five hundred square feet. On the opposite side, adjoining the living room, would be a library and music room equal in size to the dining room.

Our house "flowed," pulling us together as a family, and dissolving us when any of us desired privacy. It would be possible to use the living area for entertaining without involving conflicting age-groups, and to keep the library, the bedrooms, and other rooms on the inner circle available for privacy. The large dining area and the kitchen would involve the entire family in the preparation of meals.

With the great improvements in cement-block construction, David was certain that the exterior walls, a merging combination of glass and random color blocks, could be built inexpensively. Our Living Home would embrace us in a continuity of both indoor and outdoor living.

Tanya and I discussed the conjunction and privacy of the two master bedrooms. Since, in our matriarchal setup, Horace and David would travel between Tanya's room and mine, it seemed convenient to locate them next to each other. While access to either room could be from the outdoor area through the sliding glass walls, or from the dining-room area, we were in laughing agreement that the dividing wall should be sound-proofed.

My only fears were the land cost. Since we were constructing for two families, we were allotting only a typical ten thousand square feet per family. But in a world of increasing population, with the urban crowding and willingness of people to accept compression, we wondered if we could get the land we wanted within reasonable commuting distance. A few weeks later Peter came up with a unique solution for that problem.

I couldn't shake the feeling that Peter's interest in the Herndon-Shea family was a little like the curiosity of the medieval baron toward the peasants on his estate. I even suspected that his trip from the luxury of Santa Monica Hills to our middle class neighborhood was in the nature of a slumming expedition. But I couldn't dampen David's or Horace's enthusiasm.

By nine o'clock Friday night, when the Albertis still hadn't arrived, they were a little less sanguine. At last Tanya received a phone call from a woman who identified herself as Fritzi, saying not to give up, they would be a little late.

Tanya was amused. "Maybe she's as nervous as you are," she said to me.

"That's all we need," I replied. I watched Sylvia and Jun Makura, who had arrived at seven o'clock and calmly joined the kids, swimming naked and happily with them in the pool, while Horace, David, Tanya, and I, all still properly dressed for a backyard barbecue, couldn't make up our minds whether to join them, and thus be faced with the problem of welcoming Peter and Fritzi in our birthday suits. "If the Albertis arrive half crocked," I said to Sylvia and Jun, "you both better put on your clothes in a hurry. There's going to be no S.O.S. party in this house!"

Sylvia, who had been helping Horace and David tuck the children in bed in the Herndon house, where we decided they would be out of the confusion of the party, had just pattered across the lawn between the two houses, her perfect brown breasts swaying lightly against her chest. I wondered how Horace or David could resist the temptation to touch. Tanya didn't seem to be bothered with Sylvia's assumption of our maternal duties.

Now Sylvia lay on a pool-side chair and grinned happily at me. Abruptly, in a point-blank defenseless way that has become a way of living with all of our friends, she said, "I know we've only known each other two hours, Nancy, but I've a feeling you're a little antagonistic toward me. Why?"

I shrugged, neither affirming nor denying. When Sylvia and Jun arrived, Sylvia had quickly hugged Tanya and me. But the gesture was lost in my queasy memories of Boston, where

Horace first told me about Sylvia. She was breathtakingly, coolly, a lovely woman. Her almond eyes, full lips and light brown oval face were an exotic mixture that was enhanced by the unsophisticated girlishness of her manner. Horace had slept with this beautiful woman; any man would want to. At least Jun, a six-foot blend of Japanese and white American blood, who hugged Tanya and me with an unforced joy, telling us he loved us both for our daring to live, counterbalanced Sylvia. In contrast, the four of us seemed quite homespun and unglamorous.

Near the pool, while Horace was making drinks and David was lighting the charcoal, Horace had suggested it would be interesting to see if we could bypass the usual social amenities and plunge into intimate, defenseless conversation. "Most people are afraid to speak the thoughts they think without censorship," he had told Sylvia and Jun. "In the past five months the four of us have become convinced that defenseless thinking is the sine qua non of survival."

Tanya's opener had a breathtaking simplicity. She smiled coolly at Sylvia. "Nancy and I are scared to death of you," she had said. "I presume Jun knows you've slept with Horace. We wonder if you still have an occasional rendezvous."

Sylvia's face sparkled with good humor, and to my surprise Jun didn't seem shocked. "Once Horace needed me," she had replied. "Not for sex alone, Tanya, but for an amalgamation of sex and intimacy. Isn't that really the key to sexual satisfaction? Horace and you had lost intimacy; the innermost, intrinsic self of each of you withdrew a little. The minute that happens in a relationship, each person becomes even more encased in his basic loneliness." Sylvia looked straight into my eyes. "And then the search is on. I think the search for intimacy is equal to the sexual drive, and that it's unfortunate they rarely coincide. Even Jun and I haven't fully bridged the gap. Isn't that what impelled you toward David, Tanya?" Lost in her thoughts for a moment, Sylvia had watched the kids swimming in the pool. "Amazingly, the four of you seem to have solved the problem. To answer your question, Nancy, I can't give Horace anything he isn't getting far better than I could give it to him."

Jun had smiled. "Sylvia's warning you. She thinks if she finally agrees to marry me, within a few years we might realize ourselves better in a similar arrangement. I still feel it's quite Utopian. What amazes me most is that females, if they have security, apparently aren't quite so possessive as males."

Sylvia laughed. "We've had centuries of conditioning. Females owned by males have only had one way to express their resentment! Give themselves to another male. Good

Lord, I envy the kids. I haven't swum naked since the Alberti party. Do you mind if I join them?"

In a twinkling Sylvia had slipped out of her dress, bra, and panties. To the delight of Susan, Mitch, Sam, and Jimmy she dove into the pool with them and exhorted us to join her. Jun shrugged at Horace, who gave him the go-ahead. Fearing the imminent arrival of the Albertis, we watched them frolic. Strangely, I felt more inhibited dressed than I would have undressed.

An hour later, shrugging good-naturedly at my comments that Sylvia, naked, was an open invitation to Peter for fun and games, Sylvia and Jun lounged near the pool and asked searching questions about our living arrangements. With the amazing ease acquired from professional training, Jun led me into a confession. Yes, I was afraid; not of our marital arrangements or that we couldn't cope with our internal problems, but that the outside world would screw us up. "We're not legal," I told him nervously, half distracted by the thought that the doorbell might ring any minute (and then what should we do; invite the Albertis to take their clothes off?) and by Horace, who, not a bit concerned about our unknown neighbors on the hill, had turned on the floodlights.

"Since we're being totally honest," I told Sylvia finally, "I think you and Jun should get dressed. You asked me why I felt antagonistic toward you. You give me the impression that you're showing off." I ignored Tanya's sharp intake of breath. "You knew damned well, when you took your clothes off, every penis in the crowd shivered a little in delight."

I've learned since that nothing pleases Sylvia more than a frontal attack. "If that's true, I'm delighted," she said calmly. "I'm sure you and Tanya could have created the same sensation, and I'm elated the male enjoys seeing the female naked. I'm not afraid to say I enjoy the sight of Jun's maleness; it gives me a warm feeling to see the essential fragility of his body. If his penis is stirring just a little, he still knows that at the moment I'm content that it's flaccid. Many people think that nudity should be reserved for the bedroom. If it weren't, they believe sexual desire would gradually disappear. That's quite silly, really." She looked at Tanya. "I know none of you believe that anyway. Horace has told me you're often naked together. Well, group nudity is not intimacy. Final intimacy between a male and a female quickly restores the sexual drive. While Jun and I haven't asked you yet, I'll wager that you and Tanya wouldn't wish to copulate in front of one another or together with Horace and David as a foursome."

Sylvia's challenge was punctuated by the doorbell chiming impatiently. "I still wouldn't want to greet Peter and his wife naked," I told her sarcastically. "Why don't *you* answer the door?"

To my amazement, Sylvia scrambled up the back stairs to the living room. I shrugged at Tanya's amused smile. Soon Peter, fully dressed in a light-green Italian suit, sauntered into the yard, followed by Fritzi in a sheer yellow dress printed with surrealist flowers, her dyed blond hair faultlessly puffed. Sylvia, naked, brought up the rear. I quickly gulped my fourth Scotch. Spying Jun naked, Peter boomed, "What the hell is going on? Are the two of you putting on a show while the others watch?"

Fritzi, smirking, held my hand, "So you're the baby Peter tried to screw?" All of them merged in a blur of my temporarily contained wrath.

"Sorry we missed your cookout," Peter said as he embraced me with a fatherly hug; he held me almost a minute before I managed to squirm out of his grasp. "I got tied up with an afternoon crowd that hasn't left our place yet."

Glaring at him, I restrained a scorching comment as to why he bothered to come anyway. I sensed it wouldn't do any good. Peter had transferred his attention to Tanya, coolly passing his hand in appreciation over her swollen belly. "So you're the Shea half of this nutty ménage. Next time you should take your pills! Why haven't you taken off your clothes?" He laughed good-naturedly as he took the drink David offered him. "I haven't seen a thoroughly pregnant naked female since Fritzi was expecting. My God, Horace, this house of yours is a shit box. I know that damned Greek, Nick Finos, who contracted this area. He just slapped them together. It's a wonder they survived the November rains. Let a good quake come, and every damned house will slide down in the harbor." Swaying on the edge of the swimming pool, he ignored David and Horace's hopeless expressions, and kicking the coping. "Christ, this crappy little pool isn't big enough to take a bath in. Look, the damned thing is eroding on you."

By this time Peter's high-handed takeover of our party had nearly boiled away the alcohol in my blood. Horace and David's attempts to divert him from an extended discussion of how peasants like us were being sold highly overvalued properties led him to give us a history of his youth and his extraordinary financial success. "I got where I am because I only stole from the rich," he said. Peter was obviously inflated with his own ego.

Slumped in a chaise, Fritzi smiled at him sarcastically. "Robin Hood Alberti, his friends call him, only sometimes with his bow and arrow he thinks he's Cupid."

Still standing on the edge of the pool, beaming at all of us, he focused on me with a huge grin. "Been taking any boat rides lately, Nancy Herndon?"

That did it; I gave him the push he was asking for. Unfortunately, as he tumbled over backward with a wild yell of dismay, he caught my arm. Screaming and pummeling him with my free hand, I went sputtering to the bottom with him. Elated that the party had livened up, Fritzi jumped in with us. In minutes Sylvia got her wish; Tanya, David, and Horace stripped off their clothes, and all eight of us were in the pool. If any of us had been completely sober we might have realized that our shrieking was alerting our neighbors, but at the moment we were too involved in our own silliness. We had broken through the communication barrier.

Chapter 14

〜〜〜

Squirming out of my soaking clothes, I was caught between tears and laughter. Peter insisted that my aggression proved that I really liked him. He doubled over with laughter as he piled his clothes in a soggy heap. Bending over the mess on his hands and knees, his behind in the air, his balls dangling, ignoring Fritzi and Sylvia, who giggled as they slapped his behind, he finally extricated his billfold from a coat pocket. He handed it to me. "Here's Fritzi's wedding present to the Herndon-Sheas." He exploded in laughter. "The marriage of the century. By God, I like you, Nancy. Fritzi always said I needed a daughter. I should have adopted you instead of trying to screw you." He sighed and slumped blissfully down on the flagstones, grinning at us as we peeled apart ten soaking one-thousand-dollar bills and laid them side by side on the edge of the pool.

Fritzi sensed that we considered Peter's flagrant gift the gesture of a half-crocked millionaire. "He means it, Nancy. I want you to have it; I made him take it out of the bank this morning." She hugged me, her naked breasts smothering me for a second. "You see, I wouldn't have minded wrecking some floozie with those pictures, but after Horace told me you had a couple of kids and were a damned nice person, I really gave Peter hell."

"Maybe you saved me as well as Peter," I told her. "He obviously didn't shanghai me for that boat ride."

Tanya, who was proudly showing her belly to Peter, explained that at the moment her baby wasn't kicking. She said she had an idea for the money. She sent David upstairs after the plans for our house, and unrolled them on the picnic table. "You keep the money, Peter." She giggled. "Buy these two crappy houses from us, and help us build our new home." In a few minutes we were all huddled around the table while Peter, still quite high, but remarkably lucid, at first insisted we were all quite mad, but then, in response to our enthusiasm, slowly became intrigued.

Just as our nervous tension had quickly given way to the hilarity of our dunking, so our natural gaiety now swiftly

231

merged into a deep interacting personal interest in each other's ideas. I was both surprised and exhilarated. Beyond our two-family nudity, it was my first experience with a larger group of men and women who were naked together. Tanya and I discussed it later. From the female standpoint perhaps there was some sexual interest and a comparison of the male penises, all of which were a little shrunken from their exposure to the cooling night air, but there was something else, too. There was an engulfing sense of wonder, as Sylvia had pointed out, at the essential fragility of the human being and his inability, shorn of clothing, to pretend or role-play something he really wasn't. Perhaps the deep reason that nudity has become popular is that we are living in an age when no man accepts another as infallible. We have the faint perception that man, without clothes, is quite humanly vulnerable. With nothing to lean on, he begins to recognize the universal human interdependence. We should make war naked.

Munching a dried-out steak sandwich that Tanya had warmed up for him, Peter rolled up the plans and gave them back to David without commitment. He flopped in one of the chaises. "I'll think about it. I never make a decision when I'm half-boiled." He grinned at Tanya and me. "Jesus, I don't believe the two of you can share Horace and David without coming to blows somewhere along the line. One of you is going to get more partial to one of the men. Fritzi doesn't even understand how you, Nancy, can accept Tanya's pregnant by *your* husband." Peter shook his head and compared our madness to his own daring, some thirty-five years ago, when he had bought several thousand acres of orange groves a few miles south of Hollywood and Vine. "But I only had the bank's money to lose; the four of you will lose your minds. Four human beings can't mesh their lives. All man wants of man is a temporary refuge. Then he backs off into his own damned selfishness." He looked in a kindly way at Fritzi, who was lying on an air cushion, her legs in the air on Jun's knees. Jun was sitting in a chair, and Fritzi's open crotch was completely visible to him. "Look at her." Peter chuckled. "At her age, she's still displaying her candy store. Thirty-six years ago I rescued her from the sad fate of a movie starlet. No damned talent; just sex. You'd never think she was the mother of two boys." Peter shrugged. "Damn it, Fritzi, I never have figured out what makes you tick."

Fritzi blew a puff of uninhaled smoke in the air. "That's why you haven't divorced me, sweetie. I'm an enigma. If it hadn't been for me, you'd be broke; I saved your money. If it hadn't been for me, you'd have lived like those Hollywood stars and pissed it away." She sighed and was silent a moment, lost in her thoughts. "Maybe these kids are right. They're not embarrassed to admit they need each other. They've learned, if they go looking for an eternity, that just plain sex isn't the answer. I'd rather have a big family and grandchildren drooling over me. Our boys are in their middle twenties. They live in the East to escape their vulgar parents. Maybe you'll let us adopt you." Fritzi's mood suddenly brightened. She shifted position and flicked David's penis with her big toe. "Hey, YOU! If I adopted your wife, would you snuggle with me a few afternoons a week? I promise Peter won't take any pictures."

It was impossible to get angry with Fritzi. Rambling on in a voice husky from too much drinking and cigarette smoking, she tried to convince David how good she was in the sack.

David grinned at her. "If I can call you Mommy when you cuddle me on those big tits, it's a deal."

Horace turned off the floodlights and lighted a pool-side flame. The unusually sultry spring night and too much drink had made us all languid, happy to drift along with the meandering conversation, which ranged from a detailed discussion of how Tanya and I could adjust ourselves to two different men, to an involved discussion in which the males disagreed with the females over the impossibility of two females ever being willing to be defenselessly honest with each other, especially in the kind of environment that the four of us had created.

"For Christ's sake, we all have to play games with each other," Peter said. "I'm five or six different people. Who I am at a particular moment depends on the situation and the company present. If the sharks I deal with knew that basically I was a happy little kid who likes to build sand castles instead of buildings, and prefers to rub bellies with females over anything else, they'd eat me up."

I guess it was Peter's confession that gave Sylvia her idea for a Catherine wheel. It was her version of a new method of creating group empathy. Jun had swung the conversation to the merits of marijuana over alcohol as a medicine to make human beings interact more easily with one another. He suggested that tomorrow, when we would all be suffering from hangovers, we remember that we could have achieved the same relatedness with pot, but without any aftereffects. Fritzi and Peter had tried marijuana, and Peter said he was damned if inhaling the weed into the depths of his lungs made him see things any more clearly or made him better able to emote with a group.

"I like booze," he said. "It reinforces my philosophy that you have to pay for your sins."

233

Sylvia suggested that Maharishi Mahesh, an Indian yogi and guru, had a more valid approach to life, through meditation. She said that Mahesh, like his predecessor, Swami Vivekananda, who came to the United States some hundred years ago, had a Vedantic philosophy. According to Mahesh, a half hour of meditation each day, fifteen minutes in the morning and the same at night, brought your desires in tune with nature, in accordance with the flow of creation. Properly understood, meditation was the only source of happiness. No form of stimulant, such as drugs or alcohol, could equal meditation.

David challenged Sylvia, telling her that all the crackpot panacea solutions like the Maharishi's were latched onto by neurotics. "California is full of quacks supported by bored housewives who don't really want to solve their problems. They just find it titillating to tell their friends that they really have the secret."

Sylvia calmly replied that our corporate marriage idea might be a chip off the same block.

"The difference is we aren't proselytizing for it," David answered. "At least, if we manage to keep Sea in check."

Fortified with another drink, we finally agreed to try Sylvia's Catherine wheel on Tanya's broadloom rugs. Of course, we should have got dressed, and we might have done so if Fritzi's clothes had not still been wet. But ascending the back stairs, with every male patting every female behind ahead of him, and all of us giggling and laughing at how silly we looked, we agreed with Sylvia that, anyway, getting dressed would defeat the purpose of her Catherine wheel.

All we had to do was lie head-to-head in a circle, and meditate. Because we were not facing each other, but were joined by holding hands, presumably our private thoughts would surface in a fantasy situation which Sylvia promised to provide if she ever managed to calm our silliness and stop our grumbling about the insanity of it. She finally got Horace on the floor, to his left Fritzi, then David, Tanya, Jun, me, Peter, and finally herself, all in a circle staring at the ceiling. "Now," she said, "if you'll be quiet and listen, the idea is that we can vocalize to a sympathetic unseen audience. If we succeed with the fantasy I'm going to give you, we can slide into each other's thoughts, expand them, or carry on our own track. Really, it's . . ."

Sylvia was about to say "fun" but, when the Albertis arrived, she had forgotten to lock the front door. The picture of us, hip to hip, leg to leg, holding hands, stark naked, our heads forming the hub of the wheel, will probably be appearing in sex-orgy magazines to torture us (or, as Horace now says, for us to laugh at) the rest of our lives.

The front door burst open. Flash bulbs popped, three policemen, one with a camera, the others with guns in their hands, and a policewoman the size of a female wrestler, shouted at us in wrathful triumph, "You're all under arrest!"

Chapter 15

Tanya told me she couldn't live long enough ever to forget our sudden transition from silly happiness to sheer horror. Our female screams of dismay and ineffectual clutching for anything to cover our nakedness drowned out the wrath of Peter and Jun, who were demanding, in gutter language, that our captors get out of our house.

While one of them held us at bay with a drawn revolver, coolly advising us we'd have a hell of a time proving it was an illegal search and entry, since John Vestal, one of our neighbors on the hill, and a former State Senator, was supposed to have sworn out the search warrant, the others tore the house apart, pulling out drawers and sniffing ashtrays. We were not only guilty of lewd and indecent exposure, having, as we were told, copulated in the back yard while our neighbors watched but, in addition, we had all been smoking pot and corrupting the morals of children.

The police paid no attention to Jun, who demanded to see the search warrant. They stared lasciviously at Tanya, me, Fritzi, and Sylvia as we cowered before their obvious sexual excitement. I had an eerie feeling that if it weren't for the moral commitment of their uniforms, their bull-like bellowing would have been a prelude to rape. "Jesus Christ," one of them gasped, touching Tanya's belly, "one of these pigs is pregnant. Damned near ready to drop it, too! Who in hell is the father?" he demanded, ignoring the tears on Tanya's cheeks.

"Group-fuckers don't give a shit who the father is," another advised him. "The whole lot of them should be run out of the state. This is just what Vestal has been looking for."

In near hysteria myself, I watched the policewoman lead the children, all in their pajamas, in through the front door. "Found them in the Herndon house next door," she announced as the kids, shrieking their fear and dismay, ran to Tanya and me. Their obvious fright and their bewildered fear and alarm as they realized their parents were going to be taken away in a police wagon reminded me of pictures I had seen of the Jews being ushered off to Belsen and Dachau while their friends watched. Jun and Peter, their penises bobbling in response to their wrath, shouted angrily that we were not guilty of any crime of misdemeanor, but they seemed sadly ineffectual.

The disgusting female representative of the law, bulging in her uniform, corralled the children. "Don't you worry," she told them imperiously, while she glared at us, "I'm staying here with you tonight. We aren't going to hurt your fathers and mothers; we're just going to teach them a little lesson. They're going to learn that they can't bring up children this way."

Unable to turn up anything immoral except the clothing we had discarded near the swimming pool and Peter Alberti's ten one-thousand-dollar bills still wet from their dunking, they shoved us down the front walk wrapped in blankets. At the curb a police wagon, its beacon nervously revolving, and a mobile television crew, recording the event, had attracted our neighbors from blocks away. But we evoked no sympathy, only silent disdain and hoots of laughter. After centuries of bloody wars against power gone amok, it is frightening how easily man casts his lot with the authority of the uniform. We had no defenders.

Five days later I appeared on the Joe Kraken Show, defending corporate marriage against a panel composed of the men who had instigated the raid, John Vestal and the Reverend Harvey Strate. In our age of instant mass-media exposure, it is possible for a complete nonentity such as myself, to become famous or notorious overnight. Perhaps if it weren't for the furious anger sustaining me, and the unforgettable picture of the children sobbing as they begged to go with us, I might have remembered my former shy self and been thoroughly frightened. But in less than ten minutes the old Nancy had been effectively erased. When I think about the indignity we suffered and the even greater provocations to which some of our Negro leaders have been subjected, I wonder if the police, with their new, so-called humane methods of subduing rioters, are aware of man's intrinsic need for dignity. Even if we were evil, if our actions were really against all standards of morality (I knew they weren't), we had an inalienable right to the respect of our fellow humans.

Huddled in the rear of the police wagon, with sheets and blankets our sole covering, only Peter, Jun, and myself were able to rise above stunned rage. Tanya was almost catatonic. "My God! My God!" she kept repeating. "The poor kids! Did you see the expressions on their faces? And that awful policewoman. What will she tell them?"

I knew that in the coming days their minds would be corrupted by a new and equivocal image of their fathers and mothers—a tarnished image of perverted parents who laughed at the sacredness of marriage as they sought a return to the Roman Saturnalias, with masses of females and males copulating together and reveling in a drunken orgy drenched in sweat and semen—pullulating bodies experimenting with every known sexual deviation from whipping to sodomy. It was a nightmarish vision, of course, but it had some truth in it, and I could not drive it from my mind.

Most people are easily cowed. Herding is one way; naked herding is even better, particularly when the victims have already undressed for you. Even Sylvia had lost her shell of youthful uncompromise, and was weeping on Jun's shoulder. Horace tried to reassure her that word of this evening would never reach Frank Kitman, but neither Sylvia nor Horace himself was convinced. Both knew that Sylvia was especially vulnerable: a person of Negro and Chinese descent would too nearly fit the middle class image of a far-out, nude, pot-smoking swinger. When the other suburbanites read about us in the newspapers the next day, they wouldn't think, "There, but for the grace of God, go I," but would congratulate themselves that their own transgressions were minor by comparison.

"There's more to this than meets the eye," Jun told us. "One of those cops mentioned John Vestal. Vestal was involved with Proposition Sixteen, the anti-obscenity proposal that was defeated a few years ago, and he's running for re-election to the State Senate this fall. The police can't hold us; we haven't broken any laws, but we'll be great publicity for Vestal. We're living examples of the moral decline of Southern California."

I remember David and Horace casually remarking that some neighbor on the hill had been watching the Shea swimming pool. David wasn't so unconcerned now. "For God's sake, Jun, you're a lawyer," he said. "What are you going to do? I'm going to be in trouble with some of my customers. For instance, Sanderson Greetings. Henry Sanderson is a pillar of respectability, and all his suppliers contribute annually to his various church activities; it's an unwritten part of his contract."

Peter snorted. "To hell with Sanderson; I'll give you more business for your plant than that creep. You're all acting like idiots. These morons broke into your home, and even if they have a warrant, there's no law against being naked in your own home. I'll shove the knife right back in their slimy chests. Is our police force a Gestapo? This is illegal search and entry."

238

Jun grinned at him without humor. "They knew it. My guess is they'll go through the whole bit of fingerprinting us, take mug shots, charge us all with immoral behavior, wife-swapping, contributing to the delinquency of children, and then justify the raid on the suspicion that we were having a pot party. Of course, they'll release us on bail, and in the end there'll be no formal charges. The whole thing will be dropped."

I was as close to hysteria as Tanya. "It's the old political trick—brand someone guilty and everyone believes the worst. We've got to fight to clear ourselves. We are *not* guilty."

Fritzi chuckled. "By any middle class standards I've ever heard of we're guilty as hell. Eight naked people lying on the floor have to be guilty of *something.* In Los Angeles most people aren't so emancipated that they take their clothes off when company comes. Even the nudists have been unable to start a camp in this area."

"It isn't being caught naked." I shuddered. "It's what the papers will make of it."

"That's easy," Tanya sobbed. "I can see the headlines: 'Prominent Nude Swingers Hopped up on Pot,' 'Children Watch Parents in After-hours Sex Orgy.'" Tanya clung to me as the wagon skidded onto the freeway. "The kids are going to get a liberal education in ugliness."

I tried to hold back my tears as I looked at Horace and David. "Either we believe in what we've been doing, or we don't," I said. "If we act guilty, then we haven't any faith in ourselves." The police wagon was slowing down. Through the grille we could see the sidewalk in front of the police station. We had been well advertised; fifty or more men and women with mobile television cameras and reporters with flash cameras were milling noisily around the rear of the wagon.

"I don't know about the rest of you," I said as I threw my blanket on the floor, "but I'm walking out of this truck stark naked with my head high. Let them put *that* on television."

Peter cheered me. "You're damned right, Nancy! I'm with you. Let's give the bastards something to think about."

But though we walked naked through the crowd of grinning faces, it wasn't easy to be indifferent to the popping flash bulbs and the salacious remarks. I prayed that Tanya who, with her big belly, was the most exposed of us all, could keep her composure and not collapse in tears. My own terror was balanced by furious anger. "Be the snarling tigress with her cub," I whispered to her. She laced her fingers in mine and grinned feebly at me through her tears.

Later we had to admit it was grimly funny. The police station was in an uproar. The sergeant angrily demanded that

239

we cover ourselves with the blankets the police had recovered from the police wagon. "Get these damned nuts dressed," he shouted. He cursed us and the men who had brought us in. "Clear the station of reporters, we're not running a damned nudist camp here," he ordered, but no one paid any attention to him. While Horace, David, and Jun formed a loose circle around the females, Peter, who was at least a head taller than any of the reporters, calmly let it be known that as a private citizen he was going to demand a full investigation of the police department. "Put that in your newspapers," he said. "If this kind of thing is permitted, the next step is that anyone can be taken off in the middle of the night. Then, if your political beliefs don't coincide with those of Big Brother, the police wagon will arrive and you'll just disappear."

"This ain't my party," the sergeant told Jun, who was finally given a telephone. "I'm just doing my duty." He spied Tanya and shook his head disgustedly. "I don't care whether you were smoking pot or not, the whole lot of you are a disgrace. All right," he bellowed to the police who were pushing the reporters into an outer waiting room, "if they won't cover their asses, toss them in the tank. It's damp enough back there. They can either wear the blankets or continue fucking to keep warm; I don't give a shit."

Within an hour we were released on bail and driven back home in cruise cars. Yielding to Peter's insistence that before the day was over we would be beleaguered by reporters and crank telephone calls and ostracized by our neighbors, we dressed, awoke the kids and followed Peter and Fritzi, in two cars, back to their home. It was five A.M. when the children were finally in bed in one of the cabanas; at least they had been cheered by the prospect of swimming in the largest pool they had ever seen.

Tanya smiled as Peter and Fritzi, who had found a room for Jun and Sylvia, were trying to fathom our sleeping arrangements. "Just give us the room with your biggest bed," she told them wearily. "I don't think any of us want sex. If it's all right with Nancy, I think the four of us need to be together."

Alone at last with Horace and David, Tanya and I lay naked together in the middle of the bed as she sobbed in my arms. "Sea, I'm so sorry," she said. "I wish I were dead. It's all my fault; if I hadn't got pregnant we wouldn't be in this mess."

"Maybe we'd be in a worse one," I told her softly. "We've passed the real crisis. We care for one another. We can't let the world destroy that."

240

When Peter tiptoed into our bedroom it was nearly noon, and I woke with a yell when he slapped my naked behind. Guffawing loudly at the mingled confusion of the four of us and the cross expression on Horace and David's faces as they untangled from our heap of mixed legs and arms, Peter said John Vestal would delight in a picture of us now and that he wished he had brought his camera.

I knew it would be useless to explain to Peter that we didn't copulate together. Behind him all four kids, naked and dripping from their continuous dunking in the Alberti pool, precluded discussion. They surveyed us for a split second and then, to Peter's huge amusement, leaped into bed with us as they shouted that they had been up for four hours. (I remembered groaning to Tanya, when we had first heard them, hours earlier, that we must be dreaming; we'd only been in bed two hours.)

How could we sleep so much? Had we seen the huge swimming pool right outside our door? Mrs. Alberti and a very nice Chinese, Mr. Wong, gave them breakfast. Why weren't we swimming? The questions seemed endless. Was it possible the children had absorbed the shock of our donnybrook last night and had bounced back so quickly? Horace, grasping Jimmy in a bear hug while Susan tried to yank Tanya out of bed, grinned at Peter. "Obviously, like the police, you lack perspective. If you had invaded this room and found one wife and one husband in bed, you would have accepted it as quite normal. In fact, you might have even been embarrassed. Finding two husbands and two wives together not only outrages your sense of propriety, it gives you the impression that it's a free-for-all."

Tanya laughed at Peter's puzzled expression. "In his egghead way, Horace is asking why a family composed of two wives and two husbands can't demand the same privacy as a monogamous one."

"Jesus Christ," Peter snorted. "When you get past fifty you don't give a damn about propriety. I yanked Jun out of Sylvia's arms three hours ago. How in hell can you all sleep while Rome is burning? Someone has to figure out a way to whitewash our sins. As an old hand, I suppose I'm elected." Laughing and growling at the same time, he invited us to breakfast beside the pool. "It's a beautiful morning. No smog. With Nancy's help we're going to make Vestal wish he'd stayed in bed last night."

While we ate the breakfast served by Mr. Wong, who was completely uninterested in our nudity, Peter tossed a heap of newspapers at us. "Fritzi's gone to her hairdresser's. Best source of news in Beverly Hills. In the meantime, read 'em and weep."

The war news had been displaced to page two. The sins of one's neighbors were easier to encompass, anyway. We were notorious swingers raided by the police on suspicion of a pot party. While no evidence had been found (Had we flushed the marijuana down the toilet?) statements by our neighbors and the police confirmed we were obviously high on "grass." Many of the newspapers had run airbrushed photos of us emerging naked from the police wagon, or wrapped in blankets as we came out of the house. All the papers had blurry pictures of our Catherine wheel. "Naked Suburbanites Woo Nirvana in Mystic Rites," read one headline. Parallel columns ran pictures of John Vestal, a handsome, gray-haired man in his late fifties, exhorting the crowds at his recent Crusade for Sanity rally. His message was that the voters should stem the tide of moral disintegration by reelecting Vestal to the State Senate in the fall elections.

Through blurry eyes I looked at the City of Los Angeles, spread to the horizon below us. Could anyone in those millions of homes ever understand? Or was it easier to tar and feather us than to try?

"That's not all," Peter told us. "A friend at Television City saw the first run of some movies that were made of us. Before the day is over, we're going to make television history. They're going to show us naked, as we climbed out of the police wagon. The public can decide for themselves." He grinned at me. "It was your idea, Nancy. Only people high on narcotics would dare to expose themselves the way we did."

Peter didn't give us time to commiserate with each other. While David, Horace, and Tanya listened in growing amazement, and Sylvia and Jun lay silently, with closed eyes, on air cushions at our feet, Peter insisted that we couldn't stand idly by. The whole sleazy raid was a political deal. On his insistence, Jun had telephoned the newspapers that we were suing John Vestal for moral abuse and for using the law to harass innocent people.

"I suggested a million dollars damages." Peter chuckled at our consternation. "But Jun made it a more conservative four hundred thousand. Fifty thousand apiece. Now we've got to plunge the knife in deeper. Vestal may have connections, but so do I. Tonight at six o'clock we get our chance for rebuttal. I wanted all eight of us, but News of the Week is a panel show, and they'll only take two. They're extending the show a half hour for our benefit." Peter patted my shoulder. "Since

Nancy and I seemed to have crossed astrological stars, we'll do the job together."

I listened silently, convinced that Nancy Neleh Herndon would never have the nerve to defend herself in front of television cameras while Horace and David insisted that we'd be insane to go on and, if we did, that we'd only make a sideshow out of ourselves. "Listen," David said angrily. "You're crazy. Nancy would crack up in front of that panel, and I'm not sure you won't yourself. I've watched that show; they're all tough newspaper editors. They'll make mincemeat out of you."

"I think we'd better ignore this whole business," Horace said. "What will we accomplish, anyway?" He nudged Jun's leg. "You said last night they didn't have a case against us. Certainly there's no law against being naked in your own home. As for suing Vestal, that's a joke, and you know it."

Jun shrugged. "I'm Peter's lawyer. If he wants to fight, we fight. But you're right. By Monday, whatever charges they've trumped up against us will be dropped. But I agree with Nancy," Jun waved at the panorama of the city. "Until Vestal is elected or defeated, a lot of people out there are going to be hearing a lot about the Herndons and Sheas. You're a cause célèbre, and your neighbors may not want to see you again. Also, Cal Institute will probably decide Horace and Sylvia are too hot to handle. You need some kind of defense, if it's only a counteroffensive. Of course, Peter and Fritzi don't give a damn. The public expects that anyone so wealthy is by definition immoral. Since I work for Peter, I won't lose my job. The whole business can't shake me one way or the other." He ran his finger down Sylvia's back. "If you marry me," he said, "you can tell Cal Institute to go to hell. If you don't, a lot of chicks will think I'm really with it."

Laughing, Jun scuttled away as Sylvia lunged for him. He waved at Mitch and Jimmy, who were yelling to him from the top of the diving board. "You know, you might be surprised. While we can't win a suit against Vestal, we can raise hell generally. It's an interesting question as to whether the police have the right to pre-alert the press and television when they make a raid. We can question the whole ugly business of harassment of innocents, prejudgment caused by unnecessary publicity, invasion of privacy. I think we might split the public between sympathy and disgust." Jun dove in the pool beside Susan and bounced a water ball off her head. "If these were my kids, I'd fight back."

Chapter 16

The precise sequence of events over the next few days is confused in my mind, though I know that it was the day after Peter and I appeared on a reasonably sedate interview on News of the Week that I was invited to appear on the Joe Kraken Show. To the horror of Tanya, David, and Horace, on News of the Week Peter and I had not only excoriated the police invasion and defended our right to be naked with guests in our own home but, under a crossfire of questions, I calmly revealed that the Herndons and the Sheas were not actually wife-swappers, but had embraced a much sounder concept based on group marriage and a corporate family. I suppose it was my suggestion that what we were attempting should become a legal form of marriage, which we would gladly embrace for the protection of our children, that alerted Joe Kraken's lieutenants. Here was a lamb who could easily be slaughtered, he probably thought. It was a sexy subject, too—just right for an after-ten-o'clock audience.

Most people who crawl through life turtle-fashion, being careful to hide at the least danger under their shells, believe in the principle that those who stick their necks out damn well deserve to get their heads chopped off. Perhaps the natural timidity of the average man accounts for the popularity of programs like the Joe Kraken Show. We all have a hidden desire to see people pay for their sins. Shown on a schedule which eventually exposes Kraken in all the major cities, and developed on a formula that includes destruction by insults, studied innocence, flag waving, and reductio ad absurdum, the program has made him a millionaire. By challenging those who deviate from the tried-and-true middle-class beliefs, Kraken deifies stupidity for the stupid.

After I told David, Tanya, and Horace that I had accepted, and that the Reverend Harvey Strate, head of the greater Los Angeles Council of Churches, and John Vestal would appear on the program to help rip Nancy and one other of our combined family to pieces—I wanted it to be Horace—we entered into a heated discussion that lasted two evenings. David said I had accepted only because I was still suffering from the trauma of our return from the Albertis' to San Pedro.

We had driven back to our San Pedro homes after lunch at Peter's house. Horace and David had finally agreed that it was my decision; if I wasn't afraid to appear on News of the Week with Peter (I was really trembling, but refused to admit it), Jun and Sylvia would pick me up at my house at five o'clock. While David, Tanya, and Horace were invited to the studio, they all had politely declined. "It isn't that we aren't with you," Tanya told me. "It's just that I can't stand those cold-blooded newsmen prying into our lives." I didn't urge them; I was still halfway between fury and terror at the police raid. Sylvia told me we all needed Nancy to appear on TV as she was—a sincere, pretty young mother, nicely middle class, calmly certain that we were the innocent victims of a politician's madness to be reelected; but she didn't convince me, and did nothing to alleviate my worries. What if I broke down, and couldn't think coherently? What if I appeared defensive, or actually seemed guilty? I didn't voice my thoughts, but tried to steel myself. I had to do it.

David and Horace were still arguing that a counteroffensive would only add fuel to the fire as we turned in our driveway and were greeted with a front lawn littered with garbage and debris. A crudely lettered sign nailed to a picket read, "This is a God-fearing neighborhood. Swingers not welcome!" Scrawled across our windows in soap and painted on our front door were crude messages such as: "Nude Pot Party Tonight"; "Ring the Bell Show Your Prick. Cunt Lappers and Cock Suckers Welcome"; "Fuckers Got Fucked," and so on.

Susan, Mitch, Jimmy, and Sam asked what some of the words meant; their trembling voices reflected our shock as much as their own. Shoved through the slot in the Sheas' front door, an anonymous typewritten letter addressed to "The Herndon-Sheas" abhorred the mess teen-agers had made of our houses, but asked whether we wouldn't be better off in some section of Los Angeles where our deviant ideas would be more welcome. This was a good Christian neighborhood; why did we want to corrupt it?

Scarcely able to control our mounting hysteria, trying to maintain some control of our emotions before the children, Tanya and I dazedly tried to straighten out the mess the police had made of her house. "We're not evil, are we?" Tanya finally asked before she burst into tears. "It can't be wrong for the four of us to love one another."

David and Horace hugged us. Even though I knew they

were worried, their quick responsive affection and our reciprocal need seemed so wondrous and joyous to me that I wept, too.

Two days later—I *think* it was two—David was exasperated with me. "Good God, Sea, until you went overboard on that program—I noticed even Peter was surprised—all anyone knew was that the Herndons and the Sheas were having a party. It was a warm evening, so we took off our clothes. I'll even concede that, while a lot of people would never approve, you and Peter have turned the tide a little and I've even had a few customers agree that the police and John Vestal went too far. But dragging in our marital arrangements was like pouring gasoline on smoldering ashes."

David's opinion that instead of appearing on the Joe Kraken Show I should take a tranquilizer and stay in bed a few days irritated me. While our neighbors had made no further overt protest, evidently preferring a policy of silent disdain, I disagreed with both Horace and David that we should leave well enough alone. As long as we lived in San Pedro, the Herndons and Sheas would never be completely forgotten or left alone.

A week before I would have agreed with him. I reminded him that I was the only one of the four of us who thought the less people knew about us the better; now I was convinced I was wrong. Inevitably, we had to justify our way of life. "Our neighbors for at least a mile around won't forget," I stormed at him and Horace, who was listening with a bland smile. "The kids are so bewildered they don't know what has happened. Mrs. Materi told her boys not to play with ours. Susan was pulled out of class today and interviewed by some old bitch from the Society for the Prevention of Cruelty to Children. She asked her point-blank if her mother slept with other men. Some of the girls at school are avoiding her because her parents are wifeswappers, while some of the older girls are asking her all kinds of sexy questions." I flopped on the floor beside Tanya, who was doing her breathing exercises and nodding in agreement with me. "You may have noticed that our evening meals are lacking in their usual spontaneity." I wanted Horace, who was watching us silently, to support me. "The kids know that you and Sylvia Mai have been suspended from Cal Institute. After the board of directors meets next week for their final decision, and you're both fired, what are you going to do for a living?"

Horace grinned feebly. "David offered me a job," he said.

"That's great," I snorted, "but you never seemed the type to run a lathe. The way David has been talking about losing the Sanderson account, he may be firing instead of hiring. Probably Tanya hasn't told you that Tom Bayberry telephoned to say he's cutting expenses and won't need her anymore."

Tanya shrugged. "I still don't see what you can accomplish, Sea. Joe Kraken will really wreck you. That news show was lavender and lace in comparison. Maybe David and Horace are right that, if we leave it alone, in a week or two everything will be forgotten. Frank Kitman won't fire Horace, and if he does Horace can get another appointment. Professors of sociology who have written textbooks aren't easy to come by. Of course, he had to make some gesture to cool the wrath of the parents. But the worst that will happen is that Sylvia and Horace will have to give up their experimental course in teaching pornography."

"Damn it all," I shouted. "You're all hiding your heads in the sand. If we're going to continue together, we'll never escape the label of deviant kooks until we start to call the tune ourselves. The kids will never have any confidence in us or our idea of family. People won't let them, and we'll end up a divided camp. If that's what you want, the three of you can sleep without me tonight." David grabbed my arm as I was about to stalk out of the room. (It was my David week.) Tumbling on the floor with me, he scooped my dress up over my breasts and encouraged Horace to slap my behind. "Go ahead," I cried, "but it's not funny. I'm not going to live my life cringing, on the defensive, scared to death at what people think. We're either proud of what we're doing or we should get divorced and forget it."

While I didn't convince them, I didn't dare to lay all my cards on the table, either. Maybe the idea that had crystalized in my mind couldn't ever be realized, but it would at least be fighting back for a principle. Maybe we would be laughed at, maybe people would think we were cracked, but they wouldn't be able to deny our honesty or our right to pursue our beliefs.

Needing a fighter, I telephoned Peter, and asked him to meet me at the Port-o-Call Restaurant. "Not for a boat ride," I joked. "Bring Jun Makura. You helped get me into this mess. Now you can help me untangle it."

Peter and Jun were waiting at a window table when I arrived. They had ordered me a Manhattan. "Peter says you want to get a divorce," Jun said seriously.

"He's crazy." I tried to gather my wits. I seem to be one of those females who is taken with a grain of salt. Would I be able to convince Jun I was serious? "I'm really interested in marriage, not divorce," I said.

247

"That's good." Peter seemed relieved. "If the four of you hang together, I've decided I'll build your corporate house. But there's a catch. First, it'll be in San Peur, about ten miles south of here, where I've got thirty acres of land. It's zoned for business, but it's in one of those submarginal areas that no respectable business would be caught dead in, and it isn't even good for residential development. I even checked for oil, but there's no hope in that direction. It's just one of those wasteland areas that every coastal city has. Part of it may be below sea level."

"He's putting you on," Jun advised. "It's not that bad."

"It won't be when I get through with it," Peter said emphatically. "I'm going to transform it into a new kind of suburbia based on corporate homes and group living." I was so startled I couldn't respond. "Naturally, I expect to make a buck. But I'll build the Herndon and Shea home first, for one dollar and other considerations."

I was weak with astonishment; Peter's offer was complementing my own mad scheme. "I'll have another Manhattan." I grinned at Jun. "If your other consideration is a cruise in your boat, forget it. I've been down that path. Besides, I'm faithful to David and Horace."

While we ate, Peter explained his plan in detail. It was a Peter Alberti I wasn't acquainted with, the super salesman and promoter obsessed with an idea. When we were first married, David had bought some of those pep-up phonograph records used to stimulate salesmen. Peter Alberti could have made his own. "All right," he said finally. "That's the pitch. I'm still not sure the idea is sane, but a good salesman doesn't have to swallow his own product hook-line-and-sinker. I want the four of you to know right from the beginning that basically I'm a rat. The consideration is that I plan to use the Herndon-Sheas for a million dollars' worth of free publicity. If you're all in agreement, I'll launch San Peur and your new corporate home with full-page advertisements in the *Times,* showing ground floor and perspective drawings. By the time I get through, you'll need an unlisted phone number." Peter looked at me coolly. "I hope you understand. If the public doesn't cotton to the idea, you may end up living all alone in a former dump. I'm after bigger fish. Up north a young fellow, Stanley Cole or Kolusakas, is married to the heiress of the Grove Oil Company. He's neck deep in a multimillion dollar project for a new kind of city, no heavy industry, with a maximum population of a couple hundred thousand. The citizens will earn their living within the city, concentrating on all aspects of the new education industry. Alberti Construction is bidding on that project. You can call San Peur and your corporate home progressive thinking. If I get the Kolusakas deal, I'll charge it off to advertising. Do you hate me?"

"Why should I?" I demanded. "This country was founded by people who were feathering their own nests." I crossed my fingers under the table and prayed that the combination of Peter's idea and mine wouldn't completely demoralize Horace and David. I had already told Tanya and, God bless her, she had just chuckled and assured me that no two men could withstand two females who were in agreement.

Peter broke into my happy reflections. "I'm really trying to help you in a perverse sort of way," he said.

"Who knows," I told him, "you may end up building cities based on corporate homes, or you may get branded as a visionary nut who sank a lot of money into a crackpot project." I enjoyed the crinkly grin around Peter's mouth; it helped to confirm a kind of paternal feeling I sensed he had toward me. "Really, I think the rest of my family will go along with you," I said, "but before I say yes, we'll have to see how I do on the Joe Kraken Show."

It was Peter's turn to be astonished. The News of the Week Show was one thing, but nobody in their right mind would give Joe Kraken a chance to nail them to the cross; he was a slimy skunk. "The bastard's had four wives," Peter told me, and shook his head. "You'll note his guests never discuss his personal life; that's *verboten*. If Kraken doesn't crucify you, Vestal and Harvey Strate will."

Jun agreed with him that I was too naive to go on the Kraken Show, and that the Herndons and the Sheas were a sitting duck. Why did I want that kind of exposure?

"Because I'm like Peter; I want publicity. What I have in mind, whether it succeeds or not, will at least let the four of us live together honestly." I smiled at them nervously, knowing that as I spoke the words my emphasis sounded a lot braver than I really felt. "I've decided that the only way the Herndons and the Sheas can live together at peace in this country is to make group marriage legal—institutionalize it, make it a normal, socially approved way for two or three couples to live together. Here in Los Angeles, where the divorce rate is practically equal to the marriage rate, it might be embraced as a new solution. Instead of families breaking up, they might consolidate."

I could tell by Jun's expression and the tone of his voice that he felt he was humoring a slightly wayward female. "Just how do you propose to go about it?" he inquired.

"In California, if an issue is put before the voters in a form of a Proposition, and the Proposition is voted favorably by the majority, ultimately it becomes a law, doesn't it?"

Jun nodded. "It would take several hundred thousand signatures from registered voters before it would ever get on the ballot, and plenty of money to gather the signatures."

I could feel that my cheeks were flushed from excitement. "Joe Kraken doesn't know it," I said, "but he's going to help me acquaint the entire state with Proposition Thirty-One."

"What's Proposition Thirty-One?" Jun demanded.

"I don't know, yet," I admitted calmly. "You've got to write it. It will make corporate marriage legal."

"My God, Nancy, I think you're overwrought." Peter patted my hand sympathetically. "You'd have the entire state up in arms. Really, I admire your pluck, but it's insane. The churches will light on you like a ton of bricks."

"You don't have to patronize me," I told him angrily. "A minute ago you were proposing to build a home for two families and splash it all over the newspapers. Don't you consider that a little insane?"

Peter nodded. "Most certainly, but I'm not trying to get the couples who will live in that kind of house legally married. I'm not even mentioning sex; just economics. Think of the money they'll save. How they go to bed together under the roof of that corporate house doesn't concern me a damned bit. When you get into the sex aspect, and, even worse, try to make it legal, you're whacking at a hornet's nest." Peter guffawed. "Legal? Two couples married together legally? Christ, why get into that! Just swap wives and husbands and forget it. Everybody else does!"

"Damn it! We've got a lot more going for us than just sex." I couldn't stop the tears welling in my eyes. "I'm not going to bring our kids up with the four of us labeled as wife-swappers. I want them to have the larger social approval of living in one family."

Jun had listened to me silently. "May I ask you a question, Nancy?" he said. "Where did you get the number thirty-one for your Proposition?"

"Love and marriage—for couples past thirty," I told him. "And for better or for worse!"

I couldn't tell whether Jun was laughing with me or at me. When he finally came up for air and wiped away his own tears, he kept muttering, "Why not? Why not? Out of the mouths of babes and innocents." Still laughing, he kissed my cheek. "I'll write your Proposition for you, Nancy," he said. "If it ever passes, it'll confound legal minds for centuries to come!"

Chapter 17

~~~~~~~~

When Jun and Sylvia arrived to drive us to Television City
—once again they were acting as chauffeurs—Horace and I
were still trying to convince Tanya and David to come along
and join the studio audience of the Joe Kraken Show to give
us moral support. As he came through the door, Jun slipped
me an envelope and whispered, "You're on your own."

David and Horace didn't hear him; I smiled uneasily at
David. It might not be too late to read Proposition Thirty-
One to them, but there would be no time for the discussion
that would inevitably follow. In the bathroom, while I fiddled
with my makeup, Tanya sat on the toilet and read the typewritten draft to me. When she said, "Wow, I hope this
doesn't paralyze Horace's vocal cords," she didn't help to
quiet my fears. Still, a speechless Horace seemed quite unlikely. And if he didn't like the Proposition, he had only himself to blame. After all, I was his protégée.

Before we left, David laughed as he hugged me. "When I
married you," he said, "I suspected the worst. You're the
kind of intense person who can't stop playing with matches
even when you're sitting on a powder keg. If I were at the studio, I might have to restrain myself from running up and
punching Kraken in the nose." Tanya was more practical.
"The way things are, Sea, someone really has to stay here
with the kids. I'll be praying for you both."

On the way to the studio, the envelope in my pocketbook,
I listened as Horace voiced his last-minute doubts and his
fear that we would both make asses of ourselves. I prayed,
too, that Horace, David, and Tanya would forgive me if the
powder keg exploded.

David tape-recorded the show, which turned out much better than the play I never got around to writing, and he played
it back for Horace and me late that evening. In the version
below, I've added the italicized comments:

KRAKEN (*smiling unctuously at Horace and me, the Untouch-
ables, and benevolently at John Vestal and the Reverend
Strate*) Our guests tonight, Mrs. Nancy Herndon, a

housewife, and Horace Shea, who I believe *was* Professor of Sociology at Cal Institute (*oily close-up*). I say *was*. Due to some rather wild happenings a few days ago at the Shea home, Professor Shea has been temporarily suspended from the faculty. The Institute is rather concerned, and maybe you are too, if you've been reading your newspapers. The Herndons and the Sheas may or may not be just one more collection of the sort of kooks who have overrun Southern California and are trying to destroy every belief that you and I hold sacred and that have made this country great. But this is a democracy, so we'll give them their chance to defend themselves.

On my left is John Vestal, one of our former State Senators, and now running for reelection. John Vestal, as you know, is active in the crusade to restore moral sanity to California. Next to him is the Reverend Harvey Strate, of the Greater Los Angeles Council of Churches. Dr. Strate is a champion in the cause of strengthening the family by a return to sound religious values.

In the unlikely event that you don't know all about it, Mrs. Herndon and Professor Shea and their legitimate spouses, who are not with us tonight, and four other prominent citizens of this area, were raided by the police last week at the home of Professor Shea and carried off naked to the police station. From everything I have read, it seems likely the police interrupted a wife-swapping party on the suspicion that marijuana was being used for additional tililation. Frankly, I'm somewhat amazed that Mrs. Herndon and Professor Shea dare to appear on this program; at least, their nerve does them credit. If I were in their shoes, I'd want to slink out of town before a decency committee decided to tar and feather me and ride me out on a rail. Well, if there's one thing you have to admit about our fringe groups, it's that they've lost all their modesty. They don't seem to know what shame is, and they're nauseatingly vocal. But kooky or sane, and whether they make you hold your noses or cheer, Joe Kraken believes that every citizen of this great democracy has a right to know what's going on. To get to the heart of our subject for tonight, may I ask you, Mrs. Herndon, are you the mistress of Professor Shea? I gather there's a Mr. Herndon somewhere in the boondocks.

NANCY (*jittery*) David, my other husband, and Tanya, Horace's other wife, are baby-sitting with the children. They're watching this program at home.

KRAKEN (*snorting*) Your other husband! His other wife! Really, Mrs. Herndon, you're putting me on. Having two husbands or two wives is bigamy. America may have given up on some things, but bigamy is still illegal. She's kidding, isn't she, Professor Shea?

HORACE Not at all. We simply believe that in our present-day society a merger of two small families will give all the members of them greater family identity and greater economic strength, and that it will also give the adults sexual variety within the family.

KRAKEN Then you do in fact sleep with Mrs. Herndon, and Mrs. Shea sleeps with Mr. Herndon. It seems to me those words you just said are a high-sounding way to dignify wife-swapping.

NANCY (*burning*) We're not wife-swappers. Wife-swapping is a one-night stand, usually, with numerous couples. The Herndons and the Sheas are involved in a complete commitment to each other.

KRAKEN Have you ever tried wife-swapping as you define it?

NANCY No! And I'm not interested; that would devalue sex.

KRAKEN But what you are doing *is* adultery, isn't it, Mrs. Herndon?

NANCY I read somewhere, Mr. Kraken, that you've been married several times. Isn't that a polite form of adultery as well as bigamy?

KRAKEN (*sternly*) We're not here to discuss my life, Mrs. Herndon.

NANCY Let's not call it your life. Let's call it Mr. X and the several Mrs. X's that Mr. X has copulated with and had children by.

KRAKEN They have used the legal processes available to them to maintain one relationship at a time.

NANCY For varied copulation. If one observes the legal forms, it's possible to achieve the joys of bigamy or adultery and still be considered a responsible citizen and even a good Christian.

VESTAL While you and your friends are attempting to sue me, Mrs. Herndon, as a cover-up for your activities, may I point out that at least in divorce and remarriage the rights of the children are protected. Since we are not here to discuss the other aspects of your morality, which to my mind are the *real* issue, may I at least point out that our society, quite rightly, recognizes only monogamous marriage. Your premise would destroy the family and the morals of the community. No child would know who his father and mother were, and future generations would have to be the wards of the state. The way you say you're living may not be against any California law that's enforced, but it should be. If the churches have failed, and we haven't yet heard from the Reverend Strate, then I say we need a law with teeth in it to protect us from ourselves.

NANCY   I agree with you, Mr. Vestal. Since you have such faith in the law, you certainly wouldn't object to group or corporate marriage if it were a legal form of marriage in California.

VESTAL (*disgustedly*)   I can assure you, I'm not interested in pipe dreams.

NANCY (*laughing*)   Perhaps not for yourself. But if a majority of the voters in this state demanded such a law, I'm sure you would uphold it.

VESTAL (*coldly*)   I have a feeling, Mrs. Herndon, that your brain has been damaged—I hope not by the use of drugs. Obviously, the possibility you suggest is remote.

NANCY (*trying not to laugh at Horace's surprised expression*)   Perhaps not so remote as you may think, Mr. Vestal. I would like to read a Proposition to you, and enlist your aid in getting a petition through the Secretary of State. Perhaps we may even succeed in getting this Proposition on the November ballot . . .

KRAKEN (*interrupting*)   This is not a political platform, Mrs. Herndon.

NANCY (*insistent*)   This happens to be quite germane to this discussion. I agree with Mr. Vestal. For the security of our children, the Herndons and the Sheas should be able to formalize our marriage in a legal civil or religious ceremony. I think many of your listeners will sympathize with our proposal.

KRAKEN (*resigned*)   Go ahead. Nuts and bolts cheerfully assembled on the Joe Kraken Show.

NANCY (*reading*)   To the Secretary of State of the State of California: We the undersigned, being duly qualified and registered voters of the State of California and constituting not less in number than eight percent of the entire vote cast for all candidates for governor in the last election, hereby petition the Secretary of State and request that the following proposed law, to be known as the California Corporate Family Law, be submitted directly to the electors of the State of California for their adoption or rejection at the next succeeding general election or as provided by law. . . . the text of said proposed law is as follows: The people of the State of California enact an act to permit not more than three married couples, past the age of thirty, to join together under a new civil marriage provision of the present state laws in a joint form of marriage to be known as group marriage or corporate marriage, establishing a family unit that will exist independently of the individual members and have all the rights now permitted under the existing laws of corporations, such family corporations to appoint from their legal members by marriage, or from the issue of these marriages, directors to govern the affairs of these family corporations and to continue with their full human powers to carry on the purposes of such corporate living which will be construed as follows: To create a joint family environment for the financial security and independence of its members, and to provide for all members an environment that fulfills their needs, both emotional and economic, so they can live fully self-actualized lives and develop, to the full limit, their abilities as human beings. It being a further provision of the law that such Corporate Families, once established, may, on the vote of the majority of the directors past the age of twenty-one, dissolve the Family Corporation if there are no children under the age of eighteen in the unit and if there are children under the age of eighteen, that the Corporation may also be dissolved by such majority vote if any two of the original incorporators shall undertake to assume responsibility for all children under the age of eighteen and to maintain a suitable home environment for them that shall be in conformity with the original purpose of the corporation. It is further to be permitted to the incorporators to assume for legal purposes one surname for all members of the corporate family, which may be either a single agreed-upon surname or a new joint name combining the surnames of the original incorporators.

NANCY (*pausing and smiling sweetly at the panel and enjoying Horace's astonishment*) There is more, but I think that makes the point, Mr. Vestal. If that Proposition became law, it would restore some of the moral sanity you're so anxious about.

KRAKEN (*to Horace*) Am I mistaken, or does this idea come as a surprise to you? I know it damn well shocks the hell out of me.

HORACE (*laughs*) When you're married to two women, nothing comes as a surprise. Anyway, I applaud Nancy's Proposition. It blends with an experiment now going on in several colleges where the sexes live together unmarried through the three or four years of undergraduate work. After graduation there could be eight to ten years for monogamous marriage, followed by corporate marriage. Such a way of life, if it were accepted, would not only wipe out a great deal of sexual neuroticism, but might well cut the divorce rate in half and ultimately provide all men and women with a new kind of adventure, encompassing several phases, as they grew in their abilities to handle complicated emotional relationships.

STRATE (*jarred out of his ecclesiastical reverie*) Your multiplication in marriage sounds like sheer nonsense. Marriage is a pact between two persons, one male, one female. You and Mrs. Herndon and your absent spouses evidently miss the essential quality of marriage. Marriage is not a sexual playground. It is a commitment the individuals make to God. While I'm not a Catholic, I believe that, in a larger sense, marriage is a sacrament. To quote Matthew, "And a man shall be joined to his wife, and they two shall be one flesh."

HORACE (*smiles broadly*) Really, Dr. Strate, we shouldn't quote the Bible at each other. Matthew also quoted Jesus as saying, "For after the resurrection there is no marrying, or being married, but they shall live as the angels do in heaven." Jesus, in the Acts of the Apostles, asserted: "All mine thine, and all thine mine." Isn't it possible Jesus meant a sharing of the sexual relationship as well as property? Remember, women were considered property in those days. Paul advised in Corinthians that "They that have wives be though they had none." Wasn't Paul's real meaning that men should cease regarding women as property? You won't mind if I say I'm wary of religionists who try to force biblical interpretation to fit modern conditions. The Bible is magnificent history. As history we should enjoy it, both for its perceptions and for its clues as to our failures as human beings. If you trace the monogamous concept of Christian marriage, won't you find it rooted in the patriarchal domination that may have been necessary to the Jews, in their time? Today, survival is no longer a matter of the male's skill as hunter or husbander. We've passed beyond the problem of satisfying the needs for food, clothing, and shelter. If I were a religious man, I would think the new awareness of our necessity to satisfy the hunger of man for love and understanding might put us closer to whatever kind of God may exist in the universe or in our tiny world.

STRATE (*smiling*) I admire your seeming idealism, Mr. Shea, but your actions, as reported by the newspapers, belie what you are saying. Whether you accept the Bible or not, modern psychology reinforces the Christian and Jewish laws by teaching us that neither man nor woman is emotionally equipped to share, either in the marriage or in the sexual relationship.

KRAKEN I congratulate you on your tolerance, Reverend. I would put it more bluntly. No man or woman *in their right mind* is going to share their husband or wife with another male or female.

NANCY It's quite apparent, Mr. Kraken, when you were a young man you believed the woman *you* married *must* be a virgin. Down to fifty years ago, more or less, the male *insisted* on the prerogative of being the first to pierce the hymen of his beloved. Now, most people believe premarital relationships are not only inevitable, but make good sense, and we even laugh about postmarital relationships beyond the family. We laugh, but we cry when it happens to us. Isn't it conceivable to you that we're pointing the way to the possibility of a new kind of marital relationship that preserves the family and that avoids the emotional ugliness of adultery?

David flipped the off-button on the tape recorder.
"There's a lot more." I scowled at him. "At least another half hour, unless you and Tanya got distracted and forgot to record it."

David patted my naked behind. Horace and I, both exhausted and exhilarated from our ordeal with Joe Kraken, had said good night to Jun and Sylvia in the car. David and Tanya joined us in the bathroom while we took a shower, and then, happily together again, celebrating Joe Kraken's confession, after the show, that it was a draw and he might request a return match, we relaxed together, naked, on the living-room floor.

"We recorded every last minute of it, Sea." David kissed my neck. "Even if we'd felt like it, Tanya and I didn't make love. How could we, when you and Horace were on the rack?

257

The rest of the show Kraken lost by default. He could pretend mock horror at Proposition Thirty-One, but your sincerity defeated him."

David grinned at Horace, who had assumed a yogi posture and was sitting cross-legged with his buttocks resting on his insteps. Sitting between Tanya and me who were curled in a U-shape around him and David, Horace looked like a Buddha who had gone on a starvation diet. He leaned over and yanked one hair loose from my delta. "You should yell ouch," he said solemnly. "It's a good thing this isn't my Nancy week; I'd probably strangle you, but as it is I'll leave the job to David. Good Lord, you had me completely off balance for a moment. In this marriage, no further connivance between the females is permitted. Joe Kraken knew that Proposition Thirty-One was a complete surprise to me."

It was silly, but I cried. Even though I realized that the warm love-friendship that existed between us scarcely needed legal sanctification, and though I felt the inner glow of our shared love as palpably as a touch, I was happy with our mutual conviction that society should learn how to permit us to exist. The four of us had transcended the centuries and by-passed the expected limitations of men and women interacting together to the full depth of their humanity. Our group marriage was no longer a forced solution to our marital difficulties. We had battled our way through the jungle of egocentric fears that most people acquire in the process of growing up, and now the barricades—our defenses against one another—were down. The Herndons and the Sheas no longer existed. We didn't pivot endlessly alone. The smaller circles of our previous lives had merged into a larger *gestalt,* a unitary perception of the essence of us that would always unite us.

Tanya expressed the feeling. "David and I were talking about Proposition Thirty-One before you got home," she said. "If corporate marriage ever became a legal reality, David agreed we should have a big wedding. And, by the way, you and Horace missed a beautiful point. Couples married together, after thirty, could have their children for best men and maids of honor. It would be a ceremony both of marriage and of family solidarity."

While we were discussing the reaction of the television audience, and what would happen in the coming weeks when, inevitably, Proposition Thirty-One would be tossed to the winds of controversy, Tanya invited us to press our ears to her belly and feel the quick jab of our baby's foot. In six weeks we would have another child, and he or she would be a loved and wanted addition to our family.

If the Reverend Strate could have looked in our window, I'm sure he would have erupted in rage. The four of us, indolently naked, reluctant to go to bed, might have given him the impression that we did indeed consider marriage a sexual playground, though the contact between us now was only peripherally sexual. We liked each other for our bodies, but even more because in our sexual couplings we had achieved a unique new depth of friendship. We dared to delve below our surface thoughts and to approach each other with intimate thoughts most people suppress or leave unsaid.

All three of us had kissed Tanya's belly and, unembarrassed, touched her swollen breasts and nipples in pride and awe at the miracle of conception and gestation. Tanya smiled at me. "Poor Horace and David! Look at them, Sea, like two kids in a candy store." She ran her fingers down David's chest and across Horace's stomach and sighed. "The time has come when this candy store is practically closed for business, if only temporarily. Now it's up to you, Sea: for the next few weeks you'll have to work overtime. The thought of sex, even if it were practical, leaves me a little cold." Tanya was silent for a moment. "Why don't the three of you make love together? In novels that become best sellers there's always a scene like that."

"You're silly." I laughed at the sheepish look on David's and Horace's faces.

"No, I'm not. I agree with you. In normal circumstances, the act of love is between two people. I could never blend with Horace or David together or if you were watching, but eroticism as well as love motivates every human being. Sex can be silly happiness as well as poetic happiness."

I knew what Tanya was leaving unsaid. Many people would assume that four adults living together would eventually experience group sex. Maybe some day the four of us would experiment together, but I doubted it. We might play erotically together, but the ultimate surrender, unless it was mechanical and objective, was for a male and female alone. I tried to express my feelings. "I think in the act of love we all come to each other differently. The pure joy is the conscious attempt to be the other person. Together, making love, we would be acted upon, not reacting. Right now I want to hug both David and Horace because they're silently interacting with your thoughts and mine. If I went to bed with both of them, and we made love, ultimately one would watch, and all of us would have closed off our minds. The orgasms and climaxes would be machinelike, perfunctory, with none of us

259

deeply involved." I smiled. "Believe me, if we should ever copulate together as a group of more than two, you'll be in a condition to join the fracas. In the meantime, if you don't have any imagination, Horace and David will have to take turns being continent for a week at a time."

Bubbling with merriment, Tanya kissed my cheek. "I really love you, Sea. All the time you were talking I kept thinking, 'Thank you, Somebody! Thank you, God, that the Herndons and the Sheas discovered each other.'" She took Horace's hand. "Come on, honey, it isn't often a curious female can watch the havoc she can wreak."

Not that sex is the whole of our existence. But the *understanding* of sex and the joy of ourselves as sexual creatures is related to the even more important comprehension of all facets of ourselves as amazing, living, breathing human beings. A few evenings ago, Tanya was reading aloud to us from Ashley Montagu's *On Being Human*. If people can live together, *and love* (corporately or monogamously), Montagu has discovered the key in these words.

Most human beings want to like, to love their fellow men. Yet in their everyday lives they, for the most part, practice self-love and are more or less hostile toward all those they conceive to stand in their way. The reason for this tragic disparity between what they feel to be right and what they do is simply that the structure of this society is such that the life of the person becomes reduced to a competitive struggle for existence. Under such conditions, men everywhere tend to become nasty, brutish and cruel. In such a situation it is hard for them to do otherwise, for the first law of life has always been self-preservation (the satisfaction of basic needs), and if the individual will not do everything in his power to gain security for himself who will? Self-responsibility is the basic law of human living. A man must first look to himself and his own. But he also has to see his personal interests and responsibilities as opening into collective interests and responsibilities. The cosmos itself is the smallest frame of reference in which he may think, if he is to orient his life in the direction of human values. Self and society exist together. . . . The principle of self-responsibility, for self, society and the world has relevance only *now!* Never at some later date. One may not put off being human. In a very profound way all the wisdom and the whole secret of human relations is incorporated in the Talmudic saying. "If I am not for myself, who will be for me? If I am only for myself, what am I? If not now—when?"

Isn't that really the commitment?

Publisher's Note

The reader may be aware that the Herndons and the Sheas have contracted their former surnames to coincide with their new entity, the Hershe Family Corporation. Because of the public interest in the Hershes, we asked Mrs. Nancy Hershe to give us an additional chapter bringing the affairs of the Hershe family as close to publication date as possible. In answer we received a Xerox copy of the letter that follows, on the stationery of Future Families of America, San Peur, California, written by Horace Hershe, Executive Director, to Margaret and Phillip Tenhausen, Harrad College, Cambridge, Massachusetts. Attached to the letter was this note from Horace Hershe:

The continuous newspaper publicity since the Grove Foundation first agreed to pay the expenses of any Harrad graduate or student who wished to help in the drive for signatures on the petition for Proposition Thirty-One has probably made it clear that Nancy has been working night and day to coordinate the efforts of all the workers in the campaign to put the Proposition across in November. Knowing that I had promised to write Phillip Tenhausen, Nancy pounced on the idea that my letter could serve the dual purpose of bringing Phil up to date and, at the same time, present our family from the male perspective. I immediately tried to defer the honors to David. After all, Nancy has *two* husbands and *two* male points of view . . . not to mention Tanya, who only grinned and said she might disagree with Nancy, but not in print. David's reaction was to the point: "I'll leave the daydreaming to you and Nancy. Tanya and I have to make sure we all eat!" Which I suppose has some justification. Not that David and Tanya aren't active in Future Families. Actually, they have become so involved with Peter and the Alberti Construction Company, designing and estimating interiors for the many corporate home styles projected by Peter's architects, that David jokingly told Peter it was only a matter of time before

Herndon Showcase became a subsidiary of Alberti Construction and David took over as president of Peter's firm. Noting the flicker of interest on Peter's face, we warned David that kidding with Peter is more dangerous than backing up on a freeway! In any event, when you have two wives, you rapidly discover when to argue and when to acquiesce. So here is my rather lengthy letter to Margaret and Phil. You have our joint permission to use it both as a conclusion and, we hope, a beginning.

Dear Margaret and Phil:

Nearly three months later, we still remember the warm glow and joyful return of confidence when we received your long-distance telephone call the day after the Joe Kraken Show. More than anything else (and I include Peter Alberti's kind of anti-faith in us) your belief that Proposition Thirty-One was a logical extension of the Harrad program has sustained us. *We were not alone!* Any social system, even a democratic one, tends to isolate the person or group that challenges the dominating mores. In the early years, when your conviction of the validity of the Harrad idea was denied, I am sure you sensed that this was not only inevitable but perhaps necessary. Despite Marx, man could never survive in a state of complete anarchy. We cling to the old ways with an innate realization that a bird in hand may be worth two in the bush. Hopefully, for those who innovate, whether individuals or groups, they no longer have to wait generations. Vast changes in values and philosophies of living are now achieved in decades. Perhaps, for the first time in history, man is learning to profit from past experience.

Your insistence that we should meet Stanley and Sheila Cole, followed by their telephone call inviting us to their home in Tiburon, completed the circle. Even in California we had friends who believed in us. While we didn't exactly run from the initial havoc we had created, the escape to Tiburon gave us the opportunity to marshal our forces. In the company of InSix we discovered the most delightful shock troops who ever came to the aid of outnumbered combatants.

The day before we flew up to San Francisco, Peter Alberti's full-page advertisement, announcing that his company would build the first corporate home in the United States, appeared in practically every newspaper in the state. When you meet Peter, you'll understand—enough is only the beginning for him. We were still inundated with telephone calls and letters as a result of the Joe Kraken Show. Nancy had been keeping score; about one in five in favor, two belligerent and offensive. Without consulting us, Peter touched off a landslide. In a television interview, he told reporters that his ultimate concept embraced a "new city" at San Peur based on a complex of corporate homes. To implement the idea, he would endow a foundation, to be called Future Families of America, with five million dollars in stock of the Alberti Construction Company. The purposes of the foundation: to investigate the social, economic, political and emotional relationships involved in corporate marriage. As the most likely person to direct the activities of the foundation, he suggested Horace Shea, Professor of Sociology at Cal Institute!

When I finally reached Peter by telephone and suggested he might at least have discussed his wild ideas with us (I'd already accused Nancy of knowing a great deal more of Peter's plans than she would admit), Peter just laughed. "Don't blame Nancy. The four of you rolled a snowball to the top of the hill. While you were still puffing and trying to make up your minds what to do next, I gave it a shove. What do you want to do now—tell the world you don't really believe in what you're doing?"

Peter insisted he was damned serious about the Foundation. Choking with laughter, he told me he had received at least twenty calls from top educators (including Kitman, who assured him my career wasn't in jeopardy) who praised him and offered their services. "It just goes to show, Horace," he told me, "that a proper injection of money can turn the devil into an angel. Now, courtesy of Uncle Sam, you've got the prestige you need. And think of the fun I'll have, tax free!"

When I told Peter I wasn't certain I wanted to devote my life to promoting Proposition Thirty-One or corporate marriage, he just laughed some more. "Think it over, Horace," he said. "If you don't want the job, I'll try Kitman. The salary will be twenty-five thousand, and you can have Nancy for secretary. She can run things for you. If the Proposition isn't adopted, the Foundation can always muddy up some other waters with its money. For example, it might encourage the teaching of pornography in high school. My God!"

On the flight up to San Francisco, we were still trying to make Nancy admit she had had more than a little to do with the magnitude of Peter's daydreams. "Maybe I lighted the fuse," she admitted, "but how could you expect me to resist? The firecracker was just lying there. Besides," she pointed out, "I've been giving a lot of thought to marriage and the family in the past few months. I'm convinced that every family needs a unifying, goal-directed approach to life, whether it be monogamous or corporate, yet most families don't have one. In a corporate family, the many problems of achieving deep interaction are a goal-incentive that releases the individuals from their preoccupation with self. Yet the need is the same in any type of family structure. With Peter's money we can explore the vast possibilities open to everybody."

Stanley and Sheila met us at the airport. Recognizing Nancy from the Joe Kraken Show (while Sheila was impulsively hugging Tanya, David, and me—breathlessly introducing herself as Sheila Kolusakas, sometimes known as Cole) Stanley whirled Nancy off her feet in a bear hug. "I should have brought a brass band," he yelled enthusiastically. "The Herndons and the Sheas are the heroes and heroines of Harrad College."

In the parking lot we gasped in admiration over their huge motor home, only slightly smaller than a transcontinental bus. "We tried a trailer," Stanley told us, "but it was a damned nuisance. This one functions as a combination living room and automobile during the day. At night, at least eight can sleep in it."

The interior was equipped with sofas and chairs that converted into beds, and a built-in kitchen and toilet. "We bought it two years ago so that InSix could travel together. Of course we can't all sleep in it, now." Stanley smiled at Jimmy, Mitch, Susan and Sam, who were excitedly exploring the interior. "We're InThirteen, now, unless Beth and Harry Schacht have decided to add one more to the tribe."

We were on a freeway headed toward San Francisco and the Golden Gate Bridge. Stanley drove while the kids hovered around him demanding to know what happened when they flushed the mechanical toilet and asking if they could have some Cokes they discovered in the refrigerator. The rest of us were trying to fit our questions and answers into a jubilant ten-way conversation while Stanley, completely unperturbed and smiling happily at the confusion, guided the bus through the traffic.

"Did you say Beth and Harry Schacht?" Tanya finally managed to ask him. "My God! That's my doctor's name. Harry Schacht. He practices in Beverly Hills."

"One and the same," said Sheila. "Finest medical pair in Southern California. Complete female care from gynecology to obstetrics, with Beth carrying on into pediatrics. We always told Beth she wanted to mother the world, and, by God, Harry and she ushered four of the InSix brood into the world. When all the publicity broke on the four of you, Harry was beside himself. He put two and two together and guessed you must be the female Shea of the infamous Herndons and Sheas. They're up at Tiburon now, waiting for us, along with Jack and Valerie and all the kids. Harry's going to give you hell for missing your appointment last week!"

"I hope you don't mind bedlam," Stanley said. "Altogether there'll be twenty-five of us, with five females to do the cooking."

"You may not eat!" Sheila, sitting behind Stanley, tweaked his ear. "It's Stanley's obsession that the trappings of money shouldn't dominate our personal lives, so we have no cooks or maids. Just a handyman, Jake, who's supposed to keep the house in some kind of shape, but mostly thinks he's one of the family. You've got to talk to him, Stanley. Yesterday, when he should have been fixing the roof on one of the cottages, I discovered him drinking a straight bourbon near the pool and telling Arnold and Eadie fantastic stories about the days when he and Daddy were prospecting for oil. He even offered to make me a drink so I could learn something."

"Jake gets lonesome," Stanley explained. "We only use the house at Tiburon every fifth week. The rest of the time we're in our apartment in San Francisco. I've got to find a bedmate in her sixties for Jake. Then Sheila can serve Jake and his mistress breakfast in bed."

Crossing the Golden Gate Bridge, maneuvering his huge vehicle with the dexterity of a cross-country truck driver, Stanley chattered happily. "Don't let Sheila put you on. She agrees with me. I have the same temperament as her old man, who left us millions. But spending money for personal aggrandizement bored Sam." Stanley told us in some detail about their model city project. Currently they were diverting all the Grove Foundation income into Grove City. In addition, he said, they were personally in the project up to their ears.

"Grove City is the key to the future," he continued. "Twenty-five miles north of San Francisco, it'll be fully independent of the core city and yet not isolated from it." Stanley turned off the bridge into the road leading to Sausalito. "Another thing, Sheila and I were determined money wouldn't separate InSix. This fall InSix celebrated its twelfth anniversary. The corporation we put together for our education still continues. When we graduated from the University of Pennsylvania, Sheila gave the corporation five hundred thousand dollars. A present from Sam Grove. Right now the income is being used to support Jack and Valerie. Jack was elected to the House of Representatives in the State of X* last fall. InSix owns the most popular radio station in the City of Y," Stanley went on. "We're still a long way from taking over the state, but the kids love our rock and roll station, and Jack

---

* Readers of *The Harrad Experiment* will find it obvious why the state and city are still not identified.

266

even has his own program. He plays country music on his guitar. The people love him, and in five or six years, he's sure to be Governor."

Stanley and Sheila told us about your occasional visits with them, and—by the way—we all insist that you both join us on election eve. Needless to say Tanya, Nancy, David, and I were ecstatic with the huge rambling house at Tiburon with its guest cottages scattered in two acres of redwood forest, with its veranda cantilevered over the water, with the city across the bay emerging and disappearing in the fog. All that, and the six O'Day class sailboats that we divided up among kids and adults and spent one day racing (Beth and Jack were invincible)—the heated swimming pool, where all twenty-five of us plus Jake (a hundred-and-ten-pound, tanned-black, laughing skeleton of a man) swam naked into the late hours of the morning—all became a backdrop for incessant conversation and discussion.

The kids united in cliques of five girls against six boys, and Susan, delighted at the reinforcements, and, being older by two years than any of the other girls, became their mentor. Beth clarified the sleeping arrangements for us. "We're too mobile, at the moment, to attempt corporate marriage," she said. "Besides, if we all lived together every day we'd probably murder one another." She grinned at Nancy. "But don't think we aren't going to delve into the mystery of what makes you and Tanya tick. Anyway, every fifth week we meet at Tiburon. Thank God for airplanes, even Jack and Val can get here in two hours. Since we always plan four-night weekends, the females desert their husbands and have two nights apiece with new husbands."

"Not so new, Beth, honey." Jack patted her naked behind. "Having slept with you some hundred or more times in the past four years, and even more often at U of Penn, I know your habits as well as Valerie's or Sheila's, and I can't escape the feeling I have three wives." He chuckled as Sheila bounced a beach ball off his head and pushed him off the edge into the pool. "I apologize," he yelled, "I should have said three wives have me!"

Most of the weekend we relaxed together naked or partially dressed as the evening air became cooler. The most amazing discovery was InSix's mental nakedness with each other and the four of us. They have discovered a way of penetrating one another's varied emotional reactions, enjoying themselves for their differences as well as their similarities.

"The reason we're so thrilled at discovering you," Sheila told us, "is that you seem to be managing, despite the poor start Nancy told us about. I might even say you had an impossible beginning, and without four years of Harrad conditioning. It proves that human beings have the power, if only they have the will, to achieve a greater awareness of each other. It may surprise you that Beth, Val, and I *know* our men with an intimacy that we dare to share with each other. I know, for example, that Stanley in bed with me is often more casual than he is with Beth. Harry is protective, a tower of strength in my emotional ups and downs. Jack is like a kid with a new toy. He can't believe that I love his deep, boyish affection. We've explored our reactions with one another, together and as a group, and there's no anger, no jealousy—just happy excitement at our continuously amazing differences as human beings. Our individual monogamous security strengthens the interacting unity which is an equally valid expression of ourselves."

It would be impossible to cover the range of interests of InSix. They're alive, aware, tuned in, to all the currents of man's incessant probing to know, to find answers. But in any discussion they eliminate exclusiveness and force participation. When Tanya tried to apologize for her lack of education, whether in politics, economics, philosophy, music, religion, or medicine, she was prodded, given all the known facts (even if it took hours) and forced to make evaluations. Once she was strained to the point of tears when Stanley and Jack had inveigled her into a discussion of the motivations of Communist China. Tanya took the position that communism was an unmitigated evil. A half hour later, grinning at last as they pressed her to view the world from Chairman Mao's point of view, Tanya slowly admitted that perhaps communism was the only adequate way for China to move into the twentieth century. But, before she did that, Stanley and Jack had almost literally transformed her into a young Chinese intellectual who was aware that ancient Chinese feudalism was no match for powerful (and perhaps inadvertent) modern financial and industrial exploitation.

Harry, who had been listening, related the discussion back to all of us. "The secret of loving, we've all discovered, is that we must fight continuously against the ambivalent aspects of human behavior. The deep need on the one hand—a human necessity, really—to relate to other people, counteracted by the constant trickery of the human ego to appoint itself both judge and jury."

"My God," Val said teasingly, "last night while I was snuggling erotically against Harry, he was murmuring in my ear a thought that just occurred to him. One of man's greatest problems is his delusion that the vast scientific breakthroughs in medicine, space, computers, etcetera, have by the fact of their existence rubbed off on him and, as a result, he has assumed an unwarranted sophistication and denied his own basic primitive nature."

Harry ruffled her hair. "I philosophize best in the arms of an affectionate female. The way you and I gently ate each other up was charmingly primitive. I don't want to escape it, just to be aware of it."

Despite their laughing reactions to each other's sexuality, InSix and we agreed that our marriages of four and of six assume within them one-to-one male-female relationships, and a total inviolability of the group, similar to what is expected of monogamous marriage.

"Three different men or women are all any human being can encompass in his intimate world," Beth told David. "Whether we all live together the way you, Nancy, Tanya, and Horace do, or join, on an occasional pattern, as we are doing at the moment, wife-swapping and group sex is a different phenomenon entirely. It's motivated by insecurity and a lack of personal identity. Wife-swappers flee from involvement while we love it."

As Nancy pointed out, it would be possible to write not just a letter, but a book, about any weekend with InSix. Before we flew back to Los Angeles, Stanley had convinced us that several hundred Harrad students would spend as long as necessary to gather signatures to put Proposition Thirty-One on the State ballot. After election, we plan to rent a schooner big enough to accommodate all twenty-six of us and cruise for several weeks in Mexican waters.

I guess that tells you the story—our separate corporate entities have joined hands as friends!

But of course we did not have to wait until autumn to see Harry and Beth Schacht again. In them Tanya had discovered potent allies who quelled all our fears about having the children witness the birth of our baby. At least a third of the InSix brood had seen the other half born without any ill effects. We agreed that on the big day, even if Tanya's labor took twenty-four hours, the kids could sit through it even if they had to stay home from school. Sylvia Mai, who was back in Frank Kitman's good graces, agreed to take over my classes, while David would simply telephone Bill Sapolio to take charge for the day.

The children had examined, and asked us a thousand questions about, the life-size three-dimensional models loaned to us by Harry and Beth of sagital sections of the female pelvis with a full-term baby in utero. Harry had also brought us plaster models showing the successive cross-sections of a woman's body as the baby moved out of the womb during labor.

One evening, to the delight of the kids, Beth showed us movies of the birth of Abraham, their first child, that Jack Dawes had taken when InSix were all living together at the University of Pennsylvania. "Abe makes us run them once a year on his birthday," Beth said. "Believe me, it looks easier than it was. We didn't know about Doctor Lamaze then."

Fascinated as much as the children by the amazing birth process, we all subjected Tanya to a hilarious daily physical examination. While Tanya blushed and grumbled, we insisted that she had asked for it. Her privacy as a physical person, at least temporarily, was gone. Jimmy and Sam calmly discussed the position of the baby in Tanya's womb. Mitch, with an expression of sheer beatitude—we finally took a wondrous picture of him with his head pressed against his mother's naked belly—hugged Tanya and told her, one day, that his little sister had kicked him in the ear. Susan, calmly superior to the boys, who couldn't coordinate the breathing techniques with muscular control so necessary for painless childbirth, was actually able to relax her arms and leg muscles alternately, and to hold her breath as efficiently and as long as Tanya.

At two in the morning Tanya started to contract on a ten-minute schedule. David, who was her bed-mate that week, awoke Nancy and me. A week before Harry had stirrups, a special bed, and oxygen delivered to our house. After some discussion, we turned the Shea living room into a delivery room, since the bedrooms were too small for so many spectators. It was still too soon to alert Harry and Beth, so we all sat together and tried to calm Tanya, who was alternating between jitteriness and a waning conviction that she was doing the right thing.

"There's no damned sense in being a martyr," David told her. "Harry won't care if you change your mind. We can take you to the hospital right now, and you can still have the baby without the ordeal."

"Damn it!" Tanya exploded. "It's not the baby or the possible pain. I just hope it isn't ugly for the children, particularly Susan. I want it to be beautiful, but I'm suddenly scared to death. With all of you gawking at me as if I were some ingénue, I may forget how to breathe—or blow my lines!"

"You won't, honey." Nancy put her arm around Tanya. "And you won't forget to push and when not to. You've got me, Harry, Beth, and Susan to coach you. You can stop worrying about your audience. You're *our* family, and Tancy is *our* child."

In between contractions, while David and I were trying to agree on a boy's name, neither Nancy nor Tanya would admit any possibility other than that the baby would be a girl and her name would be Tancy Hershe.

When Harry and Beth finally arrived at about one thirty in the afternoon, Tanya was contracting on a five-minute schedule. After the Schachts had examined her and had explained to the children about dilation, Harry challenged Horace to a game of chess. "You've got hours yet, sweetie," he told Tanya as he patted her belly. "Keep it cool, and remember if all doctors went to this much trouble, there'd have to be twice as many of us."

"We don't need M.D.'s for what you'll do," Beth said. "Midwives have been doing it for centuries."

Harry laughed. "Beth believes that in the future all hospitals will be equipped with mobile-home birth units manned by competent nurses who will officiate right in the mother's home. With the growing cost of hospitalization, she may be right."

At seven twenty-six, while her entire audience was yelling and cheering her on for the final pushes, actually inhaling and exhaling in unison with Tanya, the baby's head crowned. "You've done it, Tanya," Harry said sharply. "Hold it now! Don't push."

"You're turning the baby's head! I can feel you!" Tanya panted, tears of joy streaming down her cheeks. "Oh, God. I feel wide open. Oh, oh! I love you all so very much!"

"Here's the forehead; the eyes; the nose!" Triumphantly Harry held the baby up, grinning at its indignant squeal. "By God, you were right! Tancy Hershe!" There were tears in Harry's eyes as he placed the baby on Tanya's belly and we propped her up to see her child.

"If I could do it a million times, I'd still stand in awe." Harry swiftly kissed Tanya's cheek. "Come on, sweetie, you were great! One more push, please. We need the placenta."

And that, Phil and Margaret, may be the function of the Tenhausens and the Hershes. We are the placenta, the plank to bridge the impossible and bring it to life. Isn't that the essence of America, too? While we have split the State of California into two opposing camps, those who disagree with us are dreaming of a past that no longer exists. The fundamentalist preachers, who state categorically that corporate marriage is a blasphemy; the psychologists and psychiatrists, who insist that man is still too primitive for this kind of emotional adjustment; the lawyers, who claim that even if Proposition Thirty-One becomes a law the legal problems can never be surmounted; the industrialists, who shiver a little when they

271

realize a group family can live quite comfortably with fewer automobiles, appliances, and television sets (and have less time or motivation to look at TV); the faithful romanticists, who point with pride to their years of absolute fidelity to a monogamous marriage (extolling the sufficiency of two people triumphant against the world); and the prurient snickerers who conceive corporate marriage as licensed lust (They'd join us willingly if they could fuck and run away.)—all these are of the same breed. They were alive, too, when the great adventurers were exploring a flat ocean and daring to sail off the world into hell. They lived in Puritan England, preferring frustration at home to joining their brothers of greater vision who took off for a new world. They lived when the first few families dared to cross the country in a covered wagon only to arrive in California, and discover even more daring men who, believing in their God, had fled Mexico and were here before them. And they exist today in an even more frightening form—people and their leaders who would rather destroy the world than take the greater adventure and penetrate the jungle of petty nationalistic virtue.

Even though the exploration of space remains as a vast adventure for those challenged to the conquest of man's physical environment, it is an adventure for the few. In place of the substitute adventures of drugs and the thousands of mechanical escape mechanisms created by man to fill the growing voids of his new freedom from work, *we* offer the greatest challenge and adventure of them all—to really discover one another as human beings. Each day we discover anew that *we are not alone*.

While the Alberti Construction Company is rushing to complete our new corporate home here in San Peur well before November, Future Families of America have leased a former supermarket here for our headquarters. With an underpaid staff of some fifty university students we try to handle the flood of mail and telephone calls.

The key, Margaret and Phil, that quickly opens the door into a world where men and women *dare* to be defenseless, loving human beings, is a *sensual, integral* awareness. Nancy, Tanya, David and I agree—it will always unlock the door to our new home in San Peur. We look forward to November when you and InSix will join us!

Sincerely,
Horace Hershe

Postscript by
Sylvia Mai

~~~~~~~~~

As the daughter of a mixed marriage, who couldn't possibly "pass for white," with a background of early life in the city of Watts, I can't help feeling that corporate marriage, if it can be achieved in the larger sense of a love commitment, might have value for many Negro families. The pooling of resources and the creation of an "enduring family" (so lacking in many modern Negro communities) could give stability and identity to Negro children that they now rarely have. The strength of the Jews, and their amazing achievements in a world that has always denied them, can be traced back to their covenants that demanded family unity as a vital part of their religion. For many Negro and white families with no strong religious ties to guide them, Proposition Thirty-One may be the answer to disintegrating family structures. But Proposition Thirty-One passes even beyond the dream of men like Ralph Borsodi who, in his various writings, extolled the self-realization possible through communal property-sharing and homesteading. It may—I admit—require an emotional and sexual sharing beyond the capabilities of most men and women.

I know the Hershes would agree with me. The marriage commitment they are living demands a continual adjustment of four individuals on a high intellectual plane, plus the conscious elimination of jealousy and possessiveness as an expected and instinctual aspect of the human psyche. Yet, if some human beings can find their way out of the emotional jungles they have sown for themselves, if Proposition Thirty-One offers them the means for family stability, it can do much to eliminate the segmented life most of us now are forced to live. As a sociologist, I see this as its greatest merit.

We are no longer a society of people with common goals. In a technological world based on ever-growing consumption, we have created a society of at least four noncommunicating age-groups. The teen-agers, distrusting the past-thirty age-group, span a period of about fifteen years. Ultimately they become the newly marrieds, maintaining their separate existence in housing developments created expressly for the pro-creative years.

Inevitably their spawn becomes the new teen-age group. But this group is frustrated and defeated because it lives in an artificial environment that hasn't room, literally or figuratively, for both cultures. Hence this new crop of teen-agers moves into early marriage, and the original family, now without the cohesiveness of a family with young children, may slowly move toward the adventure of divorce. In any case, the original parents eventually become the really displaced people in our society—the old people.

This does not happen by choice. Man has set in motion economic wheels of which he has little control or comprehension. Read this quote from *Time*. It shows the frightening direction we are taking:

> As small firms [home builders] vanish, giant combines rich enough to build on a huge scale are taking over. Big corporations such as ITT are increasingly joining forces with builders—often by merger, sometimes through joint ventures. Last year for example, Westinghouse Electric acquired Florida's Coral Ridge Properties, and is now busy building a city for 60,000 residents near Fort Lauderdale. Pennsylvania Railroad's Macco Realty Company is developing an 87,500-acre Rancho California community near Los Angeles with Kaiser Industries and Kaiser Aluminum & Chemical Corporation. American Standard Inc., the nation's biggest plumbing manufacturer, this year joined a 4500-house venture in California's Ventura County. . . . The building company, which also retails furniture and appliances, makes an obvious outlet for such . . . consumer products as TV sets, refrigerators, and freezers.

Perhaps the deeper meaning escapes most of us. But these "homes" do not house families, simply itinerant age-groups. Two individuals clinging together in a monogamous marriage are up against forces a thousand times stronger than their precarious partnership. We have created a society where life is extended, but the meanings of living have vanished. The generations are cut off from the vital two-way flow between young and old. Finally, in the isolation of senior-citizen centers, the confinement is complete. The grandfather who might have learned to rock and roll with his granddaughter and to reabsorb the wonderful vitality of youth (while she has the joy of teaching someone older and learning how grandfather danced the Charleston or jitterbugged) now has only the company of his peers and the drained memories of his "better world." The science of gerontology can well reflect on the miracle we have created—dead minds in healthy bodies.

As the age-group segregation increases, our ingenious builders are moving into the province of insurance companies. "Pay now . . . die later." It is now possible, when you are young, to prepare to live out your remaining life in the company of those about to die. Artificial communities like Rossmoor Leisure World near Laguna Beach offer haven to hundreds of thousands of middle-aged people. Communal living for those past fifty—a place to play (not sexually) with friends your own age for the last ten years or more of your life without worries or responsibilities. From Leisure World to Forest Lawn. We have created a world where at thirty you may eventually be required to pay in advance for the security of a roof over your head in your declining years and even a cement jacket to keep the rain out of your coffin.

Here is a quotation from the literature of Leisure World which requires no comment. "Leisure World Living offers freedom to grow . . . time to learn another language, acquire a new hobby if you wish. It offers you freedom from mowing the lawn, weeding, painting your own house. . . . Best of all, it offers you freedom of choice. . . . Picture yourself in a country-club surrounding with a golf course, Olympian-size swimming pool, tennis courts and riding stables, all within walking distance. . . . And the only membership requirement is that you must be fifty-two or over to qualify. . . . Visitors of any age, including grandchildren, are welcome at any time."

From Levittown to Leisure World to the cemetery. Man is being packaged into neat little age-categories where his own personal meaning and validity are exchanged for the empty pursuit of happiness. It is a moot question who are the real dropouts from civilization, the new generation or those who have abdicated from life in Leisure Worlds, or been pushed into senior-citizen centers by their children. At least, in the seedling cry of the younger generation, "make love not war," we can detect the deeper yearning for a world where a new kind of interpersonal relationship will exist between people in all areas of life, young and old, creating a process of living from youth to old age that becomes a throbbing testing ground where the individual never loses the excitement and wonder of man.

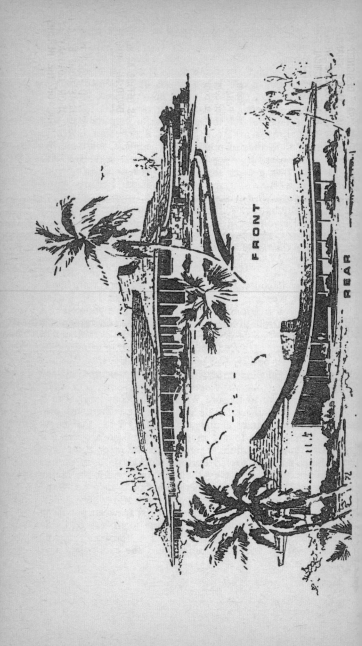

FRONT

REAR

WHILE THIS HOME WAS DESIGNED FOR
SOUTHERN CALIFORNIA, SIMPLE CHANGES
IN THE FOUNDATION STRUCTURE WOULD
MAKE THE CIRCULAR HOME PRACTICAL FOR
ANY LOCATION IN THE UNITED STATES.

1. Living Room Area
2. Dining Room Area
3. Kitchen
4. Library and Music Room
5. Living Room and Patio
6. Nancy's Master Bedroom
7. Tanya's Master Bedroom
8. Children's Area
9. Boy's Bedroom
10. Susan's Bedroom
11. Tancy's Bedroom

GUEST AREA DOUBLES AS OFFICE AT HOME
AND RETREAT AREA FOR DAVID AND HORACE

PRELIMINARY DRAWINGS AND FLOOR PLAN
FOR THE HERSHE CORPORATE HOME BUILT
BY ALBERTI CONSTRUCTION COMPANY AT
SAN PEUR, CALIFORNIA FOR THE HERSHE
FAMILY

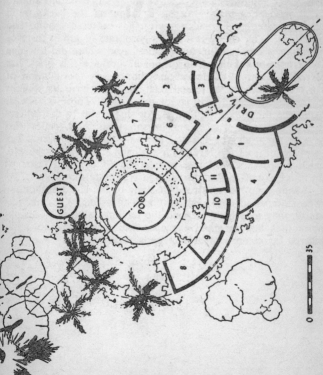

Sources and
Reading List

〰〰〰

From the inception of its campaign to have Proposition
Thirty-One appear on the California ballot, Future Families
of America has been besieged by requests for background
reading material. Particular interest has centered around two
questions: Why do we feel that a corporate or group form of
marriage is inevitable in our culture? And where did the idea
for Proposition Thirty-One originate? Perhaps this book has
helped to answer both questions, though any reevaluation of
the old shibboleths of sexual relations must have its sources
in the thoughts and writings of many men. Those who wish
to pursue the subject further may wish to refer to the following list of books, articles, and organizations. Any reader who
pursues them all will discover not only that the proposal has
validity, but that the means for realizing it, for many people,
exists *now* in the willingess to take the difficult and fascinating road to self-realization through corporate marriage.

It should not be construed that any of the listed authors or
organizations advocate Proposition Thirty-One. Yet, inadvertently, they may have mapped the territory and erected sign-
posts that the imaginative reader will know how to read.
Starred books are available in paperback editions.

BOOKS

Argyle, Michael. *The Psychology of Interpersonal Behavior*, Pelican Books, Baltimore, 1967.

Bertocci, Peter. *Sex, Love and the Person*, Sheed and Ward, New York, 1967.

Blood, Robert O. *Love Match and Arranged Marriage*, The Free Press, New York, 1967.

Blood, Robert O. and Wolfe, Daniel. *Husbands and Wives, The Dynamics of Married Love*, The Free Press, New York, 1960. An examination of the interacting phases of marriage based on an extensive questionnaire submitted largely to women in the Michigan area.

Borsodi, Ralph. *Education and Living*, Melbourne University Press, Melbourne, Florida, 1948. Borsodi's book is a detailed study of a new way of living that is actually put into practice today by many homesteaders. A two-volume paperback edition has been available from the Schools of Living, see addresses below. Some publisher should reissue it. It is quite germinal to many stirrings in the land. Melbourne University, conceived by Borsodi, is no longer in existence.

Borsodi, Ralph. *Seventeen Problems; A Study of the Basic Problems of Man and Society*, Porter Sargent, Boston, 1968.

Breedlove, William *The Freelovers*, Pendulum Press, Atlanta, 1967. A hastily written survey of communal living and free love.

Butz, Otto. *To Make a Difference, Students Look at America*, Harper & Row, New York, 1967. An opportunity to look at the kind of future the younger generation hopes to achieve.

Charles, Edward. *The Sexual Impulse*, Brussel and Brussel, New York, 1966. A sex manual, yes. But something else besides.

Christiansen, Harold T., editor. *Handbook of Marriage and the Family*, Rand McNally, New York, 1964. A thousand-page book filled with a wealth of valuable information and analysis.

Codman, John Thomas. *Brook Farm, Historic and Personal Memoirs*, Arena Publishing Company, Boston, 1894.

Colton, Helen. *What's on Woman's Future Agenda?*, Family Forum, 1539 North Courtney St., Los Angeles. A pamphlet in the same genre as the better-known Betty Friedan book listed below.

Comfort, Alex. *Sex in Society*, Citadel Press, New York, 1966. Definitely a book worth reading. Dr. Comfort is British.

Darin, Drabkin. *The Other Society*, Harcourt, Brace and World, New York, 1963. Essential for an understanding of the kibbutzim.

de Chardin, Pierre Teilhard. *The Future of Man*, Harper & Row, New York, 1964.

Dicks, Henry. *Marital Tensions; Clinical Studies Towards a Psychological Theory of Interaction*, Basic Books, New York, 1967.

Ewald, William R., Jr. *Environment For Man; The Next Fifty Years*, Indiana University Press, Bloomington, Ind., 1967. The chapter by Christopher Alexander in this fascinating book is especially recommended.

Frankl, Victor. *The Doctor and the Soul, From Psycotherapy to Logotherapy*, Bantam Books, New York, 1967. The chapter in this book "On the Meaning of Love" is well worth reading.

Friedan, Betty. *The Feminine Mystique*, W. W. Norton, New York, 1963. Miss Friedan is interested in greater opportunities for female development.

Gans, Herbert J. *The Levittowners; Ways of Life and Politics in a New Suburban Community*, Pantheon Books, New York, 1967. Not exactly in the tradition of *Middletown in Transition*, and *Crestwood Heights* but, depending on your point of view, shocking.

Greene, Bernard L. *The Psychotherapies of Marital Disharmony*, The Free Press, New York, 1965.

Handel, Gerald. *The Psychosocial Interior of the Family*, Aldine Publishing Company, Chicago, 1967.

Heard, Gerald. *Pain, Sex and Time; A New Outlook on the Evolution and the Future of Man*, Harper & Brothers, New York, 1939.

Hine, Robert U. *California's Utopian Colonies*, Yale University Press, New Haven, 1953.

Holloway, Mark. *Heavens on Earth*, Dover Publications, New York, 1966.

Horney, Karen. *The Feminine Mind*, W. W. Norton, New York, 1966. Karen Horney is always worth reading.

Hosskinson, J. Bradley. *Loneliness; An Explanation, A Cure*, Citadel Press, New York, 1966.

Hunt, Morton. *The World of the Formerly Married*, McGraw Hill, New York, 1966. If you are contemplating divorce, read this book with the spouse you are about to leave. You may change your mind!

Huxley, Julian. *The Humanist Frame; A Modern Humanist View of Life*, Harper & Row, New York, 1966.

Huxley, Julian. *Knowledge, Morality and Destiny*, Mentor Books, New York, 1966. Original title: *New Bottles for Old Wine*.

Jourad, Sidney. *The Transparent Self*, D. Van Nostrand, New York, 1964.

Kaplan, Benjamin. *The Jew and His Family*, Louisiana State University Press, Baton Rouge, 1967. Valuable insights into family as the basis of Jewish survival.

Keniston, Kenneth. *The Uncommitted, Alienated Youth in Modern Society*, Dell Publishing, New York, 1967.

Levine, Lena. *The Emotional Sex; Why Women Are the Way They Are Today*, William Morrow, New York, 1964.

Littlefair, Duncan. *Sermon Series*, published by the Fountain Street Church, 24 Fountain Street, Grand Rapids, Mich. Especially recommended is the series *The Nature of Love*.

Loomis, Mildred. *Go Ahead and Live*, Philosophical Library, New York, 1965. Mildred Loomis is the chief factotum of the School of Living Philosophy advocated by Ralph Borsodi. Be careful, she may convince you. But homesteading is still monogamously based.

McLuhan, Marshall, and Leonard, George B. "The Future of Sex," *Look* Magazine, July 25, 1967. The conclusions of these writers point to the inevitability of communal marriage.

Maslow, Abraham. *Eupsychian Management*, Richard Irwin, New York, 1965.

Maslow, Abraham. *Religion, Values and Peak Experiences*, Ohio State University Press, Columbus, 1964. While Abe Maslow may shake his head at the concept of corporate marriage, no one should attempt it without knowing his studies on the self-actualized person and being willing to say, "this is me."

Matson, Floyd. *The Broken Image: Man, Science and Society*, George Braziller, New York, 1964.

May, Rollo. *Man's Search for Himself*, New American Library, 1967. Rollo May is one of the best interpreters of man's present predicament. Absolutely recommended for anyone who wants to understand the motivations of the new generation.

Montagu, Ashley. *On Being Human*, Hawthorne Books, New York, 1966. This tiny book should be, but isn't, as well known as Eric Fromm's *The Art of Loving*.

Morgan, Arthur. *Nowhere Was Somewhere*, University of North Carolina Press, Chapel Hill, 1946. An interesting survey of some Utopias.

Murphy, Gardner. *Human Potentialities*, Basic Books, New York, 1958.

Negley, Glenn, and Patrick, Max J. *The Quest for Utopia, An Anthology of Imaginary Societies*, Henry Schumann, Inc., New York, 1952.

Nordhoff, Charles. *The Communistic Societies of the United States*, Hillary House, New York, 1961.

Noyes, John Humphrey. *History of American Socialisms*, Dover Publications, New York, 1965. Unfortunately, with the exception of this book, the writings of Noyes and reports on his successful experiments in communal marriage (Oneida lasted seventy years) are difficult to obtain. Some publisher should remedy this serious lack of information on a prolific writer.

Otto, Herbert A. *Human Potentialities, The Challenge and the Promise*, Warren H. Green, Inc., Springfield, Missouri, 1968.

A valuable collection of writers such as Maslow, in the area of self-actualization, study of the family, and the unrealized potential of man's spirtuality and sexuality.

Pieper, Joseph. *Leisure, the Basis of Culture,* New American Library, New York, 1963.

Rogers, Carl. *On Becoming a Person,* Houghton-Mifflin, Boston, 1961. Also contact Western Behavioral Science Institute for Roger's paper, "A Plan for Self-Directed Change in an Educational System." Roger's proposal for a system of nationwide encounter groups would be an essential stabilizer of corporate marriage.

Sarnoff, Irving. *Society with Tears,* Citadel Press, New York, 1967.

Schutz, William C. *Joy, Expanding Human Awareness,* Grove Press, New York, 1967. Instead of the games people play to separate them, here are games to unite them.

Simon, Anne. *Stepchild in the Family; A View of Children in Remarriage,* Odyssey Press, New York, 1964.

Soubiran, André. *Open Letter to a Woman of Today,* James H. Heineman, New York, 1967. An open letter to a French married female which proves at the very least that the marital problems of different Western societies are strikingly similar.

Spiro, Melford. *Kibbutz, Venture in Utopia,* Schocken Books, New York, 1963. In the early days of the kibbutzim, marriage, in a monogamous sense, did not exist. A fascinating excursion into a very different system of interpersonal relationships.

Stein, Robert. *Why Young Mothers Feel Trapped,* McCall Corporation, New York, 1965.

Suttie, Ian D. *The Origins of Love and Hate,* Julian Press, New York, 1933. Required reading for students of corporate marriage.

Wassell, Bohdun B. *Group Therapy,* Citadel Press, New York, 1966. Read this book with imagination and see the possibilities within corporate marriage for the elimination of role-playing.

Wattenberg, Ben. *This U. S. A.,* Pocket Books, New York, 1967. An interpretation of the 1965 U. S. Census statistics which proves, if nothing else, that statistics can be used to prove what you already believe.

Watts, Allan W. *The Book: On the Taboo Against Knowing Who You Are,* Collier Books, New York, 1967.

THE UTOPIAN NOVELISTS

The following novelists have explored or skirted the areas of group marriage or have touched on different forms of marital and premarital relationships.

Bellamy, Edward. *Looking Backward*, New American Library, New York. Reprint of a classic first published in 1880.

Heinlein, Robert. *Stranger in a Strange Land*, Avon Books, New York, 1967. Although ostensibly a science-fiction novel, this book has a here-and-now quality which makes the reader wish he lived in a world where people can "grok" each other and be "water brothers."

Huxley, Aldous. *Brave New World*, Bantam Books, New York. Perhaps the most famous, along with Orwell's *1984*, of the anti-Utopias. First published in 1932.

Huxley, Aldous. *Island*, Bantam Books, New York. First published in 1962.

Mittelholzer, Edgar. *Shadows Move Among Them*, J. P. Lippincott, Philadelphia, 1951. A charming story of a life with expanded possibilities. Why isn't it available in paperbacks?

Wright, Austin Tappan. *Islandia*, Farrar & Rinehart, New York, 1942.

Rimmer, Robert H. *The Harrad Experiment*, Bantam Books, New York, 1967. Harrad College, where male and female students live together unmarried, comes closer to reality every day. The extensive bibliography in this book is especially recommended.

Rimmer, Robert H. *The Rebellion of Yale Marratt*, Avon Books, New York, 1967. Explores possibility of bigamous marriage between consenting individuals.

Skinner, B. F. *Walden Two*, Macmillan, New York, 1962. Written twenty years ago by a Harvard professor of psychology, this book studies a closely contained intentional community. (Several such communities are now in existence, and some have splinter groups advocating group marriage.)

Wallace, Irving. *The Three Sirens*, New American Library, New York, 1964. When you finish this novel, you'll have the feeling that Wallace may have been on the right track, but got led astray by the commercial possibilities.

Wright, Austin Tappan. *Islandia*. Farrar & Rinehart, New York. 1942. This is the granddaddy of all modern Utopian novels.

GROUPS, COMMUNITIES AND INSTITUTES

Intentional communities, groups for communal living, and organizations to develop the human potential stem from a tradition as old as Brook Farm and are in keeping with the American pursuit of happiness. The organizations listed below have been in existence long enough to indicate some permanence. Hundreds of organizations or groups, many of them dependent on the outlook or premises of one or two individuals, are in existence. For a complete listing, the reader is referred to the *Directory of Social Change*, published by *The Modern Utopian*, Starr King Center, 2441 Le Conte Avenue,

Berkeley, California, 94709. This unique directory covers the contemporary scene, and lists many individuals and groups practicing various forms of communal marriage. *The Modern Utopian* is a valuable magazine for anyone interested in the rapid growth of self-realization through group endeavor.

Aureon Institute, 71 Park Avenue, New York, 10016. Seminars in personal and social growth.

Community Service, Inc., Yellow Springs, Ohio, 45387. Arthur E. Morgan, President.

Esalen Institute, Big Sur, California, 93920. A center to explore those trends in behavioral sciences, religion, and philosophy which emphasize the potentialities of human existence. Highly recommended: A two-hour stereo tape from a week-long group encounter, with Robert Rimmer and nineteen others discussing *The Harrad Experiment, Proposition Thirty-One* and interpersonal relations. Available directly. Write "Recording R-31, Esalen Institute, Big Sur, California, 93920." Price, $12.00.

Fellowships of Religious Humanists, Box 65, Yellow Springs, Ohio, 45387. Ed Wilson, Director (Publish: *Religious Humanism*).

Kairos, c/o Wishing Well Hotel, P. O. Box 350, Rancho Santa Fe, California, 92067. Seminars and workshops exploring the expanding commitment to release and energize those capacities which lie dormant within individuals, groups, organizations, societies and nations.

Mid-Peninsula Free University, 1601 El Camino Real, Menlo Park, California, 94205. Offers some eighty courses in developing all aspects of the human potential.

National Center for Exploration of Human Potential, Herbert Otto and John Mann, Directors, Stone-Brandel Center, 1439 S. Michigan Ave., Chicago, 60605.

NTL Institute for Applied Behavioral Science, 1201 Sixteenth St., N.W., Washington, D.C., 20036. Leland Bradford, Director (Publish: *Journal of Applied Behavioral Science*) (Run training centers and schools for T-groups, basic-encounter groups, personal-growth groups, etc.).

Schools of Living, Land's End Homestead, Brookville, Ohio, 45309. Also the Heathcote School of Living, Freeland, Maryland, 21053. Center of the homesteading movement based on Ralph Borsodi's principles that men and women can live fuller lives by limiting their dependency on a technological society. Financially communal in some aspects but sexually monogamous.

Topanga Human Development Center, P. O. Box 480, Reseda, California, 91335. The Center is seeking to find more creative and effective ways of living in this evolving society.

Western Behavioral Sciences Institute, 1150 Silverado, La Jolla, California, 92037. Richard Farson, Director.

284

World Future Society, P. O. Box 19285, Washington, D.C.,
20036. A neutral clearinghouse for ideas on the future and
Utopian schemes. Publishes a newsletter, *The Futurist.*

PUBLICATIONS

The following magazines are published by organizations or
individuals who are exploring the vast potential of human interaction.

Daedelus, published quarterly by the American Academy of Arts
and Sciences, 208 Newton Street, Boston, Mass., 02146. The
issue entitled *Utopia,* Spring, 1965, and *Toward the Year
2000,* Summer, 1966, are especially recommended.

The Humanist, published by the American Humanist Association,
125 El Camino del Mar, San Francisco, 94121. *The Humanist* is a clearinghouse for articles and reviews on all approaches to a humanistic philosophy.

The Journal of Humanistic Psychology, published by the American Association of Humanistic Psychology, 2637 Marshall
Drive, Palo Alto, California.

Manas (weekly). P.O. Box 32112, El Sereno Station, Los Angeles, 90032.

Medical Aspects of Human Sexuality, published monthly by Clinical Communications, 250 East 39th Street, New York, 10016.
Published for M.D.'s in the realization that the average doctor
is often as bewildered as his patient by sexual interrelations.

New Life, 15 Camden Hill Road, London, England. A newsletter
published six times a year by an English group actively practicing communal or group living.

Population Characteristics, Series p-20 #164. Bureau of the Census, Government Printing Office, Washington, D. C. Worth
reading; on the changing composition of the American family
and households.

Psychology Today, 1330 Camino del Mar, Del Mar, Cal., 92014.
An attractive monthly magazine that keeps abreast of the
new approaches to group interaction.

Current SIGNET Bestsellers

☐ **MOTHERS AND DAUGHTERS by Evan Hunter.** From the pen of the bestselling author of **The Blackboard Jungle** and **Strangers When We Meet** comes a compelling story of four women of different ages and temperaments, whose lives are closely linked by the threads of love.
(#Y3855—$1.25)

☐ **ALWAYS ON SUNDAY—ED SULLIVAN by Michael David Harris.** The inside scoop on "the worst master of ceremonies who was ever on land or sea," the loser who wins every week, the "unstar" of the Ed Sullivan show and the launcher of hundreds of stars—Ed Sullivan himself. Written by Michael Harris, CBS press representative for the Sullivan Show since 1959. (#Q3793—95¢)

☐ **DO YOU SLEEP IN THE NUDE? by Rex Reed.** Rex Reed, who revolutionized the traditional Hollywood interview, tells it like it is with Barbra Streisand, Warren Beatty, Lester Maddox, Marlene Dietrich, Sandy Dennis, Peter Fonda, and many others. It's no wonder some of them were upset when they saw their interviews in print.
(#Q3773—95¢)

☐ **THE NINE LIVES OF BILLY ROSE by Polly Rose Gottlieb.** With complete honesty and frankness, Billy Rose's sister tells all about his amazing nine careers and his five tangled marriages. (#Q3764—95¢)

☐ **ME, HOOD! by Mickey Spillane.** From the master of suspense comes another outstanding thriller. Hood (Ryan) is on the side of the law only when it suits his purpose. For ten grand and sweet revenge, he is, however, willing to tangle with the Syndicate. (#P3759—60¢)

THE NEW AMERICAN LIBRARY, INC., P.O. Box 2310, Grand Central Station, New York, New York 10017

Please send me the SIGNET BOOKS I have checked above. I am enclosing $_____(check or money order—no currency or C.O.D.'s). Please include the list price plus 10¢ a copy to cover mailing costs. (New York City residents add 6% Sales Tax. Other New York State residents add 3% plus any local sales or use taxes.)

Name_____

Address_____

City_____State_____Zip Code_____
Allow at least 3 weeks for delivery

Other SIGNET Books You Will Enjoy

☐ **THE PURSUIT OF HAPPINESS by Thomas Rogers.** The story of a family and a society, and of two young people who are led to abandon both in their pursuit of happiness. ". . . witty and polished, eminently readable, quite relaxing—and often funny enough to make one laugh aloud."—**Saturday Review** (#Q3734—95¢)

☐ **THE SHORT YEAR by Barbra Ward.** A probing novel about a young woman striving to maintain her individuality and freedom as she sets out to confront life in New York. (#T3621—75¢)

☐ **THE ECSTASY BUSINESS by Richard Condon.** The author of THE MANCHURIAN CANDIDATE weaves a wild satire of the movie industry, revolving around Hollywood's most beautiful couple. (#T3615—75¢)

☐ **HARRY MYERS RAPTURE (The Stranger in the Snow) by Lester Goran.** A splendid portrait of a self-made failure and his attempts, alternately jaunty and sad, to come to terms with the specter of guilt that haunts him. (#T3694—75¢)

☐ **GORE AND IGOR by Meyer Levin.** An irreverent, outrageous, sexy and extravagantly funny novel about the lives of Gore the California boy and Igor the toast of Moscow—both poetniks, peaceniks, loverniks and fugitives from justice. (#T3768—75¢)